# THE
# CHANGE
# ARTIST

## Here's what people are saying about *The Change Artist*

*This book is not only a completely engrossing read, it nicely describes something I wholeheartedly believe in: living your life as a work of art. I was drawn into the story easily, and as it unfolded, I found myself totally enjoying the way the main character developed. Her awakening to her self made this story much more than your average adventure. Knowing that this book is a fictionalized version of real events in the author's life makes it all the more potent. As much as I liked reading it, I can't wait to see the movie!*
— Sarah Fisk, PhD, Organizational Development Consultant, *Community At Work*

*I just finished* The Change Artist *and am blown away, speechless and impressed beyond words. I can't help but keep thinking about it and how it relates to so many aspects of my life.*
— Kathy Lynn, author of *Who's in Charge Anyway?*

*Beautifully written and rich in spiritual issues; this book deals with the depth to which we are willing to sacrifice of ourselves to survive, and the search for the return to our true human values. It is a parable for our times and an amazingly good read!*
— Julie Blue, Recording Artist and Film Composer

The Change Artist *took me on a powerful journey of re-evaluating my beliefs and expanding my compassion and tolerance for human nature. It is an insightful and impacting story which masterfully explores the power of creativity to free the human soul.*
— Adelle Bernadette, Shamanic Artist

*I was immediately taken in by the characters and their interwoven journeys; so taken in that I couldn't stop until 2:00 a.m.!! I have so longed for a parable with a female protagonist/hero a la Coelho's The Alchemist, and I think* The Change Artist *is it.*
— Carrie Gallant, Director of Gallant Solutions

*I just completed the last page of Carla's compelling book. Her characters came so to life, joining me in my days when I put the book down, becoming part of my reflections, my conversations. I found myself reflecting upon what I know, and don't know about the journey of my grandparents as I read the book — the difficult choices they made through this time in history that Carla chronicles so eloquently. A brilliant book — well researched, beautifully written. Not one you'll put down easily, nor forget soon.*
Laura Mack, Whitelight Promotions

*I had trouble putting the book down long enough to tend to life! It brought back some of my childhood memories in Holland … and it did a lot of clearing for me.*
— Greta Farina

*Well written, impeccably researched. It keeps you reading all the way through. It is a testament to creativity, to finding your own power and to reuniting some of the lost souls of the past so they can rest in peace today.*
— Lorraine MacGregor, Director of Spirit West Management

*I loved this book for the way it expands your horizons, allowing you to see behind a curtain of mistaken assumptions about people living in a complicated place and time.*
— Jana Stanfield, International Recording Artist

*It's a compelling read…I didn't want to put the book down.*
— Amrita Dhanji, Artist

*A heart-rendering book that moves the soul. It connects historical events to the present day to help heal our unconscious feelings about authoritarian structures and abuse. Bravo!*
— Ulrich Freitag, Director of the Institute for Bodymind Intelligence

*I just finished reading* The Change Artist *over two evenings and didn't want to put it down. It was engaging and a lot of fun to read. It got me thinking in many new ways.*
— Karen Kristensen, Park Design Planner

The Change Artist *was a real page turner and a moving and thought-provoking journey. Carla has an amazing brain. Bravo!*
— Donna Hutchinson, Owner of On the Edge Fitness Educators

*This book brought back many forgotten memories. The writing is beautiful and I know that all of my family will read it. It is sad that my generation closed itself up and seldom if ever talked about what they had to endure. I do understand why we did it as I belong to the same generation. I chose to write about my life during this horrible time in history and the discussions around it have been important. Thank you for writing it.*
— Bernd Muschalla, author and survivor of WWII

*This book was emotional, thought-provoking and inspirational all at the same time. It truly brought home the message about how important it is to break free of the past and live life victoriously.*
— Terry Brock, technology coach and syndicated columnist

*I couldn't put it down. The story was riveting and Carla's creative writing skills are excellent.*
— Art Pouchet, Therapeutic Counsellor

*I'm savouring the book, I don't want the story to end. The experiences and the conversations and the angst between the characters about what they are finding out about themselves and their family background is so interesting. This will be a book to read again.*
— Eileen Reppenhagen, Tax Consultant

*I love the book and I don't want it to end. It is such a page turner. It was uplifting to see how people want to get along and how trusting some can be and how others are so stuck on themselves and past beliefs, which leaves them nowhere, thus a perfect title* The Change Artist.
— Lilly Page, Flair Image Consulting

*I love Carla's blending of new-age and old-age wisdom, showing us once again that it is all one. This book has so many fascinating people and settings. It's a wonderful piece of work, totally engaging.*
— Catherine Berris, Landscape Architect

*I just couldn't put this book down. I was intrigued by the storyline and nervous for the main character! She had to put all behind her and be totally in the present to solve each situation she found herself in: such a great key to living in today's complex world. Kudos to Carla for bringing such timeless lessons to a creative and captivating story.*
— Chenoa Johnston

*A good read, with a quickly moving narrative. This novel is full of fascinating stories about a period not often covered. In addition to being well written it has great fluency and truthfulness.*
— Moira Johnston, retired editor for Elek Books, UK

# THE
# CHANGE
# ARTIST

**CARLA RIEGER**

Anand Publishing
Vancouver, B.C.

Published in Vancouver, British Columbia, Canada in 2009
by Anand Publishing

#138—2906 W. Broadway,
Vancouver, B.C.
CANADA V6K 2G8
Tel: (604) 222-2276

or

145 Tyee Road (#1273)
Point Roberts, WA
USA 98281

www.anandpublishing.com
www.thechangeartistbook.com
www.carlarieger.com

Printed in the United States

Edited by
Deon Brown
Brett Huffman

Back cover photo by Bruce Skipper

Cover Design and text layout by 1106 Design, Phoenix, Arizona

Library and Archives Canada Cataloguing in Publication: C2008-903501-1

ISBN: 978-0-9688272-8-4

## Dedication

*To my parents for giving me life, love, a home
and the freedom to choose my own path.*

*Our lives begin to end
the day we remain silent
about something we care about.*
—Martin Luther King, Jr.

## CHAPTER 1

Algeria, 1943 — The plane flies low over the desert plain. Jorg rests his head against the cannon and watches the never-ending sea of dunes below; waves within waves, mingling their varying shades of reddish crystalline. As a portrait artist, shadow play fascinates him. It's only through shading that an artist can draw focus to his subject; it's only through the dark hollows that he can carve character.

He imagines her face again, that last time when the cord of love between them snapped. If he ever lets himself paint again, he would paint the Sahara as he would his own heart: barren as far as the eye can see with an oasis where you least expect it.

He releases his grip on the gun controls. There is little ammunition anyway; he made sure of that before they left the ground. The intense vigilance serves no purpose anymore because his death wish is rising like the desert heat. The drone of the propeller is putting him into an hypnotic half-sleep. Jorg has not slept well since arriving in the desert. He finds it hard to get used to the scorching heat and the thick, dry air. It chafes at his undeserved need for solace.

In his half sleep he hears a man shouting. He awakes with a jolt.

It's the pilot, Hans, shouting, "Sandstorm!"

Jorg looks up to see a towering wall of sand heading their way.

The locals in Tunisia had warned them about it. But Hans, their madcap pilot, simply waved away their lecture on the ways of sand. "You don't know German Engineering. Ach, sand, snow, we fly through anything!"

At the time, Jorg looked from Hans to the turbaned old gentlemen. The locals had gathered to see their reconnaissance team off at the dusty outpost they called an airstrip. Jorg thought, at the time, that he saw genuine fear in those dark old eyes. Hans might know German engineering, but Jorg knew more about the wisdom of fear than anyone. He wished his best friend was right, but Jorg was no longer sure he trusted anything German.

He shudders as these thoughts race through his overtaxed system. Sand splatters their windshield. The fury of the earth is reaching up and grabbing them out of the sky.

Sand and grit fill the propellers. Hans struggles to keep control of the plane. He turns the nose upwards to see if he can get above the storm, but the plane can't climb fast enough.

They are trapped. The sandstorm swallows them whole. Sparks fly out of one propeller as it chokes with grit and the left propeller grinds to a horrifying halt.

Hans shouts "We have to crash land!"

Jorg watches as the other propeller chokes. The plane has lost its forward momentum. Hans tries to take the plane down, but he no longer knows which way is down. The plane gives way to gravity and ten tons of metal drop toward the earth …

## CHAPTER 2

Canada, 2002 — It was February when Fran Freeman, accompanied by a small group of people, exited the baggage claim area at the Vancouver International Airport. A scattering of photographers and journalists rushed her.

"Excuse me, Miss Freeman …"

"Welcome back to Canada."

"What do you think about the latest news on the Wrightway collapse?" "What will be your defence on the stand in terms of Freeman & Wilson's involvement with the audits?"

"No comment," Fran replied as she turned to answer her cell phone. She wore a shawl backwards and in her haste to get to the exit the double-tresses of the liquid fabric twirled behind her back. Flashes from the cameras caught her in mid stride, her exotic features not completely hidden beneath a head scarf and sunglasses. As the media followed, her entourage vanished into the back of a rented limo.

Jean Pierre Gagnon, a Quebecois journalist had been standing back, surveying the scene from near the pay phones. He had been following the Freeman story for the past seven months and wanted to include this case study in an upcoming article on ethics and innovation in business. He jumped on his motorcycle and followed the limo as it drove toward downtown Vancouver.

The limo arrived at the Fairmont Hotel about half an hour later. Jean Pierre couldn't believe his luck. He worked as a waiter at Griffin's, one of the hotel's restaurants.

He sat in the lobby outside the restaurant, making notes in his note-book, waiting to see if they'd come down from their room for a meal. About an hour later his wish was granted. All five of them entered the restaurant and took a table at the back. As Fran stood up to survey the brunch buffet, Jean Pierre slid into line behind her.

One of the chefs looked up from behind the counter and said, "Hey J.P., I didn't know you were on today."

"Later. Just catching the last of the brunch. It looks great today."

He flashed his perfect grin at the chef and at Fran as she turned to look at him. His tight jeans and worn out leather jacket encased his chiselled physique. "Hi, I'm Jean Pierre, but most people call me J.P.," he said extending his hand.

"Hi, I'm Fran."

"Yes. I know. Listen, I'm a journalist from the *Global Reader*. I'm doing an article on innovation and ethics in business. You know since this Enron and Arthur Andersen scandal, this business with Wrightway and Freeman & Wilson is very topical. I assure you, I know you are innocent and I believe you have such a powerful perspective to share. I'd love to interview you..."

"I don't think so. Not right before the trial," Fran answered, looking away.

J.P. handed her a pre-heated plate for the buffet.

"That's okay. I wouldn't print anything about the trial. I'm inter-ested in your father, what kind of man he was, where he came from, why there is no past on him. He just seemed to emerge from out of nowhere. I'm curious to know whether or not you found out anything while you were away. I promise I won't publish anything until after the trial is over, and you can pre-screen the whole article before it goes to print ..."

"Really, I'm rather tired from the trip," Fran replied with a sigh.

J.P. pressed on. "It may be a chance to clear your father's name. I think people would like to know the full story, not just the salacious misquotes you read in the papers. It could make a huge difference to your cause."

Fran looked over at her travel companions. They were busy making plans to go shopping. She certainly didn't feel like shopping. She felt that the *Global Reader* was a thoughtful publication. Also, Marguerite had recommended she find a way to get control of the message about her father's life. She looked at J.P.'s face. His eyes shimmered with reassurance and Fran was getting used to going on instinct more and more.

"Okay. Let's meet in the lounge here in an hour. I get to proof it before you go to print?"

"Absolutely. You have my word," J.P. smiled appreciatively as he extended his *Global Reader* business card.

An hour later they met as arranged. As they settled into the red leather sofa in the hotel lounge, J.P. pulled out his digital voice recorder.

"Do you mind if I tape the conversation?"

"No. That's okay."

"Where would you like to begin?" J.P. asked as he placed the microphone near her chair.

Fran hesitated. "There's so much to tell. I'll start near the end and work backwards. How's that?"

"Whatever works for you."

Fran shuddered as the memories of the last few months flooded into her mind.

"Last July my whole life changed, and it's been a rollercoaster ever since."

## CHAPTER 3

I t was a late summer's eve when a loud thump on the floor suddenly startled Fran out of a turbulent dream. Bewildered, she peered up at the illuminated clock on the wall. It was 1:11 a.m.

The banging started again.

She sighed and gathered herself for what she knew would be another uncomfortable interaction. As she passed her reflection in the full-length mirror, Fran noticed that she had lost more weight. It's stress, she thought. She had been worrying about the firm's partnership meeting coming up. For six nights in a row, she had been tossing and turning, wondering how she was going to make a compelling presentation about why she should be a full partner in her father's accounting firm.

Though she was almost thirty, Fran had a youthful, almost girlish appearance. From years of marathon running her physique was lean and formless; a tomboy that never grew up. On this night, her unkempt black hair and coal eyes gave her a brooding look. Dark circles and more crow's feet, a tightly set jaw; she didn't like what she saw — a seething edginess was piercing through her tightly wound surface more frequently these days. A blustery wind snuck in through the slightly opened window shivering Fran's bony shoulders. She put on an old terrycloth robe and slippers, tied her hair back neatly and threw some cold water on her face.

The banging started up again.

Taking in a long, slow breath, Fran tiptoed down the spiral staircase that separated his world from hers. As she opened the door at the bottom of the stairs, she braced herself. Her own apartment was meticulous. Fran had studied Feng Shui and had developed an aching need for harmony and symmetry in her environment.

In contrast, her father's living area was a Feng Shui nightmare. Clutter and chaos reigned. It was a foreboding space, dark and dusty; a maze of decades old newspapers, moldy books, broken down appliances, and electrical cords running haywire in all directions — a fine haven for spider webs and dust bunnies. With three TVs constantly blaring, the cobwebs ran from light fixtures down to gnarly, dead houseplants. There were only narrow passageways to get around the house.

Tattered curtains and old bookshelves blocked all sunlight from coming through the huge picture windows. Fran had not seen that million-dollar view in over ten years. It was like the long-forgotten tomb of a buried pharaoh, or a mausoleum: dead, like her father in some way; the show was over, but they'd forgotten to turn out the lights.

Any attempts Fran made to rearrange his living area, water his plants, or simply throw anything out made him quake with panic. She gave up trying years ago and decided to live and let live.

She spent as little time in his space as possible. This served her father as well. He was a private man who liked his solitude. The older he got, the more of a hermit he was becoming.

Fran entered the living room, her eyes falling on a familiar but bizarre sight. George Freeman was a whale of a man with a shiny domed head fringed by a halo of frizzy gray hair. For the third time in the last month George was stuck in his reclining chair, his enormous girth trapping him in the 'feet up' position. He hadn't been able to get out for three hours and didn't want his daughter to know. Finally, in desperation to go to the bathroom, he resigned himself to prodding his mahogany cane on the ceiling to get Fran to come down.

Last week on his eightieth birthday, George had stepped on the industrial-size scale in the doctor's office. It was something he had avoided doing for a long time, but the doctor insisted. He now weighed in at over 350 pounds, up seven pounds since last year. After several years of foot ulcers and toe problems, the doctor said if he didn't lose weight, his legs would turn gangrenous due to onset diabetes. The spectre of being fully disabled weighed heavily on him this particular night.

It was becoming increasingly difficult for him to get out of chairs. He had recently installed an elevator in his house along with handles everywhere, and a modified bathroom so that he could remain independent. He secretly endured a long list of ailments, from diabetes to sciatica to high blood pressure to arthritis. He took at least thirty different kinds of drugs and supplements a day in hopes of slowing down the imminence of death. The cocktail of drugs in his system made him feel fuzzy-headed, especially late at night.

Fran gently placed her hand on his wrist to let him know he could stop banging on the ceiling. She was there for him. Unless she came right away her father would go into a panic. Without a word to him, Fran got behind the chair and heaved with all her might, but to no avail. After several failed attempts she slumped in a nearby chair exhausted, waiting for the next instructions. He said nothing.

In a thin voice Fran suggested, "Maybe I should call the twenty-four-hour respite care line."

"No! Try again!" he barked.

"I can't do it, Dad, I'm not strong enough. I need to call. They will only be here for a few moments."

As usual, he said nothing and turned away. His silence spoke volumes. Years of fierce independence, robust energy and self-imposed exile from society, all crumbling beneath this humiliating experience.

"I'm making the call now," she said with quiet compassion. She found the phone number that she had carefully hidden by the phone. "I really think it's the only thing we can do. You don't want to stay stuck there any longer, do you?" she said as she waited for someone to answer.

A cheerful woman at the care centre answered her call.

"Twenty-four-hour respite care!"

"Yes, my name is Fran Freeman, and we have a bit of the situation here."

"What kind of situation? Alzheimer's? An accident? Interpersonal family issues?"

"My eighty-year-old father is stuck in his reclining chair. I can't push him out — I'm not strong enough. We are going to need someone quite strong to help out."

"Your father is a big one, then, huh?"

"Um. Yes."

"How much does he weigh?"

"I don't know," Fran said lowering her voice, "Several hundred pounds."

"Okay then. Eva, we have a number fifty-nine," the receptionist said to somebody else at the care center. "We need your address, name and phone number."

"It's Fran Freeman, at 80 Alder Place, West Vancouver. 604-928-3601."

"Oh. The Freeman Manor."

"That's right," Fran said reluctantly. *Why did people need to gossip about them?*

"Someone will be right over."

"Thank you."

As they waited, Fran went to the kitchen to make him some Chamomile tea. As she negotiated her way past the piles of newspapers and old furniture, she noticed that the photo of her and her father was not in its usual place on the mantle. It had fallen over when an old curtain rod fell on it. Fran found the photo on the floor. The glass was broken. She removed the glass and stood the photo back in its rightful place.

In the photo, Fran was seven-years-old, and holding a giant, stuffed, brown shaggy dog that her father won for her at the fair. George's mantelpiece was lined with photos of Fran at all ages — at three-years-old, at nine, at fifteen, and at twenty-four in cap and gown when she graduated with an MBA in accounting. Fran was his reason for being, the one person who still cared even after he had alienated everyone else. Her life belonged to him. There were no other photos of George, and none of Fran's mother, Roberta. All photos of George's former wife had been destroyed years ago.

After twenty minutes, Fran heard someone try to ring the doorbell. The doorbell hadn't worked for years and George didn't want it fixed. It just made an annoying clicking sound, like someone trying to start a car after having left the headlights on all night. Fran raced to the door and opened it just as the woman was about to pound on the doorknocker.

Eva, a stocky woman in her mid-fifties, wore a caregiver's uniform, and had sallow, saggy skin with large pores. Her exhaustion rolled off the edges of her thick Polish accent. The dark circles under her close-set eyes spoke of burdens too painful to tell.

Fran tried to have a word with the woman about her father and the house before they entered the living room. People often felt shocked and spooked by what they saw, and Fran had a 'script' she used to help them get over it. However, Eva simply pushed past Fran, manoeuvring deftly passed stacks of rubbish. After years of helping eccentric and grouchy senior citizens deal with the indignities of aging, Eva needed no explanation. She planted herself firmly in front of George to assess the situation. He said nothing to her and simply looked away. She tilted her head and drummed her fingers on her elbow; a scowl etched onto her face.

Eva moved to the back of the chair and pushed. No success. She rocked it back and forth, and George protested, "That is too rough!"

Eva shot back at him, "Then make it easy on us and lean forward!"

Then both Eva and Fran nodded to each other and took a running leap at the rocker. They hit the chair simultaneously and the force of their charge knocked the chair forward and George was free. But the sudden impact made George's reading glasses fly off his lap and he winced in pain as blood poured back into his gangrenous legs.

Leaning forward, he fumbled for his two canes so he could get up. His bladder was so full, he was sure he wouldn't make it. Eva and Fran reached forward to grab an arm, but he shook off their attempts to help him. In a foreign tongue he mumbled a few curses as he made his way to the bathroom.

Eva inquired, "Has this happened before?"

"No. It's not a problem," George muttered, as he limped out of the room. "Thank you for coming. We won't need your help anymore."

Once she heard the bathroom door close, Eva turned to Fran and said "I don't recognize the language that he speaks, where is he from?"

Fran shrugged.

"You aren't a family member, then?" Eva said as she started to take in the oddness of the house.

"I'm his daughter, actually. He's from somewhere in Central Europe."

"I'm from Central Europe and I don't recognize his accent or his language."

They could hear him still talking to himself in the bathroom.

Eva looked intrigued. She leaned in to hear better. "It's not Polish or Hungarian. Not German. Well, I know he's not Czech, or Slovak. Not even Romanian or Serbian."

Fran responded, "I have only ever heard him speak English. But lately he seems to be mumbling these strange words. I think he's just getting senile."

Eva turned to her and said, "He needs to be in a home. A skinny thing like you can't possibly give him the help he needs here."

Fran sighed, "Try telling that to him."

Eva surveyed the unkempt mess and raised her eyebrows.

"I try to tidy things up," Fran flushed, "but he just won't let me. He used to be fanatically tidy but in the last ten years he seems to have gone in the opposite direction. I cook occasionally and do errands but he prefers to be alone."

Eva repeated herself firmly, "He needs to be in a well-equipped senior care facility."

"He made me promise I would never put him in a home."

"That's rubbish. It's not good for him to be here. This house is a danger zone. That said, the only home that could take a man of his size is Blakewood and that is very expensive."

"Money isn't a problem."

Eva raised her eyebrows, "Yes. He has a big accounting firm — Freeman & Wilson, if I'm not mistaken?"

"Yes."

"For some reason I thought he had died years ago."

"He hasn't been active there for about ten years," Fran replied.

Eva leaned in close to her, "I take it your mother has passed away?"

Fran hesitated then said, "I'm not sure."

There was an awkward silence, and then Eva added, "I don't mean to intrude. It's just that you obviously need help here."

Fran continued, "I don't know where my mother is. She never kept in touch after she left."

"When did she leave?" Eva asked, her curiosity plainly evident now.

"A long time ago. When I was a child."

"Haven't you ever tried to find her?"

"No," Fran said hugging herself tightly, as if bracing herself against an icy wind.

"It's just that it's quite easy now with the internet and these agencies that help you."

"I've thought about it. But she could have easily found me if she wanted to. We're still living in the same house we lived in when she left."

"What would make a woman leave her own child?"

There was another long silence. Eva looked sideways, as if regretting saying those words.

Fran continued. "She was a singer and left to go on tour with a band when I was about seven-years-old.

"You've lived here your entire life, then?" Eva gasped.

Fran barely nodded but insisted, "I live in the upstairs apartment. It's a totally separate living space."

"And what about other relatives?" Eva asked.

"There aren't any."

Eva inquired, "What about neighbours, or friends?"

Fran shook her head, "As I said, he likes his privacy."

"So, there is no one else that can help you with this situation?"

"Listen. I understand you are trying to help," Fran said, growing uncomfortable, "It's just that my father would be upset if he knew I was talking to you about all this."

"I absolutely promise to keep this all confidential," Eva said glancing away. "I'll confide in you something, because I trust you and I want you to trust me. You are so much like my own daughter...yes, so much... loving and kind but much too easily hurt. We haven't spoken in years. We spoke angry words once and that erected a Berlin wall between us. I haven't seen my grandchildren in so many years that I wouldn't even recognize the little ones anymore. She won't let me back in their lives, but I know she misses me. I could help make her life so much easier if she let me. But she won't, so let me help you."

As Eva handed Fran a leaflet about her services as an in-home caregiver, a wave of melancholy seemed to waft up around them both.

"I work in this field," she explained, "I talk to people everyday about the pressure of dealing with their aging parents — that's my job. I want to be helpful, but only in a way that works for you."

There was a long silence while Fran hesitated, considering the offer, covering her delay by busying herself clearing some cobwebs from a door frame. Then she looked up at Eva and let a little of her distress show.

"The truth is I am desperate for someone to talk to. I don't have many friends and my life consists of working at the accounting firm and taking care of my father — there isn't much room for anything else. His health is declining rapidly and he's getting increasingly disabled. But he won't accept anyone else in his home. I once tried hiring two male nurses to help him move around — they didn't last a week."

The bathroom door opened, and both women watched as George made his way to the bedroom.

"I'm okay," he grumbled as the dagger of his thin moustache curled into a grimace. "I don't need any more help. Thank you for coming. Goodnight!"

The bedroom door swung shut with a bang.

Eva shrugged and headed for the door.

"My number is on that flyer," she said to Fran, "I know how to deal with someone like him, trust me."

She stepped out onto the front porch, then paused and turned around to face Fran. Then she reached up and gave Fran a hug.

"You don't have to do this alone," she whispered.

Fran looked down at the ground and nodded, choking back tears. The summer rain sprinkled down just outside the front porch. Eva opened her umbrella and headed out into the darkness.

## CHAPTER 4

George couldn't get comfortable in his bed. The dozens of pillows scattered around still could not cushion all the painful parts. These days he felt grateful for any area of his body that didn't ache constantly. He grabbed a handful of painkillers, shoved the pills into his mouth, and then searched for his water. He forgot to bring in a glass of water. He didn't want to talk to his daughter again this evening, and forced the pills down his dry throat. Swallowing was painful. He rolled over and succumbed again to that haunting scene.

*He looks out his bedroom window. The streets are almost deserted. A beggar woman limps along the cobble-stones.*

*She carries a heavy package. Stooping, she pulls out a crumpled piece of paper, smoothing it out in her palm. Then she holds the paper up, squinting at in the lamplight.*

*He steps back from the window upon realizing the beggar woman is coming to his house. There is a knock on the door. The housekeeper walks past his bedroom, heading for the door and mumbling, "Who can that be at this hour of the night?"*

*The housekeeper opens the small glass hatch in the front door and peers out. He can hear the beggar woman saying, in broken German, "I want to speak with Jiri."*

*He freezes at the mention of that name.*

*The housekeeper replies "I know no one by that name."*

*The woman asks, "Does a man named Karl live here?"*

*"Yes, ma'am, Karl Frei is the head of the household."*

*The woman nods, then shows the housekeeper her heavy package — which is no package at all, but a five-year old little girl, sound asleep in her arms.*

*"This young child is a relative of this family," the woman says.*

*The housekeeper recoils upon seeing the face of the little girl. "I think you must be mistaken, ma'am. That child cannot be a relative."*

*The housekeeper quickly shuts the glass hatch and dead-bolts the door.*

*At that moment Karl comes out from the master bedroom, "Who was that?" he asks.*

*The housekeeper shakes her head, frowning, and replies, "A beggar woman looking for a handout."*

*He watches from the window as the woman limps toward the lamppost and sits down in the snow, exhausted. He stares at her, transfixed. As she peers out from her shawl, her melancholy eyes register his figure in silhouette. A police officer appears from no where, shooing her and the child back out into the night.*

## CHAPTER 5

Summer still hadn't graced the wet coast of Canada by early July. Cool, damp weather clung to the land like an unwanted guest. A sparse crowd stood under umbrellas to watch the annual Canada Day fireworks, while the outdoor Kits Pool sat forlorn and empty, abandoned by the sun worshippers like a forgotten lover.

Fran glanced out into the dreary haze of misty rain outside and ached to stay curled up in bed. She had spent most of the night awake worrying about how to prepare for today's events.

Today she had to give her speech before the partners of Freeman & Wilson. They had invited her to possibly become a partner in the accounting firm. It meant a higher income, but also more responsibility; something she wasn't completely ready for. The other partners had been acting on behalf of the company without George's input, even though he still owned fifty-one percent; a fact which made some of the partners uncomfortable. One solution was to invite his daughter to be part of the decision-making, but Fran was just a junior account manager, and even she had a hard time deciphering her father's needs at the best of times, let alone acting on them.

George's razor-sharp logic and visionary thinking had deteriorated slowly into rants about the most trivial and inconsequential things.

During the last meeting he'd attended, he'd spent thirty minutes complaining how difficult it was to find good slippers. After that the partners stopped inviting him. With George aging and in poor health, they were getting anxious to re-negotiate the partnership agreement. There was no succession plan in place. The other partners had tried for years to get George to sign a shotgun clause, but he kept putting off the decision saying he needed to wait due to tax purposes. Now it was clear to them he never had any intention of signing — which meant that the company would be thrown into chaos upon his death. Some partners felt it was natural that Fran be groomed to take over her father's company but others felt that she was too young and that Nelson Gaulin was a far more appropriate choice, particularly Nelson himself.

Fran knew this upcoming meeting would be her chance to prove her leadership capabilities. For years, she had strong opinions and innovative ideas about the direction of the company but never said anything. It had been immensely frustrating to see the partners make decisions that she knew would hurt the company and its stakeholders in the long run.

Over the years Fran had decided that people just didn't care to listen to her, particularly authority figures. Perhaps this was because listening was never her father's strong suit and so Fran had resigned herself to not talking to him about her life or her views. Her resignation felt, at times, like a prison cell.

But today, her carefully constructed walls of inscrutability had to come down. Suddenly it was *very important what she thought* and how well she could convey her ideas. And the sudden glare of attention on the neglected garden of her opinion was more than a little disconcerting.

Before Fran left for work she made sure George's breakfast and lunch were ready to go: two low cal meals, packed away in Tupperware containers in the fridge. She noticed a brown paper bag at the back full of chocolate bars, donuts and cake. She thought of tossing them out, but instead turned a blind eye, shuddering at the thought of his reaction.

As she was leaving, George shouted, "Don't forget we need to go to the bank today. I want to see if the gas bill went through and I need more bread. I want the flax kind this time, not that dark rye stuff, so we need to go to that place across town. Then I need the non-shredding dental floss which you can only get at that place on Broadway. Then I have to be at the podiatrist."

Fran tried to scrawl down a reminder to herself while fumbling down the narrow hallway, juggling her briefcase, purse and car keys.

"Today is the leadership meeting, remember?" she shouted back amidst the chaos, trying to be heard over the din of three television sets blaring at full volume.

"We need to be at the podiatrist at 4:30, so we'll need to leave by at least 2:00," was all George said.

Fran felt the sinewy muscles around her jawbone tighten up. She had missed her workout regime three days in a row now. In addition she already had a huge backlog of e-mails, paperwork, phone calls, and preparation to do for a new client. The last client had requested a new account manager because Fran just wasn't able to keep up with the workload. Each item on George's list of tasks would take at least thirty minutes — the bank, the special bread store, the super market. Then the visit to the podiatrist to cut his toenails would take almost two hours. Even though Fran could easily pick all these things up herself, George insisted on accompanying her so that the job got done correctly. And even through the podiatrist offered to do house calls, George wanted to go to the doctor's office himself.

This meant Fran had to help him into a wheelchair, wheel him to the car, help him into the car, disassemble the wheelchair, load it into the trunk of the car, and drive to each location. Then at each location she needed to unload the wheelchair, assemble it, get George into it, and wheel him into the store or office. George would then complain about her driving. She invariably drove too fast and took the wrong route, and couldn't park properly. Taking care of George in this detailed way meant that Fran could only handle a small client load. This kept her personal income low and made it more difficult for her to gain the experience she needed to be a full partner.

If Fran failed to become a partner the balance of power would go in Nelson's favour. Fran's presence as partner would help give voice to the minority of partners who held a different set of values about how to run the company. Why didn't George seem to care about that? He had favoured Nelson for years to act on his behalf as managing partner. Nelson used to make good choices for the company, but lately his decisions seemed to be more self-serving. Fran looked at her father, wanting his vote of confidence before the meeting. She drew in a short breath for courage, and ventured forward, daring to turn down the volume on the TV sets.

"You know, most of the partners — Nelson, Maria, Frank, Tahira and Ramon — they want to keep Wrightway as a client. Given their history of fraudulent audits, though, the others, Gordon and Nisha, think it's a bad move. And I, umm, well, I think they may be right. But, unless I'm a partner then, ahh, then my voice doesn't count."

She waited for his answer, watching a bug crawl across the peeling linoleum in the front hall. Finally she added, "What do you think? We could put you on speaker phone during the meeting."

George was rifling through the newspaper impatiently. "Where is the crossword section? They keep changing the page."

"Did you hear what I said, dad?" Fran asked, handing him *The Vancouver Sun.*

"I don't like their crosswords!" he said, pushing it away. Fran studied his 'far away' eyes. His manner turned childlike again and his words turned into that other nonsensical language; a language with an odd rhetoric and a staccato cadence.

"I don't understand, Dad" asked Fran, lost, her discomfort growing.

George smiled and laughed at her as if he was seeing someone else in Fran's face.

She smiled back at him. "Dad. It's Fran, your daughter. Look, I'll see you this afternoon for the appointment. Okay?"

She felt somewhat glad to know that at least his senility was taking him to a place where he seemed happy again.

As Fran got into the car the sense of anxiety and gloom settled over her like a gray blanket. All her father had to do was make one comment against working with Wrightway and it would tip the favour in their direction. But he seemed to be retreating into another world as his health deteriorated. Fran just couldn't count on him anymore. In fact, no one could.

Traffic was particularly heavy that morning as Fran drove into town. Must be the rain, she thought. She had chosen what she thought would be the fastest route possible, but there were barriers on the road everywhere, and construction delays. The meeting was starting at 9:15 a.m. sharp and it was already 9:02. Fran's breath grew shallow. Why didn't she get out of bed earlier? This was clearly self-sabotage.

"There you go again, Fran, making your life more difficult again," she spoke aloud to herself.

When she finally pulled into the office tower it was 9:11. To her surprise she saw another car pull into her parking spot — clearly marked with the name Fran Freeman. It was a shiny white Jaguar convertible with the top down. It irked her that already being late, someone parked in her spot. It also struck her as odd that the top was down on a rainy day. The car was wet, but the woman driving the car was dry. She stepped out of her vehicle just as Fran pulled in behind her.

"Excuse me, but I believe this is my parking spot," Fran said trying to sound cordial while pointing to the sign.

"I'm sorry, our organization just moved into this building. I thought they told me that my parking spot was #111," the woman replied, "I'll move."

The woman got back in her car and backed out very quickly, so quickly in fact that she scraped the edge of Fran's car. A rasping sound pierced the air as the two vehicles made contact.

Terrific. Fran's day had barely begun and now it was unfolding like a bad reality TV show. Maybe she secretly wanted to fail this "partnership audition." Then she would have a great excuse to just leave the company and do something more satisfying with her life. Fran shook her head, trying to push the thought from her mind, and focus on the situation at hand.

"Oh my goodness, was that me hitting you?" called the woman from her car.

They both got out of their vehicles to inspect the damage. There was a dent in Fran's 1991 Plymouth Sundance, and a big scratch down the side of the white Jaguar.

"I'm so sorry I damaged your car!" the woman exclaimed.

"Your car is much nicer than mine, and has a much bigger scratch right there," replied Fran

"Don't worry," she said, "I'll get them both fixed as soon as possible."

The woman got back in the car and pulled into parking spot number 110, right beside Fran.

As they both walked to the elevator the woman murmured to herself "What's good about this situation?"

"Pardon me?" Fran asked.

"It's just something I ask myself whenever something I perceive as 'bad' happens…like scratching someone else's car."

"Oh."

The woman handed her a business card, "I'm Marguerite LeBoyer. Here is all my information so that we can get your car fixed. Pleased to meet you. Sorry it had to be under these circumstances."

Fran accepted the card and glanced at the woman.

Marguerite was a dark-skinned mulatto woman, with a panther-like grace. She was dressed in a high couture gray suit with crimson piping that ran the length of her impossibly long legs. Her jet black hair was straightened and coiffed in an ornate French knot, and her crimson stiletto heels made the woman tower over Fran's five-foot-seven frame.

"Nice to meet you, too," Fran said, trying to act businesslike despite her panic about being late. At the same time she was in awe of the woman's appearance and presence, and she felt drawn to her immediately. "My name is Fran Freeman and I work at Freeman & Wilson Accounting on the eleventh floor."

"You are the owner of the company?" asked Marguerite.

"No, my father is," Fran answered, glancing at her watch.

It was 9:23.

Fran frowned.

They waited in silence. The elevator was taking forever.

"I met a man the other day who said he ran the show at Freeman & Wilson," Marguerite said suddenly, piercing the silence.

Fran reacted, returning a cold smile, and clearing her throat.

"Really?" she managed.

Marguerite raised one eyebrow upon seeing Fran's reaction.

"That was probably Nelson Gaulin," Fran answered, explaining, "My father founded the company but he is eighty and not in good health. Nelson is the ... how I shall say ... the self-appointed Managing Partner right now. It's funny you should mention it, because there is a meeting today to talk about who should take on the role more officially. Some people think that I should take over from my father since he owns fifty-one percent of the partnership share and I am his only heir. Others think Nelson should take over because he has the leadership skills and apparently I don't. But why am I telling you all this?"

Fran blushed, catching herself suddenly, surprised by her Chatty Cathy routine. Talking so openly to a stranger was not like her. Yet there was something about Marguerite she liked, despite the other woman's inability to read signs or drive well.

Marguerite laughed. The sound was rich and comforting. It seemed to issue from deep in the woman's spirit, and had the effect of lightening Fran's mood.

"I've been there!" Marguerite replied, "I took over my father's organization. Have you heard of us, by the way? Artistry International. We've just moved into the third floor. We are a foundation to help artists from other countries bring their art to North America — visual

artists, musicians, poets, etc. Anyway, some people didn't want me as
the leader. I certainly had to prove myself first. I tend to base my decisions on intuition rather than facts, which bothered people at first."

Marguerite glanced over at Fran, "You're a racehorse, girl, aching to
be let out of the stables. My instinct tells me you'd make a great leader
of the company. Would you like that role?"

The elevator stopped at the third floor and the doors opened. Fran
stood looking at Marguerite, not knowing what to say.

"I don't know," she said finally, feeling appreciation for the woman's
belief in her, yet still frightened by what that responsibility would
mean.

"Give me your business card," Marguerite suggested, "I'll call a
garage and arrange for your repairs. I promise I'll drive better next
time. Good luck with your meeting."

Fran handed the woman her card and the elevator doors closed. She
was alone. In the thirty seconds that passed between floors three and
eleven, she wondered what gave Marguerite the sense that she'd be a good
leader. Could she really tell that fast? Marguerite's question had made Fran
realize that she herself didn't even know if she wanted the job. Her father
hadn't groomed her for the position the way he had groomed Nelson. She
always assumed he didn't see her as the leader type. In fact, she was sure
that the partners, her father and everyone at Freeman & Wilson didn't
want her to take over George's role. They were considering her for the
position as a gesture of politeness — but they knew she'd do a lousy job.
She couldn't even be on time for a meeting.

As Fran stepped onto the eleventh floor she was confronted by a photo.
The eyes of George and Paul, the two founders of Freeman & Wilson,
were bearing down on her. She looked to the right and Meili Cheng, the
receptionist, was imploring her to hurry, "They're all waiting for you!"

Back at home George sensed his daughter's anxiety. It triggered a long
forgotten memory.

## CHAPTER 6

*H*e jabs his comrade in the ribs and points with his chin over to the left. *Vlad can just make out a boy carrying a sack of potatoes in the lingering dusk. He is alone. It's past curfew. Something finally to curb their boredom. He adjusts the ill fitting Hlinka uniform. Starchy fabrics make him itch. They march in unison as they have practiced countless times before. The menacing rhythm on the gravel road is like an aphrodisiac; it's the hunt. It runs hot and cold in his blood.*

*The potato carrier's back seems to stiffen and he quickens his pace. He pulls his cap down lower on his face. The footsteps get closer. Suddenly the boy drops the potatoes, leaps across the ditch, and slips into the forest.*

*Vlad shouts to him, "Come on!"*

*He pulls out his billy club and leaps the ditch. It's dark in the forest, but the moon shines through in rays between the trees. There he sees the boy hiding behind an oak tree. The boy doesn't think they can see him. He snickers to himself. This is beautiful. Silently they creep, then one nods to the other. Vlad goes one way, he goes the other.*

*He grabs the boy's arm and pulls him down to the forest floor. He's quick, though, and scrambles again to his feet. Vlad grabs the boy's collar. Potato boy is struggling to get loose, shouting nonsensical words. He lunges and the boy kicks him. That's all he needed, one small provocation. Thank you. He holds the club wide and takes aim against the boy's head.*

*Smash!*

*He draws blood.*

*The excitement escalates.*

*The boy kicks him again.*

*The second blow of the club hits the boy's shoulder with a thud.*

*As he winds up for a third strike, something drops out of a tree.*

*The crash of branches startles all three of them. It's a man — dark, viciousness waving a stick like a feral ape. He stalks them. Vlad drops the boy, like the coward he is. The ape man draws closer — stick as a spear pointing, ready to pierce him in half. The boy runs behind the ape man. A twig snaps. Someone else is there. But he can't see anything now. It's too dark. The dark beings rule now. Wildness is all around him. He drops his billy club and runs, ripping through branches and thorn bushes, tearing his face up, leaping across the ditch, twisting an ankle, running hard still. He runs into civilization until the neatly carved cobblestones soothe his blood back to normal.*

## CHAPTER 7

F ran stepped into the boardroom and all nine heads swivelled, like a firing squad taking aim. The disapproving looks of the "tribal elders" pierced her veneer of cool. Nelson was at the head of the room talking about his vision of the company.

He stopped for a moment, glared at Fran and with a plastic-coated smile said, "Glad you could join us."

She stumbled over the table leg as she took a seat and tried to find her notes. They weren't where she had left them. She had worked on her speech all weekend. After shuffling through every pocket of her briefcase, Fran's heart began to sink. Nelson finished his speech and most of the partners smiled appreciatively and applauded. Frank whispered something to him when he sat down and the two men roared with the kind of "fraternity brother" laughter that put Fran on edge. Frank was still laughing as he approached the front of the room, trying to contain himself enough to see what was next on the agenda.

"Okay then, what's next?" he said, "I guess we need to talk about how to divvy up the Wrightway audit."

"Actually, Frank, I believe Fran is next on the agenda," said Gordon with a cordial but firm edge to his voice.

"Oh yeah! Franny girl is up. Show us what you got, honey."

Fran reacted. She hated being called "Franny" or "honey" or any uninvited diminutive. She rose out of her chair, and banged her shin again on the table leg. Her leg seared with pain as she walked up to the front of the room, noteless. She could feel her knees knocking together and her heart beating like a ticking bomb. Dread lay in her stomach like a cold, wet stone.

She cleared her throat and looked up at the partners seated around the boardroom table. Nelson was whispering something to Ramon. Tahira was text messaging someone on her cell phone. Marie's face was contorted as if she'd just smelt bad milk. Gordon was the only one paying her the kind of attention she needed — to believe she had a right to be there.

"My father's vision of Freeman & Wilson was to be the accounting firm of choice for companies wanting integrity, wisdom and leading-edge expertise. We have been that for several decades now and have a solid reputation," that was the opening sentence that Fran had memorized. Whew. At least she was out of the gate. But, then all of a sudden her mind went completely blank. Her breath froze and her mouth tightened. What was the next thing she was going to say? Something about how she understood the vision and could translate it. She worked out a catchy phrase. It even had a rhyme in it and some alliteration. Where did she put that three by five card? It was on her desk at home. In her panic she changed bags and forgot to include the cards. Gordon's eyes widened like he was about to witness a car crash. Fran blushed. A nervous rash started burning on her neck. Every time Fran felt humiliated or embarrassed blotchy red patches appeared on her neck. She had gotten into the habit of wearing turtlenecks to hide this problem but all of them were in the wash that day. She was wearing a V-neck cashmere sweater and the neck rash was in full view to everyone. Tahira looked up from her cell phone in morbid fascination.

"I, umm, believe I understand my father's, or I mean the company's vision. He lived it, and I live with him. I mean I live there a lot lately. Actually, I live in an apartment above his house, but you all know that.

Anyway, so I'm there all the time. But, of course you all know that, too. It's like, you know, we, aaah, talk about the vision regularly," This was a lie. Fran and George never discussed the company anymore.

"You know he isn't that social a person, especially not in the last several years. I am sort of like his, aahh, interpreter, or something like that," she laughed nervously and started coughing. It turned into one of those hacking coughs where you can't speak anymore. Nisha ran up with a glass of water which Fran sipped with relief. Now, her eyes were watering and her face was crimson red. After clearing her throat, Fran tried to talk but her throat was too constricted, so she sipped the water again. She coughed and spat water onto Ramon. He backed up his chair and started wiping himself disgustedly with a napkin.

"I'm sorry, Ramon," she croaked.

Frank came up and stood beside her and put a hand on her shoulder, "Franny, my dear, you are a walking disaster area today. Maybe have a seat and we'll come back to this another time."

Fran fumbled her way back to her seat, trying to stifle the ongoing cough. The rest of the meeting was a daze. When it finally ended, Gordon and Nisha simply stood up and left, without saying a word to Fran. She escaped to her office and tried desperately to quell the tears. There was a soft knock at the door and a sandy-coloured mop of frizzy hair poked its way inside the door.

It was Peter Wilson Jr. He was the son of the other partner, Peter Wilson Sr. After his father died many years ago people expected that Peter Jr. would become a partner. However, that was not Junior's vision for the future. He didn't want to have that kind of responsibility. In fact, what he particularly liked about being a simple account manager was that it allowed him to do what he loved most, which was to perform in musicals. He was part of an amateur troupe and was often trying to get Fran to audition. He was impossibly tall and had a willowy figure with eyeballs that seemed to look off in different directions.

"Come in, Peter," Fran managed to say.

Peter was one of the few people she felt comfortable talking openly to at the company.

He leapt into the room, singing "I dreamed a dream in time gone by, when hope was high and life worth living..."

"Not now, Peter."

"Sorry. I thought it would help. I heard it went pretty bad. No Toastmasters Golden Gavel award for you this time."

Fran dropped her head in her hands.

"I'm sorry. Hey, I don't want you to be my boss anyways. Then we couldn't gossip about everyone else," he said, trying to lighten the mood.

Fran smiled weakly. Peter walked around to her side of the desk and pulled up a chair.

"I don't have what it takes anyway," said Fran, "Why does Gordon keep pushing me?"

"You know why. Because Nelson is a snake," said Peter, "You of all people should know that."

Fran's brow furrowed and she put her finger to her mouth. She had asked Peter never to bring up the subject of her and Nelson. Six years ago when Fran started at the company, Nelson took a fancy to her. He was married to a strikingly beautiful woman named Janine who came from Shaughnessy wealth; investment bankers from way back. She was used to calling the shots in any intimate relationship and Nelson felt the threat of expulsion each morning he looked in the mirror. His trophy wife had a standard of living that the Sultan of Brunei would take issue with.

One weekend when Janine was on a New York shopping spree, Nelson invited Fran to come along while he finished an important audit for a big client. He said the audit was due the next day, and that he would have to finish the work at home. Having Fran's help would make sure he didn't have to stay up all night. When she discovered they were alone at his house, Fran felt uncomfortable but didn't leave.

As the evening grew on, Nelson's attentions toward her grew warmer and warmer. He sat very close to her while he explained his system for working. He invited her to edit his proposal and put his arm around her as she explained her comments. Before she knew it, she was in his bedroom.

As soon as the affair had started, Fran fell horribly, deeply and dizzyingly in love. As the months of secret liaisons went on she somehow managed to delude herself into thinking that Nelson would leave Janine to be with her. Then one day Candace, another accountant at the firm, asked Fran to go out for lunch. She wanted someone to confide in.

Fran never forgot those first few words out of Candace's mouth, "I'm in love with Nelson. Please don't tell anyone. We've been having an affair for the last few months and I'm pregnant. I haven't told Nelson yet. What should I do?"

Fran felt like she was caught in the middle of a bad soap opera. Her stomach flip-flopped. Her forkful of pasta fell back onto the plate. All she remembered was that she mumbled some kind of sympathetic comment to Candace and excused herself as quickly as possible, saying she had a client waiting. She left the table, went to the bathroom and hid in one of the stalls for over an hour until the shaking stopped.

Candace chose to terminate the pregnancy and move to another firm. The next time Nelson invited Fran to work late with him all she said was, "Candace told me what happened."

Nelson never said a word, but simply shrugged as if the loss of her meant nothing to him. Their affair ended at that moment. They never discussed their relationship or his affair with Candace again. They continued to work at the same firm together, for six years now, as if nothing had ever happened. No one ever knew, or at least she thought they didn't.

Over the years Fran saw other women become smitten with Nelson. They sometimes confided in Fran about their feelings. Each time this happened Fran would cringe with humiliation. She wanted to protect these women but didn't think it was her place, or couldn't find the courage to express herself. Perhaps it would mean admitting to them what a fool she had been.

As the memories drifted in and out, Fran finally realized that Peter was trying out his new audition song from *Les Miserables* on her. He finished the song with a flourish and an expectant smile. Fran smiled slightly, breaking out of her reverie. There was a knock at the door and they both turned as Gordon entered Fran's office. Fran straightened her demeanour.

Gordon was in his late fifties and had a salt-and-pepper buzz cut, and wire rimmed glasses. He had been with the company for twenty-five years and was normally a beacon of reassurance for Fran. Today, however, his gaze seemed troubled. He glanced at Peter before getting straight to the point.

"It seems to me as if you're trying to sabotage this situation, Fran," he said, "I would appreciate it if you let me know what is going on. Because if you're not going to step forward we need to find somebody else. The partners are very conflicted about this issue. If you don't step up to the plate, Nelson will have his way. And we all know what that means."

Then he left abruptly without waiting for a response.

Peter flinched, "Ouch. And he's one of the nice ones. But he's kinda right. The problem with you not taking the job is that they might make Edward a partner, or worse — Barbara! And then the company is truly going down the crapper."

Peter looked at his watch, "I'm sorry I have a client. I have to go. Let me know if you want to talk later."

He held Fran's hand like a knight at a medieval jousting festival. "You are the rightful Queen to this kingdom. I bow down ceremoniously in honour of your wisdom," he said, continuing to bow as he exited backwards out of her office.

Fran had to laugh at Peter's antics and was grateful for the comic relief. She had clients to see too, and emails to answer.

The morning dragged on until she had to get out of the office. Fran slipped past the receptionist and ran for the elevators. When the elevator doors opened Barbara was there. Fran smiled stiffly, stared at the floor and positioned herself as far away as possible. Barbara was a beady-eyed bean counter with over-dyed black hair that frizzed out in all directions.

"Fran, dear, you're not following my instructions on those remittance forms."

Fran couldn't think what she was referring to and shrugged.

Barbara retorted, "You know exactly what I'm talking about."

"I'm afraid I don't," she bristled.

"You have no special privileges here. Just remember that. Good day," she said as she bustled off at the lobby level.

Fran hated her. For years Barbara seemed to enjoy harassing her and always chose the worst moments. As the daughter of the founder some people assumed that she cut corners, that she was spoiled, or that she got special favours. None of that was true, at least not anymore, but some people like Barbara held onto things she'd done six years ago and never let go.

The doors closed and the elevator continued down to the parking level. When she arrived at the parkade Marguerite was there just getting into her car. Fran turned up her collar and lumbered toward her.

"I was hoping to see you again," Marguerite offered, "I'm just looking at your car again. I'd like to make it up to you by taking you to lunch. I was just going to go to Selby's."

Fran was silent.

"A short lunch," she assured Fran with a smile, "I promise I'm very good company."

"I'm sure you are." Fran nodded. She had to be home soon to help her father. Yet, a desperate need seemed to respond instead. "Okay. I'll join you."

"Great! Let's take my car. Jump in!"

Fran called her father to say she'd be a bit late but he didn't answer.

## CHAPTER 8

George had unplugged the phone and was sleeping as he often did in the day in short spurts. He couldn't sleep at night. It was too painful. Life had become one long bout of pain interspersed with a few minutes of reprieve when he sank back into other worlds and other times.

*The train station is packed with soldiers, sailors and airmen going off to fight. Parents, wives, girlfriends and their unborn babies stand huddled around their beloveds. They weave webs of magic protection around the men like bullet proof vests. 'Spare him', each repeats in silent mantra.*

*The father stares into his only son's face as if he knows that here and now may be all he ever has.*

*The girl is silly, giggling at everything. Why is she laughing when everyone else is crying? It's all too much for her.*

*The son knows — in that deep crevice of knowingness somewhere inside his chest — exactly what will happen. It's there — a solid, unwavering feeling — like a sentry.*

*He will never see any of them again.*

*He ignores the sentry, but the thought re-emerges again; its hard core edges staring him down.*

*He sniper shoots the sentry this time. The knowingness chokes to its death.*

*He can laugh now with that silly girl and flash his movie star smile. Please remember me as this dream man I see floating around in your eyes, he silently beseeches her.*

*The train whistle blows. His father hugs him. The son pulls away embarrassed. What will people think? The turquoise eyes are glassy pools of care penetrating his wall, searching for an unguarded entry point. The father finds one and goes inside.*

*The son feels white shards of lightening striking inside his chest.*

*The whistle blows again and the train begins to move. He pulls away from the father for the very last time. He kisses the girl's pretty red lips and touches her rounding belly.*

*Another shard of lightning pierces his finger tips. The heat burns a line up his arm and ignites something he can't quite name, but he knows it will stay lodged there for the rest of his life.*

*The son grabs his bag and leaps onto the train. They wave, but he does not wave back. The son smiles but he doesn't see them anymore. They are now nameless figures sketched onto a crowd scene.*

*This train is taking him to a new world.*

## CHAPTER 9

They roared off out of the parkade in Marguerite's convertible, the top down and the tires squealing. Fran glanced at the street. The rain was coming down steadily, and the wind buffeted pedestrians huddled under umbrellas.

"I'm surprised we're staying dry," Fran shouted, as they sped onto the boulevard.

"It's all in the intention," replied Marguerite flashing a huge grin.

They arrived at Selby's and got a window table looking out over the cloud-covered ocean.

"So how did the meeting go?" Marguerite asked.

Fran glanced out the window, her eyes watering, as wind and rain battered her reflection.

"That bad, huh?" said Marguerite.

"They don't think I'd make a good leader," said Fran.

"How do you know that?" replied Marguerite.

"I don't know, I just see it in their eyes."

"Maybe *you* don't think you'd make a good leader. As I said before, it's all in your intention."

Marguerite quickly surveyed the menu and said, "What are you going to have?"

"I usually get the goat cheese and pecan salad."

"I've never tried that before. That sounds good, but I'm going to ask them to substitute the red onions for more tomatoes."

"They don't do substitutions here."

"Oh yes they will."

"No, really, I've tried."

Marguerite flashed her brilliant smile again and said, "We just need an intention shift."

Marguerite winked at Fran as the waiter approached and said to him, "I'd like the goat cheese salad, but please substitute more tomatoes for the red onions. Thank you."

The waiter hesitated, cleared his throat and looked over at the kitchen nervously, "The chef doesn't like to do substitutions."

"What is it about making substitutions that creates a problem?"

The waiter smiled wryly and said in a quiet French accent, "She feels that certain dishes are balanced just so. If you substitute one thing for another, then it throws out the harmony," he added with one raised eyebrow, "It ruins the 'Feng Shui' of the dish."

"Aaaah. I see," said Marguerite, "Are there any substitutions that would keep the Feng Shui of the salad just right?"

"I've only seen her ever allow substitutions done in one way."

"Do tell," Marguerite cooed.

"More of each item in the salad in place of the red onions, but she insists on adding cilantro to replace the yang aspect offered by the onions."

"Done. Sounds good to me."

He turned to Fran.

"I'd like the same thing as my friend is having."

"Good then," the waiter said, looking relieved.

"What was I saying? Oh yes, your state of mind, or maybe I should say — your state of being — it's everything. It's like the software you are running on your bio-computer," Marguerite said, as she pointed to the side of her temple.

Fran felt confused.

"If you wanted to do a spreadsheet you wouldn't open a graphic design program, would you? If you want to be the leader of your company you need to run leadership software," Marguerite pressed on.

"And you think I'm running junior accountant software?" Fran retorted.

"Exactly!" Marguerite replied, "I think you need to get clear on what you want to create here, because ultimately it is your choice."

"It's not my choice. It's all up to the other partners and my father, I guess," argued Fran.

"Yes, I agree. But it is your choice about whether or not you want to be a leader, what kind of leader you want to be, and then the abilities will come from there," said Marguerite, "Maybe you just want to be a junior accountant."

"No!" Fran shot back, her eyes narrowing, "I want to lead this company."

There was a long pause. They both looked at each other, surprised by the force in Fran's voice. Then Marguerite said, "I think you just made the decision right then, didn't you?"

"Yes, I did," said Fran. She laughed and took a drink of water. She drank the whole glass in one gulp as if trying to quench a long-denied thirst.

Fran continued, frowning "I get confused, though. I don't want to be the kind of leader that my father was, or that Nelson is. That's not my style."

"That's good. Try to get clear on what your leadership style is. What's your first impulse?" asked Marguerite.

"I want to be a strong leader who has integrity and who cares as much about people as about the bottom line," said Fran without hesitation.

"That's clear," said Marguerite. "And how is it now? What kind of leader are you now?"

"I don't know. I suppose I could be a caring leader with integrity," said Fran.

"You most certainly could. But I'm asking about now — what kind of leader are you in the company, or when you are assuming a leadership role? It's important that you are honest with yourself about what state of *being* you have been choosing. No judgment about it. You can't get to where you are going unless you know where you are now," stated Marguerite.

"Alright. Right now I am a non-existent leader. I don't exercise my abilities much at all."

"What about your level of integrity, and your level of caring about people? Do you also care about the bottom line?"

"I have integrity and I care about people and I make money for the company, so I must care about the bottom line," responded Fran.

Marguerite countered, "Do you live your values?"

Fran squirmed in her seat, looking down at her fork, "Not all of them."

"Then do you have integrity?" said Marguerite, "By that I mean: do you operate in a way that is consistent with your values? Do you have the inner foundation that allows you to be the kind of leader you want to be?"

Fran looked at her blankly.

Marguerite continued, "For example, a chair with four legs has integrity, but a chair with only three doesn't. It's a slightly different concept than what you may be thinking integrity means. Most people get moralistic about it. I mean — do your values work in the context of your reality?"

Fran looked down at her fingers. The nail polish was chipping already, just one day after her $60 manicure. They obviously forgot to add the hardening polish. She wasn't getting the same kind of service she used to get, but still hadn't bothered saying anything.

"I guess I don't. I really care more about what other people think than anything else — not wanting to 'rock the boat'. I've seen things go on at the company that were hurtful to people and I didn't say or do anything about it," Fran sighed shakily and added, "And I have not always been truthful with people in this company either." She paused and took a long, slow breath, "That was hard to say."

"Okay, good. You can both recognize it and say it. Many people can't even recognize it. What about the bottom line? Do you care about that?" asked Marguerite.

"Not really. Money corrupts people. I don't think I particularly like money. It is important to earn it because it pleases my father and the partners. And, of course, it pays my bills," said Fran.

"Money doesn't corrupt people. Choosing a negative state of mind corrupts people. Money is just a form of energy. How you use that energy determines the outcome," said Marguerite.

Fran frowned, trying to fit this concept into her existing mental frame. Suddenly, a light came on in the back corner of her mind.

"I was reading about that concept recently. It's funny you should bring it up now. I hadn't connected the concept of money as energy and applied it to my own life like this before. How did you get to be so wise?" asked Fran.

"My father was a witch doctor," Marguerite deadpanned.

"Really?" asked Fran, sinking back in her chair — not quite sure what to make of the comment.

"Actually, both my parents were born into a shamanic tradition. They were healers. My father was Jamaican and my mother was British. What a combo, huh?" said Marguerite.

Marguerite hesitated, sensing Fran's discomfort with the topic. "Let's just say I grew up around people who liked to be helpful to others. And now, being helpful to you feels appropriate at this time. I'd advise you to take everything I say and decide for yourself if it's useful. Whatever works, great! Whatever doesn't — let it go. As I said, I go on my intuition. I think the important thing is for you to create an impetus to shift this situation — to create a magnet."

"What do you mean by a magnet?" asked Fran.

"I'll give you an example. When I was first considering taking over my father's company, I kept thinking about what I didn't want. I didn't want to disappoint my father's legacy. I didn't want my employees to turn against me. I didn't want to make the wrong decisions and see the organization suffer because of that. I didn't want to be working fourteen hours a day, seven days a week. Guess what happened?"

"All those things?"

"You got it. People felt I was not embodying my father's vision and turned against me. I made some wrong decisions and then I was working fourteen-hour days to try to fix them. A woman who mentored me pointed this out, and helped me turn it around. As a result, over time, with setbacks here and there, the organization eventually flourished, and I created a more balanced lifestyle. Well," she smiled, "what I call balanced anyway."

"Okay, so I just say something like, I am a strong leader and all that?"

"Something like that."

Fran rubbed her temples. Super positive people like Marguerite sometimes annoyed her. "And that is supposed to help magnetize it to me?"

"Getting clear on your intent is just the first part."

"Because I've created mission statements and affirmations like that for myself before, and still nothing changed," Fran sighed.

"Were you focusing on them every day?"

"No."

"Were you embodying them regularly?"

"I don't know what you mean by that."

"Do you brush your teeth everyday?"

"Yes."

"Have you ever gone through a period of your life where you didn't brush your teeth for several days or even weeks?"

Fran screwed up her face, "Yes, but only once."

"Setting your intention is like mental floss. It's like mentally removing the plaque. Our minds will naturally drift to negative thoughts and other people's negative thoughts 'collect' on us all the time. They are floating around everywhere. The plaque builds up unless we continually remove it and replace it with something else. This is something many people don't realize. The people who are most successful at manifesting their goals have the discipline to set their intention daily and to embody it."

"Wow. That's a big commitment."

"It only has to take a few minutes a day. The same amount of time it takes to brush your teeth."

"What do you mean by embodying it?"

"You can't switch your attitude through logic alone. Just stating what you want is a start but then it has to enter your essential nature. It has to get embedded in your cell structure. Artistry is one form of doing that. For example, I used to use the poetry of Maya Angelou because my father had all her books in our house." Marguerite sat back and smiled closing her eyes to reconnect to the spirit of the poet.

*I'm a black ocean,*
*leaping and wide*
*welling and swelling*
*I bear in the tide.*
*Leaving behind nights of terror and fear*
*I rise.*
*Into a daybreak that's wondrously clear*
*I rise.*
*Bringing the gifts that my ancestors gave*
*I am the dream and the hope of the slave*
*I rise*
*I rise*
*I rise*

Fran felt liquid fire down her spine as Marguerite spoke, "Woooee, that's powerful."

Marguerite sat in silence a moment to let the message seep through her.

Then she sat forward and said, "More powerful than an affirmation, huh?"

"I love poetry. I have written some myself," Fran smiled.

"Great. Artistry can transform like nothing else can. Use it for yourself that way. All the major paradigm shifts in history were ushered in by artists, poets, songwriters, musicians, filmmakers, playwrights, and designers. That's the role of the artist in society — to see what's beyond the horizon and portray it back to people symbolically.

"So treat your life as a work of art. You start with one thing and creatively turn it into something else, whether it's a lump of clay into a piece of pottery, a blank canvas into a Picasso, or a junior accountant into a CEO. But you have to start where you now. So you want to be a strong leader who has integrity and who cares as much about people as the bottom line, right?"

Fran nodded.

"How's it going with that now?" asked Marguerite.

Fran pulled her chin in like a boxer trying to avoid a hit, "I am a weak leader with low integrity."

"Is that true?"

Fran nodded.

"When did you choose that intention?"

"I didn't choose it," Fran answered.

"Then who did?"

"Maybe I learned it from my father, or mother, or teachers or society. Just read the papers. Everyone acts like that."

"If everyone else in this restaurant started banging their heads on the tables would you do it too?" replied Marguerite.

"Probably," Fran replied sheepishly, "I like to fit in."

Marguerite laughed out loud and a businessman from another table looked over. Marguerite winked at him.

"Yes, the brain is hard-wired to fit into the tribe," she said

"Into the tribe?"

"During our tribal days, if you didn't do what the tribe asked of you, then you'd be expelled. You wouldn't be able to survive alone in the forest without them — you would surely die. Fitting in is still tied into our survival. However, you don't actually need the tribe to survive anymore in our urban environments, so you can choose to do something different. The more you choose something other than pure survival the more you hardwire new, more evolved, functioning in your brain."

Fran was silent. The waiter came and Marguerite paid the bill. As they drove back to the office Fran seemed somehow disturbed by their conversation.

Marguerite glanced over, "Are you okay?

"Lots to ponder, I guess. That magnetism you were talking about ..."

"Yes?"

"Would an electric current be a good metaphor? You need both the negative and positive?"

"Absolutely. The negative or the present day situation that you don't want — that is like the ground, or the negative charge in the circuit. What you say you want — the kind of leader you want to be — is the positive charge in the circuit. You need both. And as soon as you have both, you set up an electric charge, a magnetic force. It's already started for you just because you talked about it. You've begun the choice process."

As they pulled into the parkade Marguerite added, "I'll just drop you off. I'm heading home for the rest of the day. Maybe I'll see you again tomorrow."

Marguerite pulled the car up to stall #111 and then braked suddenly. An ancient man in a trench coat and fedora stepped in front of the car.

As Fran rolled down the window the man stepped forward.

"Miss Freeman? My name is Laszlo Goldstein. I'm afraid I have some bad news for you. Your father collapsed today and is in a coma."

## CHAPTER 10

*He is disoriented in this endless expanse of desert. Vertigo. No dampness. The sweating has ceased. His skin is red and dry. Hyperventilating, gnawing headache, muscle cramps. His pulse is racing. His body is no longer regulating his temperature. It's soaring out of control. He could die, or worse, have brain damage.*

*He mumbles senseless words.*

*They are off course. Way too far off.*

*They haven't drunk any water for three days now. Not a sip.*

*He can't remember what water tastes like anymore.*

*He crawls up onto a rise and crouches. He stands there, shading his eyes as he peers over the flat, brown expanse to the north.*

*The sun beats down through the flimsy fabric of his visor cap, burning a hole through his scalp.*

*Nothing there; nothing is everywhere.*

*It's the emptiest of spaces where no living or dying thing exists.*

*The fight in him has died out now. Defeat washes through his dry bones. Surrender's sweet lull seeps into his marrow.*

*Stillness.*

*His hands are petrified at his forehead. A black line shimmers on the horizon.*

*He contemplates it for an eternity.*

*It's a heat-haze mirage. It plays games with his vision far too often.*

*Ha! It's a funeral procession and he's the one in the box.*

*He shakes his head, blinking his eyes. No water left in his stung, dry pupils.*

*He looks again. The line is still there. He pulls out his binoculars and looks closer.*

*It is a caravan. A camel caravan.*

*A caravan ... his muddy mind aches to comprehend what that means to him.*

*They have water sacks. They must have water sacks. Water is there hanging over their shoulders; strapped to the sides of those beasts.*

*His tongue sticks to the roof of his mouth, longing, aching, tingling.*

*He remembers stories of the Bedouin tribes that traverse the desert. He wants to believe it's real.*

*They don't know we are here. How will they know?*

*Smoke rising. There must be smoke rising.*

*He scrambles down the rise and looks for something to make a fire with.*

*He has a pen knife and a piece of flint but no tinder. No twigs, no grass, no leaves, no bark.*

*Goddamn desert.*

*His journal!*

*They have letters written to loved ones — in case someone came across their dried up carcasses on the desert floor.*

*He rips the paper in pieces and drags the knife across the flint.*

*How many times must he do this? It's not taking.*

*They will be gone soon.*

*They will be gone soon.*

*Goddamn it!*

*He can't see them without the binoculars.*

*He blows again. Light, you son of a bitch! It catches. He sees a few sparks.*

*A slender stream of smoke slides up toward the blazing sun.*

*More paper.*

*He looks up and the sky is filling with smoke, with blessed smoke.*

*He snatches the binoculars to his face again and races up the rise. Where have they gone?*

*The shimmering black line has disappeared.*

## CHAPTER 11

Fran felt her heart racing. She tried to get out of the car but her legs were trembling. She looked up at Laszlo and pleaded, "Oh my God! Is he still alive?"

"He is. But he is unconscious. They say he might not make it through the night. I didn't know your phone number, so I just decided to come to your office." He pointed to his car, a maroon Mercedes parked nearby, "Please come with me."

Fran turned to her new found friend, anxiety contorting her face, "I have no idea who this man is."

Marguerite leaned over past Fran and said to the little old man, "I'll take Fran. We'll follow you."

Fran protested to her friend, "I don't want to be an inconvenience."

"Honey, you need someone with you right now. And, fate has crossed our paths today for a reason," Marguerite reassured her.

Fran stared at her feeling utterly grateful beyond words. They sped off to the hospital following Laszlo's car.

Fran was starting to hyperventilate.

Marguerite noticed and said, "When I am anxious I find it useful to breathe consciously. Breathe in and out through your nose, rather than your mouth and this will trigger your brain to calm down. Try it. Do it slowly and constrict the back of your throat slightly, like when you are whispering. Like this."

Marguerite demonstrated a technique called Ujjayi breathing.

Fran focused on Marguerite's face and watched the air seep in and out slowly from her nose and listened to the whispering sound at the back of her throat.

Fran was grateful to have something to focus her attention on.

"Good. Do that at least ten times," said Marguerite with a soft smile.

After the tenth breath Fran was amazed by how she felt an actual shift in her entire body. It had altered her neurochemistry: less adrenaline and more serotonin. As her body relaxed her thoughts grew lighter and more optimistic.

"It will all be okay," she whispered to herself.

When they arrived at St. Paul Hospital they met Laszlo by the elevators.

"Excuse me, was it Mr. Goldstein? I don't think I know you," Fran said, still shaking as she extended her hand to him.

"Call me Laszlo. You wouldn't remember me. I am your father's lawyer and the Executor of his Will. I was over at your house this morning going over the Will with him. In the middle of it all he had some kind of seizure and went unconscious. I immediately called 911. I did CPR on him while we waited. They said that may have saved his life," said Laszlo.

"Oh, my goodness. Thank you so much for being there. I was at work. I knew I shouldn't leave him there alone. I tried to get him one of those medical alert things but he refused. He never told me he was meeting with someone this morning," she said as they mounted the elevator.

"That's George for you," replied the strange little man.

Laszlo spoke with a slight German accent and was no more than five feet two inches tall. Fran guessed him to be even older than her father, yet seemed as lively as a whippet.

Fran explained, "He hates hospitals. On the one occasion I took him to see a doctor, she told me that he was a *walking miracle.*"

"Yes, I think he has remained alive out of sheer will," said Laszlo, "He survived death so many times in his life I think he forgot that he is mortal."

"You know things about my father's life?" she queried.

"I know some things. I bet you know very little, huh?"

"I know almost nothing about his life, especially before he came to Canada."

"He was always a private man and life in Europe during the war was hard on everyone. Many people just refuse to talk about that time of their life."

When they arrived at his room, George was hooked up to an octopus of life-support mechanisms. Computer screens, heart monitors, IV drips, ventilators, charts and graphs all surrounded his bed. His skin was translucent and had taken on the color of ash.

Three nurses were tending to him like a hive of bees desperately trying to repair a body that was beyond repair. Yet modern science, and those who ran the machines, daily stared death in the face and daring to overcome it, or at least delay it. Death was a consumer and the medical staff, machines, drugs, equipment, surgeries, tests, and procedures all fed that constantly hungry end user.

Just as the doctor arrived George began to stir. The doctor rushed forward and examined his vital signs closely.

## CHAPTER 12

*His shipmates are kidnapping him.*
*They drag his flailing body to the*
*stern of the ship. He punches and kicks but they toughen against him. One death-*
*grips his ankles, one hooks his armpits. Is it a game? Would they really do it?*

*"On three!" the pocker-faced one shouts. "One, two, three!"*
*They swing his body back and forth until they have enough momentum to*
*hurl his bruised up torso over the railing.*
*They let him go and he tumbles head over foot, screaming into the ship's*
*churning wash far below.*

George opened his eyes in a panic and glanced around, feeling bewildered and trapped under the manacle of tubes, machines and wires. He
finally recognized that he was in a hospital. The last thing he remembered was talking to Laszlo and then everything went blank. He could
vaguely see the outline of his daughter and Laszlo — two people he
hoped would never meet while he was still alive. Fran leaned forward
and held his hand. Her hand felt warm and reassuring.

"He is stabilizing," said the doctor. Then she turned to Fran and
asked, "Are you his daughter?"

Fran nodded.

"I'll need to talk to you in the other room."

George watched as Fran followed the doctor and sat down in the next room. Laszlo sat on one side of his bed and a luminous, dark-skinned woman stood behind him.

George remembered when he met that funny little man. He was a scrawny guy even back then. It must have been 1938 when George first laid eyes on Laszlo Goldstein at a tavern in a run-down district of Vienna. George was only sixteen and Laszlo was just a few years older. Yet the underground operation that Laszlo ran spoke volumes of his renegade nature. It was because of Laszlo that his life went in the direction that it did, or that he had a life at all.

And ironically the man who gave him a new chance at life a few times before just saved his life again. He was the one person who could be counted on to keep secret lives a secret … or so he hoped.

George wondered who the raven-haired beauty was. She reminded him of Aliba, the woman whose love once kept him alive.

The woman reached out and held his hand. Her smile was dazzling. For some reason, as soon as she did that, all his pain subsided. He felt strange. In fact, he felt like he was no longer in his body but floating above it. Maybe he was already dead. Is this what death looked and felt like? It must be, and this woman was an angel taking him to Heaven — or maybe Hell. He glanced over at the heart monitor and his heart was still beating. He was alive. He felt relief and disappointment all at the same time.

"Hello, Mr. Freeman. I am Marguerite LeBoyer. I work in the same building as Freeman & Wilson and was with Fran when she heard you were in hospital. I brought her here today. Mr. Goldstein here apparently saved your life."

George blinked, absorbing her words. He wanted to respond in appreciation to her and to Laszlo, but there was some kind of contraption in his mouth. He looked over at Laszlo. His attorney was peering back at him over the top of those same reading glasses he'd had for decades.

Fran came back into his room with the doctor. George saw a child making notes on a clipboard. She looked like she was thirteen years old. How could that little girl with the stethoscope be a doctor?

"Can you hear me?" the doctor asked him, "If so, blink twice."

George did as he was told but he didn't trust her. She began explaining his condition and he struggled to follow her. He wasn't sure exactly what she said, but by the end of her monologue everyone in the room was looking at him like he was a dead man. She told his daughter that he would need around-the-clock palliative care.

George wasn't buying it. He lived most of his early life under the spectre of death. He was stronger than death, didn't they realize that? Why would this time be any different? He couldn't die because what waited for him on the other side of death was too terrifying to face. He would do what he always did: become a soldier and face the enemy head-on. He just had to get back to his house. It was safe inside there. If they left him here in a sterile institution he would surely die.

Luckily his daughter spoke up.

"I think I can speak for my father when I say that he would prefer to be in his own home," she said choking on her words, "Is there a way we can arrange for that?"

"Of course. I can let you speak to someone about that in palliative care."

George sighed deeply and his vital signs calmed down. His house was a shield against death and his daughter knew that.

A few days later ambulance attendants carried George in a stretcher up the front steps of his mansion. It took six men to carry him; three on each side. George could see they were sweating; their faces red with exertion. He felt guilty. Guilt lived with him constantly like an unwanted guest. He felt guilty for being alive, and now guilty for trying to stay alive. He was a tiresome, selfish burden on other people and he knew it.

Once they entered the front hall George noticed that his things had been moved. Fran must've done it. How dare she? The room was almost empty of his beloved possessions. What had she done with them all? Thrown them out? He was furious. The room was almost empty and he felt naked and exposed to the sunlight now pouring through the picture windows.

As if Fran was reading his thoughts, she said, "I'm terribly sorry, Dad, but I had to remove all your things so that we could bring the bed in and so that we could get the stretcher into the living room here."

"Bring them back," protested George.

Eva, the respite caregiver, stood on guard in uniform like a sentry, "No more of your silly junk anymore, Mr. Freeman. We need the space to move around."

It wasn't junk. That woman was so ignorant, just like the housekeeper at his father's house in Vienna. She judged him and he hated her for that. As the ambulance staff struggled to move his enormous bulk onto the bed, George had another thought that filled him with terror. What if he couldn't beat death this time? He would never see his daughter again, or his house, or any of his things, nothing of this world anymore. He had pushed that thought as far from his consciousness as possible for years, but now Death stood waiting for him — peering at him from the foot of his bed in the form of a Polish woman with folded arms, impatiently drumming her fingers on her forearm.

After surveying him carefully, Eva added more morphine to his IV. A feeling of pure bliss filled him to the core. A strange thought occurred. Maybe death was going to be better. The last few decades he had felt very little gratitude for being alive, even though he lived a life of comfort, opulence and safety that he never dreamed would be possible. It was ironic that as a younger man he felt more alive — perhaps because at that time he was always so much closer to death. George smiled up at Fran and felt deep gratitude for her love and her loyalty to him.

Marguerite dropped by just as the ambulance attendants were getting ready to leave. As Fran and Eva received final instructions from them, Marguerite pulled a chair up next to his bed.

"Fran got you the deluxe model," she said with a smile, "An entirely adjustable bed — fit for the king that you are."

In a raspy voice George replied, "I've never been a king. My grandfather was, though."

"You come from royalty?"

"Everyone just called him the king of the village but we were very poor."

"You have a rags-to-riches story to tell then?"

"Yes, I acquired many riches in my lifetime."

Fran came back into the room as George was telling Marguerite about how he designed the house, about how he restored the 1964 Valiant convertible he had in the garage, and about how he used to compete in bike marathons.

Marguerite then said, "Was that around the time you met Fran's mother?"

His eyes turned to ash at the mention of Fran's mother. He didn't respond. Sensing the situation Marguerite said, "You must be tired from all this transition. I'll let you rest. I'll drop by again after work tomorrow. Let me know if you need anything."

"Thank you Marguerite. It's very kind of you to drop by for a visit," Fran interjected.

As Marguerite stood at the front door, she said "I want to take you to see something. Can you spare an hour tomorrow?"

Fran replied, "I don't think I should leave my father right now, but maybe if he starts to improve."

"I'll check back tomorrow and see how he's doing. Goodbye Mr. Freeman."

George didn't respond.

Marguerite left and Fran started doing some work from home. Eva, after checking on George, went into the kitchen to have a cup of tea.

George's eyes were closed but he could feel a burning, pressing feeling in his chest. He must be having a heart attack. He didn't want those memories back. Now they were flooding back into his mind, like a dam that had burst open; gushing past the iron gates he had placed there decades before. The picture of Roberta's face infiltrated his inner landscape again. He had destroyed all her photos and all their mementos. The one image that couldn't be deleted from his memory was the first time he saw her.

He had been in Canada many years by then and Freeman & Wilson was well established. He was one of the town's most eligible, interminable bachelors. A client invited him to a supper club called "The Cave." The featured act was a Latin band. When the lights went down George struck a match to light his cigarette and as he took his first inhale, the lights came up on Roberta. There she was, under the spotlight in sequins, chiffon and a feathered headdress, her gloved hands held high above her head, eagerly awaiting the first note to strike. The shadow plays around her sculptured face, the waves within waves of ringlets on chiffon on breasts, the eyes that saw the truth that he couldn't see anymore. He fell into an abyss of longing that would be his undoing.

It wasn't long before George was showering her with gifts. Soon they were dating regularly. He was twenty years her senior but that didn't matter to either of them. He followed the band, flying from city to city, waiting for her after each show.

When Roberta got pregnant with Fran, George was overjoyed and insisted they get married. He built her the dream mansion overlooking the ocean, a feat of architectural innovation at the time. The band found a replacement for Roberta.

However, after a few years the replacement didn't work out. The band leader showed up on her doorstep one day begging Roberta to come back to the band. Not long after that, George woke up one morning alone in bed. He went into his daughter's room and she was asleep, curled up in bed with a large orange teddy bear. He went downstairs and there was a note on the mahogany dining room table. He sat down to read the note. He had to read it many times over to try to make sense of its contents. The only things she took were one suitcase, her costumes, and a photo. He had raced off in his Valiant convertible to find her. The train carrying all the band members had left the station fifteen minutes before he arrived.

He had no way of contacting her. She left no forwarding information. He tried to write and phone her family, but no response. After a while George gave up. He went into a life defining depression that he never truly awoke from.

He reached for his beloved painkillers but ended up knocking the bottle on the floor. Eva entered the room and picked up the bottle.

"How many do you want?" she asked.

George held up all ten fingers.

"You want ten pills? That could kill you."

He looked at her like a sullen child.

She counted ten pills into her palm and handed him a glass of water, muttering to herself, "I guess it's a moot point now."

He gratefully swallowed them and closed his eyes; willing all painful memories to be banished from his system.

As he fell into a drug induced dream state his throat constricted. The memory of a something was still lodged there. He swallowed but it grew more intense.

## CHAPTER 13

*I*t is twilight and the icy winds penetrate his uniform. How long has he been standing here holding this icy cylinder? His feet are stumps of ice.

There is a hex on him. The gun owns him now. It is located squarely in his trigger finger. He has stopped counting the ducks; the farther away the more of a thrill. He wishes one of them would run. It would kill the boredom. He watches them, penetrating them.

Someone is watching him.

It must be Ackermann. No, he is occupied.

Someone is watching him.

The top of his head is burning; tingling; pouring in radiating heat-light.

He wills it to stop. It gets more intense.

Someone is watching him.

The gun sparks a current. He jumps his hands away ... scorched. He never touched the trigger.

He grabs the binoculars and shoves them too swiftly against his sunglasses. The nose piece gouges his flesh. He rips the glasses off his face and pulls back his visor. He must see for sure. Who is that?

*The sea of faces are white with terror. They all look the same. It was a mirage. One more scan of the crowd...*

*There ... unmistakable ... those eyes ... stepping towards him and away from the crowd.*

*He is fossilized in that gaze. Black magic. Ackermann's orders roar in his head, but he would rather die.*

*Something burns at his feet. He looks down. His boots are covered with crushed flowers. When did he walk so mindlessly through the sacred garden?*

CHAPTER 14

Marguerite came to visit the Freeman Manor a week after George arrived home from the hospital but he was sleeping.

"What was that thing you wanted me to see?" Fran asked, "It has been an intense week. I could use a break."

"It's a surprise. Come let's go."

They grabbed their coats and bid goodbye to Eva who was busy making medical notes.

They sped down the highway in the white Jaguar. Marguerite felt it was time to broach this subject, but didn't quite know how to start.

"I know it's none of my business, but I notice your father does not like to talk about your mother."

"No, I learned to stop bringing that subject up long ago," Fran muttered. "I'm surprised he even talked to you as long as he did. He generally distrusts women."

"You're a woman."

"I try not to be one around him."

Marguerite cringed, "Aren't you curious about what happened to your mother, where she went, where she is now?" asked Marguerite.

"Of course I am, but he asked me to promise never to try to find her. He said she lived a dangerous life and would be a bad influence on me. Then later, when I was a teenager and really wanted to find her, he said she died. But I'm not so sure he was telling the truth. I once called a parent finder group and registered, but nothing happened. I guess she has to register, too. Maybe she is dead. I've never tried checking into that, but their band traveled all over the world, she could be living anywhere, in any country, and her last name could have changed. I wouldn't know where to start."

"Do you take it personally?"

"Do I take what personally?" asked Fran.

"That your mother left you?"

"I don't know," Fran said feeling a dimness set in. Of course she took it personally, but couldn't admit it. Although she tried to reason with herself that some women just didn't want to raise children, deep down she felt there was something critically wrong with her. Otherwise, her mother would have stayed, or at least taken Fran with her when she left. Perhaps it was why she never stood up to her father. He was the one who didn't leave. Her whole life revolved around making sure he wouldn't abandon her, too. Even though she was now an adult, the thought of losing her father felt strangely terrifying.

"It would be normal to feel that way if you were just a child when she left," Marguerite reassured her.

"I suppose so," Fran replied sensing the darkness of those feelings now cramping her space.

They pulled into the Pacific National Exhibition parking lot and Fran followed Marguerite to the carnival rides.

"This is what you wanted to show me?" she asked.

"They just opened the fair this week. They have the best roller coaster!" exclaimed Marguerite.

"I've been on that roller coaster once a long time ago and I didn't like it and neither did my stomach, nor did the guy next to me on whom I threw up," said Fran remembering the moment painfully. She was twelve and the boy she liked was sitting right beside her. He had invited her.

She was mortified. After that the boy put his attention on another girl who was far more adventurous. The thought of repeating that experience was in itself nauseating. She started to slow down her pace.

"Yeah, but that was years ago. The trick to not getting sick is to let go of the handlebar," said Marguerite.

Marguerite bought them both a ticket and started lining up for the front car of the rollercoaster.

"You must be crazy! Really, this is not my thing. I'll go get a corn dog and sit over there watching you," Fran said as she walked back down the ramp eager to get as far away as possible.

Marguerite pulled her back up the ramp laughing, "Come on, when was the last time you went on?"

Fran replied, "When I was twelve. A boy I liked named Dean made me go on and he regretted it afterwards, just as you will. That's a very nice cashmere suit you are wearing. I'm sure you don't want it ruined."

"That won't happen because you are going to throw your hands in the air and enjoy it," announced Marguerite.

As they waited for the car to pull up Fran went into trial lawyer mode to defend the motion sick twelve-year-old inside.

"If I remember my facts correctly, this roller coaster was built in 1955 and has not had safety upgrades since then. There is only a waist belt, no shoulder harness, or anything to protect your head. And, by the way, the sign explicitly states to keep your hands in the car. This ride is known to escalate from zero to seventy miles per hour in less than four seconds. Letting go of the handlebar could result in not only receiving a fine from the fairgrounds, but falling out and crashing to your death amongst the steel and concrete forty feet below."

"That's very impressive. But I've been riding this rollercoaster hands-free for over a decade and I'm still here. Jump in!" said Marguerite.

The car pulled up and passengers poured into the seats. Marguerite pushed Fran in first. The bar came down and the ride lurched forward. Fran white-knuckled the handlebar and looked down at her feet.

"Now just breathe and focus on the excitement, not the fear. Holding on doesn't make you more in control, it makes you more *controllable*. As soon as we get to the top of the first hill and we start to go down that's when you hold your hands up high like this and scream as loud as you can. This is going to be so fun!" Marguerite demonstrated with enthusiasm.

Fran felt her diaphragm tighten up and her breathing become shallow as Marguerite pointed to the view that was taking shape below. The rollercoaster slowly climbed higher and higher. Fran could hear her heart thumping in her ears, and her stomach churning. They were almost near the top. Marguerite was chatting away about the beauty of the North Shore Mountains and trying to get Fran to look up. Then a young girl in the seat behind them shouted, "Oh my God!" which immediately made Fran contract into a ball of tension and grasp onto the handlebar with all her strength as the ride thundered down the first hill.

Marguerite was screaming and laughing with her arms high in the air, "Let go, don't hold on!"

The ride came down and then up again.

Fran held on, turning greener by the second.

"Look at me, Fran, look at me!"

Fran looked over and Marguerite was almost standing as the ride went flying down the next hill. She was laughing, tears were streaming down her face and she looked so happy. She wondered how one person could be having so much fun while another person could be feeling so miserable while sharing the same experience.

"The ride is almost over, Fran, go for it!"

As the ride came up the next hill, a series of thoughts and memories flashed before her eyes: the pain and hardship of living life so cautiously. How many opportunities had she lost? The relationships she could have had. The places she could've traveled. The career she could've had. The ease she could've felt in her body. The moments of joy and happiness that were now gone forever. Soon, she would be thirty-years-old and soon after that life would be over. She would be facing death, just like her father. Things that happened when she was twenty, or even twelve years old seemed like yesterday. The notion that 'life is short' suddenly went from an intellectual concept to a deep-seeded experience. There was no time to waste. Her hands loosened their grip and floated an inch off the handlebar.

"Good, now look up into the sky not down at the tracks!" shouted Marguerite.

As the ride reached the pinnacle of the next hill, Fran looked up at the brilliant blue sky. The G-force of the ride pulled her arms up high in the air. As the car sped up it pulled her into a standing position as it thundered down the track.

Fran reached her hands high in the air and screamed so loud that she was sure the dolphins in the Pacific Ocean could hear her. As the ride started going up the next hill, gravity pushed them both back into the seat.

Marguerite was laughing uncontrollably and her wild abandonment to the experience affected Fran until she was also laughing hysterically.

The ride went high again and then started spiralling down a chute. Fran felt herself being whipped around and she just let it happen. She relaxed into the motion of the ride and let her body fly in one direction and then the other. The laughter kept her body fluid with the motion, and her breath deep and exhilarating. She felt a warm, soft glow that transformed everything inside her. As she felt the heat in her body rise with the summer air, she knew a door had been opened. A door that could never be closed again.

CHAPTER 15

As they disembarked from the ride Fran's entire body felt light and energized. In the past she often got carsick, airsick, and even train sick. Her stomach generally felt tense all the time so any kind of rough movement made it worse. The few times in her life when her stomach felt at ease were like foreign moments, tastes from an exotic, serene land. This was one of those times. It was as if she was looking through a bright prism, and everything seemed different. She noticed the abundant color of the trees and flowers. She noted the wide variety of people's facial expressions. The smell of buttered popcorn and candy floss tantalized her taste buds.

Then they walked by a midway shooting gallery. A powerful memory flooded back into Fran's head.

She was only seven-years-old. One day her Father surprised her with a trip to the Pacific National Exhibition. She had never been there before and they rarely did anything "fun" together. Fun didn't seem to be part of her father's vocabulary. He tended to work most of the time. After a day of watching her go on the rides, they stopped at that very same shooting gallery. It hadn't changed much in twenty plus years, except the blue paint was now peeling, the prizes were bigger and fancier, and the boy attending the booth wore pants that were much too large, with fluorescent orange boxer shorts that were hanging out.

Back in 1978 the attendant sported sideburns, a headband, with a paisley vest. The top prize then was an enormous stuffed dog hanging from the rafters. It was brown and white with long, shaggy hair and big red felt paws. Her father had put down his money and picked up the rifle. He looked it over with the curiosity of a gun expert. Then he turned, and calmly shot a bull's eye. The attendant was engrossed in the Ram Dass bestseller *Be Here Now,* and didn't notice that his customer was waiting for his prize.

"Which one of these bears would you like, sweetie?" asked George.

Fran coyly pointed at one of the miniature yellow ones.

The attendant glanced up, noticed the bull's eye and raised his eyebrows. "I get three more tries, right?" asked George.

"Right."

With one cool move he lifted the rifle again and shot another bull's-eye.

"Wow, man. Way to go. Now you get to choose from one of these," he said gesturing to the shelf behind him and looking down at Fran.

She pointed at a medium-sized fluorescent pink elephant, and George nodded. Without waiting, George then went for round three — another bull's eye!

"Listen mister, you are now up to the Chatty Cathy doll. I haven't given a Chatty Cathy away in weeks," he said as he handed over the doll.

Fran felt like she was in heaven.

"By the way, no one has ever gotten four bull's eyes in a row. If you get it, you win — that!"

Fran followed his finger to the far right corner where the gigantic dog hung like a Grecian God. His kind eyes and wagging tongue begged to be owned.

"Oh, Daddy, that would be so wonderful — can you get it for me?"

By this time a small crowd had gathered to watch. The attendant reloaded the rifle, and George put the gun to his shoulder. This time he hesitated a moment. The pressure was on.

He shot the gun again — *another perfect bull's eye.*

There was a round of applause from the crowd and the attendant rolled his eyes in disbelief. He fumbled around trying to unhook the dog from the rafters and finally handed it over to them. George held it over his head like the Stanley Cup while they headed for the park exit.

That day George was her hero. The clouds of their lives had parted for a moment and light shone down on them again. Fran felt like she was walking on air, like the princess she was always meant to be. The fears of the past had just been a terrible mistake and this was who they really were — free for that moment of whatever dark spell that had held them before. Another little girl walked by with her father. She pointed at Fran's large dog and turned to her father expectantly.

The father turned to George and said, "It cost me a pretty penny just to win this." He held up a miniature teddy bear, "How did you ever win that?"

"I guess it was just my lucky day," George laughed. He handed the man his camera and asked him to take a photo. And then he smiled. Fran had stared at her father, almost not recognizing him; to see him happy, transformed from the melancholic spirit that usually ran the show, his vitality and good looks radiating through.

As the two men chatted, Fran noticed she could barely see the eyes of the dog in and amongst all the fur. When she finally found the little, beady orange buttons she turned to her father and announced, "I shall call him Fur Face."

"Fur Face it is then," laughed her father.

Fran had loved that dog for many years. After she got tired of it, George took the dog and propped it up against the main living room window. And there Fur Face stayed for days, weeks, months, years and decades. In fact, to this day Fur Face was still there, looking decrepit and dusty now, staring forlornly out the window, as if searching for that magical, happy place they had visited ever so briefly all those years ago.

On the way back home Marguerite asked how she was doing and Fran recounted her memory.

The older woman smiled.

"It's sad, though, that we had so few of those moments. Or that I don't have more fun in my life," Fran mused.

"It is sad, but there is always a chance to choose again."

The car rounded the corner and pulled up in front of Fran's house. She hesitated, looking at Marguerite gratefully. "It's been a powerful experience for me — that silly ride. Let's go again!"

Marguerite smiled and said, "Sure. And, by the way, it wasn't the ride."

*He wraps a tiny stuffed bear in brown wrapping paper and stuffs a note inside. It's written on company letterhead. Too formal, but that's all he has.*

*Condolences upon condolences.*

*He writes in his small, neat handwriting the address on the front and walks it to the post office.*

*"It will take several weeks," the clerk warns him.*

*He nods. He was expecting that.*

*The lunch whistle blows. He must get back to work, no time to go to the diner today. He buys a sandwich to go and brings it to his desk. After each bite he goes through another ledger. Every third page he stops and imagines her face. He envisions her miniature hands ripping through the brown paper and seeing the kind face and the open arms of the bear. She smiles and laughs and hugs it close to her heart.*

*He feels a warmth in his chest. He will bring her to him. He needs her as much as she needs him.*

*Each day he prays that the package makes it across the sea into the right hands. He checks the mail and most days there is not even one letter, not even a bill. Weeks go by, then months, then years. Nothing comes back.*

*He finally takes her photo and hides it away where he will never have to look at it again.*

George awoke when Fran entered. She decided to sit down and tell him about her experience at the fairgrounds. She vividly described how Marguerite talked her into going on the rollercoaster and about passing by the midway where he had won Fur Face. Fran couldn't help but notice that George gave her his full attention. Normally, his attention span was about five seconds, which she had attributed to his loss of hearing.

But today, for some reason, he was totally present with her. At the time, Eva was monitoring some of his vital signs.

"Look at that. His heart rate is much more stable and his blood pressure is down. That's amazing. You should reminisce about carnivals more often," smiled Eva.

Fran took this opportunity to courageously ask, "What ever happened to that man, Laszlo Goldstein? Who is he, and why hasn't he come by to visit?"

Suddenly his vital signs dropped. Eva looked annoyed with Fran for disturbing him with the question.

George finally replied, "He's just a lawyer I once had. He, umm, he made up my Will a while ago. I think he is having health problems of his own." He smiled but then grimaced at a shooting pain somewhere deep inside his withering body. "We old men tend to do that."

There was a long silence as Fran waited for more information. When it was clear that none was forthcoming she let it go. She sensed his unease rumbling beneath the surface, like a wounded beast.

The next morning, the receptionist at Freeman & Wilson called and said it was urgent that Fran attend an important meeting.

"It won't take very long," Meili said under her breath.

"What's it about? I'm uncomfortable about leaving my father right now."

"I can't really say what it's about. It's one of those secretive partner meetings, but I get the sense you wouldn't want to miss it," replied Meili.

Fran reluctantly agreed. George seemed to be doing well and was mostly sleeping.

At Freeman & Wilson, the CFO, Justin Web, met privately with Fran in her office. He closed the office door behind him as he entered and lowered his voice. Justin was a middle-aged accountant with short grey hair, wearing a pressed gray suit, with gray eyes and an ashen complexion. A trail of grey billowed behind him wherever he went.

He said, "There was an investigative reporter here earlier today asking questions about Freeman & Wilson's dealings with Wrightway. The partners have decided it is best that nobody comment to the press at this time," he hesitated, "… about anything."

"Wrightway is being investigated?"

"Yes, but it's probably because their stock tripled in the last six months. Wrightway also gave significant funding to Rich Valeway's campaign and he got in. I'm sure his opponents are behind this investigation. Wrightway deserves our loyalty. It's all political infighting. I'm sure it'll blow over soon."

Just then there was another knock at her door. Fran rose to answer it, but Justin was already there, as if expecting someone. Frank, one of the partners, entered the office, nodding to the two of them. Justin shook his hand, his greeting collegial, too casual. Frank was a pudgy, balding fifty-three-year-old who kept dying his grey hair a weird reddish color.

He often had food stains on his tie, like he did today. Frank enjoyed his Chinese food. His cherubic smile, red hair and huge, round glasses made him look a bit like a carnival clown.

"Hey Frankie, are you coming to watch the hockey game at Malone's tonight?" Justin asked.

"Can't make it. Gotta stack of work. Thanks anyways."

Justin turned back to Fran, "Thanks for coming in to chat with me today. By the way, how's your father doing?"

"Well, for a dying man he is better than expected. He's generally been in good spirits."

"That's great, Fran. He's been holding on a long time. It's good to hear that old George is actually in good spirits. I'll let you chat with Frank," Justin said as he slipped out of the office.

"Please have a seat," Fran offered.

Frank shut the door in the same surreptitious way that Justin had done a few minutes earlier.

"I'm sorry to have to tell you this, but the partners have decided that Nelson should take over as Managing Partner when George is gone. I know he isn't a majority shareholder like your father, but he's been leading the show now for several years already. The partners want that continuity. They suggested that perhaps you can take on the position later, when Nelson retires."

Fran's hands clenched in her lap. She had mixed feelings about the verdict — disappointment, distrust, hurt and also a huge sense of relief.

"I understand, Frank, if that's what the partners think is best," she said as straight-faced as she could. Right now she had too many other things to focus on.

"Not everyone thinks its best, but the majority of people do at this point in time. Do you have any idea how George plans to pass on his share of the partnership in the company? Our assumption is that his fifty-one percent will be passed directly onto you. This means you can veto decisions if you absolutely need to. Or, perhaps you and your father would like Nelson to buy you out?"

"No!" Fran reacted more vehemently than she intended. She cleared her throat and dropped her chin. "I'm not sure what my father has in mind. He hasn't discussed it with me, Frank. But he recently met with his lawyer to talk about the Will."

"With Phillip?"

"No, a lawyer he used to have — a Mr. Goldstein."

"He's making changes?"

"I don't know."

"Has he discussed his changes with you or anyone here?"

"Not to my knowledge."

Frank forced a smile across his broad cheeks. "Oh that George, he certainly can be ..."

"Difficult to deal with?"

"I was thinking — secretive. But, you don't need me to tell you that. Maybe he'll talk to me. Do you think he'd be open to a visit?"

"Probably not, but you can always try. But don't tell him I said that ..."

"Listen, Franny, we need to get a sense of what's going to happen here. I don't want to be crude about this, but your father may only have weeks or just days to live. Do you think anyone else will be given ownership in the company? Are there other siblings, your mother, or anyone from his family of origin?"

"No, no other siblings, and he hasn't spoken to my mother in over twenty years. I don't think he has any other family that is alive."

"Yes, I know he never likes to speak about his past. Surely you've seen photos though."

"No. He said all his photos disappeared during World War II. He left everything behind in Europe when he came to Canada."

"Maybe you can chat with Mr. Goldstein and see what he knows."

"I never got his number and my father didn't seem to want to talk about him."

"You'll be talking with that lawyer sooner or later. Why not talk to him now so we all know what's going on?"

"I'll see what I can do, Frank."

Fran felt uncomfortable trying to get information behind her father's back. He had a habit of cutting people off when they did things he didn't like. He hadn't, for example, spoken to Frank for over five years. At all partner meetings, George made sure there were plenty of Krispy Kreme doughnuts — George's favourite. Usually George ate the lion's share of those doughnuts. Once Frank made a joke about how Freeman & Wilson was helping raise the share price at Krispy Kreme. George stopped talking to him after that. Even after five years he refused to acknowledge Frank's presence.

As Fran was leaving, she met Marguerite on the elevator.

"Do you have time for lunch?" Marguerite asked.

"I should get home. But I am hungry. I'll just call Eva and see how things are going."

After Fran got off the phone she said, "Eva thinks everything is okay, so let's go to Selby's again. I'm starving." They decided to walk because it was a beautiful day. Fran told Marguerite about what Frank was asking her to do and how uncomfortable she was about it.

Marguerite looked sideways at Fran and said, "Do you want my opinion?"

"Of course, I find your insights very helpful."

"Okay. But you might not like what I have to say."

"It's okay."

Marguerite looked up at a V-line of geese flying across the sky. Her red-tinted sunglasses boldly framed her feline eyes.

"I think you have a right to ask about the Will. He is dying and he has a sizable estate and a company in limbo. What do you gain by avoiding asking him about it?"

"Did I ever tell you that he wins the marathon trophy for silent treatment? He might die any day now. I don't want our last time together to be tainted by anger and resentment."

"Yes, and he could have written something in his Will that is harmful to his heirs or to the company. Wouldn't you like the chance to reverse that before it's too late?"

Fran was silent.

"It may be your last chance to actually have an authentic conversation with him. You act like a child around him while you're almost thirty years old. I suggest it's time to let go of your past relationship with him and start again on a different basis. I would also suggest you do this as soon as possible. You are the one that has to live with the decisions in his Will."

Fran felt humiliated and almost decided to not enter the restaurant. She hesitated at the door and looked over her shoulder.

"I told you that you wouldn't like what I had to say. Listen, it's just my opinion. Take from it what is worthwhile, and leave behind the rest. I'm not saying it out of malice, I'm saying it as a friend."

Fran's eyes were starting to get glassy, "You're right. I'm sure everyone thinks I'm a complete loser still living with my father."

"It doesn't matter what people think. It matters what it's doing to you."

Fran entered the restaurant and Marguerite followed her to the corner table.

"I wouldn't know where to begin to change our relationship now. He acts like the world is out to get him so I try to be the one person who isn't. And besides, when he's dead and gone I'll have to grow up, won't I?" Fran surmised.

"Why don't you do it now? There must be something you gain by staying childlike with him, and not communicating your needs."

"I don't know. It's a habit. Maybe it just feels more comfortable."

"Are you really that comfortable? It seems to me you walk on eggshells around him. Perhaps you're avoiding responsibility."

"For what?"

"Think about it. If you stay acting like a child with him then you don't have to face the difficulties and challenges of being an adult. But you also miss out on all the fun and freedom. Don't you ever think about that — the price you pay?"

"Yes." Fran paused and she willed her eyes not to tear up. She looked around the restaurant. There were three other people from Freeman & Wilson sitting at a nearby table.

"This is really uncomfortable to talk about. I bet you think that's why I have no life," Fran said as her hands started trembling in her lap.

Marguerite put her hand on top of Fran's. "No. But that seems to be what you think. It may be that your father is very open to discussing his Will with you. You have an idea in your head about what he is going to be like. You expect the past to repeat itself. But many people make big personality shifts when they know they are going to die soon."

"Yes, I've thought of that. And I can also see another price I may pay beyond the issue of the Will. There's a whole world about my father I may never know unless I ask him now. Maybe he knows where my mother is, maybe he has other relatives, and maybe *she* has other relatives. Maybe I would better understand his eccentricities, and his obvious pain, if I knew what he had to deal with in his life."

Marguerite continued, "I remember the day I stopped calling my father 'dad' and called him John instead. I was about twenty-five-years old. It was terrifying for me. I was choosing to redefine our relationship from father-daughter to two adults, and there was a power struggle between us for a while. He had to let go of his position of authority over me. But, later he grew to like it. I believe that redefinition helped him see me as capable of running his organization."

After ordering and receiving their food, they ate in silence and Fran remembered all the times she talked with her father, like she was still seven-years-old. She felt embarrassed just thinking about it.

Marguerite piped up first, "I would talk to him first before Frank drops by for a visit. Then see if you can meet with Mr. Goldstein. Once you know the contents of the Will you can decide how to proceed. Only then should you talk to people at the company. They may have their own agenda, if you know what I mean."

"Did I tell you they've decided to choose Nelson as Managing Partner? I'm out of the running. They said that maybe I could take over the position after Nelson retires in ten years."

"And how is that for you?"

"Well … many people in the company don't trust him. In fact, there are some investigations going on in our company right now. I don't know what's going on, but I suspect that Nelson has been cooking the books for one of our biggest clients, Wrightway. Ever since Nelson took over he keeps saying 'Freeman & Wilson has got to be more innovative, to keep up with the times.' I think Nelson puts innovation in the wrong places. He doesn't seem to think of the big picture when he makes some of those 'innovative' decisions."

"You mean he doesn't attach the innovation to some kind of principles or values?"

"I guess that's what I mean."

"He's not the only business leader choosing 'innovative accounting practices,' it's becoming a trend. Did you read in the papers about Arthur Andersen? They're going to go down with Enron."

Fran sighed and nodded.

"Do you know anything specific about his dealings with Wrightway?" asked Marguerite.

"I don't have any substantial evidence, but there is some. It's not just speculation. Other people are suspecting it, too. I just get a bad feeling whenever Nelson starts talking about Wrightway."

The waiter brought the bill and Fran suddenly noticed the restaurant was almost empty.

With a sense of urgency in her voice, Marguerite replied, "Then you definitely have a responsibility to take leadership here. Think of the consequences if the company goes under because of Nelson's choices. All the employees, their livelihood, their retirement savings in the company stock, all the years your father put into the company, all the people that your company serves — they could all be negatively affected.

"Something like that happened in our organization. One of the key stakeholders was misappropriating charity funds. My father sensed it was going on, but was afraid to confront the man he thought was responsible. Many people ended up getting hurt and it took the company years to recover. People had lost faith in us. They wouldn't do business with us after that. We literally had to rebuild the organization. We had to create a whole new foundation with a new name.

"My father never really recovered emotionally from that. His health went downhill after all that happened. He sat me down with his lawyers, accountants, and business consultants to sort out the details. He gave us a clear picture of where he saw the foundation going and how it should be restructured. After he died I knew how to proceed, which made a big difference to my effectiveness as a leader."

"Okay, you've convinced me," Fran said. It was heartfelt. She leapt to her feet and started putting on her coat. "I want to get home as soon as possible while my courage is up. Oh my goodness, look at the time. This has been an absorbing conversation."

Marguerite dropped Fran off at her car.

On the way home Fran checked her cell phone but the battery had died. She'd forgotten to charge it again. She put her foot on the gas. A black cat raced across the road right in front of her and she jammed on the brakes. The cat narrowly escaped and Fran could feel adrenaline coursing through her veins. When she pulled around the corner at the top of the hill and the house came into view she saw an ambulance parked outside. Eva was at the door as Fran rushed in.

Eva exclaimed, "I've been trying to call you for the last hour! Where have you been?"

"I'm sorry, my cell phone battery died. I lost track of the time. What's going on?"

"I'm so glad you're finally here!" Eva gasped.

*He clambers down the knoll until he can touch the weeping willow tree. Its droopy branches kiss the rippling surface of the duck pond.*

*She is there this time, for the first time in ages, sitting on the bench.*

*Waiting.*

*What is that song she is humming? He knows it but he can't remember the words. She turns to look at him. It's been such a long, long time. He wants to walk over but his legs won't move. A crimson-spotted winged creature wafts by, painting its silhouette against the blue sky.*

*She points at it, her eyes expectant.*

*His legs start to move. He knows what it is.*

*"Butterfly!" he says.*

*She nods and laughs and encircles him in her arms.*

*His heart feels whole again.*

Fran raced into the living room where George's bed was set up. There were four ambulance attendants trying to revive him. One of them looked at the others and was shaking his head.

Fran peered over to see the heart monitor — her father's pulse was barely there. She held her breath. Her own heart was thundering in her chest. Then she watched in terror as the line on the monitor changed pattern.

It flat lined.

Fran stood in stunned silence, staring at the thin, blue line that stretched out into infinity. From the corner of her eye she could see the ambulance attendants pulling back from her father like bloodied warriors after a lost battle. The thin blue line became blurry and she felt herself became dizzy.

The one person who had always been there in her life was now gone.

## CHAPTER 16

"I'm sorry ma'am. We tried everything."

One of the attendants walked over to Fran and put his hand on her shoulder. She stood motionless, still watching the heart monitor. A cold stillness filled the room, encasing her, seeping into her skin. Her father seemed different now. The familiar body that lay there was now so foreign. The hair on the back of her neck stood on end. She took in a deep breath, and suddenly felt *relief*. The feeling took her by surprise. Instead of grief, she felt relief shower through her like a waterfall.

The ambulance attendant offered Fran and Eva some time alone with the body.

"He was saying some words right before he passed away," Eva said, "One of them I heard him say was … Francesca. Is that your full name?"

Fran nodded. She never liked that name. It sounded too frilly. "Fran" was a much more practical, simple, no-nonsense name. By the time she was ten-years-old she'd requested that her name be shortened to Fran. It felt bittersweet that he had called out her childhood name at the very end. He hadn't said that name in years at her request. Perhaps he had wanted to say some things to her he had never been able to say to her before. She felt an icy pang of regret at the thought. Why had she not talked to him before he died? Her last conversation with him was about Laszlo Goldstein. It might have given him the impression that all she cared about was his estate.

"That was a lovely memory you brought to him of the fairgrounds. He was very happy remembering that."

Fran stared down at the floor and didn't respond. She felt over-whelmed by the comment, struggling to get control of herself. The memory of his laughing eyes the day before flashed in her mind. She made him feel happy for once. He always seemed so unhappy and in turmoil that Fran often felt somehow responsible. Yet, nothing she did could take away the burden of pain he carried. What had happened to him and why could he never let it go?

Finally she said, "It's funny because I always thought of him as someone who frowned upon fun things like amusement parks or parties or movies or recreational activities. He didn't have time for fun. He worked seven days a week. Then, after he stopped working full-time at the company he immersed himself in academics."

"Yes," Eva responded, happy that Fran was talking. "He said that he was a member of Mensa. Isn't that an organization for people with a very high IQ?"

"Uh huh. He spent a lot of time on the internet discussing intellectual issues with other members. Academics were always a big interest in his life. I think he would have preferred to be a researcher or philosopher rather than a businessman." She paused and then added, "but I'm just making that up. I really didn't know him."

"Maybe people at his memorial service will tell stories that will explain his life from their perspective."

"He told me he didn't want a memorial service."

"These kinds of services are not for the departed, they are for the survivors. If you want a memorial service, we should organize one. I will help you."

"Eva, thank you for the offer," Fran said, her eyes stinging. "But he cut off most people in his life. Who would come? Maybe some people from the company because they feel obliged."

"Perhaps if you make an announcement in the paper, people who used to know him might come."

"Yes, I suppose that would be a good idea. Eva, I have to tell you something. I felt such relief when I first realized he was dead. Relief for him, for me, for everything, I guess. But now that is gone. Now, I feel regret. I was rushing home to have a very important conversation with him and now I can't have it. I feel like I've lost the chance of a lifetime — to somehow help him, or help me. I'm not sure which."

Eva sat close to Fran with an arm around her shoulder. "You seem like someone who doesn't cry very often."

"Never, actually. Or at least I can't remember the last time when I did," replied Fran.

"Listen, I know what it's like to alienate most of the people from your life. Like your father I had stopped trusting people. I felt hurt so many times. But because you and your father decided to trust me to help you in this situation — it somehow shifted something in me, do you know what I mean?"

Fran shrugged.

"I guess what I'm trying to say is that I understand hurt and loss, so you can cry around me anytime. No apologies necessary."

Fran heard her words but still couldn't bring herself to cry. A cacophony of emotions swirled inside her head and chest. As she sat there with her head in her hands, Eva motioned the attendants to remove the body.

It was two weeks later that Eva arrived at the Freeman mansion carrying a newspaper. She held up the paper. "The announcement came out in the news today."

"Let's see," Fran said, looking at the scanned photo of her father she'd taken about ten years ago, standing outside the doors of Freeman & Wilson. She had sent that into the newspaper.

Eva read the short description, "George Freeman, aged 80, died peacefully in his home on July 28, 2001. He was one of the founders of Freeman & Wilson Accounting which appeared for several years on Canada's top 100 places to work list. Known for integrity and philanthropy, George Freeman's visionary leadership helped it grow from a two-person operation up to Vancouver's largest independent accounting firm in record time. Freeman & Wilson dominate the film, entertainment and broker-dealer segments of the marketplace and are one of the province's leading taxation firms. George Freeman is survived by his only daughter, Fran Freeman, an accountant at his firm."

"That looks good."

"It will be interesting to see who comes to the memorial service. Have you heard from Laszlo Goldstein yet?"

Fran shook her head, "No. And I can't find a copy of the Will anywhere. I typed the words 'Laszlo Goldstein+lawyer+Vancouver' into Google and nothing came up."

"Perhaps I can try calling all the L. Goldstein's in the phonebook," Eva offered, looking around for the phonebook.

They were there to deal with the house and all his belongings and it had turned out to be a huge job. Fran wanted to sell the house as soon as possible. There were too many painful and stuck memories here and it needed renovations badly. She wanted to just clear the clutter, sell it and buy a small place close to the downtown area. Eva helped her sell off anything of value and they hired workmen to take the rest outside to a dumpster in the front driveway.

"Wow, this newspaper is from 1964," said one of the workmen.

Two other workmen walked by carrying a La-Z-Boy rocker and one of them muttered, "This is, like, broken down La-Z-Boy rocker number five."

A fourth workman chimed in, "That's nothing. I carried out forty-five dead houseplants. And I mean *dead* from, like, six years ago."

The first workman nodded, "And did you see the room back there filled with exercise equipment? You can hardly see them because of the cobwebs."

Eva looked at Fran and said, "Yes, it reminds me of the scene from the movie *Great Expectations.* Remember that old lady still in her wedding dress in the house with cobwebs that hung from the decomposed wedding cake?"

"Yes, I remember," moaned Fran feeling embarrassed. "In fact, I realize he even kept every detergent sample that ever came in the mail. There are about 217 of them over there, in case any of you need one."

"I think we can all agree, he was a collector," added Eva.

"I've just ordered another dumpster because this one is full," Fran announced.

"That will be number eight!" exclaimed a workman.

"Those dumpsters are expensive. They're at least $800 each, right? I never realized how expensive it was *not* to throw things out. By the way, there are about fifty bottles of pills in the bathroom cupboard. I guess you want me to just chuck them all out? Those must have cost a lot. Did a doctor really tell him to take all that?" asked Eva.

"That was just half of it. I'd say he took about a hundred pills a day. Some for his heart, some for his kidneys, some for his diabetes, some for his depression, some for his headaches, some for joint pains. I don't know where he got all the prescriptions, or maybe some of them were over-the-counter or herbal supplements."

"All those in combination would have been enough to kill a man," added Eva.

Fran led everyone down to the basement for the final room to clear. She opened up a closet, to find it packed to the brim with dusty boxes and old suitcases. She opened the first one.

"Ah ha! The box of every toaster he ever owned. There are four in here. He kept them in case the new one broke down. He could then use the parts from the old one to fix it."

"Did he ever do that?" asked Eva.

"No. As soon as he put the old toaster in this box, he forgot he had it."

Fran handed the big box full of toasters to a workman to take it to the dumpster.

She was just about to open another box when she suddenly sat back on the floor and leaned against a wall.

"I'm exhausted. I can't keep doing this. I have too much work to do back at the office. It's all junk. I say we just chuck the rest."

"Fine by us," said one of the workmen and the other two nodded.

Fran started handing off unopened boxes to the workman. When they were down to the last one, Fran noticed it was surprisingly heavy. She handed it to a workman who carried it up the stairs. As she stood there looking at the empty cupboard, a strange feeling washed over her. She immediately bounded up the stairs after the man. Just as he was about to throw the box into the dumpster she shouted, "Wait! Don't throw that one out!"

The man put the box down.

Eva came over to inspect the situation and asked, "Why not?"

"I don't know, it's just somehow different-looking than all the other boxes. Look how overly taped up it is and it's bulging at the seams. Let's bring it back inside."

He carried it back inside the house and laid it down. Fran scratched some dirt from the label. She could just make out the words "George Freeman." She tried to rip off the tape with her fingernails but it was too thick and too old.

One of the workmen pulled out a utility knife and tried to saw through the eight layers of tape. After several awkward minutes, he finally sprung it open. A flurry of contents fell onto the floor. The women swivelled their heads sideways to make sense of what they saw.

Laying there at their feet was a scattering of photos, documents, letters, and mementos. Some of the photos seemed to be of George as a young man in Europe. The documents were mostly in other languages.

"He told me he lost all his photos back in Europe." Fran remarked, curious.

"Maybe he forgot it was all here, like the toasters," said Eva.

"Or maybe he just didn't want me to find them."

They sat on the floor studying the photos. There were photos of George marrying a gorgeous girl who looked like Bridgette Bardot. There were photos of the same woman holding a baby. Then Fran pulled out a photo of George standing in a uniform, next to an airplane.

Eva looked closely at the cap on his head, "There is a swastika on his cap. Was he a Nazi?"

Fran recoiled at the image. Her knowledge of World War II and the Nazis was scant to say the least. Yet, she was aware that the Nazis were responsible for the genocide of approximately six million Jews. Her heart felt tight in her chest. Was that what he was trying to hide? She glanced at Eva whose face was now contorted in derision.

"I have no idea," Fran replied.

Eva picked up the photo and underneath it was an autographed photo of Adolf Hitler.

"Look at this! It proves your father *was* a Nazi!"

Fran studied the infamous face that had become synonymous with evil.

Eva spat out, "Well that explains a lot."

"What does that explain?" asked Fran, defensively, but Eva didn't answer; she just kept looking at more photos.

There were photos of George in uniform, as a young man on a bike holding a trophy, as a child on a carousel.

"I can't believe it. I can't believe I worked for a man like that!"

"What do you mean?"

"If I had known. If I had just known, I would never have stepped foot in this house."

Eva picked up another photo of him holding a rifle, "Do you have any idea what the Nazis did to my family?"

"You're Jewish?"

"Yes, we were Polish Jews. All of my family members were sent to concentration camps and were tortured or died a horrible death there. I lost everyone I knew. I was just a child, and I barely survived," Eva dropped the photos and wiped her hands fastidiously on her handkerchief as if to rid herself of the memories, "How come Canada let someone like him into this country? How could I not have known? I usually never trust a man of his generation with a German accent."

"You said you didn't recognize his accent and that you were normally an expert at that," Fran questioned, intrigued now.

"Yes, but I always detected some German," Eva shot back, "He must have worked hard to cover up his former identity, which proves he was a war criminal."

Fran suddenly stood up feeling somehow insulted, "Aren't you jumping to conclusions? We're talking about my father here. He wouldn't hurt a fly, you know that. And, why would you not trust anyone with a German accent? I'm sure there are lots of people with German accents who are trustworthy."

"Don't you understand? The Germans are monsters! It's in their blood. I don't think I can be in this house anymore. I have to get out of here," Eva said as she collected her coat and headed out the door.

Fran ran after her, "Wait, Eva. Don't go."

The door slammed and Fran stood looking out the window as Eva raced out of the driveway.

Fran looked down at the photo of the man in uniform. If it wasn't for the eyes she never could have believed this handsome, athletic-looking man was her father. His whole demeanour was different.

Fran came back in the house and the three hired men stood in the foyer, looking down at the floor. They had heard the whole conversation. Fran felt too confused and upset to explain, so she paid each one and sent them home.

Then, picking up the cordless phone, Fran dialed the number for Eva's cell. There was no answer. Fran's stomach was tense. She wondered if Marguerite would know how to find out about her father's past. She called Marguerite's work number. The receptionist told Fran that she was booked up for the whole day.

Who else could she talk to about this? No one came to mind. A feeling of isolation descended upon her.

On impulse she leapt into her car and drove down to Marguerite's office, hoping to catch her between meetings. Fran rarely did anything impulsively nor reached out to others but life was handing her too much to deal with right now.

When she arrived, Marguerite and some staff members were meeting with the CEO of a credit union and a First Nations chief. She waited until the meeting ended then slipped into Marguerite's office, closing the door.

"I know you're busy, but this will only take a moment ..."

After hearing her out Marguerite sat back in her chair and said "Let's try to find Laszlo. He may be your only link to the past. I have to get to another meeting now, but my receptionist can get you the number of the Law Society — you might get his number through them. I can come by first thing tomorrow and go through the box with you but it will have to be early, say 7:00 a.m.?"

Fran nodded gratefully and headed down to the parkade.

On the way home she called the Law Society on her cell phone.

"I'm interested in connecting with a practicing lawyer named Laszlo Goldstein," Fran told the receptionist, then waited while she checked the database.

"There is no lawyer by that name practicing here in this province, but you could try the law societies in the other provinces. Would you like their numbers?" said the voice on the other end of the line.

"No, not right now. Thank you."

When she arrived home the front door was unlocked. Fran was sure she locked it when she left. Maybe Eva came back. She went down stairs to the box of photos she had found. As she turned the corner into the rec room she heard a loud crash at the other end of the basement. *Someone had just gone out the basement door.* She ran to the door to see if it was Eva, but heard only the sound of thumping feet as someone ran along the side of the house.

Afraid to chase the intruder, Fran ran upstairs to see if she could see the face of the person from the upstairs window.

There was no one in sight.

She picked up a hammer from the workbench and slowly walked around the rest of the house.

It was silent.

When she felt sure no one was there, she locked all the doors and windows and sat down on a chair to catch her breath. Her heart was thumping. Should she call the police? Nothing of value seemed to be taken, there was no forced entry. Back in the rec room, she examined the box of photos and papers.

Some photos were missing!

Who would do that?

Fran tried calling Eva again but there was no answer.

She curled up on the sofa and felt very alone. The house no longer felt like the fortress it once was. It was a perilous place now and she felt vulnerable. She considered going to a hotel or to someone's house for the night rather than stay there alone. Yet, strangely, some inertia or paralysis stopped her, and she curled up on the sofa instead. She pulled a blanket around her and further studied the items in her father's box.

There was a well-worn book of quotations in English. Several quotations had been underlined in what looked like black fountain pen. The copyright on the book was 1926. Some of the pages were so thin they were disintegrating. She flipped through the pages and her eyes were captured by an underlined quotation from Dante's *La Commedia Divina: In the middle of the road of my life I awoke in a dark wood, where the true way was wholly lost.*

"How appropriate," she said out loud to herself.

She opened a sketchbook full of exquisitely drawn portraits of individuals, couples and families. Some of the ones of women had their names written underneath. Margarethe looked like a movie star with her hair in a French twist and sophisticated eyes. Silvie was curly haired with high round cheeks and a mischievous grin. Renate had long hair in pig tails, a freckled face and round, melancholy eyes.

The realism in the work astounded Fran. She wondered where the drawings came from. Each sketch was signed in the bottom right hand corner, "Jiri". Who was Jiri? At the bottom of one picture was the name, "Francesca". She had long, wavy dark hair and wide-set dark eyes just like Fran. How fascinating, she thought. But who was she?

There was one sketch of a young teen wearing a Navy man's cap painting in front of an easel. Another was of a boy in uniform waving a Nazi banner. Then another seemed to be a portrait of her father in a winter coat and fedora.

Some of the documents and letters were in German and some were in a foreign language she didn't recognize — Fran would need a translator to read them. She kept looking. There were photos of a child on a carousel, and a band playing, and a large tent with an illegible sign on it. In one photo there was a little boy she guessed to be him, standing next to a stocky, sweet-faced man. It looked as if one side of the photo had been torn. She studied it more closely. The boy and the man seemed to have been close. They were holding hands.

It suddenly dawned on her that this large man in the photo was his father — her grandfather. Would he still be alive? Probably not, she guessed. George looked to be seven, and his father to be in his mid-thirties. That would make her grandfather over a hundred years old now. There were no photos of his mother. Was she the person that he had ripped out of the family photo? George had destroyed all the photos of Roberta after she left. What had George's mother done to deserve a similar fate? She thought of the newspaper article about her father. From many people's perspective in Canada, he was a man who seemed to have it all. How did he become so alone, so eccentric, and so weighed down by the end of his life? She started to feel fatigue creeping over her. She wrapped the blanket around her like a cocoon and fell into a deep sleep.

The next morning Fran awoke to the sound of Marguerite knocking at the front door. Fran dragged herself up and staggered to the front door. Peering out through the window in the door Fran could see that Marguerite was holding up the morning paper. On the front cover was the photo of her father in uniform. The caption read "Freemen & Wilson founder — Nazi War Criminal?"

She unlocked the door in three places and swung it open, staring at the paper in shock and horror.

"Who would have done that?" she gasped.

"Quick, close the door. A media truck has just arrived."

She pushed Fran into the interior of the house, as Fran looked out the window, stunned, "There are media people coming to talk to me?"

"Yes, I suspect so. Don't answer the door."

Before the sentence was even out of her mouth, there was a knock at the door.

"This is insane! It must have been Eva who leaked this news. You didn't, did you?" cried Fran.

"Of course not. It might have been Eva, but why would she do that? I thought she cared about you and your father," asked Marguerite, "I read the article. They have no proof of this war criminal claim. It's all speculation. I can't believe the editor would let a story like this run. It's like tabloid reporting."

Fran's cell phone rang.

"Don't answer it. It's probably the media," said Marguerite.

"Only three people have my cell number — my father, Eva and Meili, the receptionist at Freemen & Wilson."

They looked at each other as the phone continued to ring.

"Okay, answer it," instructed Marguerite.

Fran picked up the phone.

It was Laszlo Goldstein.

## CHAPTER 17

When the call ended Fran turned to Marguerite and said, "He saw the news. He is in the hospital and apologized for not contacting me earlier. He is dealing with complications from leukemia. I'm supposed to come to the hospital alone as soon as possible and his assistant is bringing the Will. I'm going there now. I'll call you back once I've talked with him."

Fran put all the remaining photos and documents in a briefcase and grabbed her coat.

"Put on my coat, hat and sunglasses," suggested Marguerite.

Fran looked over at the clothes Marguerite was handing to her and shook her head, "I don't usually wear purple zebra coats."

"Exactly. Nor an African Zulu hat. They need to think that it's me leaving the house, not you. I'll put on your coat and hat. Then later I'll slip out the back."

"Alright," Fran said slowly. "But that means we'd need to exchange cars too."

Marguerite nodded. "Alright. Put these on then."

Fran put on the purple zebra raincoat and fuzzy Zulu hat, and then Marguerite added the finishing touch to Fran's face — the Sophia Loren sunglasses. They both stood looking at Fran in the hallway mirror and broke into laughter.

"Perfect. They'll never know the difference."

Fran rolled her eyes, "Yeah, right. Despite the fact that I am several inches shorter than you."

"Do you have any stilettos?"

"I have one pair that I can't stand wearing for more than five minutes."

"Good, go put them on."

Fran rummaged around in the back of her closet and produced the five-inch stilettos with sequined ankle straps.

"Oooooh, where did you get these?"

"Lavana, the marketing manager, lent them to me for a staff Christmas party and didn't want them back."

She forced her feet into the narrow toe and was immediately five inches taller. Fran fumbled her way to the front door and Marguerite helped her along by the elbow.

"You need to stick out your derrière, it makes it much easier."

"Who invented something as wretched as these to wear?"

"A man, of course."

Marguerite hugged her at the door and tucked her curly black hair under the hat, "You look striking in this outfit. You should wear bright colors more often. Don't say anything to anyone when you walk to the car."

In a sensual Jamaican accent, Fran said "Ms. Freeman has no comment at this time. Please leave the property. Thank you."

Marguerite looked at her, incredulous, "That's amazing. You sound exactly like me. I didn't know you were such a good mimic!"

"You name 'em I can do 'em," Fran smiled. Then she turned and opened the door.

Several people from the media swarmed her the moment she stepped out. Marguerite peeked through the curtain and watched as Fran sped away in the Jag.

Once safely inside the car, Fran laughed, delighted at fooling the media with their ruse. She looked in the rear-view mirror, surprised to see she was actually having fun while her world and her father's reputation tumbled down around her ears. She shook her head, puzzled by her own reaction, then focused on the car, enjoyed the sensation of driving the brand new car. It seemed silly to be so impressed with leather interiors and heated seats when she had so many other important things to focus on, but she couldn't help herself. At each traffic light she played with more buttons on the dash.

When she arrived at the hospital's underground parking lot the only spot she could find was far away from the elevators. She limped her way to the exit on to the other side of the parkade when a young man about twenty years old with a buzz-cut and a goatee approached her and asked for the time.

When she looked down at her watch he suddenly tried to grab her briefcase.

Then another young man grabbed her from behind and she felt something cold and metallic in the back of her neck.

"Drop it. I have a gun at your head."

Her breathing stopped and she froze on the spot.

Suddenly a security guard came around the corner and shouted, "Hey!"

The two young men let her go immediately and raced out the exit, dropping their "gun" as they ran.

Fran stared at the object, her knees shaking.

It was only a flashlight.

The security guard ran up to her. "Are you all right, ma'am? Did they hurt you? Did they steal anything?"

Fran looked down. The briefcase was on the ground. They never did get a hold of it.

"I think I'm alright. What was that all about?"

"Just teenagers trying to purse snatch, ma'am," the guard replied, "It happens from time to time around here. I'm very sorry. I was just getting a coffee. Usually they try to get into unlocked cars and steal loose change. It's not like them to actually accost someone."

After that, the guard escorted her to the security desk so that she could make a police report. Fran was still trembling as she sat down to talk to the other security guard. It occurred to her that those teenagers were specifically going for the contents of the briefcase, not money. Whatever was in that briefcase had to get to Mr. Goldstein as soon as possible.

Fran squinted as she eyed the man writing out the report. He painstakingly printed out each letter as if he was the Queen's calligrapher.

Finally, Fran lost her cool and said, "I don't think I need a report filled out. Thank you. I'm in a bit of a rush. Let's just let it go."

With that she exited the office and headed for the elevators.

As she waited for the elevator to come, Fran's instincts were at their peak. Aware of all sights and sounds near her, she noticed an unusual willful streak come to the fore. If anyone tried to take the briefcase this time, she would knock their knees out with her five-inch stilettos; a move she once practiced endlessly in her Model Mugging self-defence class. The fantasy of actually using this move on a real criminal seemed appealing. That thought surprised her. Was it from wearing Marguerite's clothes or was it some kind of legacy re-emerging through the long-forgotten photos?

When she arrived at Laszlo's room there was an attractive young woman sitting near him. Laszlo was attached to an IV; the morphine pump was making its rhythmical breathing sound, his heart monitor bleeping across the screen.

He looked frail, thin and pale.

But when his eyes fell on Fran, his demeanour changed immediately; his lawyer self came to the forefront. The woman took the ventilator out of his mouth and he beckoned her forward.

In a hoarse voice he said, "Ms. Freeman. Thank you for coming. I'm very sorry about the loss of your father. He was a good man."

"Was he?" Fran replied directly, searching the man's face, "Or was he a war criminal? I'm sorry. I'm just a bit upset. All this talk about my father being a Nazi, and someone just tried to mug me in the parkade, and get this briefcase away from me. I thought they had a gun at my head! I don't understand what's going on."

She thrust the case forward.

"This is full of photos and documents that I found in my father's house. I've never seen them before. Please tell me how you know my father and what all this means. I know you're very sick and I don't want to tire you, but I really need to know what is going on here."

Laszlo held his hands up, beseeching her for calm, "Slow down. One thing at a time. By the way, this is my granddaughter, Lena. Lena this is Ms. Freeman, the daughter of that man I was telling you about."

Fran flushed with embarrassment. It wasn't usually like her to be so emotional in public.

"I'm sorry. Pleased to meet you," Fran said holding out her hand.

Lena reciprocated the gesture. Fran couldn't tell if she was Italian or Asian or Black, or maybe a mix of all three. She didn't look at all like Laszlo. Her chestnut hair was swept up in combs and her highlighted ringlets cascaded down to her waist. She had large, light green eyes that were fringed with sparkly green eye-liner, and her full, sensuous lips were cased thickly in cherry lip gloss. In her leopard skin, leather-fringed pant suit, she looked like she was ready for "Star Search." Yet, her appearance somehow made Fran feel less conspicuous in her zebra coat and stilettos.

Laszlo continued, "I will tell you what I can. I'm sorry about what just happened to you in the parkade. Quite frankly, I'm not surprised. We need to talk about that."

Laszlo held his shaky hand out toward Lena who promptly handed him the Will and his reading glasses "Your father's Will states that all his wealth, his house, vehicles, assets and shares in Freeman & Wilson go to you … and your sister."

"My sister? I don't have a sister."

There was an awkward pause as Fran looked wide-eyed at both Laszlo and Lena. Then a memory of a photo filled her head. She fished around in the briefcase until she found the photo of a baby and held it up so that they could see.

"Is this child my sister?"

"Yes, that's probably her. But she's not a baby anymore. She was born in 1943. That means she is about fifty-eight years old now. I believe she lives somewhere in the outskirts of Vienna. Obviously, she had a different mother, but she is a blood relative and is entitled to her share of the estate."

Fran noticed an uncomfortable feeling well up inside. Why should she have to share the estate with a total stranger?

Laszlo continued, "Up until my visit with your father a few weeks ago, you were the sole heir. When we talked on the phone about his Will, I reminded him that he had another child. I said I would need to contact her upon his death. It seems he had forgotten all about her, but I hadn't. It's amazing what age will do to the mind."

Fran felt overwhelmed by a mixture of emotions, "Tell me more about her."

"Her name is Helena. She was the only child of your father and a woman named Uta. Your father was presumed dead in 1943. Soon after that he escaped to Canada and couldn't contact his wife. Uta died a few years after the child was born so Helena essentially grew up as an orphan. She's had it difficult, but she has managed to do well for herself. Now she runs a fairly large business making and dispensing … what was that, Lena? I think it was herbal remedies."

"You've talked to her?"

"No. I found her website. The one thing I do know is that she thinks your father died fifty-eight years ago. She has no idea he was

alive all this time and that he accumulated great wealth — or that she
has a sister for that matter.

"Oh my God ..."

"Her mother was Austrian, but born in what was then called
Czechoslovakia. Your father supposedly died in a plane crash in Northern
Africa during the war. Uta had to go back to Czechoslovakia after
the war. All people of German heritage then were rounded up by the
Communists and put into work camps. Helena's mother died very
young of pneumonia due to a lack of proper medical care and poor
living conditions."

"I didn't know the Germans were rounded up after the war," Lena
exclaimed.

"The Communists wanted to do to the Germans what the Germans
had done to the Communists."

"And to the Jews," Fran added.

"Yes, and to the Jews."

"To your people?"

"I'm mixed blood actually. My father was Jewish and my mother
was a German National. That made me only partially tainted in their
eyes. But most of my father's family ended up in the gas chambers. I lost
my grandfather, my uncle and two aunts who had helped raise me. It
was a horrible time. My father and I were imprisoned for a while, and
he was even tortured. My mother stood outside the building where we
were imprisoned for days and weeks along with the wives and mothers
of the other Jews imprisoned there. Finally, through a friend in high
places, she managed to get us out of prison and then out of the country.
We went to England and got involved in an underground movement,
forging documents and creating false identities."

Laszlo opened his mouth to continue, then convulsed suddenly,
hacking, his lungs fighting for air. Fran looked on in alarm, frightened
for him, sensitive after the trauma of her father's death. A nurse entered
and pressed a nebulizer tablet to Laszlo's mouth, forcing air into his lungs.

After a moment he started to calm.

When the nurse took it off his mouth he said, "I'm sorry about that. My energy is very low right now. It must be your father haunting us. I can feel the hairs on the back of my neck standing up. He's over there in the corner watching us."

Fran peered over at the corner of the room. Lena laughed nervously, then excused herself and left the room. Laszlo watched her go, shaking his head.

"Lena doesn't like it when I talk about ghosts. Don't you feel it?"

Fran didn't believe in ghosts either but didn't want to appear rude.

"I suppose so."

"Maybe he is getting angry with me for telling you all this. Hey, George what does it matter now?!" Laszlo laughed but then started coughing again.

"Maybe you should rest now," Fran cautioned.

"I might be dead tomorrow. I'll keep going as long as I can."

Fran nodded gravely, knowing better than anyone the truth of his statement.

"So what is my father's story and why would he never talk about it?" she asked again.

"I don't know the full story. I know he got involved with the Hitler Youth at one point in time. Oh, he doesn't like me telling you about that. I hope he's not a poltergeist or he could unplug my morphine," he winked at Fran.

Fran was now getting spooked. Perhaps it was just Laszlo's suggestion, but she now sensed an unusual presence in the room.

"Were you his friend?"

"I was probably one of the few people in his life he would call a friend. Right, George?"

Laszlo stared in the corner, smiling, as he asked the question. Fran pressed on, trying to ignore the man's disturbing belief he was communicating somehow with her father.

"And yet you were Jewish and he fought for the Nazis?"

"There's so much that you don't know about him. He was a complicated man living at a complicated time in history. I know it may be hard for some people to believe, but even those who got enamoured by Nazi ideology weren't all bad people. They were forced into it and often heavily brainwashed. They got caught up in the hype. They saw Hitler as someone who was going to save them from economic ruin. Someone who was going to give them back power, dignity, and economic stability after the mess of World War I."

Fran nodded. Laszlo certainly was talkative for a man with leukemia.

"The politicians, or I should say 'the powers that be,' they do that all the time ... and it's even more sophisticated these days."

Fran furrowed her brow.

He continued, "I mean they brainwash people into a certain mindset. Then people later realized that they made a horrible mistake to support them. To be sure, some people never wake up from that, but I know your father deeply regretted something. He carried a lot of shame his whole life and didn't seem to know how to let it go. I don't know if keeping people in perpetual damnation helps them reform — I think not."

She nodded in agreement although she wasn't sure she agreed.

He continued, "I was studying at Oxford in the '50s when J.R.R. Tolkien was a professor there and *The Lord of the Rings* had just been published. I remember talking to him in the local pub one day. We chatted away over a pint of Guinness about the meaning of The Ring and The Ringwraiths. They fascinated me and I wondered if it was an allegory of the Third Reich. Have you read that book?"

"No, but I heard they are turning it into a movie."

"A movie?! Impossible to do. Tolkien would roll over in his grave. At any rate, he told me he hated thinking of his book as an allegory of any particular current event, especially of the Hitler regime. He wanted the themes to be timeless, a mirror of the human psyche, not any particular group. I thought about it later and it does have a universal application. I've lived over eighty years and I can tell you — Ringwraiths are everywhere. They are in us. In the book the supposedly good characters are vulnerable to being seduced by the Ring. It's like there is something in everyone's heart that could get corrupted given the right circumstances.

I knew who your father was deep down. Yes, I call him my friend, despite his involvement with the Nazis. I don't take things personally. I know people who have held hatred in their hearts for decades about what happened during the war. Then, even their children hold the same hatred and it carries on down the line."

Fran thought for a moment of Eva, "Yes, my father's caregiver was like that when she saw the photos."

"Call me naïve, but to stay hateful is to victimize yourself and your loved ones all over again. I know in many ways that the persecutors suffered as much as the victims. We victims might get to feel righteous in our suffering, but what about all the people who got seduced into the ideologies of the time who were young and didn't know any better? Many lived out the rest of their life in shame, with no redemption."

"But it seems like some of them felt no remorse."

"Yes, there are people in all countries, cultures and races who feel no remorse. But I believe they are the exception. There can be no forward movement as a human race if we can't forgive ourselves and each other. There, that's my soap box. Sorry to bore you with it all."

"No, I appreciate your point of view. It is good food for thought."

"I tell you, though, if I even suggest forgiving anyone on the Axis side of the war I am passionately rejected by some members of my community. This whole 'never forgetting' thing …," he said, propping himself on one elbow and locking Fran's gaze. "You just can't do that and have your freedom at the same time."

He flopped back down on the bed and moved around to get comfortable again. Fran felt concerned that he shouldn't be exerting himself like that, yet she could sense he had much more to say and that he was looking for someone to listen, to be his witness.

He continued with his eyes half-closed, "But some people don't want that freedom. In fact, sometimes I don't want it. So I have a big dilemma, my dear. I don't want to lose my identity, but I also don't want to go to my grave feeling hatred and resentment — I would feel like I haven't learned life's greatest lesson."

"And what's that?" Fran asked intrigued, "I mean what do you believe is life's greatest lesson?'

"To love people, to forgive them, to feel gratitude for life. I don't want to die not having learned how to do that."

Fran nodded. The room became cold and silent in that moment. She could now definitely sense another presence in the room. She thought perhaps her father hadn't learned what Laszlo called 'life's greatest lesson.' She wondered if that's what a ghost was — someone still hanging around trying to 'get' what life was all about.

"So my father wasn't a war criminal?"

"Listen, at the Nuremburg trials they created a definition of a war criminal which included such things as genocide or the mistreatment of prisoners of war and considered it in violation of the conventions of warfare. However, they soon realized that it wasn't just the Hitler regime that committed war crimes, all sides in the war were guilty to some degree or another, so they changed the rules to apply just to the Axis.

They argued that if someone wanted to make a case against the Allies, it would need to happen at another time. So, to answer your question I think all decision makers on both sides of the war are guilty of war crimes. And, by the way, the real decision makers are always far removed from the headlines. That aside, I suspect your father never got high enough in rank to be put on the stand at Nuremburg."

"Then why would the media suggest that he was a war criminal?"

"Maybe they found some evidence that I don't know about. I was out of touch with your father between 1938 and 1945. On the other hand, maybe someone is trying to discredit him."

"You mean someone at Freeman & Wilson? Why would someone do that?"

"Maybe they think it will help them wrestle ownership away from you and your sister."

"Does anyone else know about the contents of this Will?"

She suddenly realized that Laszlo had his eyes closed.

She gasped and looked over at the heart monitor.

"Don't worry, I'm not dead yet," Laszlo smiled, still keeping his eyes closed, "No," he continued on, answering her question, "Only you and I and Lena know about the Will. Keep it to yourself, until you can talk to your sister. I have an address. Go to Vienna and sort it all out with her. I think you should go as soon as possible. In fact, I had Lena actually buy you a plane ticket. You leave tomorrow morning. Some people call me pushy. I like to call it enthusiastic."

He smiled again at his little joke.

"You what?" Fran replied, caught off guard, "Well ... I ... that's very thoughtful of you, but I can't get on a plane tomorrow. I have the house to deal with, and everything at work, and the memorial is on Sunday."

Laszlo locked her gaze again, suddenly deadly serious.

"I'll be honest with you. I don't think staying now is a wise idea. And I don't think that mugging in the parkade was just a couple of kids looking for some cash. I'm doing this because I think you're in danger here, Francesca. Leave the country as soon as you can."

He handed over her copy of the Will and an address for Helena.

"Lena will take care of the administrative things. My cell phone number is on there. If you encounter any trouble in Vienna, call me. And don't tell anyone where you are going other than your lovely friend from Jamaica. I like her. She's good with the hair styles."

He smiled again, looking sideways at the Zulu hat on Fran's head.

"Mr. Goldstein, this isn't a good idea. I don't fly. I get airsick. I've never been overseas before. I don't speak any German. Why don't we get Helena to come here? I'll buy her a plane ticket."

Laszlo made a clucking sound in his throat, like the kind Fran had heard Eva make with her father, something from the Old World and another time. Something that said the course was already set, and she was just stalling the inevitable.

"She doesn't even know you exist," he said resting, his eyes closed. "You must go to her."

Laszlo coughed again and it spiralled into another choking fit. A doctor rushed in, and a nurse escorted Fran out of his room.

"Visiting hours are over now," she said, "You can come back tomorrow."

Fran hobbled back to the waiting area. The stilettos were killing her. She noticed that Laszlo's cell number started with a 416 area code. That's probably why she couldn't locate him in BC, she thought. He was based in Toronto.

Lena was standing in the waiting room holding Fran's plane tickets as she approached.

"Here are tickets. Your sister lives in Kittsee, about a half-hour train ride from the Vienna train station. There are some good pensions there. I visited it once. Just ask when you arrive."

Fran held the tickets for a moment and then shoved them back in Lena's hand. "Thanks, but I won't be using them. I hope you can get a refund."

"Non-refundable," Lena said handing them back. She then turned and scurried onto the elevator. Fran stood there, not knowing what to say. What was a "pension"? She should have asked. The flight left at 7:00 a.m. the next morning. She had very little time to make up her mind.

A nurse approached her, "Is your name Fran Freeman?"

"Yes."

"There are several men waiting for you in the lobby, plus some people from the media."

"Please, I can't see any of them right now."

The elevator doors opened, and Nelson Gaulin, the Freeman & Wilson lawyer and a man who looked like an FBI agent stepped into the hallway and started walking directly toward Fran.

## CHAPTER 18

The three men approached Fran and stopped in front of her and the nurse. Nelson said, "Can you direct me to Laszlo Goldstein's room?"

Fran hesitated, shaking inside, then felt a surge of hope as she realized they didn't recognize her.

The nurse replied, "Its room 302 down that hallway."

The FBI-type man glanced over at Fran and winked. Then the three men turned and walked away, heading at a clipped pace down toward Laszlo's room.

"Thank you for not telling them my name," Fran whispered to the nurse, "Is there a way I can get to the parkade without bumping into the media?"

"Yes, I'll call security and they can escort you out the back exit."

The security guard arrived a few moments later and Fran made it back down to Marguerite's Jag without seeing anyone.

As Fran drove back home a million thoughts raced through her mind. Should she actually be going home right now? Where else could she go? What is in this briefcase that is so valuable? How could she avoid getting on that airplane? Maybe she could convince someone else to travel there instead. Maybe Marguerite would go. Maybe she would at least accompany her.

She called the number for Meili, the receptionist at Freeman & Wilson. Fran knew that whether or not she went to Europe she was not going to work right now. Also, staging a memorial was out of the question. As the phone rang, she took a deep breath and slowly exhaled. She hated lying.

"Listen, Meili, I seem to have come down with a very bad case of the flu. I just don't feel able to organize my father's memorial service. I am going to stay with a friend until I get better. Can you please cancel the memorial service for now? I will also not be coming to work next week. I will need you to cancel all my appointments. Please give them to Peter Wilson."

"Of course I will, Fran. I really feel for you — having to deal with your father's death while all this bad press is going on. Is any of that information true? I would never have considered your father capable of war crimes."

"There must be some mistake. It seems to be based on hearsay instead of evidence. At any rate, it is the first I ever heard of any of these claims. I can't really talk right now, though. I'm sorry to dump all this on you, but I'm flat on my back."

Fran winced as a car beeped its horn to her right.

"I totally understand," Meili reassured her, "I'll take care of it. If I were you I wouldn't be coming to work either. It's been a media zoo here between that article on your father and all the investigations with Wrightway. Everyone is asking where you are. I'm not giving out your cell number and I just keep saying 'no comment' just like you asked."

"Thank you, Meili, you have no idea what that means to me."

After Fran got off the phone she called Marguerite.

"I have a lot to tell you. But I would like to tell you in person. Can you meet me at my house?"

"Yes, I can meet you. Are you okay?" asked Marguerite.

"Two men tried to steal the briefcase from me in the hospital parkade. And Nelson Gaulin, our lawyer and some investigative-looking type came to the hospital just when I was leaving. I managed to leave before they recognized me."

"My God. This is really getting out of hand."

"There's something else I need to talk to you about when I see you in person."

When Fran arrived at the house the media trucks were blocking the driveway. Marguerite arrived at the same time and hopped into the passenger side of Fran's car. She directed Fran to drive up onto the lawn, and around the truck in her driveway. They opened the automatic garage door, pulled the car in, and closed the garage door.

The dead doorbell clicking sound went on incessantly as they made their way upstairs to Fran's apartment. When they arrived at the top of the stairs Fran gasped.

Her entire apartment had been ransacked.

Her mirrors, lamps and ornaments were lying broken on the floor. All her drawers were dumped out. Her bedroom window had been smashed and was wide open.

Marguerite looked around to make sure nobody was still hiding somewhere in the house while Fran sat on the edge of the bed in shock. Marguerite sat next to her on the bed and placed one hand on her back. The younger woman was trembling so Marguerite got her a glass of water.

"Now, do that breathing exercise with me again. Take in a long slow breath through your nose, slightly constricting the back of your throat. Then out again slowly through your nose. Let's keep doing that for a few moments," Marguerite instructed.

After a few minutes Fran could feel her adrenaline levels decreasing and pulse slow down. Finally, Fran told the story of all that had happened that day, and then she added, "That's all confidential. You can't tell anyone what is in the Will."

"Of course not," Marguerite asserted, "But I think it's a good idea for you to go to Vienna and follow Laszlo's advice. I'll help you get packed."

"No. I'm not going," Fran protested, feeling pushed beyond her comfort zone again, "I don't fly. I just need a place to stay until everything blows over. But I've got an idea. Why don't I stay at your place and you can go to Vienna on my behalf? I'll pay for everything."

Marguerite didn't answer, but dropped her chin and raised her eyebrows. Fran's brow crinkled in realization that no one was going to let her go on this one.

"Okay, what if you just came with me?" she relented.

Marguerite smiled, "That's a lovely offer, but I'm on the verge of completing several important deals with major contributors. We risk losing those funds if I suddenly disappeared to Europe. Besides that, your sister probably wants to meet you, not me."

"I'm much too upset to travel. I just don't think I could handle something like that right now."

Marguerite stood up and looked out the window. More media trucks were arriving. She thought out loud to herself, "What's good about this situation?"

"Nothing is good about all this!" cried Fran.

"Look, Fran, there's always another perspective to every situation. It's totally normal to have resistance to change. But you're not going to let a bit of discomfort stop you now, are you?"

Fran nodded, "Yes, I am."

Marguerite had to smile, "You have to go, Fran. If you go to Europe you might be able to clear up the story around your father. You have a lot to talk about with your sister. If it's just about fear of flying, remember how things changed for you on the rollercoaster. Just let go. Maybe you won't get airsick this time."

"It's more than just getting airsick. I've never really traveled by myself. I know that sounds lame, but I don't think I'd handle it very well."

Fran shuddered remembering the trip to Montreal she took with her parents. She was only six. The runway was so icy that the plane skidded out of control and plowed into a nearby freeway. She wasn't badly injured, but after that she took pains to travel by car or train instead. Her mother left them soon after and Fran always wondered if that close call with death had triggered her leaving.

"You'll be fine. There's an important reason all this is happening. That's my instinct on all this. Let's pack your bags and get you to the airport. You can stay at an airport hotel tonight."

"I can't leave the house like this!"

"I'll arrange for someone to come fix the window right away and clean things up."

"No!" Fran cried out covering her eyes. Even though the fear constricted her thinking, she noticed herself tiring of her own spineless nature.

Marguerite sat down next to her on the bed and said, "You will regret it if you don't go." She put her arm around Fran's shoulder. "Vienna is beautiful this time of year — the gardens, the architecture, the music, the history. I love it there. You'll be in awe. It's a very different feeling there. Europe is an experience you don't want to miss out on. And you'll be reconnecting with your roots."

Fran's head was pounding. Everything was pointing toward her having to get on that damn airplane. Fighting it felt like too much work. She wiped the tears from her face and stood up. Then, she went to her closet and pulled out her suitcase.

## CHAPTER 19

An hour later they were driving to the airport. Marguerite chose a circuitous route to lose the people who seemed to be following them, and she put the hotel room under her name. Then she hugged Fran goodbye.

The Sheraton Airport Hotel lobby was virtually empty when she checked in. A bellboy escorted her to the Club Floor which was guarded by an extra concierge. Her suite looked out over the airport runways that twinkled like a diamond necklace in the blackness of the night. The thought of getting on that airplane tomorrow made her stomach turn.

She watched television to quell the nervousness, but the movie channel was playing *Fearless,* a film starring Jeff Bridges about an airplane crash. Fran switched off the TV and the bedside light, and then curled into a ball on the bed, clutching her pillow, willing herself to fall asleep. After several hours of staring at the wall, the ceiling, turning the television on and off, pacing the room, and repacking her suitcase, the alarm finally rang. She was relieved to finally get to leave the hotel room.

At the airport Fran's mood improved to find that Laszlo had booked her a first-class seat direct to Vienna. As she stood waiting in the departure lounge, a short, elderly man in uniform approached her.

"You aren't allowed to board the flight without a smile."

"Pardon me?" Fran asked, frowning even more.

"I'm the smile police. Smiling helps the plane take off. Can I please see your smile?

Fran managed a weak smile and said flatly, "That's very cute."

"You know what they say at Boeing, don't you?"

"No."

"Planes fly because the passengers take themselves lightly."

"I don't like flying," Fran said trying not to sound as annoyed as she felt.

"What's not to like? You get to be high up in the sky, far away from all your problems. You get a different view of life."

"You certainly are positive."

"I'm actually a spiritual teacher — a psychic, disguised as an airport security guard," the old man said with a twinkle in his eye.

Fran looked at the old man slightly perplexed, then something in her realized he seemed so completely loopy and innocent it would take her mind off the flying to play along.

"Oh really? Okay. Then how about giving me a thirty-second psychic reading? I need all the help I can get."

The old man suddenly grew serious, the loopy smile fading. He half closed his eyes and drew in a long, slow breath.

"Very interesting. There are two parts of your persona that need to be merged. You have a good heart and are compassionate on the one hand, and on the other you are a powerful leader. But you don't trust yourself yet. You don't see how to be a leader with a good heart. You feel isolated and lonely for people who really understand you."

Fran stared at the elderly man, surprised by his sudden gravity and accuracy.

"Well, I don't feel lonely anymore because you certainly seem to understand me."

"Good. You will be alright. Everything will be alright. Have a great trip. I'm going on my break now. I need a burger and maybe some large fries."

And with that the little man waddled off down the hall toward the Food Court.

Fran looked after him, half-amused and half-reassured. She shook her head, and smiled. That encounter, strange as it was, helped her calm down.

Two hours later, she was in the plane. She took her seat, and immediately swallowed several air sickness pills. By the time the plane was ready for take off, Fran was already falling into a deep sleep.

## CHAPTER 20

She woke up in the plane, about an hour before landing. She was amazed at how calm she felt. Until it was time to land, that is.

A thunderstorm was howling over the land and the plane was shaking badly. To Fran's fragile state of mind, the blasts of wind seemed like the screams of spirits angry at her arrival. Whatever equilibrium she had gathered from the old man's kindness and her restful sleep was torn from her in those frightening minutes. Her fingernails almost ripped the upholstery as the plane made a rough landing, partially skidding across the tarmac as Fran fought with every once of her will not to scream.

Finally, the plane was on the ground and slowly rolling to the gate.

Once everyone else had deplaned the flight attendant came over to help Fran get herself together.

"That was a rough landing, huh? Here, let me help you."

The flight attendant escorted Fran out of the plane and an airline representative sat with her in the terminal until she felt better. Finally, Fran pulled out the piece of paper that listed the name of the town outside of Vienna where Helena lived. The airline rep spoke perfect English, which was a relief to Fran. The woman told Fran the town was near the Slovak border and called a taxi to take Fran to the Sudbahnhof, or South Train Station.

As the taxi drove through Vienna Fran marvelled at how beautiful the city was. The church steeples, the architecture, the ornate statues, everything was fascinating. She gave the taxi driver her credit card once they arrived at the train station.

The station was packed with people. Everyone was straining to read the information on the departure monitors. Each information booth had a long line in front of it.

Fran walked up to the front of one of the lines to see if she could just ask a quick question. The ticket agent looked overwhelmed, and barked something at her in German. Fran tried finding someone in the line who spoke English. Finally one woman responded, "Yes, I speak English. The train workers just called a strike. Some trains are still running, but I'm not sure which. Where are you going?"

"Kittsee."

"That's over there on Platform number three. It's the one that's marked 'Petrzalka'. I think that one is still running. You better get there quickly, though. It's supposed to leave in seven minutes."

"Thank you!"

Fran started for Platform three, walking quickly while trying to pull along her oversized suitcase. Suddenly there was an announcement on the loudspeaker and people started running in another direction.

She showed her piece of paper with the word "Kittsee" on it to several people, all of whom ignored her. Finally an elderly gentleman, wearing a yellow Fedora hat, beckoned her to follow him. He grabbed her hand and pulled her through a maze of construction, all the while jabbering at her in another language. Several times she tripped or lost hold of her bag until the man grabbed her huge suitcase and heaved it over his head, bullying through the crowd like a Sherpa on steroids.

They emerged in another part of the station just before the throngs of people arrived. He pushed her and her bag onto the train and he waved at her from the platform as the train moved away.

She waved back and yelled, "Thank you!"

People started filling up the seats all around her so Fran grabbed the nearest one. She tried to ask the woman next to her if this train would take her to Kittsee. The woman didn't seem to understand English and nodded unsurely.

Across from her sat a man holding a multi-coloured, six-string guitar. He smiled at her and started to strum his guitar. Then he began to sing a quiet song in what sounded like Italian.

Fran couldn't help notice how striking the man was. He had long, dark hair, tied in several braids that were interwoven with ribbons down his back. He had a dark complexion and high cheek bones. His eyes were kind, and had an exotic quality to them. With his wide-brimmed leather hat and neatly-trimmed moustache he looked like a wandering troubadour. She couldn't place his heritage, but she guessed him to be in his mid-thirties. He wore an unusual hand-embroidered jacket emblazoned with Sanskrit symbols.

Two people on neighbouring seats looked over at him and furrowed their brows as he continued to play. Eventually, a conductor spoke to him in German, in a rather rude tone of voice. The guitar player obliged in good humour and stopped playing. Fran was disappointed. She had found the music enchanting.

Fran asked the woman sitting next to her again about the train's destination. The woman answered in broken English that Fran was probably on the wrong train. Together they looked at a map to try to figure out how far off course she was.

After about five minutes of getting nowhere, the guitar player grabbed the map out of their hands and in a perfect British accent said, "This train indeed stops in Kittsee, and I am getting off at the next stop after that. I will inform you when we are about to arrive."

"You speak English!"

"Yes, I'm from just outside of London, as a matter of fact."

"Why didn't you say something before?"

"My apologies, I was rather enjoying watching your interchange. The name is Jasper, and yours …?"

"I'm Fran. Fran Freeman. I'm going to visit my sister in Kittsee, but I've never been there before."

"I'm going just beyond Kittsee to visit my father in Slovakia. Where does she live in Kittsee? Or is she coming to pick you up?"

"No, she doesn't know I'm coming. It's a surprise. I'm actually thinking of getting a hotel for the first night. Is there a place you'd recommend?"

"Yes, I can think of a few places near the train station. I'll point them out to you when we arrive."

Fran smiled in relief. They sat in silence for a while and she looked out at the countryside. It was flat farmland, but she could still see the Vienna Tower off in the distance. The names of the towns they stopped in seemed so foreign to her: Gramatneusidedl, Gattendorf.

Fran noticed Jasper pulling out a British music magazine. It occurred to Fran that she must look rather unkempt after that long flight, so went to find the restroom. The woman who spoke broken English was standing outside the restroom when she emerged.

"Don't talk with this man. He is probably thief. No good hotels by train station. Best to go into town center. Get taxi to take you there."

"What makes you think he is a thief?"

"I know. Trust me. Must get off at next stop, otherwise I help you more. Be careful."

She thanked the woman and watched her disembark. When Fran got back to her seat, Jasper struck up a conversation. After the woman's warning she felt on guard with him, but at the same time she sensed that he was trustworthy. She remembered Marguerite's words about going on instinct.

"Is this your first time in Europe?" he asked.

"As a matter of fact, it is. I am quite taken with the architecture here. I've seen photos, but it's so much more vivid in real life."

"Yes, you should get your sister to take you to Stephansdom and the Rathaus."

It sounded like he said "Rat House", and she wondered if it was some kind of rodent petting zoo.

Jasper recommended a number of other attractions in and around Vienna and Fran took down some notes, enjoying his rich descriptions and the sing-song quality of his voice.

As the train pulled up to Kittsee, Jasper pointed out some places to stay nearby. Then the conductor came by to help unload her bag and collect her money. She thanked Jasper, and followed the conductor to the exit door.

She reached for her wallet but it was not in her purse. She looked in her other bag. It wasn't there. The train was waiting for her to get off, but the conductor wouldn't give her the large suitcase until she paid. She started looking on the floor and then went back to look under her seat.

"What's the problem?" Jasper asked.

"I can't find my wallet. It's not in my bag."

She looked again inside her purse.

"My passport is gone, too, and all my ID and my cell phone and even my plane ticket."

She felt adrenaline course through her veins. Fran immediately wondered if Jasper took it, but couldn't bring herself to accuse him of that.

"I'll pay your train fare. How much is it?"

"Thank you. That's very kind, but I don't want to get off this train with no money for a taxi or a hotel."

"I'll lend you money for that, too, if you like."

The train started to move again.

"What's happening?" Fran cried out, now starting to panic.

The conductor spoke in German and Fran said, "I'm sorry but I don't speak German."

"I think he said that you can't get off the train until you pay."

"This is just great. Now what am I supposed to do?"

"Do you have traveler's cheques?"

"No, I brought cash. Just Canadian cash. I was going to go to a bank tomorrow and exchange some."

"That kind of cash wouldn't have gotten you too far. Listen, I have relatives just across the border in Slovakia. You can stay there tonight. A hotel manager won't let you stay without a credit card or passport. You can call home tomorrow and wire for some money ..."

"You're very kind, but I'm just not sure ..."

"Oh, you'll love my father. He's a right character and he loves visitors from other places. Additionally, he is a phenomenal musician. He's won awards and I'm sure he'll play for you."

At the next stop in Petrzalka, Jasper paid for both of them and got off the train. He reached out to help her, but she stood on the train frozen in indecision.

"This is the end of the line, I'm afraid," he explained.

Her normal 'risk assessment' mechanisms were not working so well. Was it because she was so travel weary or so hung over from the travel sickness pills, or because this man had so much magnetism? Much to her bewilderment, she found herself taking his hand and following him off the train.

He continued, "Under the usual circumstances you must go through customs and present your passport because we are now in another country. Of course, they won't let you in without a passport, but I know another exit. Follow me."

In that moment, Fran snapped back to her former self. What was she thinking sneaking into a formerly Eastern Bloc country? How would she get back into Austria now without a passport? She should have stayed on the train and gone back to Vienna. She slowed her pace and looked back at the train, then back at Jasper.

He was already fifty feet ahead with her suitcase in hand, beckoning her to follow him. Something kept her moving forward.

They arrived at a fence with barbed wire across the top. In one place, the wire fence was broken. Jasper pushed both their bags through the mesh, then he squeezed himself through, ripping his jacket collar. Once through, he tried to pry open the fence wider for her to step through.

Fran looked around almost sure they were going to be arrested by border guards.

"This is illegal."

"Sometimes bending the rules is necessary, don't you agree?"

Fran shook her head, unmoving.

"Come on then!" Jasper insisted, straining to hold open the fence.

Fran grimanced and ducked through the fence.

Once they made it out onto the street a group of people came running up to Jasper and crowded around him. They smothered him with hugs and started loading their bags onto a funky, flat bed truck. Fran noticed that many of them had dark skin and were dressed in colourful but ragged clothes.

She started to look for a way to get back inside the train station.

Jasper introduced them all to Fran in a foreign tongue. She knew it wasn't German. It was probably Slovak. Although she really wasn't sure what they spoke in Slovakia. It was obvious to her that he was explaining the situation to them. They nodded and looked at her curiously. Several children crowded around Fran, and started grabbing her coat and trying to open her bag.

"Don't do that!" Fran cried.

Jasper came to her rescue and pushed them away.

"Fran this is my clan, or at least some of them."

Fran smiled reluctantly, and held her bag closer to her chest. They all piled into the back of the truck, but the driver ensured that Jasper and Fran got to sit up front in the cab. They drove for what felt like an eternity, into the Slovak countryside.

They finally arrived at what looked like a dishevelled array of mismatched dwellings. Jasper helped Fran out of the cab.

"Welcome to the Olino commune," he said proudly as the children swarmed around them, "a rag-tag team of artists, musicians and entertainers!"

Olino consisted mostly of a few ornately carved caravans with no wheels and small ramshackle homes all set in a roughly circular formation. Each abode had its own satellite dish. There was a grassy area in the centre which was fronted by a meeting hall. To the left was a tiny wooden caravan that looked at least fifty years old, covered in vines and overgrown with camellia bushes snaking up the side.

The pre-fab houses were covered with yellow siding and had brown tile roofs caked in debris with exposed corrugated iron sticking out dangerously in all directions. The areas in front of the houses were littered with children's playthings, old tires, jars, wood stacks and lopsided flower boxes. The skeleton of a Yugo sedan sat propped up on bricks in front of some shanty huts. The home was patched together with tarpaulin lashed onto wooden posts, and the tarp was ripped and flaking off in several places. She could hear radios and TVs blaring everywhere.

An elderly gentleman in a broad-rimmed hat sat playing a guitar, held a steady gaze in their direction. Several others danced around him like orbiting moons, keeping rhythm with shakers. Fran could smell leaves burning, over a hint of hyacinth and night blooming jasmine. Surrounding the community was a lush forest of flowering deciduous trees, evergreens and broom bushes. Over on one end was a quaint duck pond and on the other end was a small, rushing river.

In Vienna she had noticed how neatly arranged the brick homes were, and how meticulously they kept their gardens. Along with that exactness seemed to come an austere nature within the few Viennese people she met, something that felt cold to Fran. All that now stood in stark contrast to the chaotic, wild and ramshackle nature of this environment and the impoverished inhabitants here who had a more unbridled vitality.

"My father thinks of himself as the king around here, so we get the fanciest abode," he said to her, radiating bliss. Jasper was certainly the sort of man that made Fran's breath quicken.

They entered a three room house packed to the brim with knick knacks. There were a variety of musical instruments tacked up on the walls, along with paintings, photos, posters, banners, ribbons and awards on every square inch of wall space. His father, Gustav, shuffled to the door and greeted her in a Slovak accent. "We very honoured you are here." He had black-gray hair flattened from too much hat wearing. His sideways grin and lively eyes felt welcoming to Fran.

He beckoned her to sit down at the small kitchen table, and Jasper talked to his father in another language. Their accent started on a low pitch and ended high; it was musical, fast and erratic. He seemed to be talking about how Fran and he met, and what had happened on the train. Jasper then showed Fran into a little back room that was filled with old records. There was a cot already made up.

"That's where you'll sleep tonight. It's not the Hilton, but hopefully it will do."

"Thank you. I am grateful. Is there a bathroom?"

"That's out here. It's kind of a shared outhouse. Again, not quite the Hilton, but think of it as an adventure."

Jasper pointed the way to the outhouse. It was getting dark, so he gave her a flashlight. "They have chosen to live off the grid here, so no electricity. I'll wait for you here," he assured her.

Fran was now deeply regretting coming with Jasper to this place to stay. There were strange smells and there was no power — only propane lamps. What was she thinking?

As she came closer to the entrance of the outhouse an ancient woman seemed to appear out of nowhere and said in thickly accented English, "You need more light?"

Fran stepped back, terrified. The little woman looked like a raisin. Her skin was thickly wrinkled and her eyes were sunken into her head. She looked to have been about a hundred and twenty years old.

"I'm sorry, I didn't see you there. You speak English?"

"Yes, I know lots of English. You need I hold the lamp for you?"

"Umm, sure. Thank you."

She opened her shawl to reveal two stumps for arms.

Fran recoiled in horror. Either this woman was born with no hands or they had been amputated at the wrists.

"Don't worry, I do okay with these," the old woman cackled, amused at Fran's expression.

On her arm hung a propane lantern that cast greenish shadows on the hollows of the old woman's disfigured face.

"I make light here inside the door for you," she said placing the lantern on the outhouse floor.

There was a putrid smell, so Fran covered her nose as she entered the outhouse. She closed the door. When she had finished her business and opened the door again, Fran jumped upon seeing the old crone still right there.

"Welcome. I am glad you came here. I do palm readings. Show me hand."

Fran hesitated. The old lady wagged a stump at her impatiently. She timidly held out one hand. She placed one stump under Fran's hand and used the other to feel the lines in her palm. Fran shuddered as the deformed arm touched her.

"Hold the lamp next to your palm so I see better. That's right. You have many lucky stars. That's good. A good, long life line. You have big loss with money, though?"

Fran said nothing, afraid to speak. Had Jasper told this woman about the train, or was she genuinely picking up something? She noticed that the old woman was waiting for an answer.

"Ah, no. No big loss of money, thank goodness. My father did very well with money, so I guess I get to benefit from that."

"He did, huh? Lucky you. Unlucky in love, though. But that will change with Saturn return."

"With what?"

"How old are you?"

"I'm twenty-nine."

"Yes, love is on the horizon. Please, hold the lamp on your face. I want to see you."

Fran squinted as the light hit her eyes.

"You are very beautiful. Very happy you come here to us."

Just then Jasper came walking up, much to Fran's relief.

"There you are. I was wondering what happened. I see you've met Sophia. She is our greatest elder here. Ninety-five just two months ago, right, Baba? She has many brilliant stories to tell. What have you been telling our visitor?"

The old woman laughed; her sunken lips opening and revealing the remains of stained lower teeth.

Fran glanced away trying to hide her discomfort, "She has been reading my palm."

"Sophia is very good at that, much too accurate for my liking."

The old woman struggled over a tree stump, so Jasper helped her. At her full height, she seemed less than five feet tall.

Sophia turned suddenly, staring at Fran, saying nothing for a moment, studying her curiously. Then she curled her sunken lips into a smile again.

"I go home now. Nice to meet you, pretty lady. Hey, Jasper, you take good care of our guest, huh?"

Sophia held out the stump of her arm to shake goodbye. Fran didn't quite know what to do. She reached over, grabbed the smooth round knob, and shook it lightly. Sophia's toothless grin grew wider, and then she turned and hobbled away.

"Let's get you settled. I'm sure you are very tired after all your travels," Jasper said as he led Fran back to his father's house.

"Is there a phone here? I'd like to cancel my credit cards."

"I have a cell phone but there's no coverage here. There is a pay phone about twenty minutes drive from here. Did you want to go now? Or we could go in the morning."

"I guess we could go in the morning."

A few minutes later, Fran was settling into her tiny cot for the night. Despite her discomfort about traveling and being in this rough setting, Fran felt fatigue rush over her as she lay her head down on the pillow.

Within five minutes she fell into a deep sleep.

## CHAPTER 21

*ran listens to her cell phone messages.
Marguerite tells her to return home to
Vancouver immediately. There is important news she must share in person. What
was it her friend had to tell her that was so secret that they had to meet at the
amusement park? And now she is there, but something has happened. The area
where the rollercoaster used to be is now a huge construction pit.*

*She hears someone calling and she turns. A boy at a nearby shooting booth
is calling her over. He is waving a rifle at her shouting, "Try your luck! Win
a big prize!"*

*A man in a white top hat pulls her away from the shooting booth and ushers
her into a House of Mirrors. She enters and sees only mirrors on the ceiling and
the floor. She looks at her reflection on the floor and sees the image of her face
looking down multiplied thousands of times. Then all of a sudden, she falls
through the floor!*

*She wakes up with a shudder.*

Completely disoriented, Fran thought for a moment that she was in her
own bedroom. Suddenly she remembered where she was when she saw

all the old photos of musicians on the wall. The bizarre experiences of
the last twenty-four hours came rushing back to her.

She desperately needed to go to the bathroom, but dreaded having
to go to the outhouse. She would definitely get some money wired
over from Laszlo that day so that she could move into a hotel. As her
father's executor he had access to her father's bank accounts. He should
be able to do that right away.

Gustav and Jasper were nowhere to be seen when Fran came out of
the tiny bedroom. As she walked over to the outhouse, the encamp-
ment looked even more impoverished than the night before. There was
more refuse and litter than she remembered. The little old lady was no
longer at the entrance of the outhouse.

In fact, there didn't seem to be people or children anywhere.

She suffered her way through the outhouse experience and tiptoed
back to the house stepping over empty cucú bottles lying in the grass.
Once there, Fran washed her face in the kitchen sink and tried to fix
her hair. The water coming out of the tap was murky and tasted funny,
but she found some orange juice in the fridge, and poured herself a
glass. As she drank the juice she savoured the crisp, acidic taste on her
tongue and the way it quenched her dry throat.

Putting the glass in the sink and wiping her mouth, Fran noticed
all the photos and plaques.

One of the largest photos said "Brno 1983" and featured seven
musicians playing at a dinner club. Gustav was the violin player, and a
teenage Jasper was their guitarist.

There was a more recent publicity photo of another band. In it,
Jasper appeared to be the front man and vocalist. Behind him were four
young men and one woman. One man was playing the electric fiddle,
another man was on piano, a third was playing bass, and a fourth on
drums. The woman was dressed in a sequined orange belly dance outfit
and was playing the finger cymbals as she danced.

There were also photos of Jasper as a child with his mother and
father.

His mother was bedecked in sequins and a headdress. She was a statuesque beauty. To her side was a banner that said "Chipperfield's".

Gustav in his younger years had the sturdy athleticism of a boxer, with a high forehead, mischievous eyes, dark, bushy eyebrows and a barbershop quartet moustache.

Fran marvelled at the exoticness of the couple and their impishly handsome six-year-old. She wondered where his mother was and why his father lived here in Slovakia while Jasper lived in England.

There was one building in the area that seemed to be a community hall. Fran could see from the window that there were people inside. She wondered if she should walk over.

Suddenly, the door of the community building swung open and people began to emerge. Many of them wore colourful shawls, unusual hats, and layered skirts. Fran looked down at her sensible, beige leisure suit and felt oddly out of place.

A middle-aged woman wearing a crimson head scarf danced in a circle with a toddler. Two young women walked hand in hand both wearing dresses threaded with silver and little mirrors sewn into the bodice. An elderly man wearing a bolero hat with a golden fringe dangling from the brim joined them in the dance.

There was an alluring quality to this mysterious, passionate tribe. People moved with a fluid harmony in and amongst each other like a school of fish in an aquarium: interweaving, laughing and playing with each other. Fran was used to a world of grey indistinguishable suits, walking with eyes fixated on the concrete, brooding over their impossibly long "To Do" lists.

She watched as Gustav and Jasper made their way back to the house.

"You are awake," said Gustav with great enthusiasm as they burst in the door, "How did you sleep?"

"Very well, thank you. I was quite tired. By the way, I meant to say last night that you speak English very well. Where did you learn it?'

"I live in England for many years working with the circus. Chipperfield's Circus. I was musician. I meet Jasper's mother there. She was equestrian performer. We travel, all three of us, for many years with that circus. What a life!" he explained, looking over at his son.

"Quite right. And I can tell you that it was a fabulous life for a child," grinned Jasper.

"I'm glad you found orange juice. I make you favourite breakfast, American flap jacks. You like that?"

"Yes. Thank you."

"I love flap jacks. You must eat that all the time in America," beamed Gustav.

"I'm actually Canadian, and I don't eat those very often, so it will be a nice treat for me too."

"Canadians and Americans — same thing?"

"Most Canadians don't think so, but many people probably think that we are alike. It is like New Zealand and Australia, similar but not the same."

"It's like us, Papa, we sometimes look like we fit in with the people around us, but we are different."

"He fits in wherever he goes. Me, not so much. I am the weirdo one!" Gustav laughed and made a silly face, "It must be time for breakfast music!"

He picked up his violin and began to play a Csardasz, a traditional dance song. Soon Fran noticed several people outside the house dancing to his music. Some of the children cupped their hands around their faces and peered through the windows. At first she thought they were looking at Gustav, as he skipped about playing his violin, but soon she realized they were all staring at her. Gustav beckoned them to come in, but they all scurried off.

"Come back! Where are you going? Come meet Francesca! Silly little people — just scared of strangers." Gustav grinned at her, from ear to ear. His gold-capped front tooth gleamed in the morning sunlight.

"Let's serve Francesca on our best china," Gustav exclaimed.

He used his violin bow to open one of the top cupboards. As he did, his shirtsleeve fell below his elbow, and Fran noticed a tattooed number on his forearm.

"Jasper, get the good dishes."

Jasper was tall enough to get the dishes out without standing on a chair. It was the first time Fran noticed that Jasper stood about a foot taller than his father.

Fran asked, "I noticed that plaque on your wall. What does the inscription say?"

"I don't remember. What does it say again, sonny boy?"

"It's in Slovak, from the Minister of Cultural Affairs, thanking my father and his band for culturally enriching the Slovak people with their music," replied Jasper.

Fran smiled, "That's impressive."

"I used to be big shot around here," Gustav said as he stirred the pancake ingredients with what looked like a broken off stick. "We were bigger than Bratsch and Tomatito put together. But I'm not bitter."

"Yes, he's bitter. He made it big in Eastern Europe but never really broke into the scene in Western Europe," Jasper added.

Gustav laughed, "He is, though. Sonny boy here used to be just back up guitarist with my band. Then he goes back to England and *boom!* He's front man, sing and write hit songs. He's a big shot now. You should let him play you his Number one hit: *Divine Shine*. Other good one is *Serenade to Josephina*. He always writes good ones when he's breaking up with someone."

Fran's ears perked up. She assumed someone as handsome as Jasper had a woman waiting for him back in England.

"So Josephina is your ex?" Fran inquired, looking anywhere but at Jasper.

"She left him. But he still loves her madly."

"I love her now as a friend, Papa. I'm okay not to be married to her anymore," Jasper said his cheeks flushing.

"You finally over her?" Gustav asked as he poured batter into a frying pan, "That's great blessing. This guy just works. All work no play makes Jasp a dull boy, huh? Time to get on with life already. How about you? You got kids? You got husband?"

"No and no."

"Why not?"

"Papa, I believe that is called prying. Don't ask her such personal questions, and stop talking so much. Eat already. You're too skinny."

Gustav laughed out loud and thwacked Jasper playfully with the frying pan flipper. "Hey, you want coffee?!"

Before Fran could protest he poured unstrained cowboy coffee into her mug.

Fran politely picked at the soggy pancakes and sipped at the granule-filled coffee. She listened keenly for the next hour as Gustav told lively stories about each of the photos on the wall.

After breakfast, Jasper took her on a tour of the artist's colony of Olino. A small river ran through the community. It seemed to be the main water source for drinking and cleaning. There was clearly no proper plumbing or waste water management in Olino.

Jasper crouched near the bank and splashed some of the water in his face. "If you need to bathe there is a spot around the bend where the women wash."

Fran recoiled at the thought of bathing in the river, or worse, drinking from it.

Jasper stood up and winked as if reading her thoughts, "It's really not safe to drink, but we're working on some solutions."

He gazed at the swirling waters finding their way around the rocks. He mused, "Whenever I come back here I remember how much this simple life here stirs me. These people have lived and breathed life from this river for generations now."

Fran smiled as toddlers splashed in the shallow stream across the way and imagined children playing there hundreds of years ago.

Jasper glanced at her and continued, "In some ways I think we are all this river." As he said the next words his eyes fell on the back eddies, "*Eventually all things merge into one, and a river runs through it …*

Fran's eyes lit up and she repeated the rest of the words with him,"*… The river was cut by the world's great flood and runs over rocks from the basement of time …*"

Jasper looked over at her stunned.

They continued, "*… On some of the rocks are timeless raindrops. Under the rocks are the words, and some of the words are theirs…I am haunted by waters.*"

A stillness descended on them and Fran's heart felt as pure and thirsty for merging as the river that cascaded around them. "I love those words," she replied, feeling the fresh, misty air on her face.

"How is it that you can recite the last lines of 'A River Runs Through it' by Norman MacLean?" he asked in disbelief.

"I could ask you the same question," Fran smiled. She liked that he appreciated the artful arrangement of words.

Jasper studied her for a moment, his mahogany eyes filled with curiosity. He added, "Several times when life felt full of obstacles, my father would take me down here to the river and ask me 'What would water do?'"

"That's an interesting question," Fran replied.

"Yes, if you think about it, water just kind of flows. When it hits a rock what does it do?"

Fran watched the traveling water swirling around a slab of granite in front of her, "Umm, it goes around the rock … and over it."

"Exactly, and if you could watch the water long enough what does water eventually do to rock?"

"It wears it down!"

"Yes." Jasper laced his fingers behind his head and stretched his back, "I meditate here every time I visit Olino. I imagine I am water flowing over and around all my obstacles.

*The hardest stones are dissolved by the softest water.*
*And water is not trying to do anything.*
*It simply goes on flowing.*
*All the sands in the oceans are nothing but past Himalayas.*

"Who said that?" Fran asked.

"An Indian mystic named Osho."

Fran thought about her own life recently. She had been identifying mostly with rocks, not water. She imagined for a moment that she was a timeless raindrop finding its way back to its source. A slim slice of possibility pierced her mental framework offering an idea for how she could deal with the mess she now found herself in.

Jasper arranged to borrow a car from one of the few people in the community who owned one. It was a green Renault with squeaky tires, shredded upholstery, and a cracked window.

As they were driving into the nearby village to use the phone, Fran was wondering why his father kept calling her Francesca. She was sure she introduced herself as Fran. Why would he make the leap to thinking her name was Francesca? It could be Francis or Francine. On her passport the name was Francesca. She was starting to suspect again that Jasper stole her passport and that's why Gustav knew her full name. She wanted to bring the topic up, but didn't know how to approach it.

Instead she asked, "I noticed your father has numbers tattooed to his forearm."

Jasper seemed to flinch and didn't answer at first. Fran suddenly knew the answer and wished she hadn't brought up the subject.

"It's from World War II, yes of course. I'm sorry I asked," she apologized.

"Not to worry," Jasper assured her. "He spent time in a Nazi concentration camp. So did several other people in our community, including old Stefan and Sophia. In fact, that is how Stefan lost his hearing and she lost her hands. Those three survived, but an enormous number of people from the original Olino community died through illness, torture or the gas chambers."

Fran recoiled and tucked her hands under her armpits.

"I'm so sorry to hear that. They are Jewish?"

"No. Many people think that Hitler only targeted the Jews. However, of the twelve million people killed by the Third Reich, they estimate that about half were Jews, the others were Romani, people from Poland and other Slavic countries, Communists, Pacificists, disabled people, homosexuals, freethinkers and artists or anyone who spoke out, even just casually, against Hitler. The people of Olino were a mishmash of everything Hitler didn't like."

Fran was silent and stared out over the expanse of farmer's fields. "I never knew all that." She decided it would be best not to talk about or show Jasper any photos of her father. Changing the subject, she asked, "I take it your father doesn't read?"

"His parents never sent any of their children to school. It just wasn't done back then. He reads music, though. He just can't read the words."

"Do you read?"

"Yes, I went to school up until I was seventeen, then I became a full-time musician. How about you?"

"I am overly-schooled. I have an undergraduate in English, and an MBA in accounting. Although, when I was young, I used to take lots of singing and dancing classes. My mother was a professional singer and dancer. I wanted to be like her."

"That's interesting. So performing is in your blood, just like in mine."

"Yes, but you actually did something about it. I dropped most of that when I was young."

They drove in silence for a while.

"Are you going to call your sister?" Jasper finally asked.

"Yes, but first I will call to cancel my cards and then call someone back home for money. My sister doesn't know I'm coming. In fact, she doesn't even know I exist."

Jasper glanced at her curiously, "Really?"

She felt uncomfortable revealing her family secrets. It could lead to the revelation of her father's involvement with the Nazis. They drove in silence for a while and Jasper glanced over at her expectantly again. She decided she would just keep the story simple.

"Yes, you see, she's my half-sister. When my father moved to Canada, he didn't keep in contact with anyone in Europe. He recently died, and she is named in the estate. But she thought he died about fifty-eight years ago, so it will be a shock for her to meet me."

"To say the least."

Fran grew silent. That was enough of the family details. It was time to put the shoe on the other foot.

"So you grew up in England but you occasionally come to visit your father here?" she asked.

"Yes, my parents split up when I was about seven years old."

"Same as me," offered Fran.

As soon as those words escaped her lips she regretted them. It wasn't something she ever mentioned to strangers. Yet, somehow with Jasper she couldn't help herself. She wanted someone to talk to about all these things. It was too much to keep to herself. He seemed trustworthy, but was he?

Jasper continued, "You, as well? My mother remarried and I grew up with her and my stepfather. However, I loved playing music so, when I was a teenager, I joined my father and his band on the road. They were a top band in the '70s and '80s around these parts. Then later, I started my own band with some of my musician mates back in Britain. Mostly folk music and rock fusion. We tour Europe, the Middle East and recently in Africa."

"Have you ever played in North America?" asked Fran.

"No, but I'd certainly love to."

"I actually have a friend who helps artists from different cultures get grants and opportunities in Canada. I can get you some information on what they do. In fact, my friend Marguerite is one of the people I'm going to call today. You should give me your e-mail address. You do have e-mail, don't you?

"Brilliant. Yes, I'm email-savvy now. I became a techno literate overnight when I started managing our band."

They soon arrived at the village. Jasper stopped the car in front of a pay phone by a coffee shop. Then he helped Fran connect to the international operator so she could cancel all her cards.

Once that business was complete Fran decided to try Lena's number. There was no answer. Fran left a message. Then she called Marguerite, but the line went dead. The coffee shop owner shrugged and told Jasper in Slovak that the phone often went dead for no reason. Fran grew frustrated and realized she should have called last night. It was still too early in the morning back in Vancouver. A feeling of panic rose in Fran's throat. She had no money, no ID and was stranded in a shantytown in a foreign country.

Jasper noticed her frustration.

"Why don't you try calling your sister? Perhaps we can go over to Kittsee where there are far more phones."

"What if she doesn't speak English? I certainly don't speak any German. Do you?"

"A tad. What do you want me to say to her?"

"Tell her I am a long-lost relative who would like to meet with her as soon as possible. Here's the number."

He smiled and their hands touched as she handed him the piece of paper. Fran's heart skipped a beat. There was an unearthly luminosity about Jasper that overwhelmed her at times. As he strode off to try the phone again, she couldn't help but feel like she'd met him somewhere before. Although she was also sure she'd never met anyone quite like Jasper.

He returned a few minutes later shaking his head.

"The phone still doesn't work. Let's just go there. It's about an hour drive," offered Jasper.

"Can I cross the border into Austria without a passport?"

"If you go to the right border guard. Karol is the guy you need to see."

She thought about it for a moment. If Jasper went with her then he would hear about her father. On the other hand, her desire to connect with an actual blood relative as soon as possible was so strong. Plus, maybe Helena could lend her some money for a hotel.

"Okay, that's very kind of you to take me. Let's go."

On the drive there, Fran felt her curiosity building.

"Jasper, I notice there are beautiful, old caravans at Olino that look like they have been there for decades. Did the inhabitants of Olino used to travel in those?"

"Actually, my father brought them over from Britain. He inherited a few from a carnival owner he worked for. The community of Olino used to be the site of a carnival. They were a traveling carnival until the mid 1920s, then it stayed in one place. There were rides, a shooting booth, fortune tellers, musicians and shows. Stefan, one of the oldest in our settlement, ran the rides. Sophia was a dancer and a fortune teller."

"Was there a House of Mirrors?" Fran asked, remembering her eerie dream.

"I don't know. Probably. My father was just a little boy, but he ran the shooting booth. He has some great photos. But during the war they rounded up everyone, and put them in concentration camps. The few survivors who came back to our settlement had nothing.

They tried to re-start the carnival, but when the Communists came into power they confiscated most of the carnival property. They gave people all jobs in factories. In the short term it seemed to be helpful, but in the long run this led to a whole generation of people who lost touch with the trades of their forefathers.

When they arrived in Kittsee they located Helena's home through the phonebook. It was a townhouse in a quiet, well-trimmed neighbourhood.

There was no answer when they rang the bell.

"She runs her own business. Maybe she is at work. It's some kind of herbal company. They make and dispense herbal remedies."

Jasper's face lit up, "It must be The Wichtige Gesundheit Company. They are located here and I'm fairly sure they make herbal remedies."

"Maybe. I don't know the name of her company. Do you know where it is?"

"Yes, I have driven by it several times," replied Jasper.

"Let's go."

They drove another ten minutes and parked right outside the company. At the reception desk Jasper asked in German if Helena worked there. The woman nodded and called Helena's local number.

A few minutes later a rotund, bubbly woman entered the foyer. Her bearing suggested a rare kind of comfort in her own skin and her aquamarine eyes glistened with curiosity of a child.

*"Kann ich Ihnen helfen?"*

Jasper asked, *"Sprechen Sie Englisch?"*

"Yes, of course," she replied in her well-studied British accent. "Are you the people from BHMA Organic?"

Fran hesitated, feeling nervous. It was an awkward thing to tell someone, and quite frankly she didn't know where to begin. Finally, she blurted out, "Listen, I don't know how to say this, but the fact is ... I may be a relative of yours. And I was hoping I could have a few moments of your time?"

Helena raised her eyebrows then furrowed them. She glanced over at the receptionist who was now looking Fran and Jasper up and down. The two women shared a knowing glance as if a situation like this was commonplace at Wichtige Gesundheit.

"Really?" Helena said skeptically. "How do you mean?"

"May we talk privately in your office?"

Helena sighed and checked the schedule turning to the receptionist for a chance to "huddle" and discuss a game plan. They talked softly together in German and then both fixed their gaze on their odd guests, as if to try and sense their authenticity. Jasper smiled his winning smile, and Fran followed suit. Helena couldn't help but return the smile and then beckoned Fran into her office.

Jasper took a seat in the waiting room and pulled out his harmonica to play. The receptionist looked up from behind her counter and scowled. Jasper nodded knowingly and put the harmonica back in his pocket.

Helena pointed to a chair and Fran sat on the edge of the seat, knees and toes turned slightly inward. Helena folded her arms across her chest and tilted back in her chair. Fran could tell the woman was somewhat uncomfortable. What if her "sister" flew off the handle at hearing the news? They both sat staring at the floor for what seemed like an eternity when finally Fran said, "I know this may come as a shock to you. But I think we share the same father."

Helena cleared her throat. Something about this possibility was irritating her.

"My real father died when I was just a baby. If you mean my adoptive father …"

"I mean your *real* father. I believe at that time he was called Jorg Frei."

Again, Helena sized up the young woman with the lanky figure and dark features. Fran was keenly aware they looked nothing alike.

"That can't be so. He died during World War II."

Fran's lips tightened and she set her jaw. She had to plow through this situation. Her heart ached, imagining Helena as a child alone in the world thinking she had no parents.

"He didn't die, at least not until recently."

Helena's stern face collapsed into a puddle of confusion. She leaned forward and said, "What did you say? What do you mean by that?"

"He died six weeks ago, not fifty-eight years ago."

"That can't be so. I was at his funeral, *and* I have his death certificate."

Again, Fran's heart filled with compassion for her.

"As I understand it, he was missing in action and then presumed dead. But what actually happened was that he escaped to Canada. He changed his name from Jorg Frei to George Freeman. For some reason he couldn't or didn't want to contact your mother or anyone else in his family after that."

Helena looked down at a ring on her middle finger and started to turn it in one direction.

"This sounds rather far fetched. I don't mean to be rude, but I have a very full schedule today, and I'm already late. If you are looking for some kind of charity … yes we are a very philanthropic organization, but you need to go through the proper channels. I don't appreciate this approach, Miss. It's not necessary to bring up painful memories from my past in order to get a hand out."

Fran flinched. She felt as if she'd just been slapped across the face. It took a few moments for the stinging to die down before she could even speak.

"I'm sorry. But, I think you are mistaken. I work for my father's accounting firm in Vancouver. I earn a good living. I'm not looking for a handout. I know it sounds far fetched. *I* didn't even know about *you* until a few days ago. It's all very bizarre and I'm sure it must come as a shock. I don't know why the lawyer didn't call you himself."

"What lawyer?"

"The lawyer handling the Estate. He knew about you and convinced my father to include you in his Will. I think I have something that might help. Do you have any photos of your father?"

"Why?"

"Would you recognize him if you saw a photo?"

"I was very young when he died, and my mother died soon after that. I was shuffled around between many families until I was finally adopted. I lost most of my photos along the way. I just have one of my father now."

Fran pulled out a photo of her father in a uniform, and placed it on Helena's desk.

Fran sat and waited as Helena put on her reading glasses to study the photo. On the wall was a mural of a large heart, inside of which were photos of about forty people with hand-written thank you notes under it. There were several plaques of recognition to Helena and her company for their philanthropic efforts.

After a few moments, Fran sneaked a look at her half-sister.

Helena was crying.

"What's wrong?" Fran asked, not sure if the tears were good or bad.

"Let me show you something," Helena fumbled in her purse and pulled out her wallet. Inside the wallet was a cracked and slightly torn photo. She smoothed it out, and laid it down next to the photo that Fran had given her.

It was an identical photo.

## CHAPTER 22

As Fran poured out the details of her father's life in Canada, Helena leaned back in her executive chair. She gripped the arm rests and sat incredulous as if watching a psychological thriller unfold before her eyes.

Finally, Helena blurted out, "Why would he cut off from his life here so abruptly?"

Fran added, "And why did he change his name and his accent and hide his former life?"

Helena shrugged and shook her head.

Fran felt uncomfortable as she asked, "Could he have been a war criminal?"

Helena jolted in her chair at hearing those words, "No!" but a moment later added, "I have no idea."

Both women looked away.

"As I said, my mother died when I was young and I was shuffled from home to home until someone adopted me," Helena continued, "I have just a few photos of my real parents and almost no details."

"I was hoping to get some evidence while I am here — evidence that he was *not* a war criminal because someone in Vancouver is trying to vilify him," Fran said as she pulled out the lurid article from the Vancouver newspaper.

Helena picked up her reading glasses again and studied the article. As she did her face turned grim. After a few minutes she said, "This is a lot to take in all at once."

"I know. I'm sorry to come unannounced like this, but that's what the lawyer seemed to suggest would be best. I think he is the one who knows the most, but he is dying of leukemia in the hospital and so I've had limited contact with him."

Helena looked confused. Finally, she looked at her watch and said, "Where are you staying?"

"That's the other thing. I lost all my money and ID on the train. I think it was stolen. The man out there in the waiting room kindly let me stay at his father's house. But it's kind of strange there, and so I tried calling some people today in Canada to get some money and sort things out, but I couldn't get through to anyone."

"Oh my goodness, I'm sorry to hear that. I can certainly lend you money and let you stay at my house. I have a spare bedroom."

"I would be so grateful," Fran said sighing in relief. Then she added, "I guess I am looking for a hand out!"

They both laughed and Helena added, "And why don't you and your friend come for dinner?"

"Okay, I'd certainly be delighted. I'm not sure what Jasper's plans are, but we can ask him."

Helena asked, "He sounds like he's a Londoner."

"Yes, he is just here to visit family. He's quite an accomplished musician apparently and has a touring band — some kind of folk-rock fusion. His father's community is just across the border in Slovakia, a place called Olino. They have been very welcoming to me, and I have enjoyed getting to know him and his family."

"Good. I shall look forward to meeting him, too, then."

Helena came around to the other side of her desk and held out her arms for a hug, "What can I say? It's an odd situation, but it's also nice to know I have a sister!"

Fran hesitated a moment, not used to hugging a complete stranger. Finally she stepped forward to meet her and replied, "Me, too."

Once out in the foyer, they told Jasper about the plan for Fran to move into Helena's townhouse and the invitation for dinner.

"I would be delighted to join you for dinner," replied Jasper.

The receptionist overheard their conversation and whispered something to Helena.

After her brief conversation, Helena returned to them and said, "I'm afraid I have an unexpected visitor at my house today."

"Who is that?" asked Fran.

"It's my son."

"I didn't know you had a son!"

"Yes, I actually just re-met him after thirty years."

Fran cast a nervous glance at Jasper and he, in turn, appeared confused.

Helena caught the exchange and moved in closely. She sat down next to them and said, "I was only fifteen years old when I got pregnant. My Slovak parents put me in a special home for unwed mothers until he was born. Parent finders finally reconnected us. He is, of course, forty-three years old now," Helena smiled, "You know, it suddenly seems very odd to me that this middle-aged man is my son, when I have a sister who is so much younger."

Fran offered a stiff smile.

Jasper sensed the discomfort and exclaimed, "That's splendid! We all get to meet him then."

Helena parked her car in front of her townhouse and Jasper and Fran pulled in behind her in the Renault. There was a motorcycle up on the lawn and the lights inside the townhouse were on. A man opened the front door and stood on the porch. He had a receding hairline, straggly brown hair and a greying goatee. He was dressed in work boots and smudged coveralls.

Helena waved at him and he nodded back at her. Her son leaned against the ledge of the porch and folded his arms. He made a kind of snorting sound that reminded Fran of a bull ready to charge. He surveyed Fran with interest, but narrowed his eyes upon seeing Jasper step out of the rusted green car.

Helena appeared stricken with tension. She stood next to them and whispered, "Apparently he needs a place to stay tonight and has let himself in. Just wait here a moment."

As she walked up the front steps, Helena spoke to him in Slovak. She was fumbling with a large box that she had just retrieved from her trunk. Fran wondered why her son didn't offer to help. He responded in Slovak obviously trying to explain the reason for his unannounced arrival. Helena placed the box on the ledge of the porch and listened distractedly as she tried to catch her breath.

Jasper whispered to Fran, "He's telling her he just got fired from his job last week and that his girlfriend threw him out. He has no money and nowhere else to go."

"Wow. This sure is Helena's day for taking in unexpected relatives," Fran whispered back. She couldn't help but notice how electrifying it felt to stand so close to Jasper.

"I don't care for how he's speaking to Helena. It strikes me as rather disrespectful. D'you know what I mean?"

Fran nodded and watched as Helena glanced at them and back to her son.

Helena then beckoned them toward the house, so they proceeded up the walkway.

"Fran and Jasper, this is Marek."

Marek glared at Jasper, wrinkled his nose and said, *"Zigeuner."*

Jasper stopped in his tracks and folded his arms across his chest. He tilted his head slightly and looked at the man as if he were a ten-year-old caught bullying on the playground. "And if I was?"

"He doesn't really speak any English," Helena retorted grim-faced.

When Jasper repeated his words in Slovak, Marek sneered and looked away. Fran noticed that Marek had a small swastika tattooed on his left forearm. She had read that a few Neo-Nazi groups were still thriving in Austria despite efforts to disband them. Fran also noticed that, ironically, he had the full Serenity prayer tattooed on his other arm.

Helena spoke again to him in Slovak and it sounded like she was reprimanding him. Marek went inside the house and slammed the door. Helena flinched at the sound. She stood looking down at the ground toeing the peeling paint.

"I'm so sorry. He grew up poor; he didn't get a good education, you know? I feel so guilty about this. Believe me, I don't discriminate against Romani people. It disturbs me that my own son is like that. I ask him to leave. This is my house and you are my guests."

Jasper tilted his hat forward and dropped his head as if to hide who he was from the world. He stepped forward quickly and put his hand softly on her shoulder, "Wait, Helena. I'll leave. You stay here, Fran. I'll bring your things tomorrow."

His eyes were stern as he glanced back and forth quickly between Helena and Fran. Finally, he reached for Fran's hand to shake it goodbye.

Fran felt her whole arm tremble as she touched him. Much to her own surprise, she suddenly blurted out, "Wait. I'll leave with you, Jasper. We can talk again tomorrow, Helena."

"I really do feel awkward. I'm so sorry. Please, do call me tomorrow. I'm sure he'll be gone by then."

"Are you sure you'll be okay here alone with him?" asked Jasper.

"Yes, of course. He is not so bad as he looks. He is just afraid and lost right now, and I need to support him. I couldn't do it then, so I'll try to do that now, yes?"

Fran and Jasper nodded, said their goodbyes and got back in the car.

After a few minutes of driving in silence, Fran said, "I don't mean to pry, but what does that mean — *Ziguener?*"

A pained expression appeared on Jasper's face and he drummed his fingers rhythmically on the steering wheel as if keeping time to a hard rock tune, "It's a German word for Gypsy or Romani."

Fran knew what it meant to be ostracized and felt both compassion and embarrassment for him in that moment. There was also another emotion lurking beneath the surface that she couldn't quite name.

"I'm sorry that happened," she finally blurted out, "I was so excited about finally meeting my sister and getting to share everything about our lives and our father, and then that happened. It's so strange that he would act like that to you."

"Not so strange. It happens all over the world. Romani have been persecuted for a thousand years. The irony is that I would actually *like* to claim that as my cultural background. Gypsy music has greatly influenced me as a musician. But I can't say I'm one of them."

"How so?"

"I was never raised in a Romani community. My father had a bit of influence from his parents. But even they both left their communities to join the Olino circus. Carnival or circus people have their own unique culture that is different from Romani or mainstream or anything else. That's the culture I feel in my bones, the passion to entertain, to make music and to live a creative life."

He was now nodding his head in unison to what seemed like a faster tune.

"I see." Fran said while trying to think of something more intelligent to say. "Still, I'm sorry that happened."

"You don't need to be sorry. I don't, as a rule, take it personally."

"That's great that you don't. I wish I could do that more often," Fran said, hoping to appear both complimentary and compassionate at the same time.

"Here's how I look at it," he said smiling, "Suppose I turned to you and shouted 'midget!', how would you react?"

"You mean as if you thought I was a midget and that you didn't like midgets?"

"Precisely."

"I would laugh — under my breath, of course, and then feel sorry for you."

"Why's that?" grinned Jasper.

"Because I'd think you weren't quite 'playing with a full deck' as they say. To qualify as a midget I'd need to be under three feet tall."

"Then this is precisely the same situation, hmm? I feel compassion for him because he doesn't know who I am, really. He has, in his dense little head, a list of characteristics about what he calls in that tone of voice — a *Ziguener*. We all have our prejudices, don't we? He's simply being more overt than other people. But, of course, he makes his own life more miserable because he looks at someone as wonderful as me," Jasper paused for dramatic effect flashing his grin, "and sees a threat. What a pity, really."

"Yes, you *are* quite wonderful," Fran said. Then, upon realizing what she'd just said, quickly added, "... for driving me all the way to Kittsee and back."

They both laughed and Jasper said, "Let's let it go then and go have some fun back at Olino!"

Gustav and several other musicians were playing in the meeting hall when they arrived. The two of them sneaked in the back of the hall and sat there until Gustav noticed they'd arrived. He motioned Jasper to come play with them.

Jasper grinned, shaking his head, then gave into this father's pleas and grabbed his guitar, taking a place at the back of the stage. Sophia, the old woman with no hands, was sitting in a chair nearby. She motioned for Fran to sit down beside her. Fran hesitated. That woman was difficult to look at. Many of her teeth were chipped or missing and she had a bulbous nose that hung over her upper lip.

Maybe there was another place she could sit. After glancing around she realized the hall was packed. There was no where else to sit and

Fran didn't want to appear rude, so she slipped into the seat next to the old lady.

Just as she did a woman across the aisle glared at her. The woman was about thirty years old and had a boy on her lap. She seemed penetratingly beautiful to Fran with her mane of auburn hair and copper-coloured eyes.

Sophia noticed the interchange and whispered, "That is widow Cecilia. Don't let her get you. She mad at everyone," Sophia patted Fran's hand with the stump of her arm. After a moment, Sophia added, "Especially you."

"Why me?" asked Fran.

"You take Jasper from her."

"What do you mean by that?"

"We all see big hearts come off of Jasper's head whenever he look at you. Cecilia has been trying to catch him for years. He once maybe a little bit interested in her, but then he went back to the UK. She kept a big flame for him. She doesn't like that you came here with him."

Fran leaned back in her chair, suddenly feeling queasy. Jasper *has hearts coming out of his head for her?* That was too strange to believe. She looked up on stage, just as the musicians were pushing Jasper to the front to play one of his songs. Jasper settled onto a stool, tuned his guitar slightly, then looked up at the audience. The spotlight caught the radiance of his mahogany eyes. He paused, then nodded to the bass player, and they all began to play.

A soft, dancing minor chord played seductively as Jasper's resonant tenor voice filled the hall. The song was in English, and told the story of lovers who came from two vastly different parts of the world. It seemed part Celtic, part Spanish and part Klezmer.

Fran was transfixed for the entire song.

The next tune was a dancing song. As soon as the beat started, people leapt to their feet and pushed back the chairs, even the elders of the tribe, Sophia and Stefan. They swayed lightly back and forth to the music, lost in the trance of the melody.

Fran felt paralyzed.

The only time Fran danced was when she went to rave events in Vancouver, and that was her "alter ego". There was a temp secretary at Freeman & Wilson who invited her along one day about four years ago.

This rave community was mostly twenty-somethings covered in tattoos, piercings and dreadlocks. They took on mythic names like Mercurio, Lupo or Xen, and were intent on saving the planet by re-programming the collective unconscious through techno music and crop circle imagery. Fran felt at home there for some strange reason. It was the farthest away she could get from her mundane life. She had taken on the mythic name Rhea, a Greek Goddess who was known as "the mother of all gods." She had bought a whole set of tribal clothing and kept it in a secret place in her closet. One day she even got a tattoo of a coiled snake on her lower back that no one at Freeman & Wilson had ever seen. It was her private rebellion from the conformist world of corporate accounting.

Her circle of ravers was not into the drug scene, which suited her well. Drugs never attracted her. Yet, she found that trance dancing was a powerful way to calm her nerves and revitalize her soul. After a year of going to this event every month, Fran became interested in spoken word poetry. She'd spent hours watching and trying to mimic the poets who performed at each event. During her lunch breaks she wrote, re-wrote and endlessly practiced her lyrics, trying them to different rhythms and tunes.

Then, one day about two years ago she decided to perform at an open mic night. And much to the amazement of the other ravers who saw her as guarded and aloof, Fran performed with an unbridled vulnerability and authenticity. Yet the truth is, Fran could never have done that, but Rhea could. After that, Rhea's rap poetry was a regular request at open mic nights.

But tonight, in this music hall in a foreign country, Fran couldn't dance.

Because tonight she was Fran. Or maybe she was feeling more Rhea than she ever had, and was afraid to see where that would lead. Either way, she was paralyzed. She watched the event from the other side of a strange, haunting gulf, that some part of her yearned to cross.

And she was the only one not dancing.

She had never seen a group of people dance with such uninhibited joy — old people, young people, fat people, thin people, all dancing their hearts out. There she was a multi-millionairess, lost in her insecurities and worries, and here were people who possessed hardly anything and so full of joy. The irony struck a painful nerve.

When everyone sat down for the next song, Fran felt relieved.

A woman strutted to centre stage and turned her back to the audience. She was wearing a polka dot, blue and white, low cut dress with ruffles at the base. In her hair were combs and crimson ribbons. Her flamenco shoes were fire engine red.

Suddenly the music started and she whipped her head around to face the audience. It was Cecilia. She glared at the audience as she stomped her feet and moved her arms around in wild patterns. Her curvaceous frame undulated to the drum and the bass rhythms of Jasper's guitar. He seemed transfixed by the power of her dance and Fran felt the heat of jealousy in the pit of her stomach. She wanted to bolt out the door, but she was mesmerized by the intensity of Cecilia's movements.

When the song ended, Cecilia stood in a statuesque pose with a triumphant glint in her eyes as people roared and cheered. Then she sat down at the back of the stage beside Jasper and started whispering to him. They laughed together. Fran knew it was silly to be jealous. There was no chance for a relationship between them. She would soon be going back to Canada.

The next song highlighted the guitar playing of one of the other players, and Jasper sat on an odd looking box with a hole in it, and played it like a drum. When the song ended Gustav got on the microphone. He was talking in Slovak and Fran didn't understand. He seemed to be talking about her, and pointing outside the hall. Finally, he translated what he said so that Fran would understand.

"Francesca, our lovely guest, the whole community has agreed that you should stay with us for a while, so we have found you a home in this community. Look out the window."

Fran looked, and saw one of the old caravans with a wreath of flowers on the door. People started pouring out of the building to go see how they fixed it up. Fran followed, completely bewildered. They hardly knew her. Why were they being so inviting? Maybe it was because Jasper had told his father that he wanted her to stay.

The jealously in the pit of her stomach suddenly transformed into excitement at the thought that Jasper was interested in her. She found him fascinating and at the same time this rustic and alien environment chaffed at her already frayed nerves. She felt encased in glass, unable to reach out to these people for fear of shattering completely.

Inside, the caravan was neat and tidy, with flowers in a vase on the tiny kitchen table. On the walls were several faded images taped up, one of Jesus Christ, another of Mary Magdalene, another of St. Jude, another of Quan Yin and finally a photo of Lenin. Probably vestiges of Communist rule, she thought. Someone had brought Fran's bags over and put her belongings on the shelves. It felt disturbing to Fran that someone had gone through her personal things.

As everyone was gathered around to look at the caravan, Cecilia walked to the front of the group, holding an envelope. Fran recognized her father's photos and mementos. She began to speak to the group, holding up photos of George in a Nazi uniform and handing them around to the group. Fran tried to get the photos back, but it was too late.

One man looked up at Fran, and then spat at her feet shouting in Slovak.

A group of women echoed his words and started to wail. Another man pulled up his shirtsleeve and showed her the concentration camp numbers. Cecilia was shouting at her in a foreign dialect and inciting the crowd to anger. When he saw what was happening, Gustav grabbed the photos back from people, and reprimanded Cecilia and the others for being so rude to their visitor.

To Fran's horror, Jasper looked at the photos and said, "This is your father?"

"Yes, I just found these photos after my father died. I didn't know anything about his life in Europe. I came to find my sister, and to find out what happened during the war."

People were negotiating intensely with Gustav. Jasper studied the photos, looking dismayed, "He was a Nazi?"

"I don't know what he was. I just found this photo myself. It's not like I'm a Nazi, why are they so angry at me?"

"Some people here still hold onto the past, and some have let it go. Don't take it personally."

Just at that moment, Cecilia whispered something into Jasper's ear, and started pulling him away. He left without a word to Fran. As people continued to argue, Fran went inside the caravan. She grabbed her turquoise carry-on bag and threw her father's mementos and a few small overnight items inside. When she opened the caravan door people were still arguing and didn't even notice her.

Jasper was nowhere to be seen.

She crept behind the caravan, and then headed briskly toward the road. She didn't know where she was going, or what she was going to do.

All she knew was that she had to leave.

## CHAPTER 23

Eva sat in her car outside the Freeman residence, calling Fran's number for the eighth time. Again, the recorded message said that her voicemail box was full.

Then she saw a strangely familiar man. As he approached the house, Eva got out of her car.

"Excuse me. I think you and I met before. You came to my house that night to ask for some photos. I went and got them for you and dropped them off at that office building. That was you, right?"

He was in his fifties, heavy set, balding and looked like he hadn't slept in a week.

"I'm sorry, ma'am, I'm doing an investigation here and I'm not at liberty to speak to you right now," he said curtly.

"I thought you said you were a relative. You said you could tell me about George Freeman's involvement in the war."

He didn't answer, and instead walked toward the Freeman residence. Not one to be shrugged off, Eva followed him, "Then you never called me back and you published those photos in the paper without any permission."

"Listen, sweetheart, I don't have time for this."

"What are you up to anyway?"

"As I said, I can't disclose that. Now, please, I have work to do here."

He started walking down the side of the house. Eva continued to follow him.

He turned and looked her squarely in the eye, "I appreciate your help, but I've asked you twice now to leave me alone."

"I trusted you and you lied to me. I deserve an answer!"

"I'm a private investigator. It's my job to lie."

"If I knew you would publish those photos I would never have helped you."

"That's why I lie."

The man directed his flashlight up at Fran's bedroom window. Eva could see that the window had been smashed and boarded up.

"I'm calling the police."

He interjected, "I wouldn't bother. They know what's going on. By the way, where is Fran Freeman these days?"

"I thought you said you didn't want to talk to me? This is all about money, isn't it? You just want your hands on the Freeman money," Eva shot back, as she started punching numbers into her cell pad.

The man grabbed the cell phone out of her hands.

"Listen, I know all about that nasty business at the Blakewood Nursing Home. You wouldn't want that story plastered across the front page, now would you? Why don't you tell me where Ms. Freeman is hiding out, and we'll keep that story under wraps."

Eva shuddered, remembering how the head nurse had accused her of hitting a resident. When the old man died soon after the incident, all fingers point at her. No one believed her side of the story.

Eva made a grab for her cell phone again, but the man was too quick.

"That story wasn't even true," she pleaded, "It was a complete misunderstanding. At least try to get your facts straight."

"That's not what the Director of Blakewood said. Who are people going to believe — you or him?"

"I see. It's not just lying that you are good at, you do it all: blackmail, extortion, character assassinations."

"You forgot murder and torture. We are a one-stop shopping mall for all your evil deeds. Look, I don't have a lot of spare time to chit-chat. Either tell me where Fran Freeman is, or I go to the papers."

"First off, I don't know where Fran Freeman is. Secondly, go right ahead and print whatever story you want about me. I'm too old to give a damn what people think."

"Do you care about ever being able to walk again?"

Eva stood strong. She sensed the man was bluffing and that he wasn't even a private investigator.

"Oooh, stop, you're scaring me," she countered.

Eva smirked when she saw the man's posture weaken. He suddenly seemed like a child to her; all fury and no substance. She ripped her cell phone out of his hand, got back into her Mini Cooper, and roared off down the hill.

CHAPTER 24

At St. Paul's Hospital Marguerite wandered down the maze of corridors, peering into each room in hopes of finding the little gentleman with the oversize glasses. Finally, she approached a nursing station and said, "I'm here to see Mr. Laszlo Goldstein."

The receptionist crossed her arms tightly and replied, "He's not seeing any visitors right now."

"Can you tell him that it's Marguerite — Fran Freeman's friend?"

"I already told you, he isn't seeing anyone."

Marguerite set her gaze and flared her nostrils as she leaned forward slightly over the counter, "It's urgent."

"That's what they all say," the receptionist said leaning back in her chair.

"Who are *they*?" Marguerite challenged back.

"People posing as relatives of Mr. Goldstein or friends of Fran Freeman. I don't know what is going on with all you people, wanting to bother a critically ill man, but he's fighting for his life right now. Please respect that."

Marguerite backed down and chose her next words carefully, "I understand. You are protecting him and that's important. Can I leave him a note?"

"I suppose so."

Marguerite scribbled a note to Laszlo with her cell number. Then, she sauntered slowly around the corner to wait for the elevator. As she waited, Marguerite noticed an exotic-looking young woman approach the reception desk.

She overheard the receptionist say, "A woman just left this note. She said it was urgent."

A moment later the young woman turned the corner, and clicked down the linoleum hallway in her fuchsia pumps. Fran had told her about Laszlo's granddaughter. As she passed Marguerite asked, "Are you Lena?"

"Yes, I am. Who are you?"

"I'm Marguerite La Boyer, Fran Freeman's friend. I need to know if Laszlo has connected with Fran."

"Oh, *you* are Marguerite. We've been trying to get in touch with you, too. Please come with me."

Lena told the bodyguard at the door that it was okay, and they entered Laszlo's room.

"Mr. Goldstein, do you remember me?"

He waved at Lena to help him remove the ventilator. He nodded enthusiastically as he coughed a few times. Lena handed him a glass of water.

"How could I forget you!" he finally said in a raspy voice, "I love your sense of color. Listen, I need your help."

Marguerite had to smile. She marvelled at his cheeky sense of humour, especially under the circumstances.

"I need yours, too. Fran called me and left a message saying she lost all her valuables, but left no return number to call, and she hasn't called back since. Do you have her sister's number in Vienna?"

He closed his eyes and nodded as if to endure a wave of nausea. "She called me too, asking for money. Poor thing lost everything her first day there." He exhaled slowly and then opened his eyes. His watery eyes danced again with vitality. He continued, "She had to cancel all her cards and thought I had access to her father's accounts."

"You mean that you don't?"

Lena placed a pillow behind his head so that he could look more directly at Marguerite, "No. The Will is being contested. The lawyers at Freeman & Wilson are saying it's a fraud. Unfortunately, I now don't have access to any of his accounts and I'm too ill to be dealing with it anyway. I've tried to give the situation over to my partner, Stephen Weil in Toronto, but ..." Laszlo broke down coughing again and Lena handed him a handkerchief. Marguerite watched with compassion as he tried to regain his composure. She was starting to feel guilty for encouraging him to talk when he was so ill.

"Your partner in Toronto won't ...?" Marguerite urged him on softly.

"Oh yeah ... he's buying into the hype about George, so won't go near it. So, it's back in my hands. This makes the lawyers at Freeman & Wilson very happy, because they say George re-did his Will under duress from me. They say I threatened him with disclosing his hidden past, and so the whole thing has to go to court. It's a big mess."

"I'm so sorry you have to deal with all this right now. How can I help?"

"I will give you contact information for Helena, Fran's half-sister. Tell them both what is going on, and wire Fran some money from my account if she still needs it. Tell her to stay where she is for now."

"I'll definitely do that right away. How can this dispute be resolved?"

"They'll try to hang the whole thing up in court, continue with their character assassination of George Freeman and his heirs, so they can wrestle back control of the company."

"Is that possible?"

"Anything is possible when you have high-priced lawyers manipulating the system. Fran and Helena risk losing everything, the house, all his assets, the company."

"What can she do from Europe? Shouldn't she come back here?" Marguerite asked, worried that Fran's case would be lost if Laszlo died before it got resolved.

"Part of the problem is this whole war criminal thing, because the truth is …" he began wheezing and gasping for air. His hand waved around at his side for the ventilator. Lena jumped up to hand it to him and he gratefully placed it over his nose and mouth and began breathing deeply. His eyes clenched shut and Marguerite stood up to go find a nurse, but Laszlo waved his hand for her to sit down again.

"It's okay," Lena said, "He's okay now."

After a few more breaths he took the ventilator out and Lena helped him sip some water. He swallowed and continued, "Fran needs to be there in Europe to help sort that war criminal thing out. In fact, tell her to contact my old friend Simon Wiesenthal in Vienna. He'll get his people on it."

"The Nazi Hunter? You know him?" asked Marguerite.

"Yes, we're old acquaintances. He has centers all over the world, each with a wealth of research on who was earmarked as a war criminal."

Marguerite smiled, "Sounds good. I'll contact her and keep you posted. How can I reach you?"

Lena said, "Here's my cell number. You can call me."

"Thank you."

"By the way, it's 2:00 a.m. in Vienna right now. You better wait a few more hours before you call," warned Lena.

Marguerite touched Laszlo's hand lightly and he squeezed it back with vigour that took her by surprise. Then he winked at her. Marguerite rewarded him with her dazzling smile.

She left and returned back to her office.

"No word yet from Fran Freeman?" Marguerite asked her secretary.

"No. Doesn't she have your cell phone number, though?"

"Yes, she has. But my phone has been turned off and I thought she might have called you. I'll keep it on now. What time is my flight for Vegas?"

Lynette pulled out the travel folder, "It's at 7:00 p.m., and I booked you at that great place near the underwater Cirque de Soleil show.

"Wow! Well done."

The dazzling lights of Las Vegas sparkled like a reflected chorus line off the chiffon bed linens of Marguerite's hotel room. It was 1:00 a.m. in the city that never sleeps.

Counting nine hours ahead, Marguerite calculated it would be 10:00 a.m. Vienna time. All she had was Helena's work number. She should be there by now. With the help of the international operator, Marguerite placed a call to Fran's sister.

A young woman answered the phone, *"Guten Morgen. Wichtige Gesundheit."*

*"Guten Morgen. Sprechen Sie Englisch?"* Marguerite asked using her best German accent.

*"Nein. Je parle le français."*

*"Je parle français très mal. Je suis désolé.* I want to speak to Helena," Marguerite said, perched calmly atop her king size bed in the half-lotus position.

*"Helena ist nicht hier. Elle n'est pas ici."*

"Fran Freeman?"

*"Nein."*

Marguerite tilted her head forward and straightened her back, "Can you give me Helena's home number? *Le numéro de téléphone de la maison de Helena?"*

*"Ce n'est pas possible, je suis désolé."*

"Please tell Fran Freeman to call Marguerite as soon as possible."

*"Très bien."*

Marguerite hung up the phone. She slid off the bed and stood looking out of her ninth-floor window at the city below, wondering about her friend, her concern etched in the dark, ebony lines of her face. She felt a wave of tiredness from the travel and intensity of the last few days. She could think of no other solutions.

As Marguerite settled into bed she looked at the conference brochure. The event that had brought her there was a meeting of artists,
promoters, fundraisers and funding organizations. She recognized one
of the speakers listed on the brochure. His name was Serge Wiscano.
He was an old family friend and a music promoter like her father used
to be. Memories of the different bands her father had promoted over the
decades flickered through her mind, whispers of conversations, sounds,
unforgettable images, the giddying rush of traveling with the musicians
when she was a child, walking down a deserted street in New Orleans
with her father holding one hand, and his pal, B.B. King, holding the
other, while a lone trumpet played on a balcony in the French Quarter.

There were so many memories.

Sometimes she wondered if it had all really happened, so magical
had her childhood felt at times.

But there was one band in particular that had stood out to her then,
perhaps because she had been a teenager. Serge Wiscano had given her
free tickets and it was the first time she ever set foot in a nightclub. And
it was one of Serge's new acts she had gone to see.

The music she witnessed that night was like nothing she had ever
heard before. It was haunting, sorrowful and joyous at the same time.
And the players looked and dressed differently, more flamboyantly, than
what she'd seen before — the guitar player, the bass player, the singer.
Suddenly she felt a chill run down her spine.

In a flash, she realized why Fran had seemed so familiar to her.

What was the name of that band? Gitano Españo ... something
like that. The singer was very striking in how she looked and how she
moved. Marguerite now knew without a doubt who that woman was.
The next morning, she would meet with her father's old friend.

She would see if Serge Wiscano could lead her to Fran's mother.

## CHAPTER 25

Fran heaved her bag over her shoulder and stomped through the dust and rocks of the Slovak countryside. How dare they spit at her! She was shocked by her own behaviour, her abrupt departure, and now the storm of fury welling up inside her. The multi-coloured emotions of this clan of people were somehow permeating her skin.

She suddenly snapped back to her more familiar self. Fran realized she couldn't see more than a foot in front of her. She stopped in her tracks, the awareness of her isolation stabbing at her, sending forth waves of fearful thoughts and fantasies in her mind. She was alone with no money or ID, stranded in a foreign country, and now she was walking in the dark with no idea where she was going. She felt like a five year-old running away from home.

Only there was no home to go home to.

Her father was dead. His business was in turmoil. She had no family and no future.

The fact of her total wretchedness washed over like a wave, and she stopped, sinking onto a rock, and wept. The tears poured out of her, unchecked for several moments, with no apology or reason, with no one there to see them and no way to control them.

Then after a moment, she shook her head, fiercely. It wasn't true, she realized. She had family. She had a sister. She had friends, Marguerite and Laszlo. They wouldn't want her to give up here.

She rose and walked on, the tears still wet on her face, moving with no destination — just to get away. But from what? She had no answer for herself.

The clouds drifted by, revealing a half moon which provided just enough light for her to keep moving forward. She stared at her feet, trying to concentrate on the ground, on where she was going. But she couldn't stop the images crowding her mind. The man spitting at her feet, people shouting, the old crone with no hands and Jasper running off with Cecilia. She felt cold, and her head was pounding.

After she had walked for about fifteen minutes she realized she would need to walk at least an hour before getting to the nearest village. That seemed too far, so she stopped on the road and made the hard decision to turn back.

Just then she heard a car coming.

She desperately hoped it was Jasper.

When the headlights came closer, Fran turned to look. She squinted and shielded her eyes. The car pulled over just in front of her. It turned out to be a rusty pickup truck. There were three men sitting in the cab and about six people in the back, some of them children. They talked to her in a foreign language and she shrugged. Finally one of the men said in broken English, "You want we take you to village?"

Fran hesitated.

She remembered that there was only one phone there. It was inside the café, which was probably closed. She wouldn't be able to phone Helena from there and she didn't remember seeing any hotels.

She replied, "No, thank you."

"Where you need to go?" the man asked.

"I really need to go all the way to Kittsee."

He turned to the driver and spoke for a couple of minutes.

"We can take you there now."

Again, Fran hesitated.

These people were dark-skinned like some of the people at Olino. There were several women and children in the back of the truck who were beckoning her to jump on. She stood at the side of the road, looked at the truck, then back where she came from. Maybe Jasper was worried about her. It was inconsiderate of her to leave without saying anything.

"Thanks, but no thanks."

The man seemed to be able to read her mind.

"Roberto," he said, pointing to the man at the wheel, "He come back later tonight. He tell them at Olino where you went."

Fran realized they knew who she was — the strange visitor from Canada. A vision emerged of sleeping at Helena's town house tonight. She could borrow some money, use the phone and use a proper bathroom. Helena could drive her back here tomorrow to get the rest of her belongings.

"Okay. Thank you."

She hopped onto the back of the truck. The children moved over to give her a spot and the truck roared off into the silence of the night.

She smiled at the women and children, who beamed back at her. Several of the children crawled over to her curious, like puppy dogs. They swarmed her, touching her hair and pulling at her pant leg. A middle-aged woman sat watching with bloodshot eyes. As Fran tried to push the children away the woman leaned over and drew the children back to her. A teenage girl was wrapped in colourful cloth and had a diamond nose piercing. She wouldn't make eye contact with Fran.

It was starting to get cool, so Fran hugged herself tightly. The teenage girl offered her a blanket, which she gratefully accepted. When Fran noticed the driver drinking out of a beer can, her mood darkened.

Maybe she had made a mistake accepting this ride. Fran wondered how she could get them to stop the truck and let her off. They were driving in the middle of nowhere. She would wait until she saw a house or some lights and then bang on the side of the truck.

After about forty-five minutes of driving through darkened countryside, Fran resigned herself to stay put until they arrived in Kittsee.
Almost everyone had fallen asleep in the back, but Fran was far too
anxious to sleep. Plus, her backside was starting to ache.

She heard Marguerite's voice in her head asking, "What's good about
this situation?" Fran waited for an answer, but her mind felt as blank
as a frozen field in winter.

She looked around for something soft to use as a cushion and noticed
a cloth bag. She didn't know to whom it belonged, but since everyone
was asleep, she decided to pull it over to her side. When she did, some
of the contents fell out.

Inside the bag were several wallets, passports, cell phones, wrist-
watches, rings and other valuables. She quickly stuffed the contents back
in and looked around to see if anyone saw. Everyone was still asleep.

It suddenly dawned on her that these women and children might
be thieves and this was their loot. Perhaps there was a wild chance that
her valuables were also in that bag. She sat silently for a moment then
scooted the bag under her legs. Using the blanket to shield what she
was doing, Fran started to search the contents of the bag. Other than
the moonlight there was no light, especially under the blanket.

Then she remembered that she had a tiny flashlight on her key
chain. She struggled to find it in her bag. Finally, she was able to pull
it out and shine the tiny light inside the bag. There were Austrian
passports and German passports, a couple of passports from the Slovak
Republic, an American passport and one Canadian passport. Her heart
thumped loudly in her chest as she flipped the pages of the Canadian
passport.

It was hers.

She studied the photo. It was taken about four years ago when Fran
was experimenting with a new look. Back then, her hair was straightened and streaked blonde. She looked so different.

She was stunned to actually find the passport, excited to have it back
but now afraid of her fellow travelers.

Fran rooted around some more until she found a brown leather Holt Renfrew wallet filled with Canadian money, her credit cards, driver's license, library card and Vancouver's Best Coffee frequent drinker card. Nothing had been removed. They hadn't even taken the cash! She breathed a sigh of relief. Finally, she located her silver Nokia cell phone. The battery was dead. It never occurred to her to check her cell messages from a pay phone. The adaptor for the cell phone was back in her larger bag at the camp. She would retrieve all that tomorrow.

Carefully, she transferred the treasured items into her pockets. Just as she was doing that, the truck pulled to a sudden halt.

Right away several men in uniforms surrounded the truck. The beam of a flashlight blinded her eyes. The women and children awoke in a daze as the men shouted at them to get off the truck. They slowly climbed out of the back, still disoriented from sleep. Fran scrambled onto the pavement as well, clutching her carry-on bag. One of the men grabbed it out of her arms and threw it back on the truck. A police wagon pulled up, and the officers pushed everyone into the back of their truck. A uniformed police man got behind the wheel of Roberto's pick up truck, and started driving it away.

"Wait! I need my bag!" Fran cried out.

Two men barked something back to her in German. Startled, she kept quiet. The other passengers kept protesting as the truck drove off. Everyone was gesticulating wildly in their own language, as the officers barked back at them in German. Even the smallest child was shouting at the tallest officer. It occurred to Fran that a scene like this would never happen in Canada.

The police wagon pulled away, and everyone kept shouting. In the midst of this cacophony of dissent, Fran simply hugged her knees to her chest and buried her head.

After about a ten-minute drive, they were at a customs and immigration office. As the policemen let them out of the back and herded them into the station, Fran noticed the pick-up truck parked nearby. Uniformed men were looking through all the contents.

Inside the station, the officers shoved all the women and children in one room, and the men in another. Some female officers gave orders in Slovak. Fran watched as each person emptied their pockets and she followed suit. The female officers frisked everyone for weapons. When they got to Fran, they stopped, and began discussing something about her. They started asking her questions in German.

"I don't speak German. I only speak English."

One of the women spoke back in English, "Roberto says you are one of them, but clearly you are American."

Fran looked at the other women, who were dressed in the coarsely woven, second-hand clothing and handmade scarves that were commonly worn in the region.

Fran was wearing a pair of stone-washed jeans, a silk blouse, cashmere sweater, and a suede three-quarter length coat with a silver brooch and matching earrings.

"I'm from Canada, actually. I'm trying to visit a relative in Kittsee. They were just giving me a ride."

"Do you have any ID?"

"As a matter of fact, I do."

She glanced over at the women and children furtively, and then produced her passport.

"I'm surprised they didn't steal it from you. There is a bag of stolen goods on the truck."

"Yes, I know. They did steal it the other day when I was on the train. I just found it, before you stopped the truck."

One of the officers studied her, frowning, and said, "That seems rather unlikely. And why would someone like you agree to get a ride from people like this?"

Another officer spoke up, following the reasoning of the first one, "Perhaps she is their ringleader. This photo in her passport doesn't look anything like her. Maybe she smuggles these items back to the United States for them."

"Do I look like the kind of person that would do that?"

"Yes, you do actually." One woman replied, "We see all types here. These people are known as thieves around here, and we've been trying to find out who is organizing them, and where they take their stolen goods."

Fran felt an unfamiliar defiance rise up in her, "If I were their ringleader why would I be riding in the back with them? Wouldn't I be waiting somewhere with a truck to receive the stolen goods?"

They all looked at Fran and seemed surprised by her retort, the ineptness of their logic hanging in the air, embarrassingly, for a moment.

"We'll need to detain you until we can sort this out," one of them barked.

"Look here," Fran pressed on, undeterred, "I have other ID. I have a driver's license and credit cards all with my name on them. Look at that driver's license photo. It looks just like me now. It's a more recent photo."

They studied her cards and took them into another room. After a few minutes a woman came back and said, "Okay, this checks out. You can leave," and handed her back the turquoise carry-on bag.

Fran took her possessions back, relieved, and then asked, "Can I make a phone call?"

"Right over there," the woman replied, pointing to a phone on the wall. The giant clock on the wall said 1:00 a.m. Fran was sure that Helena and her son would be asleep. She thought about calling a taxi, but couldn't remember the address of Helena's house. Plus, she was desperate to get out of there.

She dialed the number.

Helena answered tentatively, *"Ja?"*

"Hello, Helena. It's Fran. I'm sorry to call so late. Were you sleeping?"

"No. Not yet. I was up working late."

"Oh, good. Well, I'm glad I didn't disturb you. I have a big favour to ask. Can I stay at your place tonight?"

"Yes, of course. Where are you?"

"I'm at the customs and immigration office near the Austrian-Slovak border."

"That's very close. I can come get you if you like."

"Could you? That would mean a lot to me. Thank you."

"Is Jasper there with you?"

"No. It's just me. It didn't work out for me to stay back at Olino. I'll tell you more about it when I see you."

"Good. I can be there soon."

"Thank you so much!"

Fran hung up the phone and breathed a huge sigh of relief. Then she dialed the number for Marguerite's cell phone, using her long distance calling card. Marguerite answered within two rings.

"Hello?"

"Marguerite. It's Fran."

"Fran! Oh my God! I'm so glad to hear from you. Where are you? What's been happening?"

"It's a long story. I was kidnapped by a band of Gypsies who stole my belongings. I have just escaped from them, and am waiting for my sister to pick me up."

"That sounds like an interesting adventure!"

"Why am I not surprised you would see it that way?" Fran laughed.

Just then an officer shouted at her from across the waiting room, "One phone call, miss, two minutes only. There are other people waiting for the phone."

Indeed, there were now four people lined up behind her.

"I'm sorry, Marguerite, I have to get off the phone. I just got my cell phone back, and I will recharge it soon. Helena's phone number is 011-43-1-408-53-4." Fran could hear loud music playing in the background, so she asked, "Where are you?"

"I'm in Las Vegas at a conference. Speaking of Gypsies, I'm about to have lunch with a man who used to be the promoter of Gitano Españo."

The woman behind Fran in line began speaking to her impatiently.

"It looks like I really have to get off the line," Fran informed Marguerite, "That sounds interesting, though. You'll have to tell me about it later. I have to go. It looks like I have my ID back and I can probably get some money at the bank tomorrow. I'll call you soon."

She hung up the phone and sat down to wait for Helena. After a few minutes, Fran's mind wandered to Marguerite's words: *Gitano Españo*. Where had she heard that name before? Before she could puzzle it out, Helena's car pulled up. Fran walked out of the station and got in the car.

As they drove back to the townhouse, Fran filled Helena in on the events of the evening, and her journey back to Kittsee.

Helena listened, amazed, then asked, "So they stole from you?"

"It seems that way."

"And the people that stole your things are from Olino?

"No, I don't think so, but they seem to know the people at Olino and they must have been at the train station to have stolen my things."

"So was Jasper involved?"

"I don't know, but a woman on the train warned me that he was probably a thief. But I'm not so sure."

"Some Gypsies make their living as thieves."

"I'm confused about all that because Jasper said he can't claim a Romani heritage. And I'm not totally sure what that means. Is it Gypsy, or that he is from Romania or Rome, Italy …"

"No. Romani or Roma is a term now used to describe a specific cultural group of people who were thought to have migrated here a thousand years ago from India. They used to be called Gypsies, and sometimes still are."

"I always thought Gypsy referred more to a lifestyle than an ethnic group."

"It's a tricky subject because there are some people who live a wandering lifestyle outside of mainstream society who are called Gypsies. Then there are other people who live in communities all over the world who share some similarities in terms of language and customs who now call themselves Romani or Rom. Many of them don't live a wandering lifestyle and haven't for centuries and don't like the term Gypsy."

"Wow. I didn't know all that. So some Gypsies or Romani steal for a living or people assume they do?" asked Fran.

"Maybe they steal more per capita than other groups. But, maybe that is because they are shunned by society, not given work or support. Stealing becomes a way of surviving. There are many who don't steal, who are law abiding citizens, but you don't hear a lot about them in the media."

"I'm afraid to say you don't even hear about them at all much in North American media," added Fran.

"Here many people see them as parasites of society. It's a social problem that needs far more attention than it's getting, especially in former Eastern Bloc countries."

Fran sighed, "I suppose there are thieves in all walks of life, not just among Gypsies. In corporate North America there are white collar criminals who do more than steal your passport, they steal your entire life savings."

They drove in silence for a while.

Then Fran remembered something, and asked Helena, "Have you heard of Gitano Españo?"

"No. Should I?"

"I don't know. The name sounds so familiar to me. I was just talking to my friend Marguerite and she mentioned the name."

"It sounds like a brand of cigarettes."

"No. She's in Las Vegas right now, and she said it had something to do with meeting a music promoter."

"Perhaps it's a band, then."

Pieces of memories that lay hidden from each other in Fran's mind began fusing back together. As the pieces merged, Fran felt a chill on the surface of her skin, "Yes. You're right! I remember now! It is the name of a band … a band my mother was in! I was jokingly telling my friend that I was captured by a band of Gypsies, and she said 'speaking of Gypsies …' Why would she say that?"

"Probably because Gitano Españo means Spanish Gypsy," replied Helena, "Were the band members Gypsies?"

"I don't know. They could have been."

"Was your mother a Gitano from Españo?"

"I know this sounds strange, but I don't know her background either. I know she grew up in New Hampshire, and had a rich father, but I don't know anything about her heritage. I assumed they were originally from England."

"You look a bit like a Gypsy, you know. Not like me at all. I'm blonde-haired and blue-eyed. It's hard to believe we are sisters."

"Yes, you're right."

"When was the last time you saw your mother?"

"When I was about seven years old."

"She just left?"

"Yes, she went back on the road with her group. She never stayed in touch, or at least that's what my father said."

Helena looked over at Fran, her turquoise eyes watery with compassion, "So, we both grew up without a mother."

"Yes, we may not look alike but we have a lot in common," Fran smiled and added. "And it's nice to have family again."

"I feel the same way."

They arrived at Helena's townhouse and tiptoed inside, so as not to disturb Marek. As Helena got her settled on the sofa, Fran said, "Thank you, Helena. It's great to be here. This has been one of the most unusual weeks of my life."

Helena responded, "It's been a turbulent ride, yes."

They toasted with their water glasses, and Helena bid her a good night's sleep.

Fran settled into the sofa. As she dozed off, she noticed her thoughts drift to Jasper. She hoped that the driver, Roberto, had returned to Olino to tell him of her whereabouts. It occurred to her that Roberto might have been detained at the immigration office without being able to return.

Somehow she would need to get a message to let Jasper know that she was okay. The only way would be to drive back there and she dreaded doing that. Perhaps she should just forget about all her belongings and not return. That felt like the right decision. She made a firm decision to go through her Father's estate with Helena, see if she could clear his name, and then get back to Canada as soon as possible.

## CHAPTER 26

F ran awoke to the sound of Marek gunning his motorcycle engine.

She peered out the living room window to see "her nephew" taking off on his bike, leaving tire marks on the front lawn. It was odd to have a nephew who was so much older than her. It was even stranger to have a relative like Marek.

Over their morning coffee, Helena and Fran looked over the Will.

Fran skimmed through the document, summarizing what she saw there for Helena. "The Will states that all his assets, his house, vehicles, investments and shares in Freeman & Wilson go to both of us. We share it fifty-fifty."

"That's very generous of him, considering we never met," Helena replied, surprised, "That must have come as a shock to you, since all this time you thought you would be the sole heir."

"To be honest, it did at first. But I now realize his estate is worth around twelve million dollars. Whether I get twelve million or six million is not going to make a big difference to me."

"My part of the estate is worth six million?"

"Approximately."

Helena leaned back in her chair, stunned.

"That's outrageous! You don't mind giving up six million to a complete stranger?"

"Quite frankly, I'd much rather have a family member to share it all with. How many pairs of designer shoes do I really need?"

Helena laughed. "I would have loved to even have new shoes rather than the ill-fitting ones from the thrift store."

Fran, flushed with guilt, continued, "There was a while in my early twenties when I lived the high life. I had designer clothes and a sports car. I blew a lot of money at exclusive clubs meeting boring people and longing for something else but not knowing what."

"Really?" Helena said, arching her blond eyebrows.

"Then, when I started working in my father's accounting firm I got an inside view of the financial lives of some of Canada's wealthiest. It turned my stomach to see how people wasted their money. And later I came to see how tragic it was when they had everything and yet admitted to feeling empty inside. I know it's a cliché ..."

"That money doesn't buy happiness?"

"Yes. I also noticed that the people who were happiest were those living more simply and being generous with their money. I mean generous in healthy ways."

"What do you mean by that?"

"Like my father ... I mean your father ... actually, I should be saying *our* father. He would just give me money for no reason. Mostly cash. Or I'd get a huge cheque for my birthday. I think it was his way of showing his love for me. He wasn't so good at human interaction.

"I don't feel that's a healthy way of being generous with money, because I began to rely on it. For example, when he was upset with me, he wouldn't talk about it, but he just stopped giving me money. That was the only way I knew something was wrong. Oh, and also he would barely acknowledge my presence. And this could go on for weeks or even months!"

"For months?"

"Yes, he just pretended I didn't exist. If I asked what was wrong he wouldn't answer. If I asked if he wanted a cup of coffee, he wouldn't answer. If I told him I was getting on a boat to go to Ghana, he wouldn't answer," Fran coiled her arms around her waist as those icy memories penetrated her skin, "Then, one day he would just start talking to me as if nothing had happened. Soon after, I'd usually get a huge cheque left on my dresser."

"That's unusual behaviour."

"He was an unusual man."

Helena went to the stove to make more tea.

Fran continued, "I would rather have had a relationship with him, you know what I mean? I would rather have had a father that interacted with me."

"Yes, I understand. My adoptive father was somewhat like that. Rarely around, didn't interact much. It's also that generation of men."

"It's so great to talk to you about all this. I know we barely know each other, but somehow I feel so connected. Perhaps it's as they say 'blood is thicker than water.'"

Helena smiled, "I've never heard that expression before."

"At any rate, sometimes I noticed myself hoping he'd get annoyed with me for something so I would get a huge cheque. Then I could get my fix of *retail therapy*. Isn't that sad? One day I made a profound decision for myself — not to need much money. I scaled down my lifestyle considerably."

Helena stared at her sister for a few minutes digesting the information.

"I've never been very rich, so that is hard for me to relate to. But I know what you mean. I like to keep my life simple, too."

Fran smiled, "So, we'll have to make sure you expand your company into North America, in a simple way."

"I would love to do that! I can hardly wait to tell Effie."

"Who is Effie?"

"I haven't told you yet?" Helena took in a deep breath and slowly exhaled, "Effie is my partner, someone I would marry if I could."

"Oh, I didn't know you had someone special in your life. That's wonderful."

Helena smiled, busying herself clearing dishes, then paused and looked Fran in the eyes, "You're not shocked that I'm a lesbian?"

Fran laughed, "I'm from Vancouver, Helena. Same-sex couples are commonplace. In fact I forget sometimes that some people are still shocked by that."

Helena's turquoise eyes sparkled with relief. "Effie has her own place but we spend a lot of time here. Since Marek arrived, Effie went back to her house. I haven't quite gotten around to telling my son about my sexual orientation. I don't think it would go over very well with him!" she said, stifling a laugh.

"Maybe not," Fran sympathized.

"He's actually a good person deep down. He sponsors people who are part of Alcoholics Anonymous, and apparently he's very good at it. I just think I'll wait on introducing him to Effie."

"You'll know when the time is right."

"That was one thing about our father. He believed in the power of diversity. He said you can't have innovation without diversity. If everyone looks at things the same way, you get the same old thing. Freeman & Wilson was one of the first companies in Vancouver to hire and mentor people from a variety of backgrounds. To this day, even on the leadership team, there is a good balance of men and women. We have people of almost all races, cultures, creeds and sexual orientations on the payroll. We also employ people with disabilities, people with prison records, you name it. He was particularly sensitive to human rights before it was even popular."

"That's amazing to hear. Shouldn't that be evidence enough that he wasn't a war criminal?"

"You'd think so."

The two women worked silently cleaning up the kitchen as if they'd done it together for years.

"I'd love to meet Effie sometime."

"Yes, this week hopefully. Marek went back to work today and he's staying with a friend close to the factory. I guess I should really give him some money to re-train in something. Maybe counseling. He is so unhappy about his life."

"That's a great idea. You now have plenty to spread around!" Fran smiled.

"It's hard to imagine. I must say I wasn't expecting anything like a huge inheritance to come along."

"By the way, did you know that same-sex marriages are legal in Canada?" asked Fran.

"I know. Maybe we should move there!" Helena was starting to get giddy.

"I would love that. But first, you should come visit, to see if it feels right. You will need to come to Canada anyway to help me deal with the estate."

"Yes. Effie has a vacation coming up. I'll discuss it with her. What steps do we need to take next as far as looking after the estate?"

"I don't know exactly. We'll need to contact Laszlo."

"What about you? Do you have someone special in your life?" asked Helena.

"No. A fortune teller said I was unlucky in love. She's quite right about that."

"She read your tea leaves?"

"No, she read my palm; except the creepy thing is that she had no hands."

"What do you mean she had no hands?"

"Her arms ended at her wrists, but she seemed to manage with her two stumps quite well. And she was this ancient little raisin. So tiny, like a midget almost."

"Interesting."

"She said my love life would change soon."

"Is there anyone on the horizon?"

"No. I thought I liked Jasper, but now I realize that would never work."

"Why do you say that?"

"There's another woman that is part of his community and she is after him. Jasper and I had a great connection, though, and I am feeling sad about it. Somehow I miss him. But that's silly, because the truth is I hardly know him."

"When we go to Olino today to get your things you should tell him how you feel."

"No! First off, I just met him, and secondly, I've decided to let my things go. They saw those photos of George in the Nazi uniform, and they went crazy. Plus, those people stole from me. I don't want to go back there. I don't need any of those things. I'll go shopping in Vienna and get what I need. I just inherited six million dollars!"

"I hope you don't mind me saying this, but I think that is a shame, I'd be happy to take you there," replied Helena.

"Thanks, but no thanks. By the way, I brought a number of photos, papers and a journal with me. I found them in our father's basement. Many of the photos have no date or names on them, so I don't know who the people are. The papers and this journal are in a variety of foreign languages that I don't understand. Maybe you can make sense of some of them," Fran said as she handed them over for Helena's inspection.

Helena sat back down at the kitchen table and put on her reading glasses. She shuffled through the photos and found one of herself as a baby.

"I'm about six months old in the photo. It was taken just before my mother died. How did he get it? He must have been in Canada by that time. He must have been in contact with my mother."

"I don't know. Somehow he managed to stay connected. Plus, Laszlo was able to find you. It helps that you kept the name that appears on your birth certificate."

"So he knew where I was the whole time?"

"I don't know, but we can ask Laszlo."

Helena's face flushed with an emotion that Fran couldn't quite name. Her sister busied herself sleuthing through the documents some more.

"I see that some of the letters are in German. Here is one from someone named Frau Meinhardt. It is dated 1944. It is written to a Hans Hellermann at an American Prisoner of War camp in Colorado. Who was Hans Hellermann?"

Fran shrugged, "What does it say?"

"She seems to be responding to something that Hans wrote to her. I'll try to translate as I read. "

*February 15, 1944*

*Dear Mr. Hellermann,*

*I am responding to your letter dated November 3rd, 1943. I am very sorry to inform you that my husband was killed a number of months ago. They say he was executed as a traitor, but there must have been a mistake. Klaus was very committed to his country. As you can imagine, it has been a painful time for my family and I, and so it has taken me quite a few months to respond to his large stack of letter mail. I noticed your letter is from a POW camp in the United States. I can only assume you served with my husband in the line of duty. You asked about The Big Dipper. I'm not sure what you mean by that. I am assuming you mean the constellation in the sky. I knew my husband was somewhat of an amateur astronomer. Right now there is an investigation into what actually happened at Birkenau and into the events surrounding my husband's death. We miss him very much. I am sorry to deliver such sad news. Please pass this along to anyone else who knew him.*

*Yours truly,*
*Frau Marianne Meinhardt*

"Maybe she is still alive and we can go talk to her," Fran responded, her mind still puzzling over the significance of the letter.

"Yes, maybe," Helena said distractedly as she read through the pages of a journal, "This journal of his is fascinating. It is full of stories in

German, Slovak, and another language. There are also sketches and poetry. He seems to have been a very creative man."

"I don't think so. He was an accountant," Fran countered.

"But he had his own business. It takes a lot of creativity to start and build a successful enterprise. There are some logical steps to take, but then it's up to the imagination to create something new and sustainable. For him to have created a company that was so prosperous over such a long time must have required a huge amount of creativity," said Helena.

"Yes, you have a point there."

"Look, I have cancelled going into work today so we can focus on these issues. Perhaps we should call the lawyer as soon as possible."

"Yes, I agree. Although it's still the middle of the night back in Canada. Can I use your phone to check my cell phone messages? Perhaps he has left a message. I have a long distance calling card number that I can use."

"Yes. Please make yourself at home."

As Helena cleaned up the kitchen, Fran listened to her messages. There were several from Eva, one from Meili at work, another from Marguerite, and then a strange hate message from an employee at Freeman & Wilson. Fran wondered how the man got her cell number and what he was so angry about. Another message was from Peter Wilson saying he didn't believe the rumours and would stand behind her. Finally there was a message from Laszlo. As Fran listened, her stomach tightened, clenching in a knot. By the time the message was over, Fran was trembling.

When she entered the kitchen a few minutes later, Fran looked deathly white.

"What's the matter?!" Helena cried.

"I got a message from Laszlo, the lawyer. It's very bad news."

She sat down at the table to steady herself. Helena brought her a box of tissues. Fran looked up at her half-sister in terror.

"Oh my God! Where do I start? As I told you before, Laszlo seems to be the only person who knew about you, and he apparently convinced our father to add you to the Will just a week before he died. This was a huge concern to the partners of Freeman & Wilson, because it meant that they had much less control. If it was just me as a fifty-two percent shareholder, then they could get what they want — probably because they know I'm such a pushover. They are unsure how twenty-six percent me and twenty-six percent you will work out. It's an unknown element to them.

"They've been trying to discredit George with stories in the paper that he was a war criminal. That is another reason I came to Vienna — to find you and clear his name. So now, according to Laszlo, not only have they successfully discredited George, they seem to be holding me and him responsible for illegal accounting practices with one of our biggest clients!

"I should have seen this coming. I had the feeling that the Managing Partner and the CFO were doing some *innovative* accounting. I didn't do anything about it, because I had no proof. I just had a bad feeling about the business we did with one of our clients, Wrightway. So, now they are contesting the Will. They say Laszlo made my father sign under duress and they are starting proceedings against me!"

"Surely, that won't pass in a court of law," Helena protested. "We no doubt have a good case to fight both those claims."

"You would think so, but Laszlo thinks we shouldn't fight it. He thinks we should sign away the company to them. He says Freeman & Wilson has been trying to conceal a huge debt for years and now the company is bankrupt. Over a hundred people are losing their jobs and their pension plans. Not only that, they are trying to pin the responsibility on me. He says they have very powerful lawyers and lots of compelling evidence."

"That's unbelievable. But surely you have character witnesses to stand up for you?"

"Yes, but will that be enough? It's going to mean a long court battle and if they win...I'm sorry, Helena. I just told you that you have inherited six million, and now it seems that's not true. We have just lost a company that my father devoted his life to."

"And that you have devoted your life to," Helena added.

Fran nodded, her hands shaking.

"Are you saying there is no inheritance, now?"

"No. It's gone. Completely gone. The entire company is bankrupt, it's all come out now in the news. Everyone has lost their job. That fifty-two percent now equals zero percent."

"What about his house and personal assets?"

"I don't know what will happen to those."

Helena sat down, her head spinning from the news, trying to make sense of the complicated mess.

Fran placed a hand on hers trying to hold back the lava of panic rising in her throat, "That's a heck lot of money to gain and lose all in one day, huh?"

"Yes, but what's this business they are trying to pin on you? What if they win this case against you?"

"Then, I face several years … in prison."

CHAPTER 27

"How did all this happen?" Helena asked incredulously.

"I don't know. My father was ill for a decade and left the running of the company to the other partners. It's my fault. I wasn't paying close enough attention. The truth is, I was afraid to confront them when I sensed problems brewing."

"What kind of proof do they have that he was a war criminal?"

"I don't know. What did you hear from your mother about him? She married him during World War II, didn't she?" asked Fran.

"I was so young when she died. I think they only went after officers who had the most power. Many men in Germany and Austria lived their whole life in fear of that kind of retribution."

"What do you mean?"

"I read an article recently. During the trials at Nuremburg there were more than 90,000 people in the war criminal file. Most of them were never tried, it was impossible. They just went back into society, got jobs, had families, lived and died, and buried their shame."

"For the next generation to deal with," mused Fran.

"Exactly. And it's a huge cultural shame that erodes the fabric of our society. We judge ourselves, and the world continues to condemn people in the German-speaking world. Men here, in particular, have become emasculated. They are phobic about anything that may even hint at Nazi behaviour. Or, they go to the opposite extreme and become Neo-Nazis."

"Like your son?" Fran uttered while looking down at the floor.

"Like my son," Helena sighed.

"So many untold stories of suffering. Jasper said that many segments of society were targeted, not just the Jews, but also the Romani, artists, and many others."

"Then on the other side of the equation there is the story of the Germans. After the war, ethnic Germans in many other countries were kicked out of their homes, beaten, killed, raped, left to starve to death. My mother died of pneumonia because we lived in a work camp in Slovakia with no heat through the winter."

"That's horrible. Who was doing that kind of thing?"

"People who, after the war, decided they were justified in harming Germans."

Fran felt the knot in her stomach spiral deeper. It was like a twisted rope of oppression coiling backwards in time; rooting her to horrors she couldn't imagine but somehow felt captured by.

She looked out over the sea of red-tiled roofs of Kittsee. The orderly sameness of this place felt both like a prison and a salvation. If she stayed here in this obscure town maybe the authorities would never find her.

"So, everyone suffered," Fran said under her breath.

"That's what war is all about ... suffering ... for everyone."

"Even the war profiteers?"

Helena leaned back in her chair, "I think so. They have to live with themselves. It's like the story of Alfred Nobel. Do you know his background?"

"No."

"He was a millionaire industrialist and scientist. He made his fortune by inventing a new kind of dynamite, an explosive more powerful than anyone had ever come up with before. He licensed the patent to munitions makers throughout Europe. One day Nobel's brother died and one small town newspaper made a mistake and printed the obituary of Alfred Nobel instead.

"He had that rare opportunity of reading his own obituary in his lifetime and seeing what people would remember of his life. It said 'Alfred Nobel, who invented a new kind of explosive and made a lot of money building munitions, died the other day'. Nobel read that and said to himself, 'Is this what I'm going to be remembered for? I taught people how to kill other people more effectively? I don't want that to be the association with my name.'

"So he took his fortune and founded the Nobel prizes for achievements in peace-making, medicine, science and literature. And, of course, that is what we remember him for today."

"Yes, that's true. I totally associate him with peace, not war. Maybe our father was trying to turn something around from his life."

"Maybe."

Fran paused and wondered what she would be remembered for if she died today. Not much probably. Maybe being good at math. She wondered if she would ever have the courage to make her life into something more ... impactful.

"Laszlo suggested we should go see Simon Wiesenthal."

"The Nazi Hunter?"

"Yes. Apparently he lives right here in Vienna. Laszlo says he knows Simon Wiesenthal personally, and that I should try to talk to him. I even have his number."

"Let's call," Helena offered. "There's nothing we can do now until we can talk to Laszlo on the phone later today. Maybe we could even go there today."

"Sure, if you want to try. Perhaps you should call in case they don't speak English."

"Right. I suppose I should mention Laszlo Goldstein to get a foot in the door?"

Fran nodded.

As Helena went into her office to make the call, Fran rubbed her eyes in an effort to ease the fatigue. The lifelong financial security she'd always taken for granted was dissolving before her eyes like the mirage it always was. She felt as if she were free falling with no parachute, and nothing to break her fall.

A few minutes later Helena returned, looking upbeat.

"The name, Laszlo Goldstein, certainly made an impression. A woman said Mr. Wiesenthal is unfortunately quite ill right now, but his assistant can see us at noon today. I hope its okay that I booked the appointment?"

"That's amazing," Fran replied, surprised and cheered by the news, "Thank you for doing that. Perhaps Mr. Wiesenthal's assistant can fill in some gaps about our Father's past."

They arrived at the Jewish Documentation Center in Vienna a little before noon. It was a non-descript, sparsely furnished three-room office with a staff of four, including Wiesenthal. As they waited for his assistant to come out, Fran read a flyer about the Center sitting on the side table.

> *Contrary to popular belief, Wiesenthal did not usually track down the Nazi fugitives himself. His chief task was gathering and analyzing information. In that work he was aided by a vast informal, international network of friends, colleagues, and sympathizers, including German World War II veterans, appalled by the horrors they witnessed. He even received tips from former Nazis with grudges against other former Nazis.*

On the back cover she read a quotation:

> *An SS corporal told Wiesenthal: "You would tell the truth about the death camps to the people in America. That's right. And they couldn't believe you. They'd say you were mad. How can anyone believe this terrible business — unless he has lived through it?"*

A sense of dread washed over Fran as the assistant entered the room. What if she revealed unspeakable truths about her father? She didn't think she could handle any more bad news.

They placed the letters, photos and journal in front of the woman and the assistant looked at them, intrigued. She grasped each letter, document and photo gingerly, like an archaeologist unearthing a sacred tomb.

The woman was in her sixties with grey-streaked black hair messily arranged in a bun. Her honey-rimmed glasses magnified her already luminous hazel eyes.

"So you think this man was a war criminal and you want him brought to justice?"

"No, he is our father and we want to prove he was not a war criminal."

"You want to prove your father was *not* a war criminal. What's motivating you to come here then?"

"We think someone is trying to do a character assassination on him," replied Fran.

"Are there witnesses or documentation?"

"Not to my knowledge," Fran replied.

"Where is he living now?" she asked searching for her pen.

Fran and Helena looked at each other, "He passed away recently."

The woman sighed and glanced back and forth from one to the other, "Listen, my dears, our organization focuses on living individuals who need to be brought to justice. And, even if he was alive, it sounds like you don't have believable witnesses or written documentation. All you seem to have are these photos of him in a Luftwaffe uniform with a bit of hearsay thrown in. Unless the witnesses were actually there and saw him ..." she said as she scanned the newspaper article. "It sounds like this reporter has no factual back up. I don't think it would be worth our while."

"We need something to prove he wasn't a war criminal to help us win a lawsuit," Fran urged.

The woman cleared her throat and glanced at the clock on the wall. "Listen, I'll put a short amount of time in and see if I can find anything."

"Thank you!" Fran sighed with relief.

"But just because I don't find anything on him, doesn't mean he's not guilty," she warned. "I suggest you come back in a couple of hours."

The women agreed and headed back out into the tourist lined streets of Vienna.

Fran and Helena soon found an alleyway café and sat down at a table, ordering Viennese coffee. As Fran sipped the mocha java she savoured the rich aroma. After a few minutes she felt light-headed, and wasn't sure whether it was a result of the strong Viennese coffee, the anticipation of unravelling a great mystery, or the overwhelming dread of further condemnation.

Together they looked at a tourist flyer left on one of the tables. There were photos of Schönbrunn Palace, the Hofburg, the Prater, and Lainzer Tiergarten — places that Fran would love to go visit; perhaps another day when she felt more at ease. She imagined her father as a young man enjoying these sites with friends, girlfriends or even Helena's mother. The sisters finished their coffee, and then went hunting for a bank that would exchange Fran's Canadian money. For a couple of hours they wandered the streets and bought some items to replace things Fran had left behind in Olino.

At 4:30 in the afternoon, Fran tried calling Laszlo. Lena answered.

After she got off the phone, Fran returned to the park bench where Helena was keenly awaiting the news.

"Laszlo is undergoing some kind of surgery today so I could only talk to Lena, his granddaughter. Freeman & Wilson is officially bankrupt. There is a big sign on the door. No one has a job anymore," Fran sat down and held her hand on her forehead.

Helena sighed and peered up at the multi-patterned roof of the Stephansdom cathedral, "That's it then. It's all gone?"

Fran nodded, "Also, Lena said she emptied the contents of George's safe deposit box, and there is something important there for us to look at. She wouldn't say what it was, but she sent it by courier a couple of days ago to your work address which means it should be there by now."

The air was muggy as they strolled through the plaza. A busker was standing still as a statue on a box, in a silver zoot suit, his skin painted white. Children flocked around him trying to get him to move. He winked at one little girl and she burst into giggles. Fran noticed that she hadn't laughed like that in a long time.

"Let's go back now."

They turned and headed for the Wiesenthal office. Fran felt herself hyperventilating as they pressed the button for the elevator. When they entered the meeting room, the assistant said, "I think I have pieced together some interesting elements. There is good news and bad news. Which would you like first?"

CHAPTER 28

They drove back to Kittsee in silence. Fran undid her seat belt and opened the window. She leaned out to let the wind blast her face.

Helena slowed down the car until Fran sat back down in her seat.

"Are you okay?"

"No evidence, but that doesn't mean he's innocent," she said repeating the words she'd heard back in the Wiesenthal office. "What's with that?"

"There must be some way to prove ..."

"He was a guard at Birkenau. He probably had to kill people." Fran replied sickened at the thought.

"But that links him to the man in that letter, who was shot as a traitor at Birkenau."

Fran flipped through the envelope of photos again. There was a wedding invitation for Jorg Frei and Uta Schneider.

"They both look so young in this photo."

"That was taken in 1943. She would have been twenty, and he was twenty-one. I was born only seven months after the wedding."

"Really?" Fran said, surprised and curious.

"Yes, quite scandalous in those days."

"It was a shotgun wedding then?" queried Fran.

"I'm not familiar with that expression. What does that mean?"

"It means Uta's father held a metaphorical shotgun to George's head while he walked up the aisle."

"Maybe that's why he left for Northern Africa right after," mused Helena.

Helena parked in front of the main entrance to The Wichtige Gesundheit Company. It was 7:00 p.m. now, and the doors were locked. Helena let them in and found the courier package from Canada sitting on her desk. She opened it and dumped out the contents. There were American Express Traveler's cheques for Fran, and a notebook.

The cover of the notebook said, "Once Upon a Lifetime: 1001 Questions to Record the Stories of Your Life."

"What's this?" asked Helena.

Fran opened the book to the first page, which listed questions number one to number seven. Next to each question was her father's distinctly neat, yet tiny handwriting in pencil.

"I gave him this book last year as a Christmas present," Fran informed Helena, "It was my meagre attempt at getting him to start talking about his past. There are 1001 questions that elderly people can answer about all aspects of life: family of origin, school, career, marriage, military, parenting, etc. The point is to create a legacy for future generations. He took one look at it and said 'Why would you want to know anything about my life?' I said nothing, as usual. But after three months I sneaked a peek at the book and noticed he filled in only this first page."

Helena read some of the questions, "Some of these questions seem silly. It asks 'Do you still have your own teeth?'"

"Yes, but the questions get more interesting later on," Fran countered, "As you can imagine, I was disappointed when he didn't do it, but really disappointed when I couldn't even find the journal after he died."

"But it looks like he did fill out more than just the first page," said Helena.

"What do you mean?" Fran said as she snatched the book out of Helena's hands.

Fran flipped through the pages all the way until the end. She looked up at Helena, mystified.

"It looks as though he answered every single question in the book! All 1001 of them. Look here, if a question didn't apply to him he wrote down 'n/a'. *Always the accountant.* But, I don't know when he would have done this. The last time I checked the book, he hadn't filled in more than the first page."

Fran sat back in her chair, and thought through the last few weeks, "He must have been writing this out during the last week of his life."

"Then someone else must have put it in his safety deposit box," guessed Helena.

"Maybe Laszlo, maybe Eva. I don't know."

"Perhaps this book of questions will fill in parts of the picture," suggested Helena.

Fran met her sister's determined look and nodded.

Over the next hour, they read aloud each entry, working together like a pair of detectives on a case, trying to piece together the last threads of the mystery that was their father's life.

## CHAPTER 29

I t was springtime in Vienna in 1943 and the cherry blossoms were bursting into bloom. They gave off a scent of optimism that ran counter to the feeling in Jorg's heart. As he stood at the altar and surveyed the onlookers, he made his best attempt to smile.

Jorg watched as his bride, Uta, entered at the back of the church. She dabbed perspiration from her brow with a fine German lace handkerchief. Her bridesmaids each lifted one corner of her veil while her father, General Heinz Schneider, dressed in full military regalia, took his daughter's hand and proceeded down the aisle. She looked resplendent in her off-white silk gown with the pearl bodice. Jorg studied her, admiringly, but feeling detached at the same time. He was in the grip of an almost disembodied curiosity about why she was there, dressed like that, for him.

As they arrived at the altar, the General took Uta's hand and placed it in Jorg's. The General smiled and patted his future son-in-law's back. Jorg thought of the irony of the situation. He only appeared to be the perfect son-in-law. He passed all the tests to be a pilot in the Luftwaffe. He was bright, accurate, daring and an outstanding marksman — seemingly afraid of nothing.

Uta was radiantly happy. To his unsuspecting bride, he was the kind of handsome stranger that every girl dreamed about running away with. They had met just a few months ago at a Hitler Youth rally. Many girls had clamoured for his attention, but Uta stood out because of her beauty, her status in society, and her complete adoration of him. He hadn't meant to do it, but he had taken their physical relationship too far and now she was pregnant. Only Uta's mother and the doctor knew. They had to get married, even though in his heart *he knew it was the wrong thing to do.*

Jorg brought himself back to the present. No use going over it in his head again, he reasoned. He was going through with it. He glanced around, offering his movie star smile again, the one that hid all his true feelings. He noticed the church was full of only Uta's friends and family, which brought a sense of relief.

Now the moment was upon them. The priest cleared his throat and Jorg and Uta turned to face him.

Just then, a man and a woman slipped into the back of the church. All eyes turned to look.

Uta whispered to him, "Isn't that your father?"

Jorg glanced at the couple and panic rose in his throat. He said nothing at first.

"Jorg? Who is that girl with him? Your sister?"

Jorg turned to the priest and nodded for him to start the ceremony. The priest looked past him to the newcomers.

Finally Jorg answered, "It's my father … and mother."

"I thought you said they couldn't make it."

"I thought so, too, but here they are."

"Your mother looks so young."

"She takes good care of her health."

Uta looked back at her husband-to-be and stared at him. Something wasn't adding up here and Jorg could sense her distrust growing. He nodded again to the priest and the priest glanced over at the bride. She wasn't ready to start. The back of Jorg's throat was burning.

There was nowhere to sit at the back of the church, so the couple had to ask several people in the seventh row to stand up so that they could make their way to the center seats. Jorg finally looked up at his father who waved at him. Jorg nodded his head in response, and several people murmured.

Uta stared at them and then back at Jorg. As he tried to hold her gaze, his nostrils flared and his eyes blinked far too often. Finally, Uta turned to the priest and the ceremony began, but Jorg didn't hear a word of it. His mind was spinning. Why did they come to the wedding? Everyone would be talking about how that woman couldn't be his mother. How could he explain? He tried to calm down. He reassured himself it didn't matter. In just a few short days he was getting on a train for North Africa. They could speculate all they wanted then.

He would be gone.

## CHAPTER 30

The Ju 388 Störtebeker shone magnificently under the intense midday sun. Jorg straightened his cap and uniform, and placed himself next to the propeller of this state-of-the-art fighter plane.

"Take a photo!" he shouted.

Klaus clicked the shutter, and nodded, "That will be a good one to send to your new wife."

He walked around the camera, studying the new fangled contraption mounted on a tripod, "I like this compact size camera. I'm going to get myself one too as soon as this insane war is over."

"And I'm going to get myself one of these," Jorg said, as he ran his hand lovingly over the wing of the plane, "I've never been up in one of them before."

Their comrade Hans, who was studying the map of the Sahara, looked up at them, "I know a place in Marrakech that has unbelievable deals on cameras."

"What about used fighter planes?" asked Jorg.

"Sure. I know a guy who has everything!"

All three laughed.

To an outsider, they would have looked like three young men on a great adventure. They were the lords of the air; flying missions in a mysterious, exotic part of the world. Reality had yet to catch up with them.

It was early May 1943 in Tunisia. The Allies were moving in quickly and the German forces were barely holding their last remaining territory. However, the majority of the men fighting under the Axis banner didn't know how bad it was. In addition, Jorg and his comrades were lost in the propaganda of certain victory. The stark, inhuman slaughter of the Eastern front and the slow build-up of Allied forces for the D-Day invasion hadn't penetrated their consciousness yet.

They were boys playing men, lost in the desert heat. The expanse of the Sahara stretched out endlessly to the south and the azure blue of the Mediterranean lulled silently to the north. The scorching dry wind caused flecks of sand to sting Jorg's cheeks. Despite the intense weather, Jorg was grateful to be far away from Europe.

Today he would join his two newfound friends for a reconnaissance flight over the desert; Hans as pilot, Klaus as co-pilot and Jorg as the gunner. Klaus Meinhardt was older than Jorg, and also more reserved. He had sandy blonde hair, a rotund build, and a long, pink nose. With his aviator sunglasses and scarf he looked like the Red Baron. As a graduate engineering student from Munich, he dreamed of one day inventing a technology that would allow people all over the world to communicate instantaneously. Hans Hellermann was about the same age, height and build as Jorg, but had a lighter complexion. He was by far the most extroverted of the three. He had the roguish good looks of Gregory Peck which he hid behind thick, round glasses and a mop of dark brown hair. Hans kept his hair on the long side, much to the chagrin of his commanding officer. He felt it gave him a wilder look and it also compensated for the fact that he was already losing his hair in his early twenties. He had been training as a commercial pilot in Berlin when the war started. Hermann Göering, the commander of the Luftwaffe, had personally recommended Hans for the job.

The three young men had met on the boat from Sicily as part of the Fliegerfuehrer Afrika or Air Command Africa. They had established a bond upon learning that they would be on the same mission. All three shared a love of fine wines, fine women, and a deep-felt aversion for war.

As Klaus checked the instruments, Hans and Jorg packed the supplies into the holding area.

"I hear your wife is pregnant," said Hans.

"Yes. I'm going to be a father," replied Jorg, suddenly aware how strange the word sounded to him, and at the same time how close the reality now was.

"Don't give out any cigars at the mess hall tonight," laughed Hans, "I was hoping you'd help me take those two new nurses to the movie."

"Only as a favour to you, I'll force myself," Jorg said, as he winked at his friend.

"Good. I'm using you as bait, you good-looking, dark bastard," Hans retorted.

Jorg flinched at the comment, but smiled to his friend to play along.

"I'm sure you'll do alright on your own."

"But not as well as you, my friend. I told them it was you who won the Strasbourg cycling race and they went crazy! But I'll take whichever one you don't want, as long as it's Birgit."

"Isn't she going out with Alfons?" Jorg queried.

"Details, details."

Jorg shook his head, "You'd better be careful, Hans. Alfons likes his guns."

"I'm not afraid of him," retorted Hans, as he struck a menacing boxer's pose.

Klaus looked up from the instruments and chimed in, "Ach, you're one of those people with a death wish, Hans," He turned to Jorg, "You should see him ride his motorcycle out in the desert. He's insane. Just yesterday, he was gunning it at 180 kilometers per hour, on bald tires."

"And he's going to be flying our plane today!" added Jorg.

All three of them laughed and loaded the last of the supplies on the plane. Jorg checked the gun for ammunition. Although he said it as a joke, Jorg knew that this was a dangerous mission. He also knew that Hans loved to take dangerous risks. He looked up at the deep blue sky and felt a sense of peace descend on him. Oddly enough, the specter of death seemed both alarming and compelling. It meant an end of life, but also an escape from the burdens of his past. As Hans fired up the propellers, Jorg made a silent prayer to an unknown god, "If I am to die in this war, let it be today. Let it be on such a perfect day."

When the plane left the runway, Jorg finally felt free.

The thought crossed his mind that if they encountered enemy aircraft, he would fire back with poor aim. The thought was so unexpectedly attractive that he breathed a heavy sigh of relief, and sat back in the cockpit, closing his eyes as the plane gained altitude.

But then, a disturbing thought crossed his mind. That meant Hans and Klaus would have to die, too. That meant his unborn child would have no father, and his wife would be left a widow. The burden of those thoughts weighed heavily on him as they flew directly south into the never-ending desert.

After a few hours of flying with no other aircraft in view, Jorg began to tire of the intense vigilance and the drone of the propellers. He hadn't slept well since they'd arrived in Tunisia. He found it hard to get used to the scorching heat and the thick, dry air. He rested his head against the cannon and fell into a hypnotic sleep.

In his dream, he stood on a tiny platform forty feet above the crowd. It was his first live performance on the trapeze with no safety harness and no net. The woman who meant the most to him stood on the opposite platform, gleaming with confidence and poise. She nodded her head slightly as a cue to leap. Both of them swung forward holding firmly to the trapeze. His arms were shaking and his breath was short. They both swung back and forth in unison gaining momentum. His mind and body fought to remember the sequence, his muscles ached and his head was dizzy.

She swung past him and smiled. On the next pass she suddenly let go. It was the wrong moment. He wasn't ready. As she completed her mid-air somersault, she looked up toward him — arms outstretched. But he wasn't there. He was yards away still. She began to fall. He watched in horror as her small, athletic body tumbled down onto the cement floor below.

He awoke with a jolt to the sound of Hans shouting. Jorg looked up, to see a towering wall of sand coming their way fast.

Sandstorm!

It was a danger they had been warned about. The locals spoke of it with fear in their eyes.

And now it was upon them, hitting them like a howling banshee.

Sand and grit filled the propellers as Hans struggled to keep control of the plane. He turned the nose upwards to see if he could get above it, but the plane couldn't climb fast enough.

They were trapped.

Sparks flew out of one propeller as it choked with grit, and the left propeller ground to a horrifying halt.

Hans shouted something to the other two, his words lost in the din of the storm. But Jorg instinctively knew what he was saying.

They were flying with one engine now, and it was clear they would have to make a crash landing in the desert.

The second propeller died and the plane lost its forward momentum. The sandstorm engulfed them. Hans was trying to take the plane down, but he didn't know which way was down. The forward momentum gave way to gravity and ten tons of metal started dropping to the earth.

Jorg's goggles were caked with sand and he could barely breathe. His death wish was becoming a reality, and he was now deeply regretting it. The ground came up much quicker than he had anticipated.

When the plane hit the jolt obliterated everything, its impact so horrendous and final that Jorg lost consciousness.

The nose of the plane hit the sand and thousands of pounds of pressure per square inch crushed the nose of the craft and flipped it over.

Jorg awoke a few moments later, about twenty-five feet from the plane. He could barely see the heap of metal through the thick storm. For a few moments, he just lay there, stunned and disoriented. Were the other two alive? How broken was his body? He felt bruised, winded and weak, but after inspecting himself for several minutes, he seemed — miraculously — to be without injury. Relief filled his body. He knew in that moment that he didn't want to die — he just wanted to escape the horrible and haunting thoughts that kept going through his mind.

"Klaus! Hans! Are you there?" he cried out.

There was no reply.

The sandstorm was so loud they probably couldn't hear him. He pulled himself up onto all fours and crawled toward the wreckage.

Klaus was there, trapped under some metal. He was injured but still alive. His right thigh was cut open and bleeding a fair bit. Jorg took off his belt and bandana and applied pressure until he had effectively slowed down the bleeding.

"Where is Hans?" shouted Klaus.

"I don't know. The front of the plane is completely demolished. I don't think he could have survived."

Jorg crawled over and pried away a sheet a metal.

He saw a bloodied arm hanging out of the wreckage, and recoiled in horror. He reached forward placing his fingers on the pulse. Nothing.

"Hans!"

No reply.

He pried the metal back with all his might and saw the remains of his friend's crumbled body, his entire face smashed in. Jorg felt ill and fell back onto the sand. He lay on his side, trying to regain his equilibrium. Finally, he threw up.

After a few minutes holding his stomach, he managed to crawl his way back to Klaus.

He shouted, "I'm afraid he didn't make it."

They looked at each other, unable to hide their grief and fear. They were no longer innocent boys playing with guns. Jorg buried his head in his hands to escape the stinging sand, and to hide his panic. He looked around the crash site; he needed to get focused.

The fury of the storm was awesome and unrelenting. The sand was quickly covering them. They would be buried by morning if the storm kept up. A feeling of defeat washed through him.

Then he heard Klaus groaning from the pain in his leg. His friend needed someone to take care of him. It was selfish of him to be so self-absorbed.

Jorg looked down at Klaus and shouted, "We will be okay. They will come rescue us. All we need to do is survive this night in the storm."

He went about the task of creating a makeshift shelter out of parts of the wreckage: a tent, some rope, a broken off, hollowed-out cannon for air, and a red swastika banner across the top. He found a canteen of water and some rye bread, and rationed it out between them.

As night came upon them the storm howled on like the ghosts of soldiers screaming their grief at the lost promise of their too-short lives. Finally, Jorg and Klaus surrendered into an exhausted sleep.

They awoke to see the sun rising over a silent desert. The storm had passed and had buried their shelter in six feet of sand. The cannon air hole had saved them. Jorg dragged Klaus into the shade of the plane's wing. He then faced the ominous task of having to pry open the pilot's cockpit enough to get at Hans. Using a broken propeller shaft as a crowbar, Jorg wrenched the metal just far enough. He had to find a new reservoir of strength to lift the remains of his friend out of the plane so he could bury the body. After a few hours of digging a hole in the hot sun, he finally rolled the body into it and covered it up. Exhausted and dehydrated, Jorg collapsed next to Klaus and slept for the next few hours.

Finally, Klaus awoke his friend and requested they do a short memorial for Hans. Klaus offered to recite from memory his favourite passage from the Bible: Chapter one Corinthians, verse thirteen.

*Love is patient, love is kind. It does not envy, it does not boast, it is not proud. It is not rude, it is not self-seeking, it is not easily angered, it keeps no record of wrongs. Love does not delight in evil but rejoices with the truth.*

"That was Hans. I shall be forever grateful that I knew him and that through him I knew more about truth."

Jorg sat back, remembering all his moments with Hans and musing about the gifts of that friendship, "Remember that night he took us out across enemy lines?"

"Yes! I thought the Yanks were going lynch us!"

"But everyone loved Hans. We arrived to their camp and he was chatting away in English."

"Then he gave away all those German sausages for those girlie magazines and the Cuban cigars! I didn't think Wiener Wuerstchen sausages had so much bargaining power."

"I'm working on my English. I'm getting almost as good as Hans," boasted Jorg.

"Yes, you can do a perfect British accent. I heard you in the mess hall. You sound just like King George. Can you do Hans?"

Jorg closed his eyes and imagined himself as the tall Berliner. Clearing his throat he said, "Hey, Birgit, you want to come have a look at my gun collection?"

"Oh, that's too perfect!"

They both howled with laughter. The laughter eventually gave way to tears. Although neither man had probably cried since leaving their childhood, they gave each other the comfort and space to let the grief come.

Some hours later, Jorg found them some dried figs and a flask of whiskey, close to the plane where the supplies had been tossed. They consumed both ravenously. Then they looked out at the makeshift cross that Jorg had rigged up over the grave of Hans.

"I only knew him a few weeks, but I felt closer to him than to most people I have known for years," Jorg said finally.

Klaus' mood had swung with the alcohol and he was struggling with the death of their comrade.

"*Ja*. Thank the fucking war for that, huh?" Klaus replied.

Neither spoke for a few moments after that. "His parents are going to be devastated," Jorg said under his breath.

Klaus shook his head, "He lost his parents last year in that bombing of Berlin. His whole family was killed instantly."

"I didn't know that."

"That's why he started acting so strange. The crazy little shit was seething with rage about this God damn war. They sent him out here to no man's land, to do all these suicide missions because they knew he'd do them. It was just a matter of time for him, I think," Klaus mused.

"I took his dog tags and his wallet," replied Jorg, "I figure someone back home would want them."

"I don't think there is anyone to give them to. You and I, and the other guys at the base were his only family."

Jorg put the items in his pocket, looking down at the makeshift grave.

"There's someone who will want these, Hans. I'll find them. I promise," He vowed to his dead friend.

Then he turned back to the matter of their survival. He made a small fire inside a piece of fuselage using strips of cloth soaked in engine oil. They hoped the rising smoke would attract attention. He then created a makeshift shelter for them under the airplane wing.

"I wonder how far off the flight plan route we are," said Jorg.

"Very far off," replied Klaus.

"What do you mean?"

"Hans wanted to go to Marrakech, remember?"

"So you could get a bloody camera?" Jorg retorted.

"I told him not to bother but he insisted it wouldn't take very long."

"That's insane."

"That's Hans."

"So, do you have any idea where we are?"

"I do, but back at the base, they may not think to come this far south to look for us," Klaus said slowly, "But, hey, maybe the Americans will find us and we can smoke all the Marlboros we want."

"Yeah, right. Just before they put us in the firing line," Jorg replied, "Why didn't you tell me that before?"

"I figure you'd already had enough bad news for one day."

"We need to start walking out then, what's the closest settlement?" Jorg said as he pulled out the map.

"My guess is we are somewhere around here," Klaus said, pointing to the middle of Algeria, on the map, "The closest place with water would be Marada, which I imagine is north of here, maybe about a hundred kilometres. It would mean that you go on your own. I can't walk."

The two men sat is silence for awhile, and then Jorg stood up and surveyed their supplies.

"I'll rig up a stretcher and pull you," he announced.

Klaus looked at him as if he was a madman, "You're sounding as crazy as Hans."

"I can't leave you here, and no one is going to come looking for us here. We have to move before our water runs out."

CHAPTER 31

Klaus opposed Jorg's determined suggestion that they head out into the desert.

"That is pure suicide. We'll need far less water if we stay still. The minute you start moving you are going to need ten times the water — especially if you have to drag me, plus water and food. Its 120 degrees during the day."

"We'll travel at night."

"How will we find shade during the day?"

"I could rig up the tent, and we could sleep under it." Jorg answered, undaunted.

"Maybe, but it would be very easy for us to miss our mark."

"How so? We have a compass."

Klaus pointed to a range of mountains on the map, "You see that mountain range? There is so much iron in the rock that it throws off all the accuracy of most compasses in this region. We can't trust it."

"Okay, then. We'll use celestial navigation. You said that was your specialty at university," Jorg exclaimed.

"Actually, I studied astronomy, but I could fake it. But if we are off by just a fraction, we could miss that little oasis by miles. It's very small. It's just an oil patch with a few palm trees and a pond."

Jorg paced up and down the wreckage, wrestling with the problem, and finally said, "I'll go crazy sitting here under the wing of this plane day in and day out."

"Just give it one more day with the fire, the banner and the flares. If no one comes to rescue us, then let's talk about it again."

Jorg stared at his comrade, unhappy with the idea, but not looking forward to the prospect of dragging a resisting cripple across the desert, either. He nodded finally, accepting the compromise.

When the scorching rays disappeared behind the horizon, they lay on their backs, looking up at the dazzling array of stars. Klaus began to tell Jorg legends of the constellations in the sky: Aries, Ursa Major and Ursa Minor, The Big and Little Dipper, Orion, and Gemini.

"You know so much," Jorg said, after the sixth fascinating tale, "Why are you studying engineering instead of astronomy?"

"Astronomy doesn't offer a stable life, and I am married now. It was my hobby during my childhood. I applied for graduate school in Astronomy, but then I had to join the war effort."

"You can finish it when the war is over. That's what I plan to do. I have my undergraduate and one year of graduate studies, in philosophy. I'd eventually like to be a professor."

"How can you already be in graduate school? You said you are only twenty-years-old," asked Klaus.

"I skipped two grades in school."

"Oh, you are one of those super-smart people. You probably don't need to study at all."

"Not as hard as the others usually. But I like to study. I can read a book a day."

"That's amazing. What is your IQ?"

"I think I am in the ninety-eighth percentile."

"I scored in the 90th percentile, and I was at the top of my class. You should join MENSA."

"What's that?"

"It's for intellectuals, smart cookies like you," Klaus teased, "Join as soon as we get back, if we ever get back. It will open doors for you."

"I will remember that," Jorg replied, intrigued. He smiled at the thought, enjoying his first feelings of hope since the crash, "I think this war will end soon. It can't go on."

"What makes you say that?" asked Klaus.

"Three nights ago, when you were studying your English book, Hans and I met up with two American soldiers at 3:00 a.m. Remember? We traded bratwurst for a case of Marlboros."

"Oh, that's where you got them all from. Did you talk to them?"

"Yes, they are very friendly. They don't like the war either. But, here's the thing. They said the Germans are losing badly on the Russian front. They are decimating us."

"Is that really true? How come we don't know about that?"

"Hitler won't let that kind of information out in the news. He thinks that will turn people against him."

"The majority of us are against him anyway. Let them win. Let them liberate us from that lunatic."

"I feel the same way."

They sat in tense silence for a few moments.

"We could be executed for talk like that," Klaus whispered, as if afraid to be overhead. "Remember what they did to Marc when he put on that fake moustache and started marching around like Hitler?"

"Yes, I know," Jorg reached over and touched his friend's arm, "But believe me, I'd never say anything about your comment."

"Me neither."

Jorg went over to the plane, and rationed out a half a cup of water each and the last of the figs and bread.

"Eat well, my friend, today our fasting begins," He grabbed a bit of fat at his waist, making a face, "I could stand to lose a bit of my love handles."

"*Ja*. Me too," Klaus seconded, catching his cavalier mood, "Fasting is good for the soul. They do it in India all the time as a form of spiritual cleansing. I will need to cleanse myself of this war at sometime in life. There are times I wish I had more courage to oppose what has been going on. Did you hear about that girl Sophie Scholl and her brother Hans?" asked Klaus.

"No."

"They were students at my university and were caught giving out anti-Hitler leaflets. It was just a peaceful demonstration. Within five days of being caught they were both beheaded."

"Beheaded?" Jorg blurted out, stunned, "They beheaded a twenty-one-year-old girl?"

He nodded, "I knew Sophie. She was a good person and so courageous. I wish I had her kind of bravery to stand up against the Nazis."

"*Ja,* and if you did, you'd have no head now."

"Yes, but I'd have a clear conscience."

"But you haven't perpetrated these crimes."

"That's true, but I am a willing participant. Out here with death staring us in the face, I can't help but look back on my life. There is not too much to be proud of. I let my life be taken over by a madman."

"But you went to Napola, too. They forced us into accepting Nazism. It was brutal," argued Jorg.

"It was brutal. But, nobody *made me* accept it."

"Yes, but I would have been killed or tortured if I didn't play their game."

"Maybe. Maybe not. Regardless, my friend, you have to take responsibility for where your life has ended up. You can't tell me you didn't have a choice."

Jorg was about to defend his position when the thought occurred that he could have chosen differently several times. Thousands of choice points then flashed before his eyes like stars in the desert sky. In fact, every moment of his life he could have chosen a different path.

"Maybe if you were forced to go to Napola at seven-years-old like some of them were," Klaus offered.

"No, I chose to go there of my own accord at sixteen," he said feeling the shame creep into his chest.

Klaus continued, "I chose to go, too. I thought it would be good for my future. *Ha!* We are a nation of cowards, thinking Hitler would give us back our security and instead he's taking us to hell. Sophie was a sweet, caring twenty-one-year old girl when they executed her. I knew her. I *knew her*, God damn it! How could the bastards do that? How did our society become so savage?"

"That's nothing. I was at Birkenau," Jorg started, then stopped abruptly. The lump in his throat was too painful to continue.

"What? What is going on there?"

"In the news, they say it is for prisoners of war. It's not. They take Jews there, and handicapped people, and communists, and Gypsies, and anyone who says anything against Hitler. They take away all their possessions, make them strip down and tell them to go have a shower. Then they march them into a huge chamber, and instead of showers they gas the poor bastards to death. They are killing hundreds of people a day and throwing their bodies into huge pits."

Klaus stared at him for several seconds, "Tell me that isn't true."

Jorg stared back unblinking.

Klaus continued, "They said the Jews are emigrating."

"No, they are exterminating them. Women and children, too."

"That's genocide," Klaus said under his breath, "The Germans are going to go down in history as war criminals."

Jorg nodded, "I was at the gate. I was on watch with my rifle, in case anyone tried to escape. Something happened when I was there. I did something that I would be killed for if they knew."

"What is that?"

"I can't tell you."

"Why not? You know I won't tell a soul. Perhaps you need to get it off your chest."

Jorg inhaled painfully, and looked up at the brilliant starry night, "Okay, I will tell you. I will tell you everything, but you take it with you to your grave."

"I swear."

Jorg took in a deep breath and began. He poured out his heart to his friend, the story taking on a dimension and character as he told it, coming into being like a living entity, casting shadows around them as the telling lengthened into the night.

As he listened, Klaus lay against his backpack in stunned silence.

Finally when it was over, Klaus clasped his friend's hand and said, "I'm amazed you've kept it all to yourself all this time."

For the second time in a week, Jorg could feel his eyes stinging with tears.

Klaus struggled to sit up and look his companion in the eye, "Don't worry, my friend, I don't judge you for who you are or what you've done. We will *all* be standing before the creator and praying for forgiveness when this is all over."

Jorg swallowed and choked out his next words, "Thank you."

"I believe there is something that may be done if we ever make it out of here," Klaus offered. With that, the injured man proceeded to outline an idea that sparked a hope of restitution in Jorg's heart.

The next day they burned a fire all day and shot off the last of their flares. As dusk settled, Jorg said, "I think we should move out of here. I would rather die trying to save ourselves, than waste away here. When you were sleeping, I created some makeshift crutches for you."

Klaus stared at his friend for a moment and nodded, surrendering to the logic of Jorg's argument. Together, they managed to get Klaus to his feet. Then he took the crutches and tried them, finding that he was able to put a little bit of weight on his injured leg.

"It will be slow, but it might work," he offered gamely.

"Better slow than dead," replied Jorg.

Jorg loaded up his backpack with the last of the water, the map, the compass, and some other lightweight supplies. They said goodbye to Hans' grave, the wreckage of the plane, and their not-so-cozy shelter. As they headed out into the silent desert night, Jorg prayed that he wouldn't come to regret the decision to leave the plane.

## CHAPTER 32

As the night deepened and the heavens shone over the vast expanse of the desert, they plotted their course. They followed the North Star and prayed for guidance. They took frequent breaks to let Klaus rest, but still managed to cover several miles by the time the sun began to rise. Jorg rigged up their shelter and they huddled under the tent canvas, seeking its protection from the intense heat.

By midday, Klaus had become delirious and was talking to himself. Jorg had heard about what the desert could do to your sanity. His own mental state was feeling like quicksand. He crawled up onto a rise to shake the feeling. He stood there, shading his eyes as he peered over the flat, brown expanse to the north. After several minutes, he noticed a tiny, black line along the horizon that seemed to be moving. At first he thought it was a mirage. He shook his head, blinked his eyes and looked again. The line was still there. He pulled out his binoculars and looked closer. It was a caravan!

He could just make out some camels and lines of people walking. He remembered hearing stories of the Bedouin tribes that traversed the desert. Perhaps their luck was turning. He scrambled down the rise and began to make a fire. Once the smoke was rising high in the sky, he looked in his binoculars again. He couldn't see the shimmering black line against the horizon anymore. It had disappeared. He shook his head and looked again. This time he saw something.

A few members of the caravan seemed to be moving toward them.

He placed a wet compress on his friend's forehead and offered him a shot of whiskey. Once Klaus seemed alert again, Jorg explained the situation and let him look through the binoculars.

"That is amazing. It does look like they are walking this way. How long before you think they will arrive here?" Klaus asked, excited.

"I would say an hour, maybe longer," replied Jorg.

"Our luck has indeed turned," Klaus responded. He paused, thinking, "Now that it looks like we will survive I think we should commit to carrying out our plan. Bury all your identification in the sand before they arrive. We will tell them that your name is Hans Hellermann — you have all his identification, and the two of you look alike if you wear his glasses. Once we get back to civilization, we will split up. You turn yourself over to the Americans. They will not shoot you; they will just take you to a prisoner of war camp. Not so bad, those in America. I will call Colonel Reich at Marada. I will tell him that Jorg Frei died in the plane crash and that you, Hans Hellermann, were taken by the Americans."

"What if I meet up with the Germans before the Americans?"

"Then pretend you are a Bedouin. You have dark feature like them, and you are such a good mimic. Listen to them closely and practice."

"They won't let me pretend I am one of them."

"It's worth a try."

Jorg nodded cautiously.

Klaus added, "Look, I am sure they will send me back home with this injury. Once I am back home and well, I will try to see if I can go to Birkenau."

"It might be too late by now, though."

"I will go anyway. We must give it a try — as we discussed, and see if I can finish what you tried to start," replied Klaus.

By midday, three Kufra Bedouin tribesmen on camels arrived to see what the fire in the middle of the desert was about. Upon finding the two half-dead men, they offered them food, water, first aid and a safe passage back to civilization.

It was another four days before they finally arrived at the small outpost of Marada, where they could get medical help and use a radio. Jorg sat with the Bedouins, drinking the well water as Klaus received further treatment for his wounds and recovery from sun stroke.

"Give me more food," Jorg said to the other tribesmen, using the Bedouin sign language he had learned over the past few days. He had so easily morphed into being one of them that the local Europeans couldn't tell. He wore the layered and flowing white robe that deflected the sun's hot rays. He had learned how to wind the white fabric around his head and neck as protection. His skin had turned so dark from the sun that he looked identical to several of the Bedouin men.

"He is so like my brother, no?" laughed the Bedouin medicine man to his cohorts, "Okay, do Mouji again."

Jorg smiled and looked over at Mouji, who seemed eager to be mimicked. Mouji had a habit of twitching his eyebrows in bizarre patterns whenever he was excited. Jorg breathed in regally with flared nostrils, and then stroked his goatee beard as his eyebrows went in all directions.

The Bedouin men roared with laughter, and Mouji threw an orange peel at Jorg, "You are very good. You should go in show business!"

Klaus rejoined them. He was now moving more swiftly on his brand new crutches. He looked nervous, "It took me a long time to radio through. I managed to talk to a corporal. Apparently, the British have shattered our defences on the Mareth Line. We've surrendered our territory in Northern Africa. There is a good chance I will not get out either, and become a prisoner of war. They are attacking the German evacuation fleets going back to Sicily. They say I'm on my own."

"What about that fellow piloting the supply plane for the oil workers? Ask him. Maybe he'll get you out of here," suggested Jorg.

Klaus nodded and went to seek out the pilot.

After another half hour, Klaus returned, "That was a great idea. He said he will put me on board and drop me in Tripoli. I'll have a better chance from there. We leave midday tomorrow!"

"Excellent. When you get there, you could get on one of the fishing vessels going back over to Sicily."

Klaus nodded warily, and the two men went to set up their tent.

The next morning, as the Bedouins packed the last of the gear back onto the camels, Klaus and Jorg stood together looking out over the golden sand.

They stood silently for several minutes. Then Klaus looked at Jorg, and smiled, "This is it then. We part here, heading to two different worlds. It has been an incredible journey, my friend. I know it sounds trite, but you saved my life. I would never have survived out there without you. I hope I have the chance to repay you somehow."

Jorg looked down at the sand. He could feel a pressure in his chest, "You don't owe me anything. But I am going to miss you. It seems like this war is all about saying goodbye over and over again, whether you want to or not."

Klaus put a hand on his friend's shoulder, "Then I hope this is not goodbye. Write from your POW camp, and I will write you from Germany. But you must be Hans Hellermann from now on. Here is my address," Klaus handed a crumpled up piece of paper into his friend's chapped hand, "Don't worry about your situation. I have an idea. I know a man in the Munich SS. I will get him to find me a posting at Birkenau."

"How will you do it once you get there? It's very dangerous. You could be killed," stressed Jorg.

"I am a smart cookie, too," Klaus grinned, "I will be okay. It will be my way to repay you. I thought about it this morning, as I watched the sun come up. If it works, this small act will allow me to live with myself once this insane war is over. I will let you know as soon as I know."

They hugged each other, and Jorg felt the pressure in his chest melt. He released his friend and picked up his canteen. As he lashed it onto the saddle of his camel he felt the tears rolling down his sunburnt cheeks.

Klaus watched his friend join the Bedouin tribe, and then shouted out, "We will need a code name for our plan when we write to each other."

Jorg turned, hesitating for a moment.

"The Big Dipper," he shouted back.

Klaus smiled, nodding.

"Yes. That was our way home. The Big Dipper."

The days traveling under the hot sun were exhausting, and the slow pace gave Jorg a lot of time to contemplate the future ... *his new life.* If he survived the POW camp and the war, there was no way he could come back to Germany and pretend to be Hans. He would need to find yet another identity at some point in time.

For seven more days they traveled before finally arriving in Marada. During that time, Jorg developed a relationship with a young, unmarried woman in their tribe. Her name was Aliba and she was an exotic dark-skinned beauty only too ready to become his bride and consort. They couldn't communicate with language but they spent long nights entwined in each other's arms in his small tent under the brilliant starry skies, communicating with their bodies, sharing in a way he'd never experienced before. Her refined presence and unbridled display of love nurtured his lost soul back to life. As they approached the outpost, Jorg had an idea, and shared it with the shaman of the Bedouin tribe, the man they referred to as the Dervish.

"What if I just stayed traveling with you?" he asked the Dervish, "If I give myself up here, they will put me in a prisoner of war camp for who knows how long. I feel at home here with you and your people. You can put me to work on anything. I learn quickly."

"It's funny that you should ask that," The old shaman replied, "We talked about it in council this morning when you were sleeping. Aliba wants you as her husband. Many of us want you to stay with us. But El Aba, he thinks a foreigner will bring bad luck. He is the eldest. We cannot override his decision."

Jorg nodded solemnly, not protesting, but inside he was shaking with sadness and disappointment.

Early the next morning, El Aba went to tell the Americans about the German man traveling with them. Jorg awoke in his tent to the sight of three riflemen holding him at gunpoint. The American soldiers escorted him with handcuffs to meet their General.

General Wilcox stood only five feet, five inches tall, but had the bearing of a much larger man. He was lighting a Marlboro when Jorg arrived at his tent.

"Want one?" offered General Wilcox, looking up at his prisoner.

"Please," replied Jorg.

"You speak English?"

Jorg nodded.

The General studied Jorg for a moment.

"Your papers say you are Hans Hellermann, a pilot with the Luftwaffe. How is it that that you arrived here alone with Bedouins?"

"Our plane went down in a sandstorm. One of the men was killed instantly."

"What was his name?" asked General Wilcox as he began filling out his report.

"Jorg Frei," Jorg replied, without hesitating, "He was the gunner."

Jorg watched as the General wrote down Jorg's full name with the word "deceased" next to it. He took a drag of his cigarette, trying not to let the shaking in his hand show.

"Was there anyone else on the plane?" the General inquired.

"Klaus Meinhardt."

"What happened to him?"

"We parted company in Marada. He contacted our German commander and asked for a plane to pick him up."

"Why didn't you go with him?" the General asked, looking up at this question.

Jorg hadn't anticipated that question. He looked the General directly in the eye, trying to judge the man's character. Jorg thought he sensed a warmth and compassion behind the General's steely blue gaze. He would have to hope he was right in that assessment. He didn't have a choice.

"Because I can't go back to my home in Vienna," Jorg finally answered, "If I do, I will be executed."

CHAPTER 33

After the General heard Jorg's story, his response was both compassionate and skeptical.

"You will still need to go to a POW camp. You have been an enlisted man with the Luftwaffe. I have to send you there. But when the war is over — and the Germans will have to surrender soon — we will see what we can do about getting you U.S. citizenship."

"Thank you" Jorg replied, relieved. It was the best he could hope for. For him, the war was now over. A week later Jorg was on a boat to New York. Once in New York, he was loaded with all the captured Germans onto a train and shipped to a tiny place called Trinidad, Colorado. He had convinced the General that he should continue to be identified as Hans Hellermann. Because if word got back to Germany that Jorg Frei was still alive, his wife and child could be stripped of all rights, and maybe something worse.

It was a fairly easy life at the camp, and Jorg got used to being called Hans. He even acted wildly, in the juvenile way that Hans used to do. Perhaps he was paying tribute to his friend's spirit, or simply taking advantage of the rare opportunity to recreate himself as a different person.

One fellow named Anton shared "Hans'" love of joking around. Anton was a soldier from Hamburg and only eighteen years old. He was short and impish with white-blonde hair, freckles and a mischievous grin.

Together they dreamed up a series of plots to keep themselves occupied during the long days and nights in the Colorado wilderness. They short-sheeted their bunkmates' beds, made a habit of hiding the towels of showering inmates, and made friends with the delivery truck drivers so they could run an underground market of cigarettes and the cleverly-disguised erotic magazines known as Tijuana Bibles.

After losing his two close friends, Jorg felt cheered by the companionship of this amusing fellow. When he joined the Hitler Youth, he had found it hard to feel friendly toward any of the other young men. Mostly he lived in fear of being found out. Being in Africa, and now here in Colorado, he finally discovered other young men he could relate to.

"Did you ever kill anyone?" Anton asked casually one day as they were folding laundry.

"Did you?" replied Jorg trying to sidestep the question.

"I asked first."

Jorg didn't answer.

"Never. Not once," replied Anton.

Jorg continued folding towels in silence.

"Are you ashamed of me for that?" asked Anton.

"Not at all. I'm happy for you. You'll be able to sleep better at night."

"So?" urged Anton as he stepped in closer to listen.

"I don't want to discuss that."

"Come on! I won't tell a soul."

"Sorry, I won't ever tell anyone, Anton. Never."

"You're such a secretive bugger."

A sergeant walked by with a clipboard and peered up at them, "You two, I need you in latrine duty — now!"

Ⅴ

After a month at the camp, Jorg decided to write Klaus. He wanted to know what was happening at Birkenau. He had to wait several months before receiving a reply.

The day the letter came from Klaus's widow, Jorg lay in his bunk, reading and re-reading the letter. "*Klaus was executed as a traitor,*" the letter read. For three days and nights, Jorg hardly slept. He felt responsible for the death of this friend, and the guilt haunted him. Unanswered questions broiled in his mental landscape. Did any part of the plan work, or was it a complete failure? Frau Meinhardt never explained what happened. It must have failed. The death of his friend had clearly been in vain. How would he ever live with himself now?

Anton brought his friend food each day, but Jorg just pushed it away.

"Why don't you tell me what was in that damn letter?" Anton finally blurted out, exasperated, "Did someone you love die?"

Jorg said nothing.

Anton studied his depressed friend lying on the bunk, his playful disposition evaporated now, swallowed in melancholy. He sat down at the end of the bunk.

"I had a childhood friend who lived next door," he told Jorg, "We did everything together until we both had to go to the Hitler Youth camp. I told him everything; we had no secrets from each other. Our mothers were best friends, too," he signed and clutched his arms around his chest.

He continued, "They sent us both to different schools. I missed him so much, more than I had ever missed anyone before. When I went home at Christmas I brought a harmonica that I had found for him in a little shop in Berlin. I used all my savings to buy it. He was such a good player, and this was the best instrument of its kind. I couldn't wait to see him open the gift on Christmas Eve.

When I got home, my mother and his mother sat me down at the kitchen table. His mother had bloodshot eyes. She told me that one of the other boys at the camp had shot my friend by mistake. They were just playing around with the guns and one boy pulled the trigger. The bullet went right into my friend's temple."

Jorg rolled over in his bunk, and put a pillow over his head.

Anton shook his head, feeling foolish, "Ah, shit. I don't know why I told you that morbid story. I guess I just want you to understand that I know what it's like to lose a friend."

He sat on the lower bed chewing on his thumbnail for the next several minutes, staring at the cement floor. Then he brightened suddenly, "I know a joke. Want to hear it?"

Jorg said nothing.

"One of the truck drivers told it to me yesterday. In New York City, a man gives his shoes to a shoemaker to be resoled and forgets about them. Ten years later he finds the repair stub in the attic, and just for the hell of it, goes back to the shop and presents the ticket. The owner of the store disappears into the back for a minute, then returns and says, 'They'll be ready next Tuesday.'"

Jorg sighed.

Anton grinned and slapped his friend on the back, "Come on. That's a pretty funny one, huh?"

Jorg continued to lie with his back to Anton, and said nothing.

Finally, Anton shrugged and stood up to leave. All of sudden Jorg hurled the pillow at Anton, hitting him in the back of the head.

"Hey!" shouted Anton as he grabbed a pillow from another bed and hurled it back at Jorg. The two of them then engaged in a wild mêlée, grabbing and tossing pillows from at least eight bunk beds. By the time they were done, goose feathers lay everywhere, and the two young men lay on the floor, laughing until they both cried.

It would be almost two more years at the camp before the radio announcer declared that the war was officially over. On hearing the announcement, Anton, Jorg and one other soldier broke open one of the plumbing pipes and sprayed water on everyone. Inmates jumped around, soaking wet, hugging each other.

"Finally, we can leave this place and become Americans!" shouted Anton, "Come on, do your American accent for us!"

The men all shouted in chorus to hear Jorg's impersonation.

Jorg smiled and cleared his throat, then declared, "Y'all ain't a-fixin' to go back to that there hell-hole called Europe, are youse? I don't never want to go back there. I'm right tired of them yellow-bellied pole dogs. I'm a-hootin' and a-hollerin to stay right here in this big ass land o' plenty!"

The prisoners roared, cheering and slapping each other. Anton grabbed a hose and pointed it at his friend, spraying him, while five others jumped on him and wrestled. Their celebration went into the night. They were all delirious. It was over. Their long nightmare was over.

The next day Jorg sent a letter to General Wilcox asking him to look into Jorg's immigration status for the United States. He begged the General not to be sent back to Europe. The reply back arrived three weeks later and read:

> *Dear Sir,*
>
> *We are sorry to inform you that your status for immigration into the United States of America has been denied. Please accept our sincerest apologies. Our quotas for 1945 are full. Feel free contact us again next year.*

Desperate to find another way out of deportation back to Austria, Jorg contacted his old acquaintance Laszlo Goldstein, who was now a practicing solicitor in England. Laszlo, as usual, was able to work a miracle. Just the week before the prisoners were scheduled for departure, Jorg received a telegram that he would be granted landed immigrant status in Canada if he did a six-month stint at a northern mining camp.

"Look at this," Jorg said, excited, holding up his letter to Anton.

Anton grabbed the letter and read it, "You are going to be a Canadian — a Canuck! You lucky bastard. I am bloody envious. See if you can get me into the country too. I don't want to go back to Germany. Everything's gone to shit there."

Jorg laughed, "You're right. I'm sure that northern mining camp could use a crazy Kraut like you. I will write my friend Laszlo immediately and see what we can do."

That night at dusk, the two men strolled the barracks grounds, reminiscing. Then, they sat down leaning their backs against the barbed-wire fence. They watched as the last rays of sun went over the horizon, filling the sky with brilliant multi-coloured cloud formations, as if the end of the war had signalled the heavens that there was room on earth for beauty once again.

"Cigarette?" offered Anton.

"*Bitte,*" Jorg replied.

Anton passed him the cigarette, his gaze leaving the heavens, and resting on the grounds of their prison.

"Strangely enough, I think I'll miss this place," Anton said, as he took a long, slow drag off his Marlboro.

Jorg nodded, "Yes, me too. It's been a hell of a lot better to be here than on the battlefield."

"On the other hand, we get to be with women again. I don't even remember what that feels like anymore!" Anton laughed.

"Do you think your girlfriend waited for you?" asked Jorg.

"Probably not. Why should she? It's been two years. She stopped writing a while ago."

"I'm sorry to hear that. But there are plenty of great women out there. Say, do you prefer the blondes or brunettes?"

"Always the blonde ones," Anton replied with a smirk, "Hey, why shouldn't blondes be given coffee breaks?"

"Why?" asked Jorg.

"It takes too long to retrain them!" Anton said before busting out laughing at his own joke.

"Very funny," Jorg said, chuckling, "Okay, here's one. How do you change a blonde's mind?"

"How?"

"You blow in her ear!"

"*Ach*. God. That's even worse than mine!" Anton replied, giggling in delight, "Okay, here's the worst of all … what does a blonde put behind her ears to make herself more attractive?"

Jorg's reply was cut off by the sudden, sharp report of gunfire.

"Whoa, where did that come from?" he exclaimed, reacting to the sound. He looked out at the field to see if they were doing target practice, then turned back to Anton, remembering the joke, "I don't know … what?"

Anton didn't answer.

Jorg peered closer at Anton. His friend was hunched forward.

"Are you laughing so hard you can't even finish the punch line?" asked Jorg.

Still Anton didn't answer.

Jorg pushed on his friend's shoulder, and Anton's head tilted sideways.

It was then that Jorg saw the gunshot wound, right between his friend's eyes. Anton's eyes were wide open, and staring up, unseeing, at the beautiful crimson sky.

CHAPTER 34

"The guard said Anton was trying to escape," the prison warden said, as he filled out the death report.

"We were just sitting there having a cigarette, like we always do at dusk!" Jorg shouted at him, enraged and shaking.

"You will keep your voice down, soldier!" the warden ordered, "It was obviously a mistake."

"Why would he try to escape? The war is over, for God's sake!"

"He did want to immigrate to America. Perhaps he was trying to do it illegally."

"He would have told me. We were just sitting against the fence! I have been a guard at a prison camp. I know what it looks like when someone is trying to escape. That guard did it on purpose," Jorg said accusingly.

"Why on earth would he do that?" replied the warden.

"Because he is Jewish," interjected one of the other prisoners.

"He wasn't Jewish, and even if he was, he wouldn't just shoot someone without reason," the deputy warden argued.

"That same guard tried to shoot at me when I was outside having a cigarette," another prisoner added, "He is taking revenge on us Germans.

We are not all Hitlers. That guard is insane. You need to put him in the lunatic asylum."

At that, the prisoners broke into a screaming match with the warden and his deputy. Heartsick, Jorg simply left to go sit outside.

It seemed as if fate was against him. Once again, someone he had grown to love had been taken from him. But who was being punished? Him? Or the ones he cared about, for getting too close to him? The irony was that the guard could just have easily shot him. Why was he spared from death again? Did God have something important in mind for him? Or was it just to suffer another loss?

The boat ride back across the Atlantic was long, slow and painful. Why did he have to go back to Europe, Jorg wondered? Why couldn't he just go straight to Canada from the United States? As soon as the boat docked in France a courier was waiting with a package for Jorg.

The guard threw the envelope down on Jorg's bunk as he was packing his belongings to disembark.

"Package for Hans Hellermann." the man growled.

Jorg grasped the package. The return address was from a law firm in London, England. As soon as the guard left, Jorg tore it open.

There were documents and an old photo of Jorg. His name on the document was listed as George Freeman. Laszlo Goldstein had anglicized his given name. It was nice to somehow have a form of his name back.

He was eager to arrange for passage to Canada. The mining camp wanted to know what date he could start, but the French were in no hurry to release their German POWs.

Conditions in the French POW camp were horrendous, far below the standards in America. The command from on high was that German POWs should be treated reasonably well throughout the US between 1942-1944. In part, this was to encourage other Germans to surrender and in part to encourage the German military to treat Western POWs decently, which they did for the most part.

However, during the final collapse of Nazi Germany, about five million Germans ended up as POWs throughout Europe. At this point in time, the Allied powers had decided at the highest level to repudiate the Geneva Conventions. Under the Geneva Conventions, POWs were to be sent home within months of the end of the war.

The Allies instead decided to hold any POWs, who were now designated as "disarmed enemy forces" as slave labourers, providing "labour reparations" to rebuild the damage inflicted by Nazi aggression.

The Germans had held millions of French POWs as slave labourers, so they decided to be particularly harsh in return. From April through July 1945, the prisoners received only starvation rations, which kept many soldiers on the brink of death. Hundreds of thousands of POWs were kept for many weeks out in the open, with no shelter apart from what they might dig in the ground, and nothing to sit or lie on, above the mud and puddles, apart from their own helmets and greatcoats.

Jorg was held at the Rheinberg camp, which was one of the worst. Revelation of the mass murder in German concentration camps provoked hatred toward Germans in general. It was June 29, 1945, and the prisoners were huddled around a radio, listening desperately for news of their release.

General Lucius D. Clay, Eisenhower's Deputy, stated *"I feel that the Germans should suffer from hunger and from cold as I believe such suffering is necessary to make them realize the consequences of a war which they caused."*

He pressed his back against the barbwire fence, sipping on cold broth as the drizzle soaked his bones. It was seven months since he landed at Rheinberg. He now weighed only 135 pounds, which was 45 pounds less than normal. His ribs protruded and his cheeks sunk in. He pondered his responsibility in this mad downward spiral of hatred that had consumed Europe these last six years. What could he have done differently? In the haze of near starvation, he found no answers to his questions.

None of the men he knew from the POW camp in Colorado were there with him. All the other men were strangers. After losing two of his closest friends, Jorg was developing an aversion for risking friendships again. A man named Rudolf from Hamburg sat huddled up near him. He was holding a crumpled letter from his sister and moaning. He shoved the letter in Jorg's face.

"Did you hear what happened? Did you hear?"

Jorg sighed, "No, what happened?"

"Poland got all the German provinces east of the rivers Oder and Neisse," the man said, looking intently at Jorg and another half-dead soldier.

Jorg vaguely nodded, squinting his eyes as a torrent of rain splattered their faces.

Rudolf continued, "That's where my family lived. Over thirteen million Germans were ordered out of their homes in just a few hours, leaving behind all their belongings. They could only take along what they could carry or pull along in a cart. Most of the people were old people, or mothers and their children.

"My family has lived on that land for five generations, farming that land. Now it no longer belongs to them. They have nothing. They had to trek hundreds of kilometres to get to the new German border. My parents could hardly carry anything because they are old, and my father had a heart condition.

"I just found out they both died on the side of the road. No one buried them. They died of exhaustion. My sister went crazy and just abandoned her baby and her three-year-old little girl on the side of the road. She couldn't keep carrying them. I don't know what she was thinking. She just left them there to die.

"She dragged herself to the town of Goerlitz where she could cross the river Neisse. She didn't know where to go. Schools, hospitals, railroad stations, every public building still standing are occupied to the hilt by displaced people. Everyone there has a story about how their loved ones died of hunger, fatigue or random killings. She wants to kill herself now. And I can't do anything to help her."

Jorg could see tears stinging the man's eyes and anguish contorting his face, "I am sorry for your loss, so sorry."

As he said those words, fears for his own family's safety overwhelmed him. Everyone in his family was a target now, on both sides.

Another man named Marc chimed in, "It's open season on all Germans. No one cares about our story. We are the demons, the ones to blame for everything."

Another soldier, Franz, said, "Regardless of whether or not we supported Nazism."

"I never did," said Rudolf, "I always hated everything about it!"

"What are you saying?" Marc challenged him, "Hitler gave us hope. He had a vision of what the world could be, but people didn't get it. They still can't."

"I got caught up in the hype, and the power and the glory of it all when I was in Hitler Youth. But now it all seems like madness," sighed Jorg.

"Then you've lost your strength to the masses, my friend. We are the superior race!" shouted Marc.

"If you say that any louder we are all going to be shot in the head," warned Franz.

"I don't, in any way, feel superior to other people. Right now I feel utterly inferior," Jorg muttered.

"Yes, maybe we deserve what we are getting," added Franz.

"Our parents, our women and our children don't deserve it," cried Rudolf.

The other men nodded. A moment later, a series of gunshots echoed through the misty air. Through the fog, Jorg could barely make out two French soldiers tossing the lifeless bodies of several German POW prisoners into a mass grave.

By now, Jorg's wife, his family and friends would have found out that he died in the Sahara Desert. Would they have a funeral for him? What would people say about him? What did his child look like? Was it a boy or girl? His father would be filled with grief. Was there a way he could get word to them that he was still alive, without getting caught? Probably not. Jorg wasn't even sure he would survive the camp.

After ten months they finally released him. On his first day of freedom Jorg read in the newspaper that Hermann Göering, the head of the Luftwaffe, just before being sentenced to death had this to say: *"The people can always be brought to the bidding of the leaders. All you have to do is tell them they are being attacked, and denounce the peacemakers for lack of patriotism and exposing the country to danger. It works the same in any country."*

It struck Jorg that the leaders on both sides of this war had played the people like pawns, using their ingenuity, talents and their lives as fodder for their fear games. He decided to add the quotation to his quotation book in black fountain pen so he would never forget it.

As soon as he got his strength back and some money in his pocket, "George Freeman" bought a ticket from Calais, France to Quebec City, Canada. He stood on the dock, waiting to board the *Viking Princess*. He had put all documents, sketches, photos and memorabilia into one box; anything that linked him to his other lives in Europe. He took one last look at the contents then went to heave the box out to sea. Just then a dockyard worker shouted at him in French. He understood enough of the language to know that he wasn't supposed to litter there.

He stuffed the box back in his trunk, and vowed to throw it from the ship's stern once they were safely out at sea.

But that moment never came, because the seas were rough most of the journey, and George Freeman spent most of the time lying on his bed, throwing up into a porcelain basin. Even rougher than the seas were his two bunkmates, Hank and Josh. They had introduced themselves as two members of the 2nd Canadian Corps that had helped liberate the Netherlands. After several months of post-war clean up duty, the two young men were eager to come back to their families in Saskatchewan.

"You puking like this is causing my buddy, Josh, here to lose his cookies, too."

"Sorry ... I ... am very sick. I can't help it ..."

"What are you anyway? A Kraut?"

"No."

"You sure sound like a Kraut. Hey, Josh, we got ourselves a Boxhead as a roommate."

Josh was holding his stomach. He glanced up and shrugged.

"We got ourselves here a Jew Killer, ain't you boss?"

"No, I wasn't ..."

"What are you doin' coming to our country? We don't want you."

The seas lurched and the massive ocean liner keeled sharply to one side. The boys grabbed handles and poles to steady themselves. George, in his sick stupor, had forgotten to respond to him using his carefully articulated American accent. The combination of dread and nausea almost made him pass out.

"Maybe we should throw him overboard, eh Josh?" Hank looked over at Josh who nodded listlessly with his eyes half closed. He continued, "It's our patriotic duty to protect our country from vermin infestation."

George flinched and grabbed the railing near his bed.

Hank shoved George's shoulder and shouted, "Get off this god damned boat you — Jew Killer."

George peered up into the boy's anguished face.

Nineteen year old Hank Wright was not Jewish, but he signed up for overseas duty because he wanted to have an adventure, to be admired for helping save the world from Fascism, and to prove he was made of something.

It turned out to be an adventure alright, an adventure straight into Hell. The living conditions were horrible; he saw people he cared about killed, their bodies ripped to pieces. One by one he saw them fed to the soil knowing he could be next. When his unit liberated a concentration camp, he met hundreds of half-dead skeletons clutching barbed wire fences. For weeks afterwards he had nightmares about that enormous pit of fly-infested corpses, sunken eyeballs crested up to the heavens.

His overseas *adventure* would burn a hole in his soul for the rest of his life. Hank glared down at George and raised one fist above his head.

George had seen that look before from people who didn't know the truth about him. It was a look that said he was a savage; that he was a psychopathic killer who didn't deserve life.

Memories flooded into George's mind, flashes of all the faces he'd seen, of all the lives, of all places that he'd been and not been, of the person he could have been, and all the times when the road intersected. He saw all those choices splitting off into genealogical lines, like blood vessels reaching further and further into infinite possibilities, until they all merged back into one moment. This moment.

Hank pounded his fist on George's head, then kicked him in the shin, then in the back and finally in the stomach which made George throw up violently. Hank and Josh recoiled and for a moment stood there stunned. Finally, they grabbed their belongings and escaped out the exit.

He lay his head back down on the pillow, holding his aching gut, dizzy and disgusted, hurting all over. There was no one there to help him get well or to support him in starting a new life. He was completely alone. Coming to Canada would be no escape, it would just feel like another prison, and living inside the torment of his own hateful thoughts would be utter purgatory. He prayed that the two boys would come back and throw him overboard and end everything.

As he waited for their return, he went in and out of consciousness imagining what death would be like. He had a flash that he was of falling into the sea and sinking deeper and deeper into the ocean. His body felt heavy, like he was attached to a lead weight. He fell deeper into the darkened sea where the pressure would surely dissolve him, or a shark would eat him whole, or an undersea volcanic explosion would engulf him.

Finally there was silence, as if he'd fallen so deeply that he'd entered the center of the earth. It was there that the weight of constant dread evaporated ... leaving behind a nothingness ... so blissful and strange. The strangeness was almost unbearable. Something had gone ... that face ... that hollow fortress abandoned. His heart pumped fresh blood under the command of this new climate — a climate laced with soothing intoxicants.

He slept for hours after that, gently rocked by the great mother ocean. Finally at dawn he heard a knock on the door. George remained absolutely still and silent. After a few moments the ship's steward entered. He had with him a doctor and a housekeeping employee. George peered up at them, squinting into the sunlight that was streaming through the doorway. The three of them stood in silhouette so he couldn't see their faces. He wondered if they were angels or devils.

"We understand you've not been well, sir. I'm here to check on you and this lady here will clean up for you. You've had a rough night."

The doctor took a warm cloth and wiped George's face, then checked his vital signs, "You're dehydrated. Can we get this chap some water?"

The doctor sounded British, but there was another quality, something pacifying about his voice.

The housekeeper brought a glass of water and handed it to the doctor.

"Here, let me help you," the doctor whispered as he propped up George's head and helped him sip the water. He put some medicine in George's hand, "Take these. They'll make you feel better."

The new angle helped George see his face. He was East Indian, and as George would later discover, grew up in Bombay. Somehow this man reminded him of his beloved grandfather, Besnick; how he looked when George was just a boy. He was gentle-faced with lantern eyes. He wore a doctor's lab coat with a stethoscope around his neck.

The man stroked George's hair and said in his lilting Bombay accent, "You need to get some food in your stomach. The storm is over. It's smooth sailing from now on."

Over the next week of the trip, George slowly got better. Dr. Rakesh Chandra came to see him every day and they chatted about sea birds and the stars over the Northern Atlantic. He learned that the doctor was schooled in allopathic medicine in England, but then returned to India to study Ayurvedic medicine, as well. He was conscripted by the Brits as a medic on the Western Front, and had then gotten a job in a hospital in Toronto. He loved Canada and had now made it his home. Dr. Chandra understood what it was like to be an outsider, and George listened in rapt attention as he described his journey of finding acceptance in a foreign land, and how it must start in the heart.

One night George sat alone on his bed staring out his porthole at the full moon, grateful beyond words for the hand that had reached out to help him. There was a circle of haze around the moon and he could just make out the shape of the rabbit on the moon's surface. He remembered the day his grandfather had revealed that image to him, and for years he imagined that rabbit smiling at him from the heavens, soothing him back to sleep on those restless nights.

George vowed he would re-create himself all over again, to something that finally the world would love and accept. His creativity had not been put to good use so far. He would use his artistry just one more time in hopes of redeeming himself in the eyes of the Creator, or perhaps it had to be in the eyes of his own heart.

He pulled out his sketch pad and started drawing a self-portrait. On one of the shelves he noticed a copy of *MacLean's*, Canada's national magazine. He flipped through and found a photo of D'Alton Corey Coleman, president of the Canadian Pacific Railway Ltd. He placed the image next to his sketch pad and in great detail morphed his face onto this great businessman's face. After the sketch was finished he taped it onto the wall next to his bed.

As he gazed at the portrait a whole new world of possibilities opened up in his imagination. He would be distinguished, well-dressed, wealthy and respected. He would be admired for his business acumen and he would make a difference in people's lives, just as the ship's doctor had done for him. Each night he dreamed another new aspect of this persona until it emerged fully born into existence.

That was the last time in his life he ever sketched a portrait.

By the time he arrived in Canada, George's health was back to normal. As Dr. Chandra bid farewell to the young man on the gangplank, he handed George a business card, "If you ever need a helping hand, son, you just call me. You've got a lot of smarts and a lot of talent. This is the land of plenty and you can make your own way here. You remember that."

As he watched the black head of curly hair disappear into the crowd, another man came into view holding up a nine-by-twelve inch sheet with the words "George Freeman" on it.

George pushed his way through the crowd toward the man. He had worked tirelessly on his accent, listening to CBC radio all day mimicking the announcer's voice. He placed himself in front of the man and said, "George Freeman here, pleased to meet you."

"Nice to meet you, young man. I'm Walter Richardson from the mining camp. Welcome to Canada!"

"Thank you very much, sir. I'm pleased to be here," As George said those words he actually felt like he meant them.

"Where did you say you was coming from?"

"I've been in Europe on duty ... with the 2nd Canadian Corps," George replied, trying to remember what his bunkmates had said, "Yessiree, we liberated the Netherlands from them Germans."

"Nice work, fella. The world's a free place again! It's good to have you back home. I'm sorry I'm going to have to put you up in that mining camp with some of these here displaced people, refugees and greasies, but we need all the labour we can get. You'll rise up fast in the ranks though, boy, I'll make sure of it. You seem like management material to me."

The prophecy of Walter Richardson came true. After only five months working at the mining town in northern Ontario, George rose to a management level with his quickness at learning all the systems, his ability to balance the books and his acumen at financial forecasting.

When he got his first big manager's paycheque, he sent a telegraph to Laszlo Goldstein to see what could be done about bringing over his family.

The return letter came from Toronto. Laszlo had now immigrated to Canada himself. He said it would be a tricky process because they were now living in a Communist occupied territory. All ethnic Germans were rounded up and put into work camps. Laszlo helped George at least find the camp where they were interned.

George sent a letter to his father there. The letter announced that he was alive, that he had changed his identity and that he had immigrated to Canada to start a new life there. He asked his father to keep his letter confidential and address any return mail to George Freeman at his new address in Canada. There was a risk that the authorities would read the letter and try to find him, but he was willing to take that risk. Someone like Jorg Frei was low priority, given all the other chaos an emerging Communist government had to deal with.

He thrilled at writing the letter. His father would be so happy to know he was alive. They would all be reunited again. He would liberate them from the post-war chaos and the prodigal son would finally redeem himself.

These thoughts kept him going while he worked the mining camp in the dead of the Northern Canadian winter … waiting and waiting for a reply. Maybe letters weren't making it to the work camps. Maybe his father had died already … maybe …

Finally, a box and a letter arrived from Karl Frei. He tore it open. It contained family photos, documents and more of his mementos with the words:

*My Dearest Son,*

*I am grateful you are alive. You cannot imagine the heartache I felt thinking you were lost to me. It's truly a miracle! We had a funeral for you and people said many wonderful things. I wept like a baby and you know me — I never do that. Now I cry that you are alive.*

*As you surmised in your letter, the work camp is brutal. Your dear wife, Uta, got pneumonia and they wouldn't bring any medical help. I am so deeply sorry to tell you that she died a few months ago.*

*But the good news is that you have a daughter! Her name is Helena. She was born November 26, 1943, so she is almost four years old now. She has my eyes — that light blue color, and the same white blonde hair I had as a child. Unfortunately, she doesn't look at all like you!*

*Uta's mother took the child in but then they left the work camp. I will try to track them down now that I know you are alive. Once you get settled in Canada, I'm sure you will want to bring her over. See if you can get Maria and I on the boat, too. Life here is horrible — the food, the living conditions and the labour. I'm too old for all this. I'm sure you now realize what has happened to the rest of your kin.*

*I hope you enjoy the photos of your baby girl. I also included her birth certificate since you are the only surviving parent now. I also included your cycling trophy, some of your drawings and some other documents.*

*These items are your life, and as hard as it's been at times, it has also been a good life. Cherish them and keep up with your art, your writing, and your studies. You are a gifted young man and have much to offer the world.*

*I love you.*
*Papa*

George re-read the letter at least twenty times. He stared at the photo of his baby in the arms of the woman he married. That woman; that beautiful stranger that he married in Kittsee just before he left. She was dead. The thought made no sense to him. He searched around in his heart to find some grief, but there was none. He hardly knew her. But he had a child that he had never seen and never held. She didn't look like him except around the mouth maybe. Yet, his father said that he was the only parent now ... that he had to take responsibility ... and he wanted to listen to his father this time. He had a tiny, helpless, vulnerable child now.

The thought overwhelmed his already overtaxed system. How would he ever take care of a little girl while living in a remote mining town? How would he ever get them all out of a Communist country? The questions rolled around in his sun-deprived head trying to find an answer. There were no answers forthcoming, so he put the task to rest.

He decided then that once he had gotten a better job in Toronto he would begin proceedings for getting them to Canada.

The next letter came a few months later just as he was settling into his job as a bookkeeper in downtown Toronto. The letter was from Maria, his stepmother, informing George that his father had died. He died of a heart attack while doing hard labour. There was no inheritance. The government had taken everything away from them.

The news hung around his neck like a stone. He should have tried harder to bring them over. Now there was no one left for him, no family. No one except a small child. He sent a package back to Maria to give to Uta's mother and the child, if she could ever find them again. It was a tiny stuffed bear he had found in a children's store. He wrote a short note to his mother-in-law expressing his condolences for Uta. He offered to bring her and the child over to Canada: *Please tell Helena that her papa loves her and will take care of her.*

He waited weeks, months and years and never received a reply. No further word came from that part of the world. It was as if everyone there had disappeared; vanished into nothingness.

What he didn't know at the time was that Maria never delivered the package. She had died of another outbreak of pneumonia in the camp. The next year Uta's mother had died of a heart attack and his daughter had been put up for adoption because the authorities had no information on the whereabouts of the father. All connection was lost.

As his eyes stretched the gray city landscape for something, anything to warm what was left of him, he rested his eyes finally on the last slivers of the sun slipping west behind The Royal York Hotel.

George decided to move west, to get as far away from anything to do with Europe as possible.

CHAPTER 35

Fran read the last question in The Book of 1001 Questions. It asked *"What is one piece of wisdom you gained in life that you would like to pass onto your children?"*

Fran felt a flash of heat behind her eyes when she read aloud her father's answer, "That you should appreciate what you have now, because any moment it may be taken from you."

Helena looked out the window and saw a jay sitting in her favourite pear tree. She mused, "Well said, Papa."

"The more I learn about our father, the more I realize I never really knew him. All these years I just thought of him as a boring, reclusive accountant, but he had this whole other life ..."

"Yes, he had enough adventures for the both of us put together. His reclusiveness now seems to make so much more sense, no?"

"Yes, of course. Why couldn't I have been more compassionate and less judgmental all these years?" Fran asked herself.

"Most children are judgmental of their parents at some point in time. I judged both my parents for abandoning me. I did that for years, until I couldn't stand the pain anymore ... and I finally let it rest. Then you came into my life and told me that my father was alive all this time. I ... I didn't know what to say, what to do. The feelings of abandonment welled up again. But reading this journal … it helps. It helps very much. I understand now what he was dealing with."

As Fran stared at the awards of recognition on Helena's wall she marvelled at the woman's ability to let go and not hold onto bitterness.

Fran stood up and paced the room. "I want to know more. I think we should try to see if Frau Meinhardt is still alive. If we could talk to her, it might help us know what happened at Birkenau."

After a moment of reverie, Helena refocused and nodded.

Helena began a search of senior's organizations on the internet.

"Look here. There is a Marianna Meinhardt who was on the social committee of the East Munich Elderhostel Association."

Fran shrugged, "Isn't that a fairly common name?"

"Not so common. And, it's the only one I can find in Munich."

"Then, it's worth a try to call."

As Helena dialed the number, Fran went to wash and get dressed for the day.

As curious as she was about the outcome of the call to Munich, she was exhausted. The trip to Vienna had been long and intense. As she looked in the bathroom mirror, her face seemed pale and drawn. Ever since arriving in Europe, Fran had faced one challenging situation after another, and a huge wave of fatigue and sadness about her father was now weighing her down. When she returned to the kitchen Helena was making copious notes.

She looked up as Fran entered, "I'm stunned. That was her. We found her on our first try!"

"What did she say?" Fran asked quietly, almost fearing to hear the answer, so drained was she from the emotional rollercoaster of her father's memoirs.

"She said that Laszlo Goldstein also contacted her two months ago about the same matter. That must have been before George died. Laszlo was on the same trail as us."

"Why didn't Laszlo just tell me what he found, then?" said Fran impatiently.

"Maybe he wanted you to come and do the work yourself."

Fran frowned, not liking that, "What did she say?"

"After Klaus got back home from the Sahara Desert he immediately got posted to Birkenau. She said he ran a delivery truck between the town of Auschwitz and the camp. Apparently, Klaus tried to hide some prisoners in wine barrels on the back of his truck, but they caught him and executed him. She said to this day she doesn't know why he would have done such a dangerous thing."

"Maybe we'll finally be able to give her an answer."

"Grab The Book of 1001 Questions. Go to the section on 'military duty or friends'. He said something in there about Klaus. Remember?"

Fran flipped through the pages to the section on "Friends".

"Yes. Here it is. 'Question #343: Who was the closest friend you ever had?' 'Answer: Klaus. He sacrificed his life so that I could live in peace. Unfortunately, he died in vain.'"

They looked at each other.

"But what does that mean?" Helena replied.

Helena opened her laptop and launched her internet browser, "I wonder if this is what he was referring to. Klaus tried to save some people from death at Birkenau, people who George cared about.

"Maybe he had Jewish relatives that we don't know about," added Fran.

"Marianna Meinhardt didn't know about that, but she said Klaus died in the camp where Dr. Josef Mengele did his experiments."

"Who's that?"

"It's all making sense to me now," Helena said as she clicked rapidly through websites on her laptop, "Klaus hid people in wine barrels in the back of a truck. Those aren't very big. The only kind of prisoners who could fit inside those would be children or small people."

"Are you saying maybe our father had other children that were imprisoned there?"

"Not exactly. Dr. Josef Mengele and his crew were infamous for doing experiments at Birkenau."

"What kind of experiments?"

"It's very unpleasant. And, as soon as I tell you, you will know exactly where we need to go to find the final pieces of this puzzle."

Fran breathed in slowly. "Okay, I'm ready."

"Dr. Mengele was famous for doing scientific and medical experiments on children — on Romani children and their families. They created the *Familienzigeunerlager* at Birkenau, or Romani Family Camp."

Fran was silent. She felt a shock wave quake her surface, "What kind of experiments?"

"You don't want to know."

Fran's eyes grew large as the truth dawned on her, "Children or small people were the only ones who could have gotten away?"

Helena nodded and looked at her watch, "We have just enough time to get there before sundown. Let's go. Get your coat."

CHAPTER 36

When Helena's beige Peugeot pulled into Olino, the children swarmed around them like mosquitoes. Fran's pulse quickened. Was it from the discomfort of being swarmed, the unravelling of a mystery or of seeing Jasper again? No sooner had they stepped out of the car when Gustav and Jasper came out of their house.

"We so glad you come back!" Gustav exclaimed.

Fran felt nervous as she stepped forward to greet them, "I'm so sorry for leaving abruptly like that. Please accept my apologies."

"I imagine that must have been disturbing for you. Really, they are always mad about something here. Aren't they dad?" said Jasper.

"She not used to us yet," Gustav said flashing his gold-toothed smile, "You must be Helena. Sister to Francesca. Me, I'm Gustav, Papa to Jasper here."

"Pleased to meet you Gustav," she said as she pulled out candy for the children.

"Oh no, now they never leave you alone!"

"It's not got sugar in it, just sweetened with fruit. Less cavities, yes?" Helena smiled. "I have plenty more back at the office."

"We were very concerned about you," said Jasper, "But we surmised that you made your way to Helena's."

"Roberto said he give you ride. That guy, big trouble ... plenty worried then ..."

Fran jumped in, "It was okay. There were many other people in the truck, women and children. And it was kind of an adventure. We almost got all the way to Kittsee before the truck got pulled over by the police."

"The police!" exclaimed Jasper.

"Yes, they thought I was their American ring leader."

Jasper laughed, "How preposterous!"

"I managed to convince them otherwise, so then I called Helena and she came and got me."

"Good. You much too Canadian to be ring leader!" Gustav winked at her.

Fran smiled, "I got all my valuables back; my wallet, ID, passport, cell phone. They had them."

"Really? They found your ID?" asked Jasper.

"They probably steal it," quipped Gustav.

"I wonder when they would have done that," exclaimed Jasper.

"I don't know. Either at the train station in Vienna, or on the train to Kittsee."

"They give it all back?" Gustav inquired.

"I actually found my items in a bag when everyone was sleeping. I kind of 'stole' everything back. I don't think they knew."

There was an awkward silence between them all, and then Jasper flashed a sideways grin at her and said, "I bet you are wondering if I stole your things."

"No!"

"I would wonder that if I were you," Jasper added.

There was a round of nervous laughter, and then Fran said, "Okay I thought about it a couple of times, maybe just once, but my intuition told me you don't do those kinds of things."

"Jasper don't steal, and don't drink," exclaimed Gustav, "He's not like that."

"I don't drink either," Fran said, more exuberantly than she wanted to.

"Roberto and his gang are thieves and drunks, and dad here has tried to help them, but they just steal from him. We haven't figured out a way to deal with it as a community, but we are working on it," said Jasper.

Gustav chimed in, "Hey, we have your bag all ready for you. Sorry about pictures of your father in uniform. Nazis make people loco here."

"Is it because he was in a Nazi uniform, or because people here actually knew our father?" Fran asked.

Both Jasper and Gustav looked at each other and said nothing.

She continued, "I'm trying to piece together information from a variety of sources. We were just at the Wiesenthal office in Vienna going through war criminal records, and then just received this in the mail — our father's journal."

"Which we'd never before seen," added Helena.

"Yes, and we have strong reasons to believe that our father sent his friend, Klaus Meinhardt to Birkenau to help some people escape."

Fran glanced again at the number tattooed into Gustav's arm, "Did that man help you escape by hiding you in a wine barrel in the back of a truck?"

"That man was friend of Jiri!?" gasped Gustav.

"So, Jiri was his name here?" asked Fran, "Did he ever live here at Olino?"

"Jiri born here. He was like big brother to me," said Gustav, "I can't believe it was Jiri."

"Tell me, was it an accident that I arrived here on my first night in Europe?"

Gustav readjusted the yellow Fedora on his head, and Jasper shook his head sheepishly.

Suddenly Fran remembered the man with a yellow Fedora who helped her get onto the right train.

"That was you at the train station helping me!"

Gustav's bushy eyebrows lifted high on his forehead.

Jasper looked over at his father, searching for permission to tell them more. The old man nodded.

"Papa and I had your photo at the train station and we were keeping an eye out for you. He wanted to see if I could talk you into coming for a visit to Olino. It was just fate that your items got stolen, and you had to come with me."

"I use him as bait 'cause he just so cute," added Gustav, "Plus he speak English gooder than me."

"How did you get a photo of me?" Fran asked.

Gustav pulled out the photo from his wallet. She recognized it immediately. It was taken about a year ago at a Freeman & Wilson office party.

"Come with me," said Gustav, "Both of you. I show you who give me photo."

Helena and Fran followed Gustav, with Jasper tagging along behind. They walked past Helena's car and Fran noticed that the teenagers were unscrewing her hood ornament. Fran and Helena looked at each other but said nothing.

They trudged down a mud path winding behind the outhouse, past the main building, through a small vegetable garden, and past a cemetery.

Fran noticed an abandoned Merry-Go-Round under some trees. It was small, with just five horses. There was moss growing over the backs and necks of the wooden beasts, which made them look like Chia Pets.

Finally, they arrived at a tiny caravan, with no wheels, that had been placed on a wood platform. The platform stood on four tree stumps whose roots snaked out like crow's feet in all directions. There was someone inside, lighting a propane lamp just as they arrived. Gustav knocked at the door.

A moment later, ancient Sophia opened the door. Around her head was a black and white polka dot scarf tied in a bow under her chin.

"You came back! It's good. Please come in," she cried with delight.

They all crowded into her little caravan and Sophia moved some things around for everyone to sit down.

"How did you get this photo of me?" asked Fran cautiously.

"A courier package arrived here a while back from a lawyer. His name ... what was his name? Goldbloom — something like that. "The delivery man showed up here and asked if anyone knew the man in this photo," Sophia held up a photo of George. Fran knew the photo. It was taken at his seventy-seventh birthday party, "Everyone here shake their heads. No one knows big, huge man named George Freeman. No one recognized him, except me. How did he get so fat anyway?"

Sophia reached up with both arms to an old cookie tin on her shelf. "I don't know how the lawyer man found me, but he did. Here, let me show you something."

She pulled out an old and cracked photo. It was of a beautiful girl with long, wavy black hair, holding a baby, "That me — just fifteen — with new baby. My little Jiri."

"That's Jiri? That's George?" Fran and Helena both gasped.

Sophia nodded.

"So, he was your son?" asked Helena.

Sophia nodded proudly.

The sisters looked at each.

"That means you are our grandmother," Fran said finally.

"Yes, I think so. I think lawyer wanted to see if any relatives of Jiri are left here."

They all sat there for a moment, in stunned silence.

"Did you know that he just died last month?" asked Helena.

"Yes. Just found out a few weeks ago. I thought he died in the war, in 1943. We did a funeral and even have a little tombstone for him just over there," She looked down at the knobs of her arms, "All these years he was alive, my Jiri."

Helena and Fran looked over at the little woman, thousands of questions darting around their heads. Fran glanced out the window at the tiny cemetery across the road, at the place where Sophia had buried her memories of Jiri. The weight of that tragic misinformation sat on Fran's heart like a stone.

But Sophia looked up suddenly, her eyes fierce with the will to live and love; the will that had helped her survive all these years.

"It is sad. But I am so happy to have two granddaughters. I wanted to meet them, but I thought you might not want to know me. I'm a scary looking grandma, I know. We live here differently from mainstream society. We have some Gypsy blood here. Your father, he didn't like being one of us anymore. He didn't want to be my son anymore. So he ran away from the carnival. He ran away and pretended he was a different person. Please don't hate me. I just wanted to meet you once before I died."

Sophia held their gaze, looking like a child again, hopeful and vulnerable.

"We don't hate you," Helena said.

Fran nodded in agreement but remembered how much she feared the deformed raisin-like woman when she first met her.

Sophia smiled, her expression radiant, in her toothless way.

"Good. I am a good person. Never seen a lady as old as me, huh? Big news. And it's good to know my Jiri never died as a young man. He lived a full, long life across the seas. But why did he never bother finding me, and telling me he was alive?"

"I think because he thought that you had died during the war, too," Helena said sadly.

Gustav added, "It was Jiri that help us escape from Birkenau!"

Sophia looked at him serenely, "I know."

"What you mean, you know?" Gustav retorted.

"And how did someone who was Romani end up as a gunner for the Nazis?" Helena asked as she pulled out the dog-eared text, "We have some information in this Book of 1001 Questions that he filled in just weeks before his death, but there are many pieces that don't make any sense."

"He is vague in many places in this book of questions, and it's hard for us to interpret," added Fran.

"I will tell you everything I know," Sophia promised, "I have kept much of it to myself for many, many years, but you have come half way around the world to get to know your hidden family, so I will break my pact of silence for you. It is all here in my cookie tin."

## CHAPTER 37

It was 1936 and the Olino Carnival workers were trying to scare up customers on this rain-drenched Saturday.

"Try your luck. Win the big prize! Three shots for a crown! You, sir, you look like a man with terrific aim."

The man ignored Jiri, and kept walking.

Jiri scowled and reached again for his textbook. He had a big test on Monday and intended to study hard for it. He looked around to make sure his father was nowhere in sight before he resumed reading the chapter on Hegel, the great German philosopher.

"I'll try my luck."

Jiri looked up suddenly, and slammed his book closed. It was seven-year-old Gustav.

"You can't even hold a rifle, my friend. Go away, I have things to do."

Gustav whined, "Show me how you do it. You said you would last weekend. Remember?"

Jiri sighed, and then looked up and down the midway. It was a slow Saturday because of the rain.

"Okay. Place this part in the crook of your neck, put this finger on the trigger, and stand like this, so that you have some stability. Aim for the center and shoot. Here, I'll show you."

Jiri shot the rifle and hit the bull's eye.

"You always hit the bull's eye!" cried Gustav, "You never miss. That's amazing! How come hardly anyone else can do that?"

"Because no one else spends day after day here, trying to show people how to play this stupid game," Jiri retorted.

"I'd do your job, but your Papa won't let me," Gustav said trying to balance the gun on his shoulder.

"You're only seven, and I'm fifteen. That's a big difference."

Gustav fired and hit way outside the mark. He looked even younger than seven. He was short for his age but squarely built with a turned up nose; a cross between a logger and a leprechaun. One day, Jiri surmised, he would make a great boxer. Yet, he could see the beginnings of musical genius in the boy already. Gustav's father had been teaching him the violin and the boy carried it on his back everywhere he went, practicing whenever he got a moment.

Jiri was twice the boy's height. His swarthy complexion stood in odd contrast to his amber eyes. Their coppery tint held an almost ethereal and piercing intelligence. As usual he was wearing a sailor's cap and navy tunic, borrowed from his father's trunk.

"Maybe we can run your shooting booth together!"

"That would be fun occasionally, but today I need to study. Don't tell Papa."

"Why not?"

"Because my father wants me to take over the carnival from him, not be a philosophy professor."

"You want to be a stupid professor? No people like us ever do stuff like that," Gustav protested.

Jiri sighed, "Exactly. But I plan on being the one to break the pattern."

"Books make you polluted. They fill you with lies," Gustav said, trying to sound like his father.

"I *like* to fill myself with lies," retorted Jiri, turning the page of his book.

"But if you're polluted we won't be able to be friends anymore!"

"Listen, I've been polluted since the day I was born according to some people here. And at school I'm polluted because I live and work here at the carnival. So, that makes me double polluted. But you see, you are still pure even though you hang out with me. So what does that tell you?"

"That I de-pollute you!"

"Yes, Gustav, you have special powers of purification. Wherever you go you make things right again."

Gustav's eyes glowed with the possibility that this was his life calling.

Just then, Karl Frei, Jiri's father, strode around the corner with a sack of money and a pad of paper with a pencil.

"Here is the take from last night," he told his son, "Selma wants to get paid, but I couldn't make it balance. You are always so good with that kind of thing, Jiri."

Jiri took the money from his father and mumbled under this breath, "Of course I get the job. I'm the only one here who can count."

"What was that?" Karl asked.

"Nothing," brooded Jiri.

"Please go over it again for me. I have to go help Hanzi repair the fortune telling tent. I'll be back in half an hour," Karl said as he laid down the money without waiting for a reply. Then he marched off angrily toward one of the Merry-Go-Round workers who had fallen asleep on the job.

Gustav started leafing through Jiri's textbook about German philosophers. He whistled to himself, impressed, "You can make sense of these black squiggles? You are smart at everything, Jiri. That's what Mirela said. I think she likes you. Mirela and Jiri kissing in the tree! I saw you!"

"Go away. I have to do this work, now."

Gustav frowned, chastised, and walked away, with his head hanging low.

Jiri called after him, "You can come help me next Saturday, okay?"

The boy's face lit up at the possibility, and he went skipping off to join some other boys playing ball.

As Jiri started to balance out the books, a young man sneaked up behind him, and grabbed the rifle from behind Jiri's counter. The man held the rifle up to Jiri's head and demanded, "Give me all your money!"

Then he laughed uproariously as Jiri ducked for cover. He turned, and pointed the rifle at the bull's eye instead. His hand was shaking slightly as he pulled the trigger, causing him to hit outside of the mark.

"You have such bad aim, I didn't need to duck. You would not even have grazed my ear," retorted Jiri.

"I wouldn't want to win those prizes of yours, like that lovely hand-made CzechoSlovak doll in traditional dress. You only have five left, and those should really go to the patrons," Raoul grinned.

Raoul was a radiant nineteen-year-old Hungarian, with wide-set eyes and long lashes. He wore his curly locks in a ponytail and sported four rings on each hand. As he placed the rifle back behind the counter, Jiri noticed he had an acoustic guitar draped on his back, and a harmonica around his neck.

"You're obviously a lover, not a fighter," joked Jiri.

Raoul smiled, bowing, taking it as a compliment. Jiri had to admit he admired the *bon vivant* quality Raoul seemed to ooze so naturally. Jiri wished he had a quarter of what the older boy had. Their friendship had come to mean a great deal to him over the last few months and he was always ready to drop what he was doing to make time for Raoul.

"Hey, Jiri, I just found out you are an artist, too. You should give away framed versions of your sketches. I saw some of them yesterday, when I was at your caravan. Your drawings are much more interesting than these stupid dolls."

"Yeah, Mama thinks so, too. But I don't think they are good enough. People are used to winning dolls and animals, not art. Besides people might think that I am arrogant."

"Hey. Everyone already knows you're arrogant. Screw pretending to be humble. Talent doesn't need to apologize. Show what you can do. I'll be your sales man. I'll stand right out here — 'Get your traditional painting of the castle, or of the mountains, or of your lovely mistress!' — and you can sit there and draw people on the spot. You know, passersby-type people. They do that at the Hungarian carnivals all the time."

"Yeah, I suppose making drawings would be better than running the shooting arcade. But I want to focus on school right now. By the way, what were you doing at our caravan?"

"I'm in the band now. I was auditioning for your mother."

"She hasn't been in the band for years," Jiri replied.

Just then, Anika, a pretty girl from a nearby community, walked by and Raoul's head swivelled around to check her out.

"I'll catch up with you later, Jiri," he announced with raised eyebrows.

Raoul ran up behind the girl and started playing his harmonica. She glanced back and smiled.

Jiri rolled his eyes and went back to balancing the books. Very quickly, he found the mistake that his father had made, and from that he was able to recalculate everything. Once he was done, he slammed the ledger closed with a force that surprised him. He took the money and books over to the fortune telling tent.

On his way there he spotted a boy and a girl from school walking toward him with their mother. Fearing more taunts, he ducked behind a tent until they passed. He envied other children who didn't have to spend their weekends, holidays and evenings working. He had few friends because he had no time to be with them. His life was working and studies, so even though his life revolved around a fun fair, his life was anything but fun.

Jiri wandered around trying to find his father.

"Where's Papa?" he asked Hanzi.

"He got a telegram from the Navy. They probably want him to go out on the submarines again," he replied.

"He wouldn't do that again, would he? Mama won't stand for that."

"Yes, seven months is a long time to be away," Hanzi agreed, "I wouldn't like it either if he went again. That means you and I will have to take over most of his jobs again."

"Why does he keep doing it?"

"He makes good money in the Navy. We can't make as much money with the carnival now that we have to stay in one place. Everyone around here has seen all our shows and our acts. They are bored," replied Hanzi.

"Then maybe Papa should just sell the carnival."

"That isn't really your father's decision. Your mother's family has run carnivals for so many generations. Everyone in her family would be up in arms."

Suddenly they heard a voice coming from inside the tent. "I can hear everything you're saying," shouted Sophia.

"Sorry, Mama."

She shouted back, "Hanzi is right. I will make sure we never sell. We are going to create some new acts, shows, and rides so that the local people will come again."

Hanzi whispered to Jiri, "But we're going to need money to do that."

Sophia exited the tent and stood in front of them adjusting the crystal in her turban. As her hands fussed with the crystal, she clenched an ornate pipe between her teeth, her eyes squinting from the slender streams of smoke that escaped out the end.

She was petite, with vivacious eyes, high cheek bones, and long black hair that fell in curls down to her curvaceous hips.

"I just did a Tarot Card reading on a lady from town. It was all about money. The same card kept coming up, The Queen of Pentacles. She said it didn't make sense for her. And you know why?" She looked at her son and Hanzi for an answer, but none was forthcoming, "I know why, because it was a card for me. It tells me that your Papa should not go on the submarines again, and that I should go out touring again with the band."

"It said that, did it?" Hanzi scoffed.

"What? You don't believe me?"

Hanzi went back to repairing the rip in the tent and grunted under his breath, "You are too old for dancing now."

"I heard that, Hanzi. I'm only thirty! I just won the Czardas Dance contest three years ago. Regina danced until she was forty, so I still have many good years. I could make a fortune if your father would only let me go."

Just then Karl joined them, holding the telegram from the Navy, "I'm sorry, my love, but they want me. I leave next week."

Sophia threw up her hands and screamed in disgust.

Karl went into damage control mode, recognizing the signs of a good tantrum coming, "Listen, darling, when I come back, we'll be able to buy that new big top tent. Then, we can start having larger traveling acts."

"The government won't let us travel," interrupted Hanzi.

"They don't need to know," replied Karl.

"Mama wants to go on tour, dancing instead," Jiri blurted out.

"No," said Karl flatly.

"Why not?" demanded Sophia

"You have things to do here."

"Why don't you come on the road with us?" asked Sophia.

"You know I can't do that. I can't leave the carnival."

"You can't leave the carnival, but you can go on your damn submarines!"

Karl's face went red. He was triggered now. No more sweet talk, not even in private.

"I make good money when I go on the subs so that you and Jiri can live a good life, and so that I can keep this damn place going!"

"You are going to work for the Nazis. They hate us. How can you do that?"

Jiri hated it when his parents fought, which was all too often. He knew his father didn't want to go on tour with the band because there was nothing for him to do, and he didn't enjoy the company of several of the band members. Karl was an outsider. And although he ran the business that provided them with a livelihood, many of the other men in the community never completely accepted him.

Karl had met Sophia when he was renting tents to the traveling Olino carnival. He was mesmerized when he saw her, and did everything he could to win her over. He was twenty-seven-years-old and she was fourteen, and their courtship created havoc in the Olino community. Sophia's father had already arranged a marriage for her to another man when she became pregnant with Karl's child.

The decision was a tricky one because Sophia was the most beautiful daughter of Besnick, the carnival owner. In addition, many in her community knew Karl because he had worked in the carnival business his whole life. Yet, Sophia was unmarried and was now pregnant with a child of mixed blood. In earlier generations she would have been cast out of a Gypsy community for such behaviour. But times were changing and more often people of Gypsy blood were inter-marrying and adopting new customs, especially at Olino. The differences were now more about occupation. The artists and performers stood together against the producers, or those who did the practical work of running the show. More and more the producers had the last say.

Besnick only had daughters, no sons. Karl had the organizational skills to take over the family carnival business. He was Austrian and spoke many languages so because of this he was allowed to be part of the community.

However, after his birth Jiri's status was always in question. Gypsy women were the guarantors for the survival of the population, so when the women married outside of the community they put the long term survival of their culture at risk. Children of those unions were considered polluted, and that belief was still active amongst certain elderly members of the Olino community. In addition, Karl introduced books to both his young wife and his son, which further alienated their small family from those who saw themselves as the keepers of tradition.

Another alienating aspect of Jiri's life was his childhood role as the carnival mascot. Because of his exotic half-breed features they often decked him out in a variety of costumes, and urged him to create a different character every week. He was often his mother's sidekick as she told fortunes on the sideshow stage. One week he was a miniature Rasputin, the next he was an Indian mystic, and the third an Ancient Greek soothsayer. As a child he enjoyed this challenge to his imagination and acting skills. As an adolescent, however, he grew tired of the game and refused to to take on the roles anymore. He just wanted to be taken seriously for once in his life.

Jiri had watched his parents fight most of his life so he'd grown numb to it by now. Along with several others, he watched the fireworks between them for a few more minutes, then left the books and money under his father's hat. He sneaked around behind the fortune teller's tent and jumped over the fence. It was the rollercoaster partition. He looked over at Stefan, his uncle, who was manning the control booth. Stefan was busy at the lever, so Jiri leapt onto the back car of the ride just as it was leaving the gate.

"Hey!" shouted Stefan, "That's dangerous. Quit doing that Jiri!"

Jiri just smiled and waved as he settled himself in for the ride. The rollercoaster somehow helped him clear his mind. As the ride inched its way up to the first hill, Jiri enjoyed seeing the landscape take shape below him. It inspired a larger perspective on life. As it thundered down the track and whipped him around, he screamed and laughed until all the resentment and frustration had left his mind and body.

After the ride was over he felt free again. He sauntered back to the shooting arcade to finish studying. He knew his father would be leaving soon and he had to study as hard as possible before then.

CHAPTER 38

The day Karl left to work on the U-boats, Jiri trained seven-year-old Gustav to run the shooting booth. He knew his father would never approve, but he wasn't around to protest and the crowds were sparse anyway.

Inspired by Raoul's suggestion, Jiri instead brought his easel and large sketch pad to just outside the entrance of the carnival. He hung up his existing sketches to show off his talent. Within half an hour a gadjo couple strolled by and the man insisted they get their portrait done together. A small crowd gathered to watch him work. They had not seen a portrait artist in these parts for many years.

Jiri noticed a bead of sweat form along his brow line as he commenced the work. He quickly wiped it with his handkerchief. His charcoal was getting soft under the midday heat and little bits kept crumbling off. Frustrated, Jiri tried to work more slowly, to focus intently on his subjects and to capture the essence of their love for each other. He knew that is what would please them.

After about fifteen minutes the couple seemed to be tiring of sitting still.

"Please feel free to stretch. I'm almost done," he lied. There was still a long way to go. He wanted to add more layers. In fact, it was his attention to the minute detail that made Jiri stand out as an artist. However, he still hadn't learned how to do that quickly enough for impatient carnival goers.

When the drawing was finally done enough for Jiri to be willing to show the image, he stood up from his stool and announced, "Right then, it's done. Would you like to see it?"

The couple seemed annoyed by this time, but stood to come have a look. As they walked around to his side of the easel, both their faces lit up.

"It's heavenly!" the woman gushed.

"Excellent work, son," the man added as he tossed him ten crowns more than Jiri had asked for.

Over the next few weeks, Jiri managed to increase his speed and his customer flow. Word spread in the area. Everyone wanted their portrait done. On slow days, Jiri painted images of women in celebrity magazines and taped them up on the entrance gate. He was definitely bringing in more money than at the shooting booth.

"How's it going?" Jiri asked Gustav, who sat glumly behind the shooting booth counter.

"It's no fun without you."

"Aw, I'm sorry."

"Can't I come paint with you? I could wash your brushes!"

"No. You have to stay here."

Gustav began to cry, so Jiri leapt over the counter and pulled him up on his lap, "You miss me, don't you?"

The boy nodded sniffing.

Jiri noticed three robins dancing and playing together on the awning.

"I miss you, too. We'll figure something out," he said as he hugged the boy closer.

Jiri knew the carnival was not what it used to be, and the stress of that fact weighed heavily on the whole community.

"Hey, let's ask the river," added Jiri.

"What?" Gustav looked up at him squinting.

"Mama always says to ask the river when you don't know what to do. Come on!"

The two boys shut down the booth and ran out of the carnival. They clambered over rocks and down a steep trail. Gustav wanted to take a short cut through the garden of wild violets, but Jiri pulled him back. It was Sophia's sacred space and she had scolded him too many times now when he had come home with bits of her holy flowers on his shoes.

"Follow the path!" he shouted at his young companion.

Gustav looked down and tried to straighten a violet he had trampled, then he caught up with Jiri who was already down at the river bank. There they could smell a rich blend of patchouli incense and lilac tree. The boys surveyed the scene around them. Jiri's aunts were washing clothes with river rock and lye. The elders sat on the other side of the river. They were on crates and rusted out petrol drums, discussing the issues of the week. The men wore torn slacks and untucked shirts, the women wore bangles and floral dresses. The bear trainer was trying to fashion a harness onto his new cub, while the trapeze artists did their daily calisthenics.

Squatting by the banks, Jiri closed his eyes, "What would water do?"

Gustav tilted his head sideways.

Jiri continued, "That's how you ask the river for wisdom. The river will always find its way back to its source, no matter what obstacles appear before it."

"Okay. What would water do?" Gustav mimicked willing his creative brain to kick in. "Hmmm ... I dunno."

"Watch the water and ask it, then surrender to the answer. If you try too hard it doesn't work."

They sat in meditative silence merging their essence with the river's.

"I have it," Jiri finally said. "I will go become a great inventor and philosopher and become rich. Then I'll come back and give everyone all my money so we don't have to worry anymore."

"Can I come with you?!" Gustav said jumping up and down.
Jiri smiled, "We'll see."

The day his grandparents came to have their portrait done was a momentous one for Jiri. Although Besnick was now retired, he ran the carnival for thirty-one years and his approval meant the world to Jiri.

He was the one who taught Jiri to become an artist. Besnick had handed him a piece of paper and charcoal when he was only five. He explained several tricks such as how to sketch the light in the eyes to make them appear more alive. They spent countless days on the caravan steps together drawing people, flowers, birds and trees.

Besnick was talented as a visual artist, but even more so as a show man. His warm charisma drew attention like a magnet. He was athletically-built even in his late fifties and his booming voice could carry across a sea of rowdy carnival goers. As the ringmaster, he could make the crowds laugh one moment and fall into stunned silence the next.

Florica, his maternal grandmother, moved with precision. She had a stillness in her center from years of walking tightrope. Jiri immediately felt at peace whenever he was in her presence. The love between them was like an eternal life spring that went down to the center of the earth. The harmony between them stood in sharp contrast to the storminess of his parents' relationship.

The day they sat for their portrait, Jiri took his time. He wanted it perfect. By drawing their love, he hoped it would help him find the same one day. Although they both looked pleased at the result, Jiri felt unhappy with the result. He suspected they were just being polite. He vowed he would do another, better one soon.

On that same Saturday, Sophia approached the Olino band to discuss her idea. The four of them were just about to begin playing a new piece of music that Raoul had brought from Hungary.

"Excuse me, brothers," she interrupted.

The music stopped. The men always smiled when Sophia entered a room. On most days, she had a radiance and sensuality that made their pulse quicken. Raoul put down his instrument and others followed suit.

"Thank you. I think it's time that the band goes out on tour, and that I join you as a dancer again. We could do the festival circuit in Czechoslovakia and Hungary."

She braced herself for the inevitable push back. They were all silent, so she gathered more courage and continued.

"It starts in May and goes to September. If we can get a spot at all sixteen festivals we will do very well. I will pay you all your regular wage and then we give the profit back to the carnival. You, Ferencz, on violin, Joseph on the accordion, Tomáš on drums, and Raoul on vocals and guitar, and I will dance. Ferencz, you and I will get the bookings. Together we know many organizers and I can write the letters," she paused again waiting for a response.

No one said a thing.

"Well," she asked, "What do you have to say?"

"We still need a band to play at the carnival," stated Joseph.

"The second-string players can play. We have such low attendance these days it doesn't matter. We will make more money if we can tour," replied Sophia.

Most of them saw the logic in her argument and agreed.

"I thought Karl didn't want you to go on tour again," asked Tomáš.

"He'll be glad I went when he sees how much money we bring back. But, we must all agree to devote the first ten percent of the take for new instruments and costumes. In order to charge more money, we need to be seen as a first class orchestra to get it. Agreed?"

They began discussing the pros and cons of the idea. After about a half hour of looking at it from several perspectives, they voted unanimously to give it a try. They decided that if they got at least seven pre-bookings, they would go. Each band member had to put in a certain share of start up money. Then they would receive that money back when they got their first few gigs.

Over the next month, Sophia stopped telling fortunes and devoted her days to writing letters to the festivals and rehearsing with the band. Although almost everyone in the Olino community was illiterate, her husband had recognized a keen intellect in his young wife right from the start. He spent many hours tutoring her in several languages. Together they practiced reading and writing in Slovak, Czech, German and English.

At first some elders were outraged that she put pen to paper. They believed that the unchangeable word made you a captive of the past. They felt that educating children to live in the present moment was more important, so that they could be resourceful and innovative, and thrive in constant change. That is one reason they kept them out of school.

However, eventually they relented upon realizing how useful it was to communicate in writing with the outside world. As a result, Sophia became the official letter writer for the artists of this community.

A month later on a brisk day in early April, Sophia was drinking a cup of morning tea and smoking her pipe when she heard someone knock at her caravan door.

"I have three letters for you, Sophia," shouted Raoul.

Sophia swung open the door dancing about like a child at Christmas, "How exciting! My first return letters."

Instead of handing them to her, Raoul slipped past her into the caravan and made himself comfortable at her table. He waved them seductively in her direction. She reached for them, and he briskly pulled them away again.

"Very tricky, Raoul. Give them to me. And since when did you become the letter carrier?"

"I have a stake in what is in these letters, and thought I would hand deliver them to Her Majesty."

"Then either read them yourself or hand them over."

"I don't read, I intuit," he said as he held the letters up to his fore-head, "It says that we are the best band west of the Ukraine, and they want to pay us a king's ransom to grace them with our presence."

Sophia laughed, and tore the letters out of his hand.

"I certainly hope so!" she ripped them open with a pen knife and began to read, "You aren't too far off. The Holomek festival definitely wants us and so does the Lackova. The third one wants references. Do you know anyone in Sztojka?"

"That's near the Hungarian border. Maybe. I will look into it."

Sophia continued reading while Raoul started snooping through her kitchen. Upon finding some fruit and nuts, he helped himself. Sophia looked up.

"Do you mind?" he asked.

"Help yourself. The cool box is full, just for you," she said winking at him.

"I'm famished. Oh look, you have fresh cheese. It's my favourite kind," Raoul said as he stuffed his face with a wedge of gorgonzola, "I have some choreography ideas for your Miroslav dance."

"Oh really? What ideas?"

Raoul situated himself in an open space and struck a pose. He was tall and had an unusually muscular upper body from taming wild horses for trading, "You begin the piece like this, which really works. But then into the third refrain, when we hit the crescendo, your movements are low and lilting. Beautiful, but they need to be up here. Your arms are exquisite. You need to shorten the sleeves of your costume, and hold your arms high — like this. I also suggest you wear these."

He went to his bag and pulled out gold armbands that were decorated ornately in silver and garnets.

"Ooooh! Where did you get these?" Sophia exclaimed, admiring them.

"My father is a goldsmith. He made them. I'm supposed to sell them, but I want you to wear them on tour. Then when we get back, I'll sell them. Let me put them on you." He pulled off Sophia's shawl and lifted one arm, while he slid the arm band up to her upper arm, then repeated the gesture on the her left arm moving more slowly than he should, "Good. Now stand up and show me."

Just as she was about to stand up, the door to the caravan opened and Elena entered. Elena was a large woman in her early fifties with an abundance of wild, gray-streaked hair. She was one of Sophia's five aunts, "Sophia, I need you to help me with the laundry."

She looked up and saw Raoul standing over Sophia with his one leg up on her chair, "What are you doing here, young man? This is unseemly. Get out."

"We were just rehearsing for the tour, Elena," replied Sophia.

"You know better than to have a man like him alone with you in the caravan. What will people think, Sophia? Don't be an idiot."

Sophia flushed with shame and glanced up furtively at Raoul. He shrugged, grabbed his bag, and slipped past Elena to get out the door as fast as he could.

"That boy is nineteen-years-old and is a scoundrel, my dear. He just wants to take advantage of a lonely housewife like you. Don't let him. You will regret it."

"I know that, Elena. He is only a few years older than my own son. He was just helping me with the dance. We work together, that's all."

Elena peered at her skeptically and said, "Come on now. I need your help."

Over the next few weeks, Sophia received confirmations of bookings at ten festivals. The band also made plans to arrive a few days before some of the other festivals, to see if the organizers could squeeze them in. Ferencz found them five bookings in restaurants and clubs.

The day the band was planning to leave Sophia went to talk with Jiri. He was busy sketching Marlene Dietrich from a movie magazine.

"We will be gone until September. I know you have a lot to do here while both your Papa and I are away, but I do want you to study.

And I want you to keep drawing. You are gifted at so many things. Get Gustav and Peeter to help you with your father's chores. They look up to you so much and will do anything you say."

"I will, Mama. You have a wonderful tour and win a dance prize or two again just for me."

They gave each other a long hug, and when they looked back into each other's eyes providence flashed for a brilliant second. She was a grounding cord for him, but he did not know it at the time. He was forging his 'otherness' at the time, as boys of his age are wont to do.

"We all used to travel by caravan, you know, never staying in one place for more than a few nights," she mused.

"I know, Mama, you and Grandpapa told me the stories. It sounded like a wonderful life."

"I'm sorry you didn't get to be a part of that. Staying in one place is just not the same. We were born for open skies."

"You definitely are," he smiled.

"You be good," said Sophia as she loaded the last of her bags into the caravan.

"You be good, too, Mama," he whispered back to her trying to push away an uncomfortable feeling of abandonment.

As they drove away in the caravan, Sophia sat in the back, waving at her son, and beaming with pride and love. She knew in her heart that one day he would be a great man. She had no way of knowing that her relationship with him would soon be torn to pieces.

## CHAPTER 39

The road into Podunajské Biskupice was packed with performers on foot, on horseback, and in horse-drawn caravans. They were all coming for the annual festival of Sainte Sara la Kali, the patron saint of the Gypsies.

Podunajské Biskupice was a cooperative of artisans near Bratislava. They were the envy of other artisan communities in the country. Their silversmith and goldsmith work were known across Europe and they received handsome sums of money for their work. As a result, they were one of the few communities that had proper housing, their own school, a concert hall, three guesthouses and two restaurants.

As the caravan got closer to the gates, Sophia could feel the excitement and energy in the air. They passed a group of artisans decorating the Sainte Sara sculpture. She was a black goddess, dressed in blue and white painted robes, sitting on a wooden raft. Soon, she would be covered in candles, jewellery and blessings of food, and sent out a raft on the nearby pond for the ritual tomorrow evening.

Sophia and Ferencz had booked their band to play that evening as part of the festival, but the travel was slow due to the unexpected influx of revellers. When they finally arrived, a gatekeeper with lamb chop sideburns and a barrel chest barked at them to park their caravan outside the gate. They would have to walk the rest of the way to get to the guest quarters.

Packing all their bags and instruments on their backs, the band members hiked another twenty minutes through mud and pot-holed pathways. When they finally arrived, exhausted and bedraggled, the owner of the guesthouse announced, "Sorry folks, we only have one room left."

He pushed open the creaking door to reveal a room the size of a storage shed. There were several sacks of grain in one corner, a broken window, and paint flaking off the walls and ceiling. Tomáš shrugged and said, "That will be just fine. Thank you. The men will stay here, and Sophia will sleep in the caravan."

Sophia furrowed her brow, and began to drag her bag back down the stairs.

Raoul caught up with her and grabbed the bag, "It will be okay. I will hike back with you and help you fix up the caravan."

By the time they trudged all the way back to the outskirts of the community, Ferencz came running up behind them breathless, "We have to go back now. One of the other bands never made it, and they want us to play, starting in thirty minutes!"

They raced back down to the concert hall, both anxious and excited about the possibility of playing more than one set at the festival. Sophia locked herself inside a woodshed to change into her flamenco costume. It was dark and she could hardly see. After several minutes of frustration trying to organize her layered skirts and arrange her beaded headdress, she heard a knock on the door.

It was Raoul, "We are waiting for you. Come on!"

She emerged and stood in front of him with her arms held wide, "How do I look?"

A look of amusement crossed his face, and he quickly covered his mouth, "You look just fine."

"No I don't. You are trying not to laugh! Don't you dare let me go in there looking like an idiot."

Raoul stood back and assessed the situation, "Your skirt is inside out and your ruffles are all wonky. I think you put your blouse on sideways," he said trying to adjust her headdress.

Sophia smiled sheepishly and rolled her eyes, "Okay. Hide me."

Raoul stood facing Sophia, and held out his coat as a screen.

"Do that standing the other way, please," she ordered.

Raoul just smiled, and kept facing her. Sophia grimaced at him, while she lifted up her blouse, and pulled the ruffles back to where they belonged.

"That's right," said Raoul, "See? You need me as your mirror."

Then she took off her skirt, turned it inside out, and pulled it on again. Raoul helped her smooth out the layers at the back.

"You know better than to touch a woman's skirt."

"I'm not much of a traditionalist. I'm simply an artist wanting the show to go on. You look gorgeous," he said kissing the edge of her hand. "Now, let's go."

Raoul slipped onto his stool on stage and grabbed his acoustic guitar. Sophia took her place behind the curtain, stage right, ready for her entrance. She adjusted the gold coins sewed into her hair as she heard the announcer introduce them to sparse applause. They were unknowns, and not the band people were expecting.

As they started playing, Sophia felt a shiver run up her spine. The thrill and anxiety of performing always made her hands shake. Raoul nodded at her to begin. She slid on stage, arms held high, and bracelets glistening under the spotlights. Her brand new black Zapatos from Spain stamped the floor defiantly. The shaker above her head rattled in syncopation, and Tomáš glared at her to get back into rhythm. She smiled, and breathed out ferociously through her nostrils to release the tension.

As she turned back toward the audience, she knew there was one way she could win over the audience — that was to dance down the centre aisle. She jumped off the stage and landed with her Zapatos in unison to the drumbeat.

As she strutted her way down the aisle, she leaned back, letting her ebony locks cascade on the shoulders of a few male audience members. The energy in the room heated up, and the band members cranked up their pace. Her dance took on a life of its own. As Sophia's mind disappeared into the background, her body and soul etched out the meaning of the song, with every possible nuance of movement. By the time they finished their set the crowd was cheering, hollering and throwing carnations at Sophia's feet.

After taking their bows the band exited stage left and raced into the rehearsal room.

"That was unbelievable!" shouted Tomáš.

"They loved us!" Ferencz said, slapping Raoul on the back.

"They loved Sophia," replied Raoul. "We just supported her to do her magic."

"No, it was *all* of us," chided Sophia.

"But it was your idea to get us out on the road," Ferencz added.

"And what a great idea that was," smiled Raoul.

They gathered together in a huddle touching their foreheads giving silent gratitude to Santa Sara for making their dream come true.

Later that night, after a long evening of well-deserved revelry, the band members stumbled up to their storage shed of a room. Raoul offered to escort Sophia back to the caravan. The nighttime cold had a bitter edge and Sophia welcomed the blanket that Raoul draped over her shoulders. Together they had to rearrange some heavy items, to make room for a sleeping mat for Sophia.

"It's awfully cold tonight. Are you sure you will be okay here all by yourself?"

Sophia had two blankets, but still felt cold, "It's okay. I'll put on my hat, gloves and socks."

He felt her hands, they were freezing, "You are our star performer. I can't allow you to catch a cold. I'm getting in there with you."

Raoul took off his shoes, and snuggled in beside Sophia.

"People will talk, Raoul. Don't do this."

"They won't know a thing. They are all in a drunken sleep. Besides, I'll get up early and sneak back to the guest house before anyone wakes up. Don't you feel yourself getting warmer already?"

Sophia welcomed the warmth, but did everything she could not to look into Raoul's face. He was strikingly handsome — warm pools of liquid-gold eyes against dark skin, a high forehead and sensuous lips. She had noticed many of the women eyeing him from across the restaurant that night.

When she looked in his eyes, her whole body shuddered with attraction. She lay very still, trying to numb out her body's natural desires for him. It had been many months since Karl had made love to her. Their life was about bickering, working and paying bills. Romance had been a non-existent priority for many years.

Sophia's body was beginning to warm up and relax into sleep, so she turned over and faced away from Raoul. He pulled his body as close to her as possible, and wrapped his arm around her waist. She could feel his breath on the back of her neck, and finally his lips caressing her bare shoulder. It was at that point Sophia gave in. She decided that whatever the consequences, this one night of lovemaking would be worth it all.

At about 5:30 in the morning, Sophia awoke to the sound of wild pigs foraging next to the caravan. She rolled over to see the naked and beautiful man who had kept her up half the night.

"Raoul," she whispered, "You should get up and go back to the guesthouse."

"Yes, I will in a minute or so," he said as he rolled over encircling his arms around her.

"No. I think you should go now," she said, jabbing at his ribs.

"Right then," he said with a scowl. "Off I go."

He felt around for his tunic, pants and jacket, and stumbled into them, while banging his head on the ceiling. He kissed Sophia delicately on the lips and then peered out the back to see if the coast was clear.

A man was walking by with his dog, so he crept back to Sophia. This time he took her in a full embrace and kissed her more intently, lingering and nibbling on her lower lip.

"I will see you later on back at the concert hall," he said with a wicked grin as he sneaked out the back.

Word of the band's powerful sound and their vivacious dancer got around to several other festival organizers. Before long, they were booked solidly for the next few months.

The other band members pretended not to notice the way Raoul would sneak out after everyone else had fallen asleep and return just as the sun was coming up. At first Ferencz thought he was just having fun with some of the local girls but by late August it was clear that Sophia was his object of desire.

Ferencz approached her late one night, as she prepared to go to bed, "I know this is none of my business, but in a way it is my business. This summer with the band has been an extraordinary experience for me, and I think we could easily begin touring in Western Europe if we really focused. I wouldn't want anything to happen that would make our group fall apart. Do you know what I mean?"

"No. I don't know what you mean, Ferencz."

"I know your husband is an outsider, and goodness knows how hard it's been for all of us to accept him, but you are a married woman and I do respect what he brings to the business."

"I still don't know what you are talking about," Sophia countered, frowning.

"You think no one notices? You are pregnant, Sophia, pregnant with that boy's child. I've seen him sneaking into your bed. We all have seen it many times over."

There was a long silence as Sophia turned away, her face flushed with shame. She placed both hands on her slightly rounded belly. Ferencz was trained in herbal medicine, and had helped many women through hard pregnancies, including her own. In fact, when she became pregnant with Jiri, she had secretly asked him for medicine to abort the baby. He had refused, given the advanced stage of the pregnancy.

Karl and Sophia married to save her reputation. The pregnancy had been torturous for her. Karl was a large man, and Sophia a petite woman who still hadn't reached maturity. Her pelvis would not open wide enough for a natural birth, and in the end Jiri was born via a Caesarean section. At the hospital in Bratislava there were complications and the doctors told her she would probably never have any more children.

Although Sophia guessed she might be pregnant, she had assumed that it was impossible.

She looked back into the wise, old eyes of Ferencz and said, "You know I can't be pregnant."

"I know a pregnant woman when I see one. I estimate that you will give birth about February, unless of course you want to abort it."

"I never thought that I could have a child again. I wouldn't abort it!" she gasped.

"If you keep the child, you will bring shame to your community. Your husband will probably divorce you, and you won't be able to go on tour anymore, not with an infant child. I could arrange it for you, and we could pretend it never happened."

She remembered the day Jiri was born. It was an awful birth experience, but once he was in her arms she forgot the pain. The love she felt for that amber-eyed, innocent child was beyond anything she had ever felt before. She was so grateful that she had chosen to keep the child. Jiri was the best thing that ever happened to her.

She knew he would give so much to the world. Perhaps another great soul lay forming in her womb. Who was she to deny this child life?

Tears streamed down Sophia's face, and Ferencz handed her his handkerchief. She held her face in her hands and sobbed, "I want this child so much. My community loves me. If Karl divorces me, then I will just marry Raoul. My sisters can help take care of the baby when I'm on tour."

"You think that young lad will stick around to help raise a child?"

"We love each other," she protested.

"I'm sure you do, but he doesn't have the maturity."

Just then Tomáš approached, interrupting them, "Let's go get some food!"

Raoul was right behind him. He was about to speak when he noticed the tears in Sophia's eyes and the judgmental glare of Ferencz staring back at him.

"I need to go help Havel move some furniture," Raoul declared, looking wary, "I'll see you all after lunch."

"I think its best we all sit down and have a talk about this situation," Ferencz said as he grabbed Raoul by the elbow.

It was late September when the band finally arrived home. Jiri and Karl were lashing down some awnings that had been loosened by the brisk autumn winds.

Karl had returned a few weeks earlier than expected. Although he was still upset that Sophia had left without his permission, the local paper had written up news of the band's success. The Olino band members were now celebrities in the region, and he felt proud of his beautiful wife's accomplishments. When they spotted the caravan at a distance, Jiri ran in a circle around the community, announcing their imminent arrival. He had missed his mother so much.

For the last five years she had been both his caregiver and his friend, especially during the long months his father spent on the U-boats. They shared a love of philosophy, writing and art and would often stay up late reading the classics together. Even though the carnival was in her family for generations, it was Sophia who had encouraged him to pursue academics, to explore the world and to choose his own path. Jiri was grateful for that encouragement and so they kept his career aspirations as their own little secret together. One day Karl would understand.

When the band finally pulled up to the tents, Jiri raced over and lifted Sophia out of the caravan, swinging her around and placing her in front of him. He squeezed her so hard she almost fainted.

"You've gotten heavy Mama! Too many cakes at those fancy restaurants?"

Sophia smiled awkwardly and looked away, and so did all the other band members. Karl came over and took her in his arms, his eyes beaming with pride, "You did good out there. The goddess continues to grace you with great talent."

Ferencz put his arm around Jiri's shoulder and said, "My boy, you have grown at least an inch or two in these last few months. You are going to be taller than me! Show us the changes you've made since we've been away."

As Jiri and Hanzi explained some of the re-organization they'd done, Karl and several other community members unloaded the caravan.

Later that evening, Jiri noticed his mother, father and Raoul sitting in the meeting hall with his grandparents, Besnick and Florica. Jiri wondered why they all looked so serious.

When they emerged from the hall, he heard his grandfather shouting and saw Sophia run to her caravan and slam the door shut. Jiri dashed over to find out what was happening and Besnik stopped him, "Leave your mother be right now. She has some thinking to do."

Raoul was standing nearby, eyes cast down, kicking at a stone in the ground with the tip of his leather boot. Jiri looked into his grandfather's eyes and asked, "What's going on?"

Florica looked at Jiri and gently said under her breath, "It looks as though you are going to have a brother or a sister, my boy."

Jiri looked at both of them, then over at Raoul. The look in the young guitar player's eyes told him everything. Jiri felt a heat rise from the base of his spine right up to the back of his neck. His vision clouded over, and his hands clenched into fists. Before the elders could stop him, Jiri lunged at Raoul.

Within seconds the two young men were on the ground, and Jiri was kicking, punching, scratching and slapping Raoul any way he could. When Besnik and Tomáš finally pulled them apart, Raoul had a cut lip, a scratched cheek and bruises all over his legs. He hadn't tried to fight back.

The two had become friends during the previous winter playing cards together, swapping tall tales, and taking care of the horses. In fact, just a few months ago, Raoul had rescued Jiri from being beaten up by some Hlinkas soldiers in the village. He was carrying home a sack of potatoes when two boys in uniform chased him into the forest.

Raoul was watching from up in a tree and came at the boys with a large stick. For some reason, whether it was the stick or the wild look in Raoul's eyes, the boys had run away. After that Jiri felt deeply grateful, and their friendship was cemented. Raoul's behaviour with his mother felt like the worst betrayal possible and altogether too much for Jiri to contain.

He spat on the ground near where Raoul lay, then marched over to the barn and saddled up the brown mare. For the next several hours Jiri galloped as fast as the young horse would go through the Carpathian forest trails. The tears stung his eyes, the branches scraped at his frozen cheeks, and his heart felt smashed into a thousand pieces.

When he finally returned home well past midnight, Sophia was waiting for him on the stoop of their caravan.

"Please talk with me," Sophia pleaded.

He pushed past her and went inside to grab some belongings. He noticed that many of his father's things were gone. When he emerged with a bag of clothes and a sleeping mat, Sophia was cowering under the arm of her elder sister, Nadya.

"Where are you going, Jiri?" asked Nadya.

"Anywhere but here. Where is Papa?"

"He is packing up the gray caravan and is going to visit with your grandmother in Kittsee," she replied.

"Good. I'll go with him."

Sophia pleaded again, "Jiri! Please don't go. Please talk to me. I want you to understand things, to know my heart."

Jiri looked down at the ground in front of his mother's feet, and then raised his chin slowly until they were eye to eye, "I am never talking to you again. You are no longer my mother."

Then he hoisted his satchel over his shoulder and went into the barn just as Karl was leading the horse-drawn caravan out onto the dirt road.

"I'm joining you, Papa. I haven't seen Oma in over a year."

Karl simply nodded.

The news had shaken the normally even-tempered man to the core. His straw-coloured hair, turquoise eyes, and staid exterior had always set him apart from the darker features and more animated demeanour of his wife's family.

While the community shouted at each other about Sophia's condition, Karl had remained silent. He had felt ostracized too many times by the men of Olino, and secretly harboured a desire to find another place where he felt more welcome.

Sophia and her brother-in-law, Stefan, came running toward them. Stefan shouted, "You can't both leave now. Who will manage the carnival? Hanzi can't do it by himself!"

Both Jiri and his father said nothing.

"You are my family, and you are abandoning me when I need you most," sobbed Sophia.

Karl clenched his hands around the reins of the cart until his knuckles turned white. Finally he said, "I'm sorry, my love. I can't be here anymore. It's time for me to go. Jiri has asked to come with me. That is his decision."

"Jiri! I am the woman who gave you life. How can you do this to me? How can you renounce your own mother?"

Karl pulled on the reins and the horses began to move. Sophia ran after them screaming and sobbing to come back. Finally, breathless and exhausted, she sank to the ground. Jiri held his hands to his ears so as not to hear her screams, but still they pierced through him like a knife.

Finally, the sobbing stopped and he looked back briefly. He saw that she had curled herself up into a ball on the gravel road. His Uncle Stefan and Aunt Nadya were coming to her aid. He faced the road ahead again.

After that, he never looked back.

CHAPTER 40

K arl came back to Olino three times over the next six months. Once he came to gather more of their personal belongings, and the second time to train Hanzi in various aspects of running the carnival. The third and last time, he asked Sophia to sign divorce documents. Each time he visited, Sophia asked the same questions about Jiri: How was he doing? Was he studying? Why doesn't he write? Can I come visit?

Karl's answers were always the same, "He is doing well, working at a tire factory by day, and studying for his university entrance exams by night. He is still hurting from what happened, that's why he doesn't write. I don't think it would be wise for you to visit right now. He may come back for a visit here when he is ready."

"I don't understand," Sophia said placing the fruit bowl down so hard on the table that it chipped.

"The Nazis recently declared that Gypsies in Austria are being excluded from the military, from voting and from job opportunities. We suspect it is only going to get worse from there. Jiri wants to change his first name to the more Germanic version of Jorg and get new identity papers."

"What does that mean?" asked Sophia, feeling her son slipping farther away from her.

"He would like to remove you from his birth certificate as his mother. I know that may upset you. But he needs to become *Volksgemeinschaft* to avoid persecution. Remember what happened to him in the village? It is worse in Kittsee. Austria is coming under Nazi rule. It will give him a chance in life."

"But you are *Volksgemeinschaft*. You are a supposed *pure race* person. What do they call it — Aryan?"

Karl sighed. It was hard enough to see his ex-wife at all. He was human. He still had feelings. But to try and explain some of this Nazi nonsense and make her see the threat to their son, when all she could feel was a mother's need and pain, put him in a position he hated.

"They are persecuting people of mixed heritage. In fact, they say mixed blood is worse. They put those types in jail right away."

"What makes mixed blood people worse?" she asked, bristling.

"They have these crazy ideas, the Nazis. They say if you combine the degraded instincts of a Gypsy with the higher intellect of a German, you get a mastermind criminal who will be a huge threat to society. In fact, they want to sterilize all people of mixed blood."

"That's horrible," she gasped as she wrapped her shawl closer around her protruding belly.

He added, "The Nazi racial scientists are beginning to systematically interview all Gypsies living in Austria or Germany. They are developing detailed family histories to root out assimilated Gypsies from the general population. Anyone with even a Gypsy great-grandparent will be forcibly moved into a camp and sterilized."

There was Gypsy blood in her family but few of them talked about it openly. However, on a trip to Germany fifteen years earlier, Besnick had been detained and forced to carry a Gypsy identity card from then on. His dark complexion had been all the officials needed to tag him like a wild animal. Those swarthy features had been passed down to both his daughter, Sophia, and his grandson, Jiri.

Sophia asked, "But, how would Jiri be able to hide his family history?"

"There is an underground organization that helps Jews and Gypsies get false identity papers. I am telling you in case authorities ever come here to question his relation to you. You must deny it."

"Who will he say is his mother, then?" Sophia said looking down at the hem of her skirt, a black hole creeping into her heart.

"I have met a woman that I will marry next month. Her name is Maria Groisenberg and her family is Catholic. I have written her name down here. If authorities ask, you say this woman is his mother. Agreed?"

Sophia looked at Karl, her pain and grief at the request palpable.

"That is a very hard thing you are asking me to do."

"It may be a matter of life or death for him. You don't know what it's like there now."

"I will do it on one condition — that Jiri come visit me."

"Don't make it conditional. You know what he is like when he sets his mind on something. I will ask him, but you know I can't promise. Please don't let him down about this."

"Tell him not to let me down then, either," she begged, shaking.

Karl put the signed divorce documents back in his jacket pocket, and sat back in his chair, "It looks as though you will be giving birth soon."

"Yes. Six more weeks to go."

Karl studied the woman he had adored, feeling her sadness, and he felt his own heart opening in that moment.

"I'm glad for you that you got to have another baby. I know what that means to you. I hope it goes much smoother than the first time."

"The doctor says the baby is much smaller than Jiri was. He suspects it will be a girl."

Karl smiled and remembered what Sophia was like when they were first married, barely out of childhood. She was so beautiful then, and even more stunning now. He smiled sadly.

"I forgive you, Sophia," he drew in his breath slowly, and reached for her delicate hand, "I was away a lot and you were lonely."

Sophia dropped her chin, her throat constricting.

"Thank you, Karl," she paused to let the gift of his forgiveness sink in.

"I hope you and Maria have a good life together, and that you take good care of my boy. I miss him so much."

Karl took both her hands and watched with compassion as she silently wept. He looked out over at the barn and saw Raoul brushing down the black stallion, "I hope Raoul is good to you and that he helps you look after this child."

Sophia sniffled and nodded.

"One more thing," Karl added, "Don't let anyone from Olino come into Austria. It's not safe for you. I'm sure this Hitler mania will blow over soon, but it's probably best you keep a low profile for now, wherever you go."

She nodded. She knew his care was genuine. He was a good man. That's what had attracted her to him in the beginning. How dearly she wished in her heart, in that moment, that "good" had been enough for her.

Karl studied her a moment, savouring the sight of her once more, then he cleared his throat and stood up. They gave each other a long, warm hug, and just before he turned to leave, Sophia said, "Karl, please bring this to Jiri."

She rustled through a drawer and pulled out a book.

"Your book of quotations? I know how special this is to you. You want to give it away?"

She nodded, determined, "He will need it for his philosophy studies. It's okay. I have all the good ones memorized."

"And *underlined*, as I can see," Karl said, smiling, as he flipped through the book, "Good. He will appreciate that."

"I hope so," Sophia whispered.

Karl hesitated for a moment as the image of her burned into his heart then tipped his hat to the woman his dreams had been built around and left Olino for the last time.

CHAPTER 41

Jiri could not find it in himself to go visit his mother or any of the people at Olino. He convinced himself that the threat of discovery by the Nazis and his desire to make a better life for himself were good reasons to stay away. There were deeper reasons, but he wouldn't face what they were at the time. He missed Olino and his kin more deeply than he let himself admit. Life in Austria seemed a stony wasteland where danger lurked in every alleyway.

In early March, 1938 Karl sent Jiri to a tavern in a rundown district of Vienna. There he was to meet a man who could supply him with new documentation. Jiri brought along all known copies of his existing documentation, plus copies of his father's and new mother's birth certificates. He donned his father's bowler hat and fur coat as a disguise.

When Jiri entered the tavern he looked around the room, his eyes searching the faces of the working class men there, busy quenching their thirst with Heidelberg beer. The air was thick with sweat and the smell of French tobacco smoke. The bartender asked Jiri what he'd like to drink and offered him a Gitano cigarette. Jiri recoiled from it, as if someone had just tried to burn him with a torch.

"No, thank you. Just a glass of draught beer, please," he said, "By the way, do you know where a person could get their shoes repaired around here?"

That was the password phrase Jiri had been told to use. The bartender poured Jiri's beer carefully, and placed it on the bar. The foam cascaded down one side, and the bartender wiped it off with a cloth.

Jiri could feel his stomach tighten up in a knot. The bartender was a middle-aged man with a receding hairline, greying at the temples, and sported a thick pair of reading glasses.

He peered at Jiri over the edge of his horn rims, searching his expression, and then murmured, "There's a fellow in the back room. He re-soles for a good price."

The bartender motioned with his chin to a door behind the bar.

Jiri nodded, picked up his glass of beer, and pushed his way through the crowd until he was in front of the door. He knocked lightly at first. No one answered. He waited for what seemed like an eternity. Then he thumped the door louder, using the side of his fist. He held his breath, half expecting to be immediately seized by Gestapo officers.

Then the door suddenly swung open to reveal a scrawny young man with a long, slim nose, peach fuzz for a beard and glasses much too large for his face.

"Jiri?"

"Yes."

"Are you by yourself?"

"Yes. Totally alone as you requested," Jiri answered.

"Come in, then. Good to see you. Please take off your coat and give it to my associates. They'll need to frisk you, I'm afraid."

Two older men came forward and checked Jiri for weapons.

"Give me what documents you have now and we will do our magic on them," the little man said, "Marko here will take your photo. Please stand over there under the light."

As Marko prepared to take the picture, the little man added, "Marko works by day for the Office of Racial Relations. He is putting his life on the line doing this. If you ever get caught you must make a solemn oath that you will not reveal his identity to authorities."

"Of course. Never," Jiri swore.

He watched the little fellow work, silently creating the forgery, and grew curious, "Excuse me, but how old are you? You don't look much older than me, and I'm only sixteen."

"I'm younger than I look. I'm twenty, actually. People think I'm just a kid, so no one bothers me. I'm the perfect person to be doing this kind of work. "

The forger thrust a hand out toward Jiri, still holding the passport with the other.

"The name is Goldstein … Laszlo Goldstein."

Jiri blinked, surprised.

"You're Jewish?"

"Mixed blood. Like you, my friend. My father is Jewish and my mother is a German National. In some ways, people like you and me need the most help. Don't you think? We live half in one world and half in another. We live constantly in inner conflict. But maybe some day most people will be like us, and all this *ferkakte* racial hatred will die away. Maybe then we can finally have peace in this crazy world.

"I know, it sounds too good to be true when the Nazis are kicking in people's heads in the streets, but mark my words, it'll happen. It's already happening in America. Anybody can marry anybody there. I tell you, I want my genes to mix with someone as different as possible. I'm going to find myself a half-Zulu, half-Korean girl and settle down in Brazil. What do you think of that?"

Jiri looked at Laszlo, astonished, then burst out laughing.

"What's so damn funny?"

"I'm sorry. I was just picturing you with a Zulu princess twice your height with slanted eyes and a bone in her nose. If it ever happens, you must invite me to the wedding."

He chuckled, "I promise you'll be the first."

He kept working, but took a moment to look a little closer at Jiri.

"I like you, my friend. So I'm going to give you a little piece of advice. Once you get your German National stamp of approval, I would get the hell out of this part of the world as soon as possible. I hear Canada is great. A bit cold in the winter, but you get used to it. I can get you a passport to Canada, Bolivia, Argentina, New Zealand, or Australia anytime. Even to Haiti. Haiti is a little backward, but they have nice beaches and gorgeous, dark-skinned girls. By the way, for a guy who grew up in a Slavic country you sure speak German like a native. How did you manage that?"

"I'm a good mimic."

Laszlo nodded and grinned, "That means you'd be good in the theatre. I hear they need people with good acting skills in the French underground — spying on the Germans! You want to go? It's very exciting work. Can you speak German with a French accent? Come on, give it a try."

Jiri shook his head, "I'm studying right now and have a full time job. I don't have time for that."

Laszlo shrugged, "Fair enough. But when this country has gone down the crapper we'll all wonder some day if we did enough to stop it. Hitler is going to grind us down to nothing. Mark my words: don't stay here. If they ever find that you have fake ID, you'll be shot on sight. Use these papers to get out."

Jiri stood frozen on the spot, torn by Laszlo's prophetic words and advice. Jiri had just gotten a good job and would be taking his university entrance exams soon. The program at The University of Vienna was perfect for him. He didn't want to try to start all over somewhere else. It had been a hard enough transition leaving Olino and living in Vienna.

"I'll think about it, Laszlo. Thanks for the warning."

Laszlo nodded and then presented Jiri with his new documents, "My pleasure. Nice to meet you Herr Jorg Frei."

Jiri smiled, ruefully, playing along.

"Yes, thank you. Nice to meet you, too."

"So, where was your mother born?"

"In Vienna."

"What year?"

"I don't know," Jiri answered, frowning.

"It's not 1918, like it says here on her birth certificate, because that proves she's only three years older than you. So what's your mother's name and date of birth, Jorg?"

"Maria Groisenberg. She was born in Vienna on February 27th, 1903," Jiri corrected. "She's thirty-five, not nineteen."

"That's right," Laszlo grimaced, "And what does she look like?"

"Unfortunately, she is fair and blonde like my father."

"Which makes my point *exactly*," Laszlo said studying the dark complexion of the boy in front of him. "That would make it genetically impossible to produce someone who looks like you. Blonde hair and blue eyes are recessive genes. All children of their coupling would also have blonde hair and blue eyes. All of them. That's why you shouldn't stay here. This will keep you going for a while, but it's only going to get worse."

"My father thinks it will all blow over soon."

"Your father's an optimistic man, Jorg, but I'm afraid that kind of outlook could be dangerous right now. There is going to be another world war, and it's going to get very nasty. I see things that normal folks like you don't get to see. The news is covering up the truth, distorting it. Hitler wants to dominate the world and nothing is going to stop him from trying, except maybe a group of people I know in the French Resistance who have a plan to assassinate him. But you didn't hear that from me, did you ... Jorg?"

He looked up at Jiri sharply, demanding an answer. Jiri shook his head, not interested in plots, or Hitler, or any more of Laszlo's gloomy world outlook. He had some hard decisions to make. He held out his hand again.

"Thank you very much for what you've done for me here today, Laszlo. It may be saving my life. Please take this money."

Laszlo accepted the payment, nodding.

"It's not *maybe* saving your life, Jorg. It *is* saving your life. Be very careful. I'd think about maybe bleaching that black hair of yours or something, if you insist on staying. If they ever connect the dots —

that Maria never had a child and that she is only three years older than
you — it's over for you."

Jiri — now officially Jorg — nodded and left the tavern.

He kept his head low and his new documents safely tucked away in
his breast pocket as he walked away quickly, his footsteps echoing on
the cobblestones of the vacant backstreet.

A week later, Maria, his new 'mother,' took him into the bathroom and
lightened his hair to a coppery brown.

"That's a bit better," she said, looking at him sideways in the mirror,
"although it looks rather odd."

"It will have to do for now."

"By the way, we got a letter today," she informed him, "Since you
registered for university entrance exams under the name of Jorg Frei,
they have informed us that you haven't yet registered for the Hitler
Youth. It's now the law for boys of your age."

"Hitler Youth!" Jiri exclaimed, alarmed, "Does that mean they are
suspicious of me? What should I do?!"

"You have to register. If you don't, they will become even more suspicious. You just have to do a few silly military games. Just play along."

For the next three days, Jiri was so nervous he couldn't eat. In order to
calm himself he started trying to sound more German when he spoke.
He imagined himself being like the boys who used to beat him up;
practicing the bearing and the attitude as often as he could.

He found a Hitler Youth flyer and taped it to the wall. On the flyer
was a picture of a boy in uniform holding the Nazi flag and saluting.
He placed his sketch pad on a small easel and started drawing. First he
vaguely drew the boy and his uniform. However, instead of sketching

the boy's face in the picture he sketched his own face there. After he was done with the sketch, he held it in front of him looking at it from several angles. Then he taped it to his wall and practiced the salute many times over, making his body as rigid as possible like he'd seen them do in the news reels at the theatre.

The sketch stayed next to his bed for days and he looked at it each night before falling asleep. Day by day he dreamed another new aspect of this persona into existence.

Finally he presented himself at the Hitler Youth office with his coppery hair and false ID. His breathing was so constricted he could barely speak. As he walked into the office the staff all turned to look like a clan of hyenas. Upon producing his conscription notice with his new name, the intake clerk snatched it out of his hands. The crew-cut man with the box-shaped head scrutinized the document. Jorg's shoulders went stiff. The clerk finally slid the paper to one side of the desk, licked his forefinger and peeled off a sheet of paper from a stack on the right.

"Fill out this form with full details, listing any special skills."

Jorg sat in the waiting area filling in the details, willing his hand not to shake. The only skill he could tick off was 'sharpshooter'. Jorg handed the form back to the clerk.

"Sharpshooter, huh?" the clerk queried, pleasantly surprised. "Well, Sergeant Bauer will want to test your accuracy immediately. If you are good, this will be a big career boost for you. We need more shooters."

Jiri smiled, but winced inwardly. He'd already heard about Sergeant Bauer, who had a brutal reputation among the local Hitler Youth. He'd beaten one of his boys severely with the butt of a rifle because the lad didn't "Heil Hitler" as quickly as the other boys.

The clerk got off the phone, interrupting Jiri's ruminations and announced, "The Sergeant will see you now."

In that moment, Jiri decided he had to either sink or swim. The only weapons he had at his disposal were a quick mind, good mimicry and a will to survive. That was the moment that Jiri dissolved and Jorg the Nazi was born.

*"Heil Hitler!"* Jorg shouted as he entered Sergeant Bauer's office, saluting with the precision of a military zealot.

*"Heil Hitler!"* replied Sergeant Bauer, "You are the new sharpshooter? We'll see if you were lying or not. Come with me to the shooting gallery."

As Jorg followed the Sergeant down to the gravel courtyard, his heart was pounding.

"Where are you from?" Sergeant Bauer grilled him.

"I was born in Engerau just across the border. My family just moved here to Kittsee."

He was careful to say exactly the same thing to everyone he talked to — no more, no less.

"Where did you learn to sharpshoot?"

Jorg hadn't anticipated that question. He couldn't say at a carnival shooting arcade. That might give away his heritage immediately.

"My father loved to hunt and took me with him all the time."

"Well, I hope you are not wasting my time, Frei," Bauer snorted, "Hunting a deer and hunting a man are two different things entirely."

He handed Jorg a Mauser Karabiner 98k. Jorg had never used a rifle like that before. It was a sophisticated piece of machinery that he admired and feared at the same time. Jorg had only ever used a BB gun to shoot metal ducks. He took in a deep breath to calm his nerves. He had to trust that he could figure it out. The mark stood at least fifty feet away, much farther than Jorg was used to. He held the rifle, steadied his aim and concentrated with all his effort.

"I don't have all day, boy. Fire!" Bauer ordered.

Jorg ground his feet into the dirt, squinted his left eye, and willed the bullet to hit the heart of the target. After he fired, he closed his eyes and kept them closed until he heard the Sergeant say, "Excellent. In fact, amazing. Let's try a few more times, to make sure it wasn't just a lucky strike."

After Jorg hit the heart of the wooden figure eight more times, the Sergeant, whose disposition toward him had changed dramatically, said,

"I will arrange to have you sent to sniper school immediately. We need boys like you at the Waffen-SS. You will earn your Sharpshooter Silver in no time. You should feel tremendously grateful that you have such a gift — a gift that will allow you to be of profound service to your Führer. *Heil Hitler!*"

After Jorg had filled in all the application forms he walked back slowly to the flat he shared with his father and Maria. The sun was falling behind two monolithic buildings. Nazi banners hung from every street lamp, flapping in the late afternoon breeze.

Indistinguishable emotions broiled around in Jorg's head. His temples pounded. Two boys marched by him proud as peacocks in their black uniforms and swastika armbands. A gaggle of blonde-haired girls in bibbed dresses followed closely on their heels. All of them were stunning to look at. He smiled. None of them gave him any attention as they passed. They were pursuing the boys in uniform.

He stood in a doorway and watched. Six girls crowding around the two of them, laughing and flirting. He was older than those boys, taller, better built and certainly more handsome. It's just the uniform, he snorted to himself.

When he entered the flat, Maria was just serving dinner.

"Where have you been? It's so late!" demanded Karl.

"How did it go at the Hitler Youth office?" added Maria, "We were so worried."

Jorg sat down and slathered a piece of bread with butter and stuffed it in his mouth.

"Okay," he mumbled.

"What does that mean?" they asked in unison.

He chewed hastily and swallowed, "I told them I was a sharpshooter, so they're sending me to sharpshooter school. It's the Napola Academy near Bensberg. I do entrance exams next week."

"What? You're not going there!" retorted Karl.

"But, Papa, it's a big chance for me. It's a school for the elite only and they are sending me for free!"

"Have you lost your mind?"

"But it's in a castle and there are real showers and tennis courts and you can learn to fly airplanes there. Here I have to work full time and do my studies at night. There I could just focus on my schooling," he searched their expressions for some kind of understanding. "I could really be somebody if I went there!"

"That's far too dangerous," cried Maria.

Karl sighed and looked down at the special edition copy of Hitler's, *Mein Kampf*, that his neighbour had insisted he read. "Jiri, I don't understand what's gotten into you. You left here this morning terrified of Hitler Youth and now you want to join their elite school?"

"They liked me, Papa. They accepted me as one of them."

"You *want* to be one of them?"

"No, I mean I just want an education. I have so much I want to learn."

"I can't allow you to do that, son. If they find out about you ..." Karl felt his eyes sting with tears, "I couldn't live with myself if I allowed you to go to that place."

"But they are making special compensation to bring me in for senior year. It would only be for one year."

"No."

"But ..."

"I said no!"

"Why?"

"These people are insane, son. Don't you see that?"

"I can just play their game for this one year until I get my education ..."

"Absolutely not."

"But why?"

Karl threw his arms up in the air and pushed himself away from the table, his normally even-tempered disposition erupting, "Because I am your father, goddamn it, and I say so. No more discussion!"

The following week, Jorg packed his suitcase and left for Bensberg early one morning before anyone was awake. His note read, "I have to go there. It is important to me. I'm sorry, please don't be angry with me. I promise I will stay safe."

## CHAPTER 42

The Napola or National-Political Institutes of Learning were rigorous academies spread across the Reich for Germany's elite soldiers and athletes. They were designed to train the country's next generation of political and military leaders. Only boys and girls of high academic standing and those considered to be "racially flawless" were admitted to these boarding schools.

When Jorg approached the Bensberg Napola he marvelled at the castle architecture. As he walked through the marble pillars he imagined he was a prince entering his court. Upon arrival he was submitted to a series of tests. They measured the width of his head and nose, graded his eye color and hair color, and made him do a series of athletic as well as academic tests. When they stamped "suitable" on his entrance forms, the relief almost made him pass out.

The Headmaster, Wilhelm Braun, invited Jorg into his office, "Your parents must be proud of you?" he said as he drew on his pipe.

Jorg lied, "Yes, sir."

If he admitted that his father denied his request to go to Napola, the school would send the Gestapo to his father's house and force him into a labour camp.

"It's unusual for a boy of your age to be accepted. Sergeant Bauer jumped several hoops to get you in here. I hope you're worth it."

Jorg blinked, not knowing how to respond.

"You just might be. Your academic testing is superior. Perhaps you should consider politics. We are just at the beginning of the 1000 Year Reich, you know. We will need many leaders and not just for Austria or Germany. We will need them in Russia, England, Australia and even in the Americas."

Jorg raised his eyebrows. Laszlo was right. Hitler was going after world domination.

The Headmaster continued, "Why do you want to be a cadet at Napola?"

Jorg had remembered hearing all the boys recite the same sentence which he engraved into his memory banks, "Because I want to serve the Folk, Führer and Fatherland!"

"Use your time with full discretion here. Steel your body and soul and be a faithful, dependable disciple." The Headmaster rose from behind his desk and saluted, "Our flag is greater than death! *Heil Hitler!*"

Jorg leapt to his feet, *"Heil Hitler!"*

Later that day Jorg was issued an autographed photo of Hitler and a crisp, black uniform with a red and white swastika armband. His bunkmate, Michael Hahn, gave him the drill from locker tidiness, to making your bed, to care of his uniform and guns, and finally the sin of lateness. The look of anguish on the boy's face as he described the fanatical precision with which everything needed to be done made Jorg's stomach upset. His upbringing amongst a band of carnival entertainers in no way prepared him for this lifestyle.

"Be careful you never get caught with one badly folded towel when Rutger, the inspection officer, comes by. You will live to regret it," Michael warned.

"I understand," replied Jorg, "I heard there are real showers here. Where are they?"

"Down the hall to your left. Hurry, though. We need to be at assembly at seventeen hundred hours. If you're one minute late, it's game over."

Jorg rushed down the hall. He seemed to need the toilet far too often that day. His stomach continued its queasy complaints. The hot shower was like an island of refuge. After years of bathing in a cold river he thought he'd finally arrived. When he emerged he felt more relaxed and changed into his uniform. He studied his reflection in the mirror. It was the boy in his sketch. Almost. He could hardly wait until the beautiful young girls who worked in the mess hall saw him in uniform.

Just then, another boy entered and used the toilet. When he emerged he stood a few feet away, combing his hair in the mirror. He sensed he knew the boy. Jorg glanced at him then darted his eyes back to the sink. *It couldn't be,* he thought. He was sure that boy was a Gypsy that had once come looking for a job at the Olino Carnival. When he looked up again the boy was staring at him in the mirror. Something in Jorg's spine liquefied.

He turned his back to dry his hands on a towel. He was trembling.

As he turned to leave, the boy stepped in front of Jorg and whispered, "We are stalemated, my friend."

With that, he exited.

Jorg did his best to avoid the boy named Erich Hausen, who occasionally whispered taunts to him. Each time Erich whispered, Jorg ignored him.

"Our races compete against each other according to Darwin," lectured the teacher, "It's the survival of the fittest, and so a higher race will always conquer a lower one. If we exterminate the weak, we produce a better society. Jews, blacks and especially the Gypsies are underdeveloped and we therefore cannot have them polluting our pure Aryan race."

Jorg squirmed in his seat. He glanced at Erich. The other boy's shoulders stiffened.

Jorg remembered reading that Aryans were considered to be one of the root races, descendants of the advanced civilization known as Atlantis. They were thought of as the only race capable of, or with an interest in, creating and maintaining culture and civilizations. Although the Nazis claimed that the Gypsies were not Aryan, Jorg remembered hearing something to the contrary from the Gypsy Lore Society. He read that some members of the Society thought that the Gypsies were the most ancient Aryans and that is why they sought to protect themselves from mixing with non-Gypsy elements and from modernization — to remain a pure race.

The teacher continued, "Some people call the Nazis barbarians. We *are* barbarians! We want to be that way. It is an honourable title because by this methodology we shall rejuvenate the world!"

The boys clapped and cheered, especially Erich. Jorg joined them so as not to stand out, yet the logic of these arguments seemed wrong to his inquiring and well-studied mind, and not just because of his Gypsy heritage.

Jorg also remembered reading about eugenics, the improvement of human hereditary traits through various forms of intervention, somewhat like dog breeding. At different times in history it had been regarded as a social responsibility of the governing forces meant to create healthier, more intelligent people, to save resources and to lessen human suffering. Of course, there have always been those who claimed eugenics was immoral and of course no one could agree on who was the superior race.

He read that each eugenics advocate, no matter what race, color or creed felt that their group was the superior one. It was simply human nature to want your group to be the winning team.

The teacher boomed, "We must adhere to the laws of nature. Natural selection is our genetic programming!"

Jorg noticed that he didn't mention anything about the importance of diversity within nature. Sharks were not the only fish in the ocean. If they killed off all the other fish, sharks would also die. Fascist ideologies were invariably unsustainable, although Jorg knew better than to challenge the teachings in this academy.

Erich continued to be a source of angst for Jorg. The boy seemed to enjoy threatening and torturing other boys. One day during a break in shooting practice, Jorg noticed a young, blond boy with large hazel eyes named Günther Janssen. He was staring up at a tree, trying to sketch it on loose-leaf paper. The boy kept erasing his work and trying again. Jorg put down his gun and started walking toward the boy. Erich caught up with him.

"Are you thinking what I'm thinking?" challenged Erich.

Jorg was actually thinking he would offer a few sketching tips to Günther, but he suspected Erich had something else in mind.

"I'm just going to see what he's doing," replied Jorg.

"Terrorize or be terrorized, my friend," Erich whispered.

Jorg slowed his pace and felt relieved when he heard the captain calling them back. The two boys marched swiftly to Captain Hellmuth Sommer and saluted.

"Do what's necessary," he commanded, "Fritz, Michael, join them."

Jorg stalled, pretending to fix his boot strap. The boys charged across the field and leapt on Günther. They ripped his sketch to pieces, spitting on him, kicking and punching him. Jorg trailed behind them.

Erich yelled in Jorg's ear, "Kick him! Kick him!"

Jorg kicked with his boot, feigning a savage face. He barely touched Günther.

Erich took off his belt and held it high in the air. The other boys figured the game and tore off Günther's shirt. He was barely fourteen-years-old, but looked more like twelve. The boy was crying, nearly wailing in terror.

"Mamaaaaaa!" he shrieked.

Fritz taunted, "He wants his mommy. He's a little mommy's boy!"

The other boys screamed with laughter, joining in the taunts, shouting over top of each other, their bloodthirsty frenzy mounting. A pain shot through Jorg's gut, severing something.

Erich handed his belt to Jorg.

"Do it!" he shouted.

Jorg held up the belt, on the other end was a brass buckle with razor-sharp edges. He hesitated.

The boys chanted, "Do it! Do it!"

Other boys had now gathered around, along with the Captain and several other officers. The Captain came up beside Jorg's left. He was lazily holding a cigarette between his fingers. Jorg watched the smoke rise and curl.

"What are you waiting for?" Captain Sommer smiled.

Erich's facial expression implored him to do it — or die.

Jorg felt a shock of electricity run from the base of his neck down his well-muscled arm as the belt came down. It ripped at Günther's skin, tearing his flesh. The boy yelped like a whipped dog.

"Again!" they screamed.

The next time was harder and the tong of the buckle left a welt. Günther emitted a howling scream. A shudder of disgust ran through Jorg. The third strike drew blood. Günther finally went into shock, dazedly rocking back and forth on the grass.

"Enough," stated the Captain.

Jorg dropped the belt at the boy's feet and walked away, numb.

As he walked passed the Headmaster, he said to Jorg, "No pity for the weak. It's the only way they'll learn."

The crowd dispersed, leaving the boy on the grass in semi-consciousness. As they returned to the classroom, Jorg glanced out the window. The boy was still there. It was starting to rain. His made a mental note to destroy the sketch pad buried deep in his trunk.

A week later, Jorg heard rumour that Günther was sent home because of injuries sustained during a training accident.

Napola was a place designed to ferret out freethinkers, artists, or delicate souls whose consciences might get in the way of blind obedience to authority. Jorg hated their game. Yet, at that time, if it meant surviving, Jorg would have poked out both his eyes. Only later would he realize that being authentic — and therefore worthless — in the minds of the Third Reich paradoxically would require enormous strength and conviction.

Jorg used mirrors assiduously. His fierce mental focus went to work, detailing his every word and movement until he had forged himself into their image. To quell the terror inside he began eating more. Before long he was eating six meals a day. The artistry in him clung to his midsection like a claw. By the time his training ended he was shoulder deep in them, lost, desensitized, his own moral compass spinning in all directions.

The day he earned his Sharpshooter Silver, his comrades lifted him on their shoulders. The girls swarmed around him after the parade. Sergeant Bauer handed him a membership to an elite country club. For the young man who had felt like an outsider all his life, power had become an aphrodisiac.

In November 1938 he returned to his father's house in full uniform. Karl was overjoyed to see his son and reached out to hug him. Jorg recoiled from the embrace and offered to shake hands instead. Karl stepped back and looked over at Maria. They were both amazed at the transformation. He was no longer a boy, but had filled out into a hard-edged man. He knew that his son was fighting for his life to fit in, but when Kristallnacht occurred, Karl's concern turned to a deep-seated fear.

On November 9th, people from all across Germany and Austria took to the streets, smashing Jewish storefronts and burning synagogues. Jorg came home late that night and Karl was waiting for him at the kitchen table.

"Where have you been? I've been so worried about you. It's madness out there," Karl whispered, his face tense.

"I've been with some friends."

Karl studied his son, frowning, growing angry.

"You have cuts on your wrist and hands, and a bag of stolen goods in the front hall. You have been plundering and looting with the rest of those hooligans, haven't you?"

"Everyone is doing that. The Jews are all moving away anyway and they aren't allowed to take their things. The government said it's up for grabs. I got some incredible jewellery for Maria, and some tools for you, Papa. I thought you would be happy."

"What has gotten into you?" Karl erupted, "That's stealing. They are doing the same thing to your people, Jiri!"

"They are not *my* people and my name is Jorg, don't ever forget that!" Jorg barked back, suddenly angry himself.

The steely intensity with which his son shouted those words sent shivers down Karl's spine. He had lost control of his son. He had lost the Jiri he knew. Karl had seen this anti-Semitic fever overtake all sorts of people in his community, people who normally seemed decent and compassionate, but he never dreamed it would happen in his own home. He watched, as Jorg carried his newfound loot up to his room.

That night Karl sat in a chair next to his bed, staring out at the burning city. He prayed to a God he rarely spoke to, and asked for help to save his son's soul. It would take more than three more years before Karl's prayers were answered.

## CHAPTER 43

"Germany is taking over parts of Czechoslovakia!" Raoul shouted as he ran through the camp. "We just heard it on the radio. There are tanks moving across the border now. They are coming through and registering everyone's family history!" He leapt through the door into the caravan he shared with Sophia searching wildly for his satchel. "It's not safe for us to be here anymore. I say we leave for my parent's village in Hungary today."

Sophia looked up from nursing their two-year-old daughter, Lyuba, but didn't answer. She was filled with fear and confusion just like everyone else in Olino.

Stefan interjected, "Look, now is not a good time to travel. It's dangerous on the roads."

"And Lyuba is sick," Sophia added, seizing on the opportunity to stay where it felt familiar. "She has some kind of cough."

"Then I will go on my own," Raoul said, "I will find us a place to live there and get my old job back as a horse trainer. Then I'll come get you."

Sophia's heart sank. She suspected Raoul had been looking for an excuse to leave ever since Lyuba was born.

"Do what you feel is right," she said.

She wasn't going to try to stop him. It had been so difficult for her to let go of Jiri. She didn't want to feel attached to anyone like that again. He looked at her with both relief and sadness.

That night Sophia watched as Raoul left on horseback. His parting words were, "I'll keep to backcountry roads. I love you both. Wish me luck."

That was the last time Sophia ever saw him.

Raoul knew the lesser known horse trails throughout the region by heart. As a horse trader it was his job to rate the horses on speed, endurance and agility. How many times had he thundered down these tracks at breakneck speeds? That was in the daylight, though. This time he was traveling just as fast, but in total darkness, in the cold of early winter and with adrenaline coursing through his veins.

He chose the mare Night Rider for good reason. She seemed to have impeccable night vision and Raoul was praying that she would find her way without tripping over a root or log. After several hours of riding hard he slowed her down to a canter. She needed water.

Although it was starting to lightly snow, he could just make out the town of Skalica in the distance. He knew of a farm on the outskirts that had a stream running through it.

No one seemed to be around when they arrived at the brook. As Night Rider quenched her thirst, Raoul sat down to both eat some hardtack bread and drink from his water sack. After about ten minutes of dead calm, Night Rider became spooked and reared up on her hind quarters. Raoul leapt to his feet and tried to grab her reins. Soon four German Shepherd dogs were upon them barking and snarling like hungry wolverines.

Raoul leapt on Night Rider's back and whipped her with all his might to start galloping away, but she was too out of control and he could barely hold on.

Finally, the resident farmer and two men came running with rifles aimed high. One of them fired and barely missed Night Rider's head. At that point, she flung her hind legs so high in the air that Raoul's body flew forwards. He smashed against a tree and then landed on the back of his neck on the dirt. He heard a snapping sound and knew his spine was probably broken. Nerves throughout his body went haywire, and he writhed spastically on the ground. Finally, he went numb and the signals from his brain to his lower body no longer connected. The farmer and his farm hands stood around him with guns pointed at his face.

"He's Gypsy," said the farmer.

"He's badly hurt. Maybe we should call a doctor," one of the farm hands said.

"A doctor? He's just a Gypsy and the less of these people in our lives the better. They're always stealing from us. Secondly, that lad landed on his head. He'll probably never walk again, even if he does survive," the farmer added.

"Yeah, if you care about him so much why don't you just shoot him, Andrej, and put him out of his misery," the other farm hand added.

"Okay. I guess that would be a kindest thing to do. But if I do the shooting, I get his horse."

"No siree, that horse came on my land — it's my horse," stated the farmer.

"I'm the one who knows how to work with horses, he should be mine," argued Andrej.

As the two men stood arguing about the horse, the third man prodded the steel barrel of the rifle into Raoul's neck. He was barely conscious, but he could just make out Night Rider snorting and whinnying and calling out to him. He loved that horse. The steel felt both piercingly cold and yet somehow comforting.

"That's the lad who sold us Pegasus. Remember how he died two months after we bought him?"

"Typical Gypsy."

"Yeah, Nikolai, but that was because the horse ate that poison you left open in the barn," added Andrej.

"Just shoot him already," urged the farmer.

Those were the last words Raoul heard. The bullet left the barrel and lodged itself deep into the back of his neck. Night Rider bellowed at the loss of her beloved Raoul and thundered off into the misty night air.

By the time the three men had rolled him into a ditch there were ten more bullet holes in his body.

There was no word about Raoul for weeks back in Olino, but communication lines were down in the chaos of the takeover. About a month after he left, a man from Skalica came to visit. His name was Milosh and he sometimes helped during carnival time to set up and take down the tents. He asked to speak to Sophia's parents, Besnik and Florica, in private. Sophia watched them from a distance and she knew exactly what he was telling them.

Raoul was dead.

Milosh found Night Rider in and amongst his horses one morning, but they didn't know where the horse came from. When his son was out riding her, she led him to the ditch where they found Raoul's body. Milosh said it looked as though he had been beaten and shot several times, but there was still money in his pocket. They concluded that it was clearly a racial assault.

It took several years for Sophia to recover from the loss of Raoul and the guilt she felt for letting him go so easily. Her love for Lyuba was the only thing that kept her going. By five-years-old the child clearly had Raoul's features — his luminescent dark eyes, unreasonably long lashes and full lips. Her temperament was sweet and loving, unlike Jiri's darker moods at the same age. Lyuba's favourite pastime was to dance around the feet of Ferencz as he taught the violin to Gustav. Clearly she would one day follow in her mother's footsteps.

By February 1942, things were getting worse for the communities near the Austrian border. She kept hearing stories of the Gypsies getting stoned to death, children being kidnapped and sold into slavery, and caravans being torched.

In desperation one evening, Sophia wrapped herself and her daughter in blankets and hitched a ride across the Austrian border into Kittsee. She trudged through the snow, going up and down each street until she found the correct address, Dr. Ladislaus Batthyányplatz 19.

Sophia put Lyuba over one shoulder and pounded on the door with her frozen fist. It was late. It had taken her much longer to find the place than she anticipated. The small glass hatch in the front door opened, and a wrinkled face peered out at her.

"I want to speak to Jiri. Does Jiri live here?"

The old woman replied, "I know no one by that name."

She then asked, "Does a man named Karl live here?"

"Yes, ma'am, Karl Frei is the head of the household."

Sophia then pulled her blanket back to reveal the face of her sleeping angel, "This young child is a relative of this family."

The old woman recoiled, "I think you must be mistaken, ma'am. That child cannot be a relative!" She slammed the glass hatch and dead-bolted the door.

Sophia stood on the stoop for a moment, shocked at what had just occurred. Lyuba was heavy, and starting to wake up. Sophia sat down against a lamppost, and settled the child in her lap. She decided she would leave her there for a moment and try again to speak to Karl.

Before she could get up, a police officer walked around the corner. Upon seeing the dark-skinned woman sitting in the snow, he ordered her to get off the street. She tried to speak but when he held a baton over her head she scurried away as quickly as possible.

She hadn't noticed her own son watching them from the upstairs window.

CHAPTER 44

"We need gun tower snipers at the camps more than we need another airplane gunner," replied Sergeant Bauer.

Jorg and Sergeant Bauer were sitting in the Nazi officer's clubhouse in Munster drinking Heidelberg beer. It was rare for a man of Jorg's rank to be invited for drinks with a Sergeant. However, legend of Jorg's brilliance as a sharpshooter meant he could almost apply anywhere.

The downside was that Napola had not turned out to be a ticket to freedom. Instead of getting into the best university, Jorg was faced with Laszlo's prophetic words again: the outbreak of World War II. He had to join the war effort. Each day he hoped the war would end and each day it seemed to escalate.

He always wanted to fly a plane, so the closest he could get was to apply as a gunner for the Luftwaffe, the German Air Force. The Sergeant, however, had other plans for him.

"The ratio of prisoners to gunmen at these camps is insane. I'm always amazed that they don't just all revolt. We don't have the manpower to actually keep all these prisoners there," Sergeant Bauer mused.

Jorg had heard that Birkenau was where they were taking the Gypsies. He recoiled at the thought of going there, "Why round them up then, if we don't have the manpower?"

"We need to get rid of them," replied Sergeant Bauer. "You leave on Monday. And don't question me on this, Frei, or you will never get your post in the Luftwaffe."

With that, Sergeant Bauer downed the last of the foam in his mug, donned his cap and gave the *Heil Hitler* salute. Jorg stood immediately and returned the salute.

As he watched Sergeant Bauer march toward the exit, Jorg heard a voice nearby say, "And they *are* getting rid of them."

Jorg turned to look and saw a man at the next table in his late thirties dressed in an SS officer's uniform.

"The name is Lieutenant Gerstein, Kurt Gerstein. I work for the Institute for Hygiene of the Waffen-SS," he said reaching out his hand.

Jorg shook his hand. It was a soft grip, unlike most SS men.

"Have a seat," the lieutenant offered.

Jorg sat down cautiously. He had never been asked to sit at the table of an SS officer before either.

"What do you mean they *are* getting rid of them?" he asked, his throat constricting.

Lieutenant Gerstein continued, "They are using ziklon to make gas, and then piping it into chambers until everyone in the room is dead. Then they throw the bodies into mass graves. They plan to kill as many dislikables as possible, in as short a time as possible."

Jorg felt as if someone had just punched him in the stomach. Nausea overtook his entire system. He swallowed hard.

"Yes, lad, it's true," whispered the officer.

"Is — is — isn't that genocide?" muttered Jorg trying to remember what he'd read about the Geneva Convention.

"It most certainly is." Lt. Gerstein said as he glanced around the club. No one was around. He leaned toward Jorg, "It's the Nazi way."

Jorg nodded poker-faced. He was shocked yet also not surprised to hear that. He searched the man's expression and noticed that Lieutenant Gerstein's eyes seemed liquid pools of guilt.

"We didn't hear about that at the Napola Academy."

"Of course not."

"It's not in the newsreels, either."

"Son, I invented Ziklon-B to purify water, not to purify the German race," The lieutenant stood up and pushed a glass of water across the table to the young man, "Drink this. You'll feel better. Where are you posted?"

"They are sending me to Birkenau."

"If you go to Birkenau you may see it for yourself."

"I would prefer not to see that. I want to be in the Luftwaffe."

"I am seeing Göering tomorrow. I will mention it to him."

"The head of the Luftwaffe? Thank you, sir."

"If you do become a witness to the atrocities and then you make it out of Germany to Northern Africa, tell the world what you see."

Jorg couldn't believe what he was hearing from the mouth of an SS officer. The lieutenant saluted, and turned on his heel. By the time the trembling Jorg had leapt up to salute, Kurt Gerstein was gone.

It would be a few years later that Jorg learned the fate of this unusual SS officer. He had tried numerous times during the war to tell the international public about the Holocaust, but to no avail. Regardless of his attempts to stop the madness, he was put on trial as a war criminal. He committed suicide in his prison cell, just days before his execution.

## CHAPTER 45

A week later Jorg arrived at Birkenau. The new recruits received a tour of the grounds. Jorg saw a huge hole in the ground being dug out by machines.

"What is that for?" Jorg asked the sergeant doing the tour.

"None of your business, Corporal. You're just here to guard the gate."

Jorg regretted asking. He knew it was the mass grave site and that the shower chambers were the gas chambers. When the tour finished, Jorg did some paperwork, picked out a uniform, and Sergeant Ackermann issued him a German K98 Infantry Rifle.

"This is your gun tower, Frei," Ackermann said, pointing up at the closest tower to the gate, "The first shipment of prisoners arrives at eighteen hundred hours tomorrow. If any of them even look like they're trying to escape, your job is to shoot them on sight. Verstehen Sie?!"

"Ja!" Jorg saluted trying desperately to hide an ulcerous, shooting pain in his stomach.

He joined the other gunmen for dinner, but could barely eat a thing. Many of them were laughing and joking, making racial remarks. Now that he saw the ultimate ending to racial intolerance — genocide — he couldn't stomach the jokes anymore. He pushed his plate away and went to his bunk to lie down.

He saw that everyone caught up in the Nazi hysteria had become separated from their integrity by false hopes of a better life. He was one of them. He thought they could give him safety and security, but instead they had brought him face-to-face with the worst danger possible.

What if people in his mother's family arrived there? What if one of them recognized him? What if he had to actually shoot one of them? The thoughts kept him awake all night. The only way to survive was to always wear his visor cap and sunglasses constantly, have bad aim and get out of there as soon as possible.

By early 1943, the Germans were rounding people up from all around the Austrian/Czech border. When the crews first arrived at Olino they weren't sure who to take. Upon further investigation, however, the inhabitants seemed to be a mix of everything that Hitler wanted rid of: Gypsies, Jews, Slavs, Poles, Pacificists, artists, musicians and carnival freaks. Auschwitz II–Birkenau was the camp chosen for their detainment. The first transport arrived on February 26, 1943, when the *Familienzigeunerlager,* or Romani Family Camp, was still under construction.

It was bitterly cold the day the train pulled into Birkenau. Guards pushed bedraggled people off the train and steered them toward the barracks that were still being built.

Sophia hugged Lyuba close to her chest. Even after that horrendous train ride the child never cried. She lay peacefully in Sophia's arms, smiling up her mother and humming the lullabies that Florica had taught her.

As they shuffled en masse down the train platform, Sophia felt a shiver run up her spine. She turned her head slowly to the right, and looked up at a gun tower. A soldier in uniform was aiming a gun at her

from forty feet away. As soon as she looked at him, the gun dropped.
The gunman picked up his binoculars.

Without being able to see his face, Sophia knew who it was.

Even though he was far away and in uniform, she knew without any
doubt that the man standing at the gun tower was her own son.

Her heart beat so fast it threatened to leap out of her chest as she
desperately mouthed the words to him, "Help us!"

She braced for the bullet.

A moment later she opened her eyes. The gun man had dropped the
binoculars and was running down out of the tower.

Jorg's worst nightmares were playing out full throttle. Most of his family
was on that train platform: his mother, his beloved grandparents, Florica
and Besnick, Gustav, his Aunt Nadya, his Uncle Stefan, his cousins,
Hanzi, his father's second-in-command, the musicians Ferencz and
Tomáš, even Mirela, the girl he used to have a crush on.

Jiri, the lost carnival boy, had now come back to haunt the well-
trained Nazi gunman.

Jorg had run inside to the latrine. He knew he wasn't supposed to
leave his gun tower, especially not now, when all the prisoners were just
arriving. He was trembling and sweating. All the people he once loved,
and who had loved him and looked after him, were now standing on
that platform, frozen in terror, facing their imminent death.

Jorg stood numbed with indecision. If he tried to help them, he
would likely be killed. If he did nothing, he would never be able to
live with himself.

Without thinking, he acted.

Making sure no one was around, he raced down to the storage locker,
the only room he had keys for. There was nothing there that inspired
a solution. As he sat down on a box to figure out his next move, he
heard a knock at the door. It was the delivery truck driver dropping
off supplies.

This was his chance. Jorg offered to help the man unload his vehicle.
When they were both in the back of the truck, Jorg grabbed a shovel

and hit the man in the back of the head. The man fell forward, hitting his head, and sank to the floor of the truck. Blood gushed from his skull. There was no way he was still alive.

It was the first time Jorg ever killed someone, or so he thought in that moment. The reality of that fact stunned him into momentary inaction. He knew in his heart it would also be the last time he killed, so sharp was the impact on his conscience.

Acting instinctively and desperately, Jorg ripped open a box of medical supplies full of bandages and cotton batting. He absorbed the man's blood as best he could, and bandaged his head to stop the bleeding. After wiping the blood from his hands, he pulled off the man's uniform jacket and put it on.

He drove the truck to the far side of the camp where they were digging the mass grave. He drove past the graves and found an abandoned area behind an outbuilding. He then backed the truck up to the edge of the pit and rolled the man into it. Then he grabbed the shovel and covered the body with dirt.

Shaking with sheer terror, Jorg climbed back in the truck and drove back on the camp grounds, parking behind one of the barracks where the women prisoners would be staying.

There he waited, watching from the truck as the guards separated the women from the men. The women entered the barracks near where his truck was parked.

Jorg's mind was spinning. How could he sneak some of them out without being caught? Surely they would notice by now that he wasn't in his gun tower anymore. He peered over the dashboard of the truck, and even though all the other women were looking in another direction, Sophia turned her head and looked straight at him again ... always able to sense when he was there.

Sophia saw Jiri sitting in the truck, and realized this may be their only chance. Taking Lyuba by the hand, she whispered to her two sisters and mother. The five of them quietly separated themselves from the rest of the women. They sneaked out another door and were about to creep around the back of the building when a guard saw them and shouted at them, firing his pistol.

The bullet went right into the back of Nadya's head.

She dropped to the ground, dead, blood from her head splattered against the barrack wall. The other women huddled against the wall in terror, screaming.

Upon hearing the gunshot and the screams, Jorg immediately put the truck in reverse and sped away. He parked it at the docking area. Someone had been shot, but he couldn't see who. It was his fault, that person was dead. Was it his own mother? Or her little girl? That little girl was his sister. That was the child Sophia had tried to bring to them on that cold winter day in Vienna. He had seen her and had turned away from them both. The shame was so overwhelming he could barely breathe.

He needed to find another way to help them. If he stayed, he would undoubtedly be caught and killed instantly. How could he now get out alive?

Grabbing another handful of cotton, Jorg cleaned up the last of the blood in the back of the truck. In the pocket of the delivery uniform was a handkerchief. Jorg soaked it in the man's blood.

He changed back to his gunman's uniform, and headed straight over to the hospital, coughing all the way. When he arrived, he showed the nurse his bloody handkerchief and she immediately arranged for him to be shipped to a tuberculosis clinic in the nearby town of Auschwitz.

Jorg stayed at the clinic for a week undergoing tests, and was then released upon finding no TB in his system. During the whole week there he lay awake at night in misery, feeling utterly responsible for the death of those he loved.

The chef from the officer's mess hall at Birkenau was in the clinic one day getting tested.

"What's been happening there lately?" Jorg asked him.

"A delivery truck driver is missing, but they think he was trying to help Gypsies escape. They figure he somehow escaped when the guards caught the prisoners."

"Really? So they never caught the delivery truck driver?"

"Apparently not," the chef said.

"Did they kill all the people trying to escape?"

"I don't know. But those prisoners are getting shot at everyday, so I wouldn't doubt it." He leaned over toward Jorg. "It's an awfully creepy place to work, don't you think?"

Jorg froze. He had heard that informers were everywhere. They lure you into admitting your aversion for Nazi ways then turn you in for profit. At the same time, he was desperate for news about the camp.

He shrugged.

The chef continued, "I sure miss the kitchen at the Wirtshaus Alte Stadt-Mauer. It's one of the best restaurants in Berlin, you know. Adolph Eichmann used to eat there whenever he could, so he drafted me to be the chef here. It's supposed to be an honour."

Jorg nodded. The man seemed sincere so he took a chance and asked, "Have you seen any of the Gypsy women getting killed?"

"I tend to turn a blind eye to that kind of thing — too unpleasant. So, are you a Gypsy sympathizer or something?"

"No! I mean, hardly."

"I am. In the restaurant business, the Gypsy musicians keep the customers coming back. I don't like to see them rounded up and killed. But what can you do about it?"

Jorg caught a glimpse of his own face in a mirror. He looked away, frightened of the man he saw there. "Yes, what can any of us do?"

After a phone call to Lieutenant Kurt Gerstein, Jorg was overcome with relief that the officer managed to get his application approved for transfer to the Luftwaffe. Rommel's forces in Tunisia were surrounded on all sides by the British and Americans, and the Desert Fox needed as much manpower as possible.

He would be leaving in two weeks. There was nothing he could do for any of the people from Olino now without getting killed himself. It was best that he get as far away from Birkenau as possible before they traced the killing of the delivery truck driver back to him or before his mother or one of her clan decided to tell the Birkenau staff that their top gunman was "racially flawed".

The decision to leave without a plan to help them nestled itself in the pit of his stomach like a trapped scorpion.

Back home in Kittsee, he agonized about whether or not to tell his father about what happened at Birkenau. He was just there for a few days to get his belongings together. On the evening he planned to tell his father, the doorbell rang.

His old girlfriend, Uta, and her mother came unexpectedly for a visit. He was happy to see her, but knew there was something wrong.

Uta's mother was a compassionate woman in her late forties. She wore her grey-streaked blonde hair in a French knot and liked to wear the haute couture of the day. Although German occupation was militarizing the fashion industry, Uta's mother had secret friends in high places. She liked to wear her gathered A-line skirt and pink blouse with the puffy sleeves even when other women were much more functionally dressed.

The two women sat down at the kitchen table with Karl and Jorg. Maria stayed upstairs in her sewing room, which she always did when friends of Jorg came over. After a few pleasantries about the weather, Uta's mother paused, clearly uncomfortable having to speak of such things. Finally she said, "It seems as if my darling girl is in a family way. She suggests that your son, Jorg here, is the father."

There was a hushed silence.

Jorg glanced up furtively at his father. He saw the housekeeper standing within earshot, drumming her fingers on her forearm, her eyes dripping in judgement.

It had just been once or twice that Jorg and Uta had engaged in actual intercourse. How could she be pregnant? And was he really the father? There were probably a dozen young men in Kittsee who were courting the beautiful Uta. He had been away at Birkenau for the past month.

Karl must have been thinking the same thing. "How long has she been pregnant?" he asked.

"The doctor estimates ten weeks," replied Uta's mother.

Uta stared out the window, the skin on her cheeks and neck blotchy red. Ten weeks ago Jorg had taken Uta to a Hitler Youth party. It had been at the home of one of the wealthiest families in Kittsee. They went exploring the rooms on the fourth floor and found a quaint guest room overlooking the garden. He didn't mean for them to go that far, but she didn't try to stop it either.

Karl looked over at Jorg. His son was staring at the tiles on the kitchen floor. They needed to be cleaned, that place between the tiles. He would never install tiles in a kitchen, he thought — not sanitary.

"Jorg?" his father asked.

Jorg shrugged haplessly and the lines above his eyebrows creased. Karl scowled at him.

"What are you suggesting, then?" asked his father.

Uta frowned at the question.

Her mother said, "I think we all know what the right thing to do is here. I have not told her father, General Schneider. He would not take this information well. We can have the wedding at the main church. It is available next Saturday."

"If you don't want your husband to know, won't that look suspicious — having it so soon?" asked Karl.

"Your son leaves next week for Northern Africa, if I'm not mistaken. That is good enough reason to get married right away."

"True."

Jorg noticed that Uta was just about to cry.

She probably thought he didn't care about her or the baby. He stared at her, aware of her need, but could bring no authentic part of him to care deeply for her plight or the child at that moment. He knew it was selfish of him, but he wasn't even sure the child was his, and his family was being killed in a death camp.

On the other hand, Uta came from a wealthy family and was the most attractive girl he had ever met. Maybe through the Schneider family he could obtain some influence at Birkenau.

That idea is what he seized upon.

"I was going to ask Uta to marry me anyway," he said suddenly. "I'm overjoyed at this news that we are going to have a baby. I'm sorry this happened, but I'm also not sorry. We will be very happy together. I just know it," he reached over and took Uta's hand, "I would like us to get married. Do you want it, too?"

Uta's face lit up. Frau Schneider looked relieved.

"Very much so," said Uta shakily.

"My staff will make all the arrangements," Uta's mother said as she stood up to leave.

The housekeeper brought their coats, and they stood in the front foyer to say their goodbyes.

"The League of German Maidens can put on a shower for Uta," Frau Schneider informed them, moving into planning mode.

"I'll ask Giselle to be my bridesmaid!" gushed Uta.

"I don't think that would be an appropriate choice, dear," chided her mother.

"Why?" Uta asked.

Her mother looked down at her hand examining her wedding ring. "You know Giselle Koch, don't you?"

Jorg and Karl shook their heads.

"Giselle is that pretty nineteen-year-old girl with the red hair? We thought she was from such a good family. She and Uta have been friends since they both had to join *Jungmadelbund*, at fourteen, right Uta?"

Uta nodded but with a consternated look on her face.

"It turns out the poor girl has a Jewish grandmother. She has to leave the League. I don't understand what she was thinking, trying to be part of our society. Do you?"

As Frau Schneider and her daughter walked down the front steps, Jorg decided he would have to be very careful or very desperate before he sought any help from their family.

## CHAPTER 46

"Did you hear Hitler visited the Berlin lunatic asylum?" Sophia asked her friend Shayna who was squatting next to her stacking rocks into a bucket. Shayna smiled and shook her head.

"The patients gave the *'Heil Hitler'* salute. As he passed down the line he came across a man who wasn't saluting. 'Why aren't you saluting like the others?' Hitler barked. The man replied, *'Mein Führer,* I'm the nurse, I'm not crazy!'"

They both ducked their heads behind the rock pile and laughed, silently as always.

Then the two women stood up and brushed the dust from their prison smocks. Shayna glanced around to ensure the main guard was turned away, then said, "Did you hear that two Jews had a plan to assassinate Hitler? Every day at a certain time he would drive past in his motorcade at 11:00 a.m.. They waited with their ammunition, but at 11:00 a.m. he never showed. 11:15, 11:30 — nothing. Then finally at 11:45 a.m. one of them turns to the other and says 'Gee, I hope nothing happened to him.'"

Sophia couldn't help but laugh out loud this time, and quickly covered her mouth. She leaned over to her friend's ear, but Shayna, shaking with silent laughter, held up her hand in protest to any more jokes.

"Let me look at your palm," Sophia whispered, feeling defiant and playful.

"Don't try your Gypsy Fortune Teller routine on me, lady. My mother warned me about people like you," Shayna smirked.

"My mother warned me about people like you, too. Jews never tip."

Shayna made a face and held out her hand. Sophia took Shayna's hand, and rested in on her knee as she glanced at the palm, "You have a long lifeline, believe it or not."

"Okay, I will."

"You will what?"

"Believe I will have a long life and that I won't end up going for a long, hot shower in the eternal afterlife."

"It's hard for me to have that kind of faith," sighed Sophia.

"Then fake it. At the very least, you'll have a much better time leading up to your death than those people," Shayna said, gesturing to the other sickly prisoners hauling rocks.

"'The mind is its own place, and in itself, can make Heaven of Hell, and a Hell of Heaven,'" recited Sophia, remembering the quotation book she gave to Jiri.

"John Milton, 1669" Shayna said, nodding, "Sophia, you amaze me. You are a psychic *and* a great philosopher."

"What a combination, huh? But I wish I had your strength," Sophia admitted, "You don't let this hellish place touch you."

"I feel it," Shayna corrected, "But there is a place in both of us that they can never touch. Just remember that."

Sophia's friend was a petite woman with fair features. She had a smoothness to her gait like a swan gliding across a lake. Shayna was part Jewish and was a modern artist whose work had been banned. They confiscated her art and displayed it at the Nazi sponsored "Degenerate Art" exhibition. When she refused to stop painting, they arrested her.

"Let's see *your* palm," Shayna reciprocated.

She took Sophia's hand, and copied the Gypsy woman's style of laying it across her knee.

"You have a very, very, very long lifeline. It goes right down into your wrist. Okay, it must be a sign, psychic lady. We are meant to be ancient, shrivelled little raisins together on an old folk's porch, telling very bad jokes to each other. Deal?"

"Deal." Sophia spit into her hand, and held it out for Shayna.

"Yuck!"

"Do it or the spell won't take."

Shayna spat, poorly, and most of her saliva dribbled onto the dirt. They shook palm-to-palm, squishing the clear fluid together and snickered gleefully like six-year-olds, pretending everything wasn't falling into ruin and death around them.

One month later, Sophia lay on a mattress on the floor with her mother, Florica, now deathly ill with typhus.

"Please have some broth, Mama."

"No, let it be."

"I can't lay here with you and watch you die."

"I've lived a good, long life, my darling. It's my time."

Sophia nodded as the tears rolled down her face.

"Sophia?"

"Yes, mama?"

"Do you know where your name comes from?" she murmured.

"Where?"

Sophia waited in silence for her mother to gather the strength to continue talking, but she never talked again. Soon after that her breathing stopped.

The guards threw her body into a pit with all the other typhus victims.

It had been seven months of removing rocks and gravel in buckets when Sophia noticed how skinny she had become. She lived in barracks with other adult women, separated from the men and her beloved Lyuba.

Sophia never told anyone that she had seen Jiri at Birkenau, or that he tried to save them. Her family would never accept that one of their own had joined the Nazis. They would never forgive him, but she could. She prayed that one day he would come back and try to rescue them again.

It seemed like an eternity since that day long ago — when they had arrived. Perhaps he had died trying to help them that day or been killed in a battle somewhere. The thought clutched at her throat.

She had witnessed the execution of her beloved sister. She tended to her mother and other sisters as they deteriorated into death. She had seen countless others beaten, tortured or simply disappear into the shower chamber and never return. News of who was alive and who was dead didn't get passed around. Death was an everyday occurrence now, a numb reality.

Prisoners who were young and fit were put to work constructing the rest of the prison camp. Some women bonded together and developed deep friendships. These connections served as buffers, cushioning the devastating blows of uncertainty; the not knowing if their loved ones were alive, dead, or worse, being tortured.

Rumours did abound, but they didn't know what to believe. The very worst of the rumours was about "the zoo." A man named Dr. Josef Mengele headed up a research medical clinic at the camp, and apparently the children were his subjects.

Shayna also had a daughter the same age as Lyuba. Her name was Anita. In fact the girls looked like they could be twins. They had clung to each other the day they were taken from their mothers. The women didn't know it at the time, but their daughters were put in "the zoo."

Josef Mengele was a doctor assigned to do 'research' at Birkenau. He was especially interested in the subject of twins, on whom he conducted experiments. He kept his stock of twins, along with many of the Gypsy children, in special barracks known as "the zoo." The experiments were macabre and often involved mutilation and amputation.

One night Shayna crawled in bed beside Sophia and whispered, "I have done something that is haunting me, and I need your forgiveness."

"What?"

"I have become a whore. I have given myself to Dieter, the guard at the medical clinic."

"Why did you do that?"

"In exchange for information about Anita and Lyuba. A woman told me they are being kept in the barrack next to the clinic."

Sophia lifted herself on one elbow and stared directly into Shayna's eyes, "What did you find out?"

"They are alive. Anita and Lyuba are alive. They play together. I cried when I heard that."

Sophia held the woman's hand and felt it trembling. In the full moonlight she could see tears streaming down her friend's cheeks.

"Thank you, Shayna," she cried. "That was a brave thing you did. I am so grateful to know they are alive."

"I feel horrible for it," her friend whispered, "I have never been with another man besides my husband. I feel horrible and ... unclean."

"He cannot make your soul unclean, Shayna. Remember what you said; there is a place inside you they can never touch."

"I know, but I can't get back to that place right now," she said, clutching the blanket around her neck. They lay there together in silence as Sophia wrapped her trembling friend in a blanket. Then Shayna added, "And there is something else that you will hate me for."

"What?"

"For giving me information on Lyuba, he said you would have to come see him too. I didn't know he would say that or I would have asked you first. I tried to pretend that I was her mother, but he knew about you. He's been watching you. He knows that you are Lyuba's mother. He knows they aren't twins. He said he couldn't protect her if you didn't come to see him. I'm sorry. I'm so sorry."

Sophia lay back down on the bed and felt her stomach twist in on itself. She wrapped her arms instinctively around her own waist, "He terrifies me. I heard he poked out a man's eye for staring at him too long. What will he do to me?"

Shayna just shook her head, and prayed for forgiveness.

The next day, Sophia offered to help another prisoner carry some medical supplies over to the clinic. As she walked near the children's barrack she peered in the window and saw only one child there. It was fifteen-year-old Gustav, cleaning the floor. She was relieved to see him alive, although his normally robust body looked skinny and pale. He wore a green triangle on his prisoner's tunic, which all Gypsies had to wear — it was also the symbol used for professional criminals. Young Gustav was the farthest thing away from being a criminal; he was the sweetest, most loving boy she'd ever met.

When they arrived at the clinic, Dieter smiled and raised one eyebrow. "Finally you are here! I need this whole room swept now!" The other prisoner left and Dieter closed the door so they would be alone. She glanced at him sideways, trembling from head to foot.

His belly spilled out over the edge of his belt and he had some kind of rash across his neck. His close-set eyes, thin nose, and cherub mouth stood out in contrast to his meaty, round head. A diamond-shaped mole with long, brown hairs grew out of his left cheek.

"I'm glad to see you here," Dieter said in a German dialect that Sophia had to struggle to follow.

Sophia looked down at the floor, "You know about my daughter, Lyuba. I'd love to see her, even if just for a minute."

"Can't do that. She's okay. They don't do anything to her. Yet."

Sophia's heart shrank upon hearing the word "yet".

"Is there any way to prevent her from being hurt?" she asked, struggling to keep the panic from turning her words into a scream.

"I will see what I can do. It depends what you can do for me."

Sophia nodded meekly, desperate, "I understand."

He closed the blinds of his office, then grabbed her by the shoulders, turning her back toward him. She forced her eyes shut and held onto the edge of the desk as he forced himself on her. His bile breath turned her stomach. He rammed himself against her so forcefully that she shrieked in pain.

"Shut up, you little whore," Dieter growled as he slammed her head down on the desk.

The next half hour was a complete blur to Sophia. She must have lost consciousness when he struck her head against the desk. When she woke up again, he was gone. The office was empty, and she was tied at the wrists and ankles with rope. Another rope bound her to the legs of the desk. Her forehead was bruised and swollen, and her stomach was queasy. She fell into unconsciousness again, and woke up to the sound of the door slamming shut.

"You disgust me," he growled, "You have been trying to bewitch me ever since you got here. All you Gypsy females are the same. You use potions and curses. But I am stronger than that. Do you hear me?"

She nodded.

"You don't care for me. I can tell. You didn't give me what I asked for, so I haven't been able to give you what you want.

Panic coursed through Sophia's veins again, stronger this time.

"What has happened to my daughter?" she whispered.

"You don't love me, so I couldn't protect her."

"Is she dead?"

Instead of answering he just kicked her in the shins, then the legs, then in her face. After several minutes of this, he sat down at the other desk, and began doing paperwork. Sophia dared not say a word, and simply cried silently. Then he left for what seemed like several hours.

For the next thirty-six hours he kept coming and going. Every few hours he arrived again and would either beat her or rape her, then beg her to love him. Then he would sit and finish his paperwork as if she didn't exist. When he finally untied her hands and feet, she was delirious. Sophia looked up at him, through blurry eyes. This particular time she saw something shiny and metallic in his hands.

It was a two-foot long machete.

"Gypsies are the worst abomination ever to curse this earth. We are finally cleansing this land of your nastiness."

He rocked back in his metal office chair and stared at his reflection in the blade.

"I am rather unattractive, don't you think?" he said, not looking at her.

Sophia looked at the ground, and didn't move a muscle. She knew that no matter what she said Dieter would beat her again and probably kill her. She lay in a pool of her own blood and urine. Her mouth was parched from lack of water, and her lips were cracked and raw from the knife-like stubble of his three-day old beard. Her head, neck, back and genitals seared with pain.

"I probably wouldn't get an honest response from you about that, would I? I've been horrible to you. I don't know why. I don't under-stand this violent part of myself. I studied poetry in school. I wanted to be a poet. Funny isn't it? In fact, I thought of a beautiful love poem this morning, just for you. You are one of the most beautiful women I have ever seen. That's right. I need to tell you that. I've been keeping it to myself. But I honestly don't care that you are a Gypsy. If things were different, I would run away from here with you. I would hide you until this bloody war was over. Then we could live together on my parent's land in Bavaria. You would love it there. I can see you there now."

Sophia had heard something like this a few times before. One minute he was in love with her, and the next minute he was kicking her ribs so hard she threw up. Then he would kiss the places he had just kicked. She prayed that his next outburst would be the one that finally killed her.

"I hear you are a carny. What do you do at the carnival? Dance? Sing? Read palms?"

Sophia nodded shakily.

"That's marvelous. I bet you are gifted at them all. Read my palm for me."

He laid his large sweaty palm across the desk between them. She could barely hold up her head to look. All she could make out were long, deep lines on an unusually smooth palm.

"I said I want you to read my palm. What does it say?"

Sophia's ribs were hurting so badly she could barely breathe, let alone speak.

"Am I lucky in love? Will I be rich someday? Will I live a long, healthy life?"

Her head was swirling and her mouth was dry.

"Water," she managed to utter.

"Of course, how inconsiderate of me. Here," he said as he handed her a drinking glass with a straw. Sophia grateful sipped on the water, swallowing painfully.

"Now, what do you see?"

She cleared her throat and took his palm in her hand, turning it slightly until the light shed shadows on his shiny palm.

"I see a man who..." she paused to gather her thoughts. Visions of his destiny filled her mental landscape.

"Don't lie to me, now. Don't make things up. I know you are a true psychic. You see my future. Tell it like it is."

In that moment, Sophia felt an eerie calm settle on her heart. A memory emerged.

She was sitting by her favourite lily-filled pond at Olino with her little boy nearby. On certain days in mid-spring you could see the migration of multi-coloured butterflies across that pond. She sat on the ornate bench with the weeping willow tree watching over them. A large, crimson butterfly wafted by. She pointed at it and he followed her gaze. His tiny hand reached out toward it and he said, "butterfly." She swept him up in her arms overjoyed at hearing him speak for the very first time.

In that instant, all the trembling, hatred and suffering evaporated. Remembering that moment changed something. She no longer felt afraid of death. Instead, she imagined it like a warm, comforting blanket that was transporting her to a permanent state of bliss. Gazing up at him, all she saw in her torturer's eyes was a hurt child clouded with self-loathing. Compassion washed over her.

"You are a genuinely loving and creative man trapped beneath a black tar."

"What does that mean?"

"You could have been a gifted poet, sharing your wordsmithing with the world — a world aching for your talent. Instead, you got swept up into an illusory world of demons that you imagined were trying to destroy you. So you thought you'd try to kill them first. There has never been a threat, only the gift of your creativity. And you let that turn toxic inside your heart."

Dieter looked stunned, pinned to the core by her prophetic words. His yellow-tinged eyes seemed gripped with terror. Craning her eyes up to meet his, she caught him in her gaze.

"Soon you will see through the fog of your illusions and come face to face with your desperate acts of hatred. That realization will be too horrible for you to bear," She pointed to the crease in the centre of his palm, "Your lifeline is short. It ends here in the middle of your hand. That is middle life. It's coming very soon. Unless you kill yourself first, you will likely die at the hands of those you have so brutally harmed."

Dieter sharply withdrew his hand, hiding his palm under his armpit like a child who had gotten too close to the flames. With his other hand he raised the machete above his head. A lava-like rage crawled up from his belly and spewed out from his bulging eyeballs.

Sophia slowly drew in her breath and clasped her hands in prayer across the desk, gratefully waiting for death to come. When the blade came down, she imagined the room filled with angels and Santa Sara was there ready to take her home. Although she never screamed when the blade came down sharply across her wrists, she did pass out from shock.

When she opened her eyes again, Dieter lay slumped back in his chair with a long, crimson line of blood raining from his neck. The door to his office burst open and a Nazi officer surveyed the scene. On his heels came Shayna, who gasped in horror not only at Dieter's bloodied, lifeless form, but also at Sophia's severed hands lying on the floor. Fifteen-year old Gustav peered into the room with wide eyes. He had to go back outside because he was so nauseated by what he saw. The man in the Nazi uniform covered his mouth, as if to stifle his own gag response.

Then the man in the uniform reacted decisively, ripping the shirt from Dieter's body, and tearing it in two, to fashion two crude bandages to stop the blood flow from Sophia's arms. He pressed them against the stumps of her arms to lessen the bleeding. He leaned in to her ear as he did, speaking rapidly, but calmly.

"I am a friend of your son," Klaus said, "He saved my life in the Sahara desert so I have come here to hopefully save yours. I'm sorry I did not come into this room sooner. I am so dreadfully sorry. I will help you get away from here and we will take care of your injuries. I have a truck and can take you and your daughter and maybe a couple of others. Your son gave me a list of people to try to save. Where is your daughter? We must move quickly."

Shayna stood holding onto the door jam, looking tortured and weak, "Please don't kill her. It was my fault she is here. I will take responsibility for the damage that was caused here. It's all my fault."

Despite the blur and shock of the trauma, blood loss and pain, Sophia knew she must trust this man. She looked at Shayna, and managed to say, "This man is a friend here to help us. We need to trust him."

Shayna nodded, looking frightened and numb, "Okay. But we need to get her bandaged up," she glanced at Klaus, "We need to stop the blood flow before she bleeds to death! I used to be a nurse and if you let me go to the medical supply storage room right over there, maybe I can get some supplies."

Klaus Meinhardt nodded, "Yes, please do that now."

He peered out the window from behind the blinds. It was late autumn and the sun had just gone down. The excessive rains had caused leaking in the officer's mess area and men were walking in and out of the mess with tools, providing a fortunate diversion for them.

Shayna returned with bandages, disinfectant and morphine. As she tended to Sophia, Klaus covered Dieter's body with a dark blanket and put another one on the floor, over the pools of blood and Sophia's recently severed hands. He pulled Gustav back into the guard's office, to explain the situation to them all.

"We only have a few minutes to spare. I can maybe get the three of you out of here, plus your little daughter if she is nearby."

Sophia cried out, "Gustav! Is Lyuba still alive?"

He nodded, "Yes, I just saw her. She is alright."

Klaus added, "If you know where she is, go get her now!"

"Please get my little Anita, as well," Shayna begged, "They are always together. You know what she looks like? And get my husband, too. He is at the men's barrack, and my cousin ..."

"No," Klaus disagreed, shaking his head, "I can only take a few small people. You must hide in those wine barrels out there. I cannot take a full-grown man. Once we escape, I can try to arrange another rescue party. You two women are small enough, as is this young lad, and a child ... maybe two if we are lucky. And this will only work if we can get those two little girls now."

"I can't leave without my husband," Shayna said, shaking.

"Then you will have to stay here."

Sophia looked up from her bandages, as Gustav pressed down to stop the blood flow.

"Shayna, don't be crazy. Save yourself and Anita. He would want that."

Shayna hesitated in total anguish, then finally nodded as the tears rolled down her cheeks, "Run, Gustav! Go get them."

Gustav darted out the door and crept silently along the side of the children's barracks.

Inside, the children were sipping the weak broth that was their dinner. One of the boys was having a temper tantrum and the guard on duty slapped him sharply across the face, which only seemed to escalate the child's fury.

Gustav saw the girls. He had played hide and seek many times when he was babysitting Lyuba. He gestured to her, 'be very quiet and come here — I will help you hide.' She nodded in understanding and grinned. He gestured for her to bring Anita along.

Anita understood the game and followed her little friend over to Gustav. The boy took the girls, one in each hand, and they trotted back toward Dieter's office. Shayna was waiting outside. They ran into her arms. She hugged them both so hard that Lyuba gasped.

She didn't want the children to see Sophia. Klaus helped the three young ones climb inside the empty wine barrels lined up against the wall nearby. Then, Shayna and Klaus carried Sophia, now bound in gauze and drugged with morphine, and placed her inside a barrel.

As soon as Shayna was inside the last barrel, Klaus said "I'll be right back."

He raced over to the delivery truck parked around the corner. Using his handkerchief, he rubbed the blood off his hands and threw the handkerchief in the ditch. He backed the truck up to the wine barrels, and one by one, lifted each barrel onto the trolley, then wheeled them into the back of the truck. He then sprinkled the back of the truck with a mixture of tobacco soaked in gasoline, a trick to fool the guard dogs.

When he arrived at the gate, the guard was busy dealing with a host of repairmen who were coming to deal with the leaks. The delay gave Klaus time to find his gloves and put them on, to cover the bloodstains. The gatekeeper barely glanced at the back of the truck before opening the gates and waving him on through.

Once they were out of the camp and on the open road, Shayna checked on Sophia. She was grateful to see her friend in a blissful morphine-induced half sleep. The two little girls still thought they were playing hide and seek, and were crouched down, with their hands covering their eyes.

Shayna watched them, the fantasy and innocence of the girl's game contrasting painfully with the horrific reality of her friend's mutilation. How would Sophia feel tomorrow, seeing her little girl alive and not being able to pick her up and hold her? Shayna closed her eyes and wept silently for her.

Klaus drove steadily for an hour over back roads until they came to a farmhouse. Through friends, he had found a sympathetic farming family willing to risk their lives to take in five concentration camp refugees.

Upon arriving, he unloaded the wine barrels one by one into the barn, as previously instructed. The farmer and his wife helped the refugees out of the barrels. The little girls were skinny and pale, but their eyes still shone with an enduring innocence.

The farmer recoiled at the sight of the Gypsy woman with stumps for arms, blood-drenched bandages and swollen shut eyes. In a daze, the wife showed them the hide-a-way loft where some rye bread and water awaited them.

Gustav ravenously tore into the chewy dough and Shayna tore up bits of the bread for the two little girls. Finally she hand-fed Sophia, who could now no longer feed herself.

The farmer's wife turned to Klaus, "We've had refugees here before. We find their stomachs can only digest simple foods at first; they've been eating next to nothing for so long. We try to encourage them to slowly go back to regular eating or they get powerful stomach problems."

"I can't begin to tell you how grateful I am for you taking them in. I know you are putting your own lives at risk," Klaus replied.

In a low whisper the farmer said, "I didn't know we were getting women and children. They won't be much help on the farm. Plus, that one has no hands."

"It's alright. They can do other things. I will teach them," scolded the wife.

Shayna sensed the nature of the conversation and came over to join them, "I will do whatever you need around here: me and the boy. He's fifteen and normally a strong boy. He just needs to regain some weight. I will take full responsibility for Sophia and the girls. We won't be a burden."

"You are very weak yourself. You need time to get your strength back," Klaus chided.

"Yes," Shayna nodded looking down at her boney arms, "I have relatives in England who were working on getting us an exit visa just before we were taken to Birkenau. If I could somehow get a letter to them soon, to see if we could get still get those visas plus three more for the others?"

The farmer's wife replied, "We are in contact with an associate of Dr. William Perl. He has been helping many people get out of Germany."

"Yes, and Dr. Perl is in England right now. We could maybe get your letter to his associate and that could speed things up," added the farmer.

"It sounds like you are in good hands. I must go. I need to get myself and this truck as far away from here as possible, as soon as possible. They will have discovered Dieter's body by now and will be looking for us," Klaus said.

He got back into the truck and Shayna came up to the driver's window. As he started up the engine she said, "I don't know why you risked everything to save us. You don't need to tell me, but I know in my heart that you will somehow be rewarded for this act of kindness."

"I've already been rewarded, but thank you for your kind words. Please give this small box to Sophia. It's from someone very special. Inside that box is my mailing address, just in case we don't connect again."

With that he handed her the package and drove away.

Shayna brought the package to Sophia late that night and together they examined the tiny ornate box with the address for Klaus Meinhardt inside. Although Sophia would keep that box for decades, news that she survived the camp would never reach her son.

Y

Klaus drove northeast for two hours toward an abandoned farm. He parked the truck inside an empty barn and shut the doors. Then he went to get his motorcycle, which was hidden in the bushes. The plan was for him to hide out with another farm family closer to the Dutch border and work there until the war ended.

He would never make it to that farm.

Upon finding Dieter's body and Sophia's severed hands, the Birkenau officials surmised what had happened and who was missing. They sent a warning out to the local police.

Even though Klaus was driving on back roads with no headlight on his motorbike, he came around a corner and discovered a roadblock waiting ahead.

The local police arrested him and put him in the local lock-up until the Gestapo arrived. As he sat huddled in the corner of the jail just one mile from the safe haven of his hideaway, he pulled out a locket that was hanging around his neck. There was a tiny vial inside the locket with a perfect dose of cyanide to kill a man of his stature.

He studied the violet vial, feeling his heart thunder in his chest. Surely torture awaited him of the most ruthless kind. Would he give in to their cruelty and reveal the location of those he just saved? If he chose to die now, would his loved ones ever forgive him for the grief he was about to put them through? Surely the guards would kill him regardless of what he said or did.

By the time the Commandant of the concentration camp arrived, Klaus was lying stricken on the cement floor, staring at the wall. He had no pulse. The Commandant, eager to be seen as a hero, aimed a gun at the back of Klaus's lifeless head and pulled the trigger anyway. In the official documents, his cause of death would read "Executed as a traitor."

## CHAPTER 47

When old Sophia finished telling the story she closed her eyes, as if to let the memories disappear, and fade back into nothingness again. Everyone in the room sat in silence, struggling to come to grips with the enormity of what they had just heard.

Finally, Helena spoke, "What happened after that?"

Sophia smiled, leaning forward, "We stay there as farm hands. I say that as joke though, 'cause I have no hands! I farm 'mouth'. I tell them what to do. Ha, ha!"

Jasper added, "I think I know what happened after that. The farm family hid them all for several months, then Shayna's family got them exit visas under disguised names for England. They all lived together in London for many years.

"My father went off to become a musician. Sophia stayed with Shayna's family and became a writer. They were newspaper moguls, or something, weren't they?"

Sophia nodded.

He continued, "... and eventually she wrote a column for that arts magazine. She has volumes somewhere of articles about the importance of arts in culture. She often gave a voice to all kinds of emerging artists, too ... musicians, dancers, singers, visual artists and designers. Her writings became a voice for new artists all over Europe. Where are all those?"

"They all got kinda moldy, so I threw them out. Got a few somewhere," Sophia said.

She rustled around in the bottom of her cookie tin and pulled out a copy of a magazine article from 1972, "Here. This one I wrote when I just a youngster, at sixty-five. You probably wonder how I do that with no hands?"

"I didn't want to ask, but since you mention it," queried Helena.

"After the camp, at first Shayna take dictation, and when Anita grow up, she take dictation. Then I get fancy tape recorder and magazine people just transcribe everything I say."

"What about Lyuba — where is she now?" asked Helena.

Gustav's eyes grew wide, and Sophia looked at the floor. After several seconds Gustav said in a low voice, "She don't make it. At farm she die from typhus — just a few months after we get there. That death camp make us all very weak. Lyuba ... she not have strength to overcome."

"I'm sorry to hear that," Fran whispered.

Sophia smiled up at them with glistening eyes, "Want to see something amazing?"

"Sure," nodded Fran.

"I got this picture of you in the mail."

Fran leaned over and saw a photo of her at about the age of five. It was taken of her and her mother, walking in a park.

"Now. Look at this."

Sophia pulled out a photo of Lyuba, at about the same age. Everyone leaned in to study the two photos, side by side.

"Amazing. You look so similar at that age," Jasper said.

"It's incredible," added Helena.

"Since meeting you, I got to see what my little girl would look like if she had grown up."

Fran smiled at the delight in Sophia's eyes. All she could think to say was, "You must have tremendous inner strength to have survived all that."

"This lady my inspiration," Sophia said as she pulled out a much more recent photo. It showed Sophia and another ancient-looking woman sitting on a porch together, "That is Shayna and me. I go back to England for her ninetieth birthday."

"Just like she predicted — she said you'd be little old ladies together on a porch," mused Helena.

"Yes. Shayna maybe more psychic than me! Ha ha. She was always a dear friend. With her I make new meaning for life," Sophia said. "This experience in the camp — I came eventually to see something good from it. I stick to that now."

With that she shut the lid on her cookie tin and said, "This is enough for now. I am tired. Long time since I speak of these things. I like to see you both again soon. Please stay and maybe we talk more in the next few days."

Everyone climbed out of the little caravan. Gustav helped Sophia get settled in her bed, then turned out her propane lamp.

"That was amazing to hear what they went though," Helena said to Jasper and Fran as they walked back toward the meeting hall, "When did they come back here to Olino? I can't believe I've lived all this time so close to my own grandmother!"

"When the Iron Curtain came down they both wanted to come back here. This place is their roots. Some Olino people who also survived the death camps came right back here."

"Did they escape, too? And did Shayna ever manage to rescue her husband?" asked Fran.

"Stefan and a few others were liberated by the Americans at the end of the war. I don't think anyone else escaped. The horrible thing was, after the escape the Commandant walked through the camp, randomly killing other prisoners as a warning to others. Apparently, he found Shayna's husband crying tears of joy that his wife and daughter had escaped, so he took that poor man out in front of everyone and executed him. No one dared try to escape after that."

"Did Shayna ever find that out?"

"After the war it was so hard to find out if your loved ones lived or died. She searched exhaustively for years, but finally gave up. It was

only when Sophia and my father came back here that Stefan told them
he was executed. They decided not to tell Shayna."

The next day Helena and Fran returned to visit Olino. Since Fran was
flying home to Canada soon, she decided to stay there for the next few
nights. Meanwhile, Helena had to go to work and promised to return
on the twelfth of September to take Fran to the airport.

Fran spent as much time as she could with her new found grandmother.
Mostly they sat on the little bench outside her little abode in the woods.
Sophia still liked to smoke her pipe. Fran watched as the woman with
no hands placed the hand-crafted pipe between her knees and poured
the pouch of tobacco into it with both wrists. As she placed the pipe in
her mouth, a teen girl appeared out of nowhere to light it for her. The
smoke coiled up in a halo around her head and the rustic aroma of sweet
tobacco brought back memories of Fran's childhood; her father and his
partners puffing on their pipes discussing business on the veranda.

"That's a beautiful pipe, so ornately carved," Fran remarked.

"Yes, it's a *lyulykas,* it was a gift from a Ukrainian Zaporozhsky
Cossack I once knew. The wood is from the forests right here in the
Carpathian Mountains," she explained.

"Wow! I have so many questions for you ..." Fran said.

"Yes, like what?"

"Like how did you ever get from Europe to England when the war
was still on?"

"Good underground network of anarchists, and plenty of raw luck,"
she replied. "We got false ID that made us all look Aryan. And the
systems for checking were beginning to break down by that time in
the war."

Fran nodded imagining what it must have been like to live under
such danger.

Sophia continued, "That was actually the easy part. The hard part was coming to England and people not believing us — what was happening in Europe — the genocide. I didn't expect them to believe me, but Shayna, she was a well respected artist. They called it Jewish exaggeration. Hysterical women making up stories."

"So no one did anything?"

"Eventually when they heard other escapee stories that sounded similar, then they took some action." Sophia moved the pipe over to the other corner of her mouth and puffed.

"That's horrible."

"That's how it was back then."

"I hope you don't mind me asking ..."

"... no, its okay, you want to know ... I tell you. But then I get to ask the questions of you, hmm?"

"Yes, anything you like," Fran smiled relishing the idea of having someone to talk to about her life.

"So, how did you learn to let go of what happened to you? Do you forgive the Nazis and that man — what he did to you?"

"Uh huh."

Fran frowned not able to comprehend. "But it was so unbelievably evil and so many people you loved died or were killed because of them, and then the brutality you endured...." she said feeling tears well up in her eyes.

"Oh, I created years of misery over this, ruminating and making myself ill. Then I tried to forget, but that didn't help either. This all led to depression, nightmares, suicide thoughts. Shayna, too. Not a good time for us, I tell you."

"So how did it change for you?"

"Shayna started to learn art therapy and then she taught me. Together we transformed the demons," Sophia said closing her eyes. "We gave it all up to the gods, and they composted it for us."

Fran raised her eyes, curious, so Sophia continued.

"That was just the beginning. It was helping others that sealed the deed. Shayna founded a retreat in the Lake District. Many people came. You could come do poetry, song, dance, writing, drawing, music, crafts, whatever you needed to transform yourself."

Fran absorbed her words, imagining such a place and finally said, "That sounds amazing. So you compost ... and then ...?"

"And then you have good rich soil for the next chapter of life, yes?"

"And if you don't compost?"

"Then your life is shit. Ha ha!"

The teenager sitting near them asked Sophia a question in another language and the old woman responded. The girl ran off and a few moments later returned with a sketch pad and showed Fran a drawing. It was wild melange of colors and shapes with an eye in the centre. The girl pointed at her chest.

"You did this? It's very ... captivating!" Fran smiled.

The girl's eyes lit up and she curled up next to Sophia.

"I still show some of the children here, like Bozka here, how to draw her way out of a problem."

"I didn't know a person could do that with art."

"Art can help you create new meaning, if you let it."

"I heard you say that before, but what does that actually mean ... create new meaning?"

"Life is what you make it; your own show ... yes?"

"You mean as in 'All the world's a stage...'?" Fran asked noticing two little boys playing on the grass with hand puppets.

"Okay, yes maybe, like the Shakespeare quote. I can't control what life brings me, but I can choose how I frame it, how I color it. Many options available, yes? Like colors on an artist's palette. I can choose grey and black and have more misery, or I can choose purple and green, and have more aliveness ... more happiness. Whatever I want."

"So that's what you chose after the war?"

"Mostly. Sometimes I still choose the dark colors, for contrast. Shading can highlight, yet? Life is too boring with all one kind of thing."

Fran squinted absorbing the concept; nodding.

"And that is how you forgave your perpetrators ... you chose a different frame, different colors?"

Sophia nodded looking down, swinging her feet back forth like a child. She was such a tiny woman, no taller than a ten year old. Fran took in a long breath and thought she could smell violets somewhere off in the distance.

Sophia continued, "Huge dark can make for huge light."

Fran tilted her head, not understanding.

"To forgive that kind of darkness you must muster a lightness so bright."

"Yes, I imagine so. But doesn't forgiving them mean you condone what they did?"

"No. Important difference. Forgivness is not forgetting and not condoning, it is bringing the thoughts of all people to a higher place so it is less likely to happen again."

"You think that helps prevent evil?"

"Hating it is like adding gas to the fire, no? Evil can't exist where love and forgiveness live."

Fran was silent.

"I wrote about this forgiveness of the Nazis in the art magazine once and people sent me hate mail! They were outraged. It is their choice, this is mine. For me it is the past. I'm not there now. I am here with you on a beautiful sunny day. No one is doing anything bad to me now. I had my emotions then. Now it's gone. Over. This moment is much more potent than a memory, don't you think?"

As Sophia said those words Fran felt the essence of the oak trees and the barberry bushes around her take on an extra glow. "Yes, yes. I see. I know what you are talking about. I just don't do it very often. My mind wants to go to dark places in the past or worries about the future."

"It's not your mind; it's your immature self. The mind is just a tool. Give her a new toy."

"What do you mean?"

"Notice with a baby who is crying, you give her something shiny and her whole mood brightens. She has something else to focus on. We are growing ourselves up ... yes?"

"We are growing ourselves up ... I like that," Fran grinned.

"Show me your hand."

Fran held out her palm.

"These dark places you go to ... it is not always because of your own darkness. You hold the darkness of others."

"What? Why?"

"You think you must ... in order to be loved. Don't buy that one anymore." Sophia said this as if darkness was something that Fran could just remove from her shopping cart.

The old woman continued, "That is what you do with your papa ... you hold his darkness for him. Nice of you, but much too strenuous. Shine your light outside you instead. This dissolves the dark; like turning on a light in a dark room. Poof! All gone. So much easier, yes? Give that darkness back. It's not your job. It's his job. Your papa needs to do this now to move on. Your job with him is done. It is over. He is home now. Frees you up for new love, yes?"

"There you are! I knew I'd find you both here" Jasper said as he came around the corner.

"Oh, hello!" Fran said almost jumping out of her seat.

"I wanted to take Fran to see the gravestone of her father. Would you like to see that?"

Fran nodded.

"You take this young one down there. I'm all tuckered out from talking. I haven't talked this much since ..."

"...since you won the National Arts Council award!" Jasper interjected.

"Yes, not since then. I was such a chatterbox that whole week, huh?" she grinned. "You two go. I rest now."

Jasper helped Sophia climb back into her trailer to get settled.

They ambled down towards the pond and Fran admired the rows of neatly planted violets on either side of the path. The crumbling tomb-stones were barely readable beneath the tangle of moss and vines that had grown over them through the years. When they found the grave, Jasper took out his penknife and cut back the foliage. The inscription read "Jiri Frei — November 15, 1921 — April 23, 1943."

"You'll have to change the date now," Jasper ventured.

"That is a sign," Fran replied.

"How do you mean?" asked Jasper.

"My father's ashes are sitting at the funeral parlour, waiting for me to retrieve them. I've wondered where to scatter them. Now I know where."

"You will be coming back then?"

"Yes, I hope so."

"When does your flight leave?"

"Tomorrow evening," she answered quietly.

"Look, I have to go to Vienna anyway. I'll join Helena in taking you there."

"I would like that," Fran replied feeling a rush of excitement.

"Helena is coming here to get me tomorrow morning."

There was a pregnant pause as both of them stood staring at the sunken, empty gravesite.

"Does this mean you and I are somehow related?" Fran finally asked.

"Let me see," Jasper replied, considering, "My father's mother was cousins with your grandmother's father. So that would make us ... somewhat distant cousins!"

"Excellent!" Fran smiled, "I've never had any cousins, or siblings for that matter, up until a few weeks ago."

Jasper looked at her guiltily, obviously wanting to get something off his chest.

"By the way, I'm sorry I left so abruptly when all that arguing was going on that day."

"When?" asked Fran.

"That day you left. Cecilia said her son had fallen into the well, so I went racing over there. We couldn't see down the well and I had to drop a lamp down there, and we still couldn't see him at all, or hear him. Then we sent out a huge search party and finally found him sleeping over at his grandmother's house."

Fran drew in a quick breath and said, "Sophia says you and Cecilia are 'an item.'"

"Not at all. We dated for a while, but then I went out on tour and we lost touch. Then I met Josie."

"She was your wife?"

"Common law wife, but we were together for five years. I wanted a child and she didn't."

"Usually it's the other way around."

"Not among women who are traveling musicians. Children are incompatible with that lifestyle."

"Yes, I know. My mother was the same way."

"I think Josie thought I was going to abandon her, so she did it first. She left our band and joined another one. Then she hooked up with their drummer."

"I'm sorry to hear that."

"It was rough for a while, but I'm okay now."

"Time to get on with life already?" Fran said, imitating Gustav.

"That's incredible," Jasper marvelled, "You sound just like him."

"It's my one artistic talent."

"Surely you have others."

"Well, I do spoken word poetry, too. But I'm still learning. I don't usually tell anyone that."

"Why not? That sounds fascinating."

"Not to other accountants. They would think *I'm strange.*"

"Fortunately, I'm not an accountant," Jasper grinned.

"Quite."

They walked between the tombstones back to the path. "I also wanted to show you Lyuba's grave. She was only six-years-old when she died."

Fran could barely make out the inscription, 'Lyuba Bihari February 7, 1937–November 10, 1943.'

"She would be sixty-four-years-old by now, almost the same age as her 'niece,' Helena. I am still amazed that Gustav and Sophia did not become bitter after all that suffering," Fran mused.

"Yes, they are good role models that way, our elders."

As they walked down the path, Fran could smell lilac and hyacinth.

Jasper added, "There was a man who also escaped from Birkenau after them. He wrote a book called *I Cannot Forgive* about his experiences in the death camp. She hasn't mentioned it to you yet, but for the last five years Sophia has been recording her memoirs on audiotape. She told me she is going to call it *I Can Forgive.*

Fran smiled, "I wonder why Sophia's ability to forgive never got passed down to her own son."

"I don't know, perhaps because he left here and cut her off. She never liked to dwell on the past or ruminate about the future, because she said that spoils your chances for happiness in this moment."

"Interesting. I look forward to reading her memoirs. I see that I have a lot to learn from her."

"Yes, she makes a difference for many people. After Josie left and she saw me lost in negativity about it, she pulled me aside. And I'll never forget what she said. It totally changed things."

"What did she say?"

"She said that to live in a constant state of negativity is not only hard on your health, but it also stops you from learning how to change things next time. She said if you hang on to your hurt or anger, then you only contribute to more persecution and victimization of yourself and others."

"That's true."

"It helped me let go of being angry at Josie. Soon after I let her go with love and gratitude for what we shared together. I felt so much lighter after that. I had tendonitis from too much guitar playing and that eased up. I started to sleep better. And best of all, I guess I felt a willingness to love open up again."

Fran felt her pulse quicken, and she found herself saying, "I'm noticing myself opening up to love again, too."

She paused and took a breath for added courage, "Especially since meeting you."

She braced herself for the rejection that might come, and felt the red rash creeping up her neck again. Suddenly, the thought of leaving for Canada soon was comforting.

But then he smiled with such abandon that the clouds in Fran's mind blew away completely.

"You took the words right out of my mouth," he replied.

"Really?" she managed, the roar of her heart deafening in her own ears.

"Yes, since the moment I met you on the train," he nodded, with deep conviction, "I felt this sense of happiness. I get the same feeling every time I'm with you. It's strange. I don't think I've ever quite felt this way before."

"I feel happy when I'm with you, too," she confessed, feeling shields of protection breaking away inside of her.

He took her hand and they climbed down a small hill until they reached a weeping willow tree next to a pond. Under the tree was a hand-hewn bench. They sat on the bench face-to-face.

"Too bad you are leaving," Jasper said, his almond-shaped eyes locking onto hers.

"I'll be back. And maybe you can come to Canada for a visit."

"I'd love to do that. I've never been to North America."

He smiled, and Fran lost the sense of time, swimming in the moment, floating free in his steady gaze. His eyes were rich with artistry and spectacularly vivid. It was akin to the golden light dancing on the pond. His hand rested on the inside of her arm, below the elbow. The touch was the kind of touch she wanted from a lover: intimate, sensitive, yet exciting. She wrapped her fingers in his, and they instinctively leaned forward, and touched their foreheads together.

In this joining, all the stories of their kin stirred up from the dust of memory and whirled around them. They met there beyond the illusion of time for an eternity, in the roots of their common ancestry; the carnival entertainers who spread their artistry to the hungry souls of the mainstream world.

Eventually, from a far distant place, they both heard someone calling "Jasper! Fran! Dinner!"

The bell at the meeting hall brought them back out of their reverie. They stood up and their arms encircled one another as they walked in silent gratitude to the hall.

Sophia had held a place next to her for her newfound granddaughter. Jasper sat on Fran's other side. The smell of boiled cabbage stew filled the hall. Hand-made naan bread was handed from person to person, in a hand-woven basket. Even the pots looked hand-made. The contrast to Fran's consumerist, factory-made and throw-away world made her appreciate the care with which each item was made and maintained.

Everyone around her was gesturing, laughing and talking in what seemed like a multitude of languages, with their mouths full of bread and stew. Children came astoundingly close to her, resting their heads on her shoulder, clambering onto her lap. It was a different kind of space than she was used to, but a part of her longed for that kind of intimacy.

Stefan sat across from them, a gangly man in his late seventies with a halo of grey-white hair and white, bushy eyebrows. He had also somehow survived the brutal abuse of Birkenau, spiritually and physically intact. His teeth were stained and chipped now, but he laughed as if there were no tomorrow.

Fran felt a bitter sweetness that her father left this place, with it's simple charm and loving, boisterous aliveness. Yet, he had known nothing else when he left. He had wanted to experience what it would be like to be part of the outside world. She came from the aloneness of

North American culture, and found the connection between members of this community irresistible.

Just before the musicians began to play, Helena and her partner, Effie, pulled into Olino and parked. They walked to the meeting hall in a hurry. Fran met her sister at the door, and could see that her eyes were red and bloodshot, "Helena! What's wrong?"

"Have none of you heard?"

"Heard what?" asked Gustav.

"Two airplanes just rammed into the World Trade Center in New York City. It's all over the news. They suspect terrorists."

Gustav ran to get his portable television, and placed it on one of the tables as everyone crowded around. They could pick up three stations: one in Slovak, one in German, and one in English. They switched back and forth so that everyone could follow. For the next few hours they watched and the community members asked the kind of questions that people all over the world were asking: "Why do people do things like this?" "What is this going to lead to?"

Eventually, Helena and Effie sat down with Fran and Jasper at another table.

"All airplanes have been grounded," she said, "I'm fairly sure your flight tomorrow will be cancelled."

"Yes, I'm sure it will be," Fran said. Secretly, she felt relieved at the thought that she would not be leaving Olino just yet.

"You are welcome to stay here until this whole thing settles," replied Jasper.

"Or at my house," said Helena.

"Thank you. I am well taken care of. By the way, Effie, it's a pleasure to meet you, even if the world news today has distracted us all."

"Yes, my pleasure, too. Helena has been talking up a storm about you and Sophia and Olino. It's been quite a journey."

Sophia and Gustav came over with a tray of dandelion tea made from the plants surrounding the Olino pond. They younger ones asked about the views of their elders regarding the events of September 11th. After all, they were the ones who had survived so many political upheavals of the Twentieth Century.

"My point of view is, how you say, radical? But I say it anyway," mused Sophia. "This darkness ... it comes from stuck creativity ... blocked by fear. No one group to blame. Same thing all over again. Fear invites *Schadenfreude.*"

"What does that mean ... *Schadenfreude?*" asked Fran.

"It's the part of human nature that actually delights in other people's suffering," mused Effie.

Sophia added, "Just look at reality TV shows, ha ha!"

Several people nodded and laughed.

"An event like this will most certainly convince the Americans to go to war," Jasper added. "And that's what they're hoping for."

"Are you saying you think this was a pre-planned event?" asked Effie.

"Either that or they didn't try too hard to intercept the terrorists," Jasper replied.

"Interesting conspiracy theory," Effie proposed.

"It's quite a common political manoeuvre throughout history. Over and over again these coincidental events pop up that cause public outrage and soon everyone is at war. As Sophia just said, it's part of human nature to be *war mongering,* and not simply between nations, but within families and even within our own heads. Though we have the technology now to completely obliterate life on this planet, still the urge to war exists."

"That reminds me of a quotation I saw in this book," Helena said as she searched through her bag for the book that was among her father's possessions. She laid the ancient book of quotations on the table.

"Aahh! I gave that book to Jiri. It was last thing I ever gave him. He kept it all these years!" cried Sophia as she reached out for the book. She held it gingerly, studying its cover like it was the Dead Sea Scrolls. As she opened the first page she asked, "Which quotation? I used to have so many memorized."

"It's actually one that he added by hand, near the back. It was a quotation by Hermann Göering, the head of the Luftwaffe. Apparently he said this right before he was executed in 1946." Helena flipped to the last page and read it. *"The people can always be brought to the bidding of the leaders. All you have to do is tell them they are being attacked, and denounce the peacemakers for lack of patriotism and exposing the country to danger. It works the same in any country."*

"Exactly. It's history repeating itself." Jasper concluded.

Effie added, "And whatever country starts the war will take the blame in the history books, even if other nations also escalated the war. That's what they said of the Germans ... so many innocent people died while the Germans looked the other way. But many people didn't look the other way. They tried to do something ..."

"Yes, I agree. Many Germans helped us," Gustav reassured her.

Gustav had been sitting quietly watching the debate and the concerns, and especially watching Sophia. The tragedy they shared forged an everlasting bond between them. That connection seemed to anchor their vessels through the inevitable storms of their lives these last six decades. He squeezed her forearm in the tender way he had done since those first vulnerable years after Birkenau.

Sophia peered out from her maroon shawl and mused. "Yet, we have all looked the other way at some time, haven't we?"

It was a single sentence, but it hit Fran like a bullet. She thought of what had happened at Freeman & Wilson.

"But we can make new choice any time. No time like the present!" she cackled as Gustav helped her to stand up. "Don't make mistake of hating the bad guys. Then you become a bad guy, too. We humans we like to create the problems and the wars ... so it can swoop in and fix it all. Villain, victim and superhero all at the same time! Ha ha. Keeps us busy, no? There are many ways to look at these things. Look for the gift." She held up her lantern and a supernatural glow cast patterns across her deeply lined skin. As the nearby TV set blared a political promise to retaliate, she added, "Love is best retaliation."

She reached down to offer a kiss to Helena, "Goodnight, my precious granddaughters. You are meant to stay here longer, my dear," she said, patting Fran's knee.

Later that evening after Effie and Helena had left, Jasper walked Fran to her caravan. They were both reeling in shock from the world news not wanting to be alone, not knowing what repercussions were coming. They stood in silence, the sexual tension between them palpable. Finally, Fran said under her breath "Ahhh … would you like to come in?"

Jasper paused and cleared his throat. He glanced at his father's window. For a moment Gustav's curtain parted then ricocheted back.

"It's okay if you don't," Fran reassured him.

Jasper glanced again at his father's window and the old man was waving his fingers forward and winking. Jasper had to smile.

"I feel as if I'm in a fishbowl here at Olino at times."

"Oh," Fran said, suddenly aware of all the eyes peering out at them from darkened windows.

"Let's give them something to talk about then, shall we?" ventured Jasper.

With that they both entered her tiny caravan. Jasper could barely stand up inside. He sank onto the edge of the bed as Fran tried to light the propane lamp. After several attempts, Jasper tried.

"Right then, it looks as though you're out of propane. I suppose we shall have to sit here in the dark then."

"Right then," Fran said imitating his lilting British accent.

They laughed together, short and sharp. Then sat again in the dark, in the silence.

Finally Jasper said, "I feel rather like I'm thirteen years old. You know, all gambly and grout."

"All what?" Fran chuckled.

Jasper shielded his eyes and said, "Love is the best retaliation, that's Sophia's advice."

"That's right!" Fran beamed, and with that she reached over and placed her hand overtop of his. He pulled her in close and their lips touched together. As their arms encircled each other and their lips pressed deeper, Fran felt herself crossing a threshold from a world of barren isolation, into an infinite kind of connection that she swore she would never lose touch with again.

It would be four more months before Fran set foot on Canadian soil again.

## CHAPTER 48

The clouds hung low over Vancouver's inner harbour, like a swirling mass of wool in multi-shades of grey. It was early November and residents of the rain-drenched west coast of Canada had now been sun-deprived for almost three weeks straight. Wenda Simpson felt a chill up her spine as she heard the drone of foghorns over the water. She drove slowly up the winding roads that led to the top of the British properties. She was generally a cheery woman, always ready to look at the bright side of life; but she felt an ominous mood hanging over her as she made the drive that day. Maybe it was the three weeks straight of rain; maybe it was something else.

Wenda glanced in the rear view mirror, straightening her hair. She wore a new powder pink Holt Renfrew suit that had cost her a whole month's income. The suit had been a good investment, she had reasoned, because she was now a British Properties realtor and had to look the part.

Today was the first day in which she was showing a house in her new area. Most other well-established British Properties realtors had declined to be the listing agent for the Freeman mansion, so this was finally her chance to make a good commission.

In the seat beside her sat Edwin Wong, a wealthy investment banker looking to get into the Vancouver-area real estate market. His wife, Minnie, sat quietly in the back seat, crocheting.

"Normally, on a clear day you can see forever from up here," Wenda suddenly announced cheerfully, trying to drive the dark thoughts away. She pulled into the circular driveway of the Freeman Manor and parked near the front entrance. The dogwood, pine, and holly trees had grown so high, the branches were jammed up against the stucco exterior of the house. They hung so low over the driveway that Wenda could hear the pine needles scraping the roof of her car when they drove beneath them.

"As you probably heard, this is an estate sale," she informed her clients, "the heir to this estate had to go out of town, and hasn't been able to get the house ready to show properly. So, I invite you to look beyond the areas that need cleaning up, repairing or replacing. And you might be interested to know that Freeman Manor has always been a landmark. When it was built back in 1972, its innovative architecture put it on the front cover of *Canadian Homes Magazine*. Photographers regularly came here to capture its unusual features, such as the curved roof, spiral columns, and the green-tinted picture windows. The green helps to sparkle up the view. You'll see once they get these trees cut back. The owner was …"

"We know who the owner was," Mr. Wong interrupted.

"Didn't he die in the house?" Mrs. Wong asked.

"I don't know about that," replied Wenda, trying to sound as if she wasn't lying. She smiled and turned away quickly, to discourage further exploration of the owner's fate, busying herself with wedging the key into the rusted-out front door lock. After much jiggling, the door finally creaked open.

As soon as she opened the door, Wenda realized she should have come to look at the property before deciding to show it to prospective buyers. Many parts of the house were a mess. Chunks of wallpaper hung off the wall, their inside surfaces caked with the dust of neglect.

Electrical cords hung like snakes, dangling from hooks on every ceiling. Spiders had spun webs across each doorway.

This was not good. Wenda had gone deep into her line of credit to look the part for this sale. She had already skipped two mortgage payments.

"Imagine what fun you could have turning this place around. In fact, it would be great to do a 'before and after' photo. And it wouldn't take much work either, a landscaper, a couple of coats of paint, and whoopee! Also, and I don't normally encourage this kind of thing, but I bet you could low-ball the estate and get yourself quite a deal," Wenda said as she used her umbrella to remove the spider webs.

She felt choked by the dust, and discomfited by an unusual smell in the air: a combination of mold and formaldehyde.

"The wood trim is all mahogany. You'd have to polish it up, but I hear it's quite stunning."

Wenda prepared to open the door leading to the basement. Minnie suddenly whispered something to her husband, and the couple stopped dead in their tracks. Wenda turned, sensing something amiss.

"I understand the master bedroom is downstairs, and there is another bathroom and a kitchenette," Wenda continued, trying to override whatever had spooked the couple with a recitation of the residence's advantages, "We could even take the elevator down. Yes, this house has its own elevator. There is wheelchair access everywhere. In fact, you could have a whole separate in-law suite, once it gets fixed up. I also hear there is another entirely separate suite on the top floor. Essentially, you could have three different families living in this same house. Excellent for the multigenerational family wanting to live together, or extra mortgage helper!"

The Wongs weren't buying it.

"I don't want to go down there," Minnie said nervously.

"Okay, we go now," added Edwin.

"What's wrong?" asked Wenda.

"Bad spirits," replied Minnie, "Want to go now."

Wenda reacted, going into damage control mode.

"Really, it's not so bad. Let me just show you the upstairs instead. Apparently that is where the daughter lived, and it is very nicely decorated." As soon as those words left her lips she remembered hearing that the upstairs apartment had been broken into and ransacked. No one had cleaned it up yet. "On second thought, let me show you the back yard."

Edwin had already marched out onto the front porch and was calling someone on his cell phone, conversing in Cantonese. Minnie followed him out and put a handkerchief over her nose and mouth.

Wenda chased after them. "I understand that it's a bit disconcerting to see the house in this shape," she said, "But I assure you …"

"This is haunted house. Owner doesn't want anyone in here. Bad luck come to anyone who tries to buy," Minnie said as she squeezed her eyes shut and held her palms facing outwards.

"I assure you, it's not haunted," Wenda was almost begging now, feeling the sale slipping through her fingers like grains of sand in the desert.

A black Bentley pulled into the driveway and the Wong's personal chauffeur stepped out of the driver's door and came around to the passenger door, holding it open. The Wongs disappeared into the back seat. As the driver shut the door, he turned to face Wenda.

"The Wongs thank you very much for your time," he said, "But this will be an inappropriate residence for them to purchase. Good day, madame."

And with that, they departed, their car weaving its way through the canopy of mangled branches back out into the light of day.

Wenda frowned as the vehicle disappeared, then pulled out her prospect contact sheet and crossed another name off the list. At least they were willing to view the place, unlike the other people on her list.

Suddenly her cell phone rang, startling her.

"Hello, Mrs. Simpson," the voice on the other end said to her, "This is Laszlo Goldstein, the estate lawyer. We talked a few days ago. I understand you were going to show the house this morning. How did it go?"

"Oh, hello, Mr. Goldstein," she answered, "They just left. Thank you for calling and checking in. It didn't go well. Are you surprised?"

"That's unfortunate to hear. The estate is receiving a lot of pressure from the owner's debtors. We do need the place to sell. I suspect we need to focus on prospects who are the fix-it-up and renovation-types.

Wenda sighed. "These folks seemed to have the money to fix it up but they didn't like the 'energy' in the house. The wife sensed a 'presence.' Why do I keep getting flakey people? They just seem uncomfortable about the history of the owner and are using the ghost story as an excuse."

"Call me Mr. Flakey as well then, Miss, but it certainly is haunted by the owner. I knew him. He doesn't want the place to sell. He thinks he's still alive."

"Strange. That's what Mrs. Wong, the prospective buyer, said. But really, Mr. Goldstein, you don't believe such nonsense, do you?" Wenda pooh-poohed. Suddenly she heard a strange sound from inside the house. The hair on her forearms stood on end. It sounded like the creaking sound that tree trunks make during a heavy windstorm.

"Miss Simpson?" Laszlo asked, hearing the line go quiet.

"I hear a weird sound in the house," Wenda answered.

Laszlo laughed, "Probably the ghost of George Freeman."

"Cut that out," Wenda protested, "I'll go check and call you right back."

Fumbling around in her purse for her can of mace, she crept down the corridor again and opened the basement door. Maybe there's a hidden camera from the *Just for Laughs* TV show, she thought, and they're going to try and get me on camera, freaking out about something. After they get the reaction they want, the host of the show would leap out from behind a façade, clapping and laughing in delight. Okay, she'd give them the reaction they were looking for.

Of course the light switch to the basement didn't work. That's a very important part of the 'scare process,' Wenda thought. Yet, they didn't anticipate that all good realtors carry a powerful flashlight in their realtor's briefcase. As she extended the beam of light down the stairs, the creaking sound increased. It was accompanied now by the sound of; she hated to admit, heavy breathing. She giggled to herself nervously, thinking how silly all this was.

"Who's there?"

There was no answer. Maybe it was some kind of ventilation system that just kicked in, she reasoned. As she arrived at the bottom of the stairs, she pushed open the door to the master bedroom with her foot. The breathing sound was definitely coming from this room.

As the door swung open, she saw that the wall at the far end of the room had an enormous hole in it! She frantically shone the light over the room and saw bits of wood and plaster covered the floor. The breathing sound escalated.

Wenda dropped her flashlight and dashed up the stairs, scurrying down the narrow corridor. In her frenzy she caught her purse handle on the corner of a bookshelf. As she pulled hard to free herself, the bookshelf leaned dangerously forward. Dusty, disintegrating novels started falling on her. She pushed and shoved and scrambled around the debris until she finally broke free. Then she ran out the front door, slamming it shut behind her.

Tearing off down the hill in her Mercedes, she called Laszlo Goldstein again.

"I don't know what's going on there, but it was very disturbing!" Wenda shouted into the phone, "There is a huge hole in the wall of the downstairs bedroom and this creepy breathing sound. No one warned me about that! It looks like someone took a sledge hammer to the wall!"

"Just calm down, Mrs. Simpson. How big was the hole?"

"At least two feet in diameter. But it's an inside wall, so it couldn't have been done from the outside of the house."

"Was it the inside wall above the bed?"

"Yes! So, someone must have come into the house and done it."

"I'm the only person who has been in the house since you've entered it, and there was no hole in the wall when I was there on Saturday."

"So, what's going on, Mr. Goldstein?!"

"Probably a poltergeist."

"Look. I'm sure there's a more reasonable explanation than that. It was probably a teenage vandal."

"Maybe, but does it look like anything was taken?"

"No."

"Look. I'll have someone come fix it. It will be fixed by Thursday, so you can show it again by Friday."

"I don't want to be the listing agent for this house anymore."

"Mrs. Simpson, come on now," Laszlo protested, "It's just a wee ghost. I thought realtors were used to dealing with things like this. If you back out, you will be the third realtor to give up on us. Once the hole is fixed, I'm sure that will make the ghost leave."

"It's not a repair person you need, Mr. Goldstein," Wenda interrupted, "it's an exorcist!"

She promptly hung up the phone and that was the end of that.

About a week later, another Mercedes pulled up to the Freeman manor at dusk. Laszlo Goldstein rolled down the passenger side window and peered over his glasses at the house. Lena helped him out of the car and set up the wheelchair with the IV drip for him to slide into. Bettina, a German woman in her mid-fifties, stepped out of the back seat. Around her moon-shaped face her short silver hair clung close to her head like a Roman helmet. She had the bearing of a Druid High Priestess as she began sensing the energy of the house.

"How long since the owner died?" asked Bettina in her slight Dutch accent.

"About four months," replied Lena.

"I agree with you, *Herr Goldstein*," Bettina said as she scribbled notes in a notebook, "The owner, George Freeman, thinks he is still alive and he is bound and determined to keep this house."

She closed her eyes and continued as if in a deep trance, "He was a troubled person, who buried many dark emotions his whole life. Those emotions are embedded into the walls of this house; years of repression all coming out now that he no longer walks in a body."

"Sounds accurate."

A chilly breeze emanated from the house as she opened the front door. Bettina glanced back at Laszlo, intrigued, and entered.

"Can we just wait out here while you do whatever it is you do?" asked Lena hopefully.

"Yes, I will go in and speak to George," Bettina said without turning around, "I will help him move onto the next plane of existence."

"You go do that," Lena nodded.

Bettina tiptoed into the house and entered the living room. She lay down an altar cloth on the medical bed and then unwrapped the objects of ritual she had tucked away in her bag: a quartz crystal from a mine in Northern Ontario, a dried Edelweiss flower, a gold goblet into which she poured holy water from Lourdes, a set of Tibetan bells, a peacock feather and finally a small passport-size photo of George Freeman.

The creaking in the house got louder.

After just a few minutes of telepathic listening, Bettina gathered up her supplies and tiptoed back to the front door. As she exited the house, a gust of wind from the surrounding trees caused the front door to slam shut behind her. Bettina stood wide-eyed, looking out onto the driveway at Lena and Laszlo. The three of them backed toward the car and got in.

"My boyfriend is never going to believe this," Lena said finally, breaking the silence as she manoeuvred the car out of the driveway.

As they drove back down the hill Bettina asked, "Where are the ashes?"

"In a crematorium awaiting pick-up by his daughter. She is out of the country right now," replied Laszlo.

"She must return immediately or have them sent to her so she can scatter the ashes. This will help him realize that he has died," Bettina announced firmly.

"I'll get in touch with her today," Laszlo replied, "There is a trial coming up. She needs to be here for that anyway."

"About that awful business with the Freeman & Wilson accounting firm?" Bettina asked.

"Yes."

"She did all that embezzling while her father was dying?" the woman inquired, her look fierce, trying to puzzle the source of the pain she had just experienced in the house.

Lena and Laszlo looked at each other and shook their heads in disbelief.

## CHAPTER 49

I n Kittsee, the last of the multi-
coloured leaves were clutching their
branches trying to defy the laws of nature. The smell of snow was in the air.

When the car pulled up to Helena's office, the two sisters helped their
grandmother out of the car. Sophia beamed with pride as she hobbled
her way to the entrance door, taking in the majesty of the ornate hand-
carved sign reading *"Wichtige Gesundheit."*

Inside, they introduced her to several of the employees and the three
of them went into Helena's office. Helena gave a note to Fran saying
the ashes had just arrived from Canada and were awaiting pickup at
the courier office.

"So you are the big boss woman here. I am very proud of my granddaughter. All these years so close, and yet we never knew each other."

"Yes, it's tragic really. And if it wasn't for Fran …"

Fran interjected, "Actually, if it wasn't for Laszlo Goldstein, we never
would have all met."

"Of course. What is happening with him and the lawsuit?" asked
Helena.

"I'm not sure," Fran replied, frowning, "I need to check my cell
phone messages again. Yesterday, his health turned for the worse and so
they transported him back to Toronto so he could be close to his family."

As she punched in the code to listen to her messages, an ominous feeling washed over Fran. The first message was from Lena.

"I'm sorry to tell you, Fran, that Laszlo died early this morning around 5:00 a.m.. His wife and two children and all of the grandchildren were there with him when he passed. He wanted me to tell you that he was sorry he couldn't be more help in the lawsuit. We will all miss him very much. There is a funeral for him in a couple of days in Toronto. It's a huge one, since he was considered such a hero and godsend to so many people. I imagine you won't be able to make it as you are still abroad. I hope Europe ended up being a good experience for you and that you're glad you went. It was good to meet you, Fran."

Fran listened distractedly to the other messages and disconnected. She placed the phone on the coffee table and curled up on the sofa in Helena's office. The other two looked over at her expectantly.

"He died in the middle of the night."

The room went silent. While the news was expected, the finality of it felt like a bitter pill to swallow. He was gone and regret washed through Fran for not having gotten to know him better, for not listening to more of his stories and understanding his journey more deeply. Why had her father kept him out of their lives all these years when he was living in the same country? He could have been like her uncle. He could have been a friend to her father in those last lonely years.

Helena shook her head and sighed, "He sounded like such an amazing person. I would have loved to meet him and to personally thank him."

"Me too," added Sophia.

The women sat in silence giving their gratitude each in their own way for a man they didn't know, but for one who had made such a difference in all three of their lives.

Finally, Fran said, "We could send a telegram of appreciation to his next of kin and maybe they would read it at his funeral."

They nodded in unison, but all three felt somehow lost about how to acknowledge him properly.

"But what will now happen to the lawsuit?" Helena asked.

"I don't know. Lena said Nelson Gaulin's lawyers are couriering a subpoena for me to appear in court. No one else at Laszlo's law firm will touch the case. I have no idea what to do."

Sophia looked up and said, "They try to pin the blame on you for the business going bad?"

"Yes, on both my father and I."

"They got evidence?"

"Nelson's lawyers said both of us signed off on audits that were fraudulent, at least in the case of one particular development company."

"Did you?" asked Helena.

"No. I would never do that, so I'd love to see what evidence they have. Although I know my father signed off on some audits after he was already going senile, so maybe he did so by mistake."

"So you could get his doctor on the witness stand?" queried Helena.

"I guess so. I was also hoping several people in the company would go on the stand because it was clear from the beginning that our client, Wrightway, a real estate development company, was trying to defraud their clients through false financial claims. You know, 'invest in this raw land and build your dream home!' They would say that to investors even when they still hadn't secured any development permits. Then they'd want us to sign off on audits stating that the land was worth far more than it actually was."

Sophia's wrinkles sunk deeper.

"You know — to sucker people into the deal?"

"Okay, sucker! I know what a sucker is," she grinned.

Fran had to smile back, "But so far no one has come forward. People are believing these stories in the media that he was a war criminal and that I was taking bribes from Wrightway. Plus I can't afford a lawyer since I have no access to any estate money right now."

Fran slumped back, thinking, holding her head in her hands, "It seems hopeless now that Laszlo has died. He was the only one ..."

Her voice trailed off, not knowing exactly what she was trying to say.

Sophia sat near Fran in an overstuffed ottoman, her feet at least six inches from the floor. In her hand-knit shawl and layered skirts, she looked like one of the cultural dolls that Fran's neighbour used to collect for her from around the world. She touched the stumps of her arms together on her lap and whispered, "You must go home now."

"I know I should be there, but I just can't bear the idea of facing all that negative press. I was counting on Laszlo's help there to handle it."

"Laszlo helped you this far, now it's your turn to deal with it," added Helena.

Sophia nodded in agreement.

Fran sank back into the sofa. Here were two women she greatly admired who had both faced challenges she couldn't even begin to fathom. She felt a loathing for her own cowardice. It silently snaked it's way around her heart. In her fog of despair she faintly uttered, "I have no idea where to start."

"Start with end in mind," Sophia suggested.

"Yes, what would you like to have happen?" added Helena.

Fran stared at them both blankly. Nothing was coming to mind. The situation seemed bleak and devoid of possibilities.

Fran remembered hearing Sophia tell the story about her and the Jewish woman at the concentration camp imagining themselves as old ladies swinging together on a porch. They had created that outcome in the bleakest of all possible realities. Then, Marguerite's words crept back into her consciousness: state your current situation and then choose your ideal outcome. Establish a magnetic draw from one to the other. Intention is everything.

"Okay. What would I like?" she thought aloud, "I am just focusing on what I don't want and all the possible negative consequences. I know that's not going to help. What would I like to see happen? Hmmmm ... what could possibly happen that would turn this situation around?"

Fran concentrated, willing herself to think differently. She peered into the eyes of her kinswomen. Their wisdom, their toughness, and their compassion for her, shone through like a sword cutting through the hopelessness.

"I'd like to get the truth out in the open, assign responsibility where it's due. Then let go and move on."

"Then that's what you should aspire to. And what about the company itself?" asked Helena.

"Laszlo said it's totally bankrupt."

"You could salvage some aspects maybe and restart under a new name, no?" asked Helena.

"Me, start a company? I wouldn't know how to do that."

"I could help you; guide you through the process. I've started at least four companies," offered Helena.

"Wow! You would do that?"

Helena nodded. Fran felt a sense of excitement rush through her head.

"Who else could help?" asked Sophia.

"What do you mean?" asked Fran.

"Who would come forward and help your cause?"

"I can't think of anyone. The partners all seem to have turned against me, even several of the account managers and staff. Eva, his caregiver, sold us out to the press, and Laszlo is gone."

"There must be someone," added Helena.

Tears welled up in Fran's eyes as she realized how isolated she felt. There was Marguerite, but she barely knew them and wouldn't count as a character witness.

"You could come to Canada, Sophia, and vouch for your own son."

Sophia smiled and nodded, but then said, "I am far too old to travel now. But I write letter for the cause, if you think it will help."

"Who could you call to help you get a good lawyer?" asked Helena.

Fran shrugged. She was sinking back down again into a black hole of despair.

"Come on Fran, surely you know someone," urged Helena.

Fran willed herself to focus again on possibilities. She picked up her cell phone and started scrolling through her contacts. She was almost to the bottom of the list when a name stood out.

"Sheila Wilson! She's a lawyer who deals in fraud cases. I once did the accounting for one of her clients *pro bono*."

"What is pro bono?" asked Sophia eager to understand a new phrase.

"It means I did it for free. The client, a restaurant owner, was being sued by one of his customers. The customer was clearly a nutcase. We all believed in the restaurateur's innocence and wanted to see justice served, so I offered to do a forensic audit pro bono."

Sophia crinkled her brow in confusion.

Fran added, "That means I checked all their accounting records to see if there was any foul play and I couldn't find any. I went to court and testified which made a big difference to this man being found not guilty."

"Good. So this lawyer woman, she owes you, no?" asked Sophia.

"You think I should ask her to take on my case pro bono?"

"Pro bono!" shouted Sophia.

"Pro bono!" echoed Helena.

The three of them laughed.

"Call her. Call her now. You can use my landline."

Fran sat down at Helena's desk and made the call as instructed. Meanwhile, Helena took Sophia on a tour of the office and the adjacent factory.

About fifteen minutes later, Fran joined them in the lab where they were chatting and learning about how to make the herbal supplements. As Fran approached she could overhear them talking about Marek. They both turned to her.

"You make the call?" Sophia grinned.

"Yes. She had heard about the case in the media. She seemed very sympathetic but said she was far too busy right now to take on the case."

The triumvirate of women studied each other for five long seconds.

"And so?" Helena said breaking the silence.

"I said I understood and asked if she could recommend anyone. She said if someone occurred to her she would get back to me."

It only took Fran a moment to register their looks of disbelief. "I know, pathetic isn't it?"

"It's just bad habit, Francesca," Sophia reassured her. "Time to start new one now, hmmm?"

"I know neither of you would have let it go so easily, but I'm just not strong like you. Maybe I've had too easy a life …"

Fran shifted her gaze back and forth between them secretly hoping one of them would offer to make the call for her.

"No comparing our lives to yours. You had tough life, too, in many ways. You have moxie in you. I see it in your eyes."

Fran marvelled at the possibility of having moxie. Memories of heart-breaking, soul crushing moments cascaded through her minds-eye — times when those shattering incidents activated a survival response so primal it had astounded her. "I'm still not sure what to say to win Sheila over to my cause. What would *you* say?"

Helena was about to offer a suggestion when Sophia chimed in.

"Before your wise sister answers, ask yourself this question: 'what would *I* do if I were exceptional at this?'"

"What do you mean?"

"Imagine you are already good at winning people over to your cause, because this wisdom is inside."

"Hmmm … *what would I do if I were exceptional at winning people over to my cause?*" Fran willed herself to answer the odd question. "But I'm not exceptional."

"We play make believe right now, okay? Be imaginative like you are about to write new poem. Pretend you were exceptionally good at that. What would you do?"

Fran shrugged.

"One day you will go back to Canada and not have such wise elders here to help you," Sophia chided. "But we will be with you in spirit anytime when you can answer that question."

"You mean if I were as exceptional as Helena or Sophia?"

"Ha ha!" bellowed Sophia, grinning with delight.

"I suppose I would write out a list of benefits to Sheila for taking on my case and then call her back."

"Good. What else?"

"I would send her the list of evidence that Helena and I pulled together."

"Good. What else?"

Fran widened her coal-dark eyes, "I would … I dunno … I would remind her of all the work I did for her case. I would tell her how much it would mean to me."

"Now we are talking!"

Helena teased, "I would do stuff like that. How about you, Sophia?"

"Yes, you think like the plucky girls, now."

Fran looked down at the floor and smiled, "I'll go make the call, then." She turned on her heel and padded back to Helena's office.

An hour later she met up with them again in the staff lounge. They were chatting away in Slovak looking like a pair of roosting hens.

"So?" they both said in unison.

"So, this is amazing! I first wrote out a list of benefits to her and that buoyed my courage so much! Because there was lots she could gain, you know? Then I emailed her the evidence that Helena and I had collected and then called her back. Her receptionist said she was on another call and I asked her to interrupt the call!"

"Very plucky," the two of them nodded their approval.

Fran continued, "So she did interrupt the call. Then, I asked Sheila to read the evidence so far, then I read out my list of benefits. Then I reminded her of all the work I had done for her and how much it would mean to me if she took on the job. Then I told her why I thought she'd be the best lawyer for the job. I even brainstormed with her to see if there was a way she could turn over some of her existing work to other lawyers so she'd have time. To make a long story short I convinced her to take on the case — pro bono!"

"Good for you, Fran!" Helena clapped.

"Good for everyone," beamed Sophia.

## CHAPTER 50

The mid-January ground outside was cracked frozen and the icy air stung Fran's nose with each inhale. Jasper was busy making tea on the propane burner in the tiny caravan at Olino. Fran lay snuggled in bed under a puffy, hand-quilted duvet. The heater was taking a long time to warm up the caravan this chilly Sunday morning.

"Two peppermint teas at your service," said Jasper as he slid in beside her, "After this we can go jump in the river!"

Fran shuddered thinking of the last time she attempted to join the Olino folks in river bathing. She still preferred the solar shower in Gustav's house.

As Fran gratefully accepted the minty-smelling warmth, she said, "By the way, Marguerite left a message to say that she can get you a spot to perform at the West Coast Music Festival in Vancouver. It's on February twenty-seventh. Several of her promoter friends will be there and she will ensure they come see you play. Bring as many of your CDs as you can."

"Smashing! Well done, Ms. Freeman. You are most admiringly well-connected."

"It's Marguerite who is the connected one. You should be getting a North American tour in no time."

"I look forward to meeting her and seeing your fine city."

"Yes. We should all buy our plane tickets as soon as possible. I'm thinking February 15th. Effie has arranged to get the time off work to come with us, as well."

"We can ring up that travel agent in Kittsee today," Jasper said as he put his arm around Fran so she could place her head on his shoulder.

A soft knock on the caravan door broke them out of their reverie. It was Gustav. Jasper slipped on his jeans and sweater and stepped outside to speak with him. A few minutes later he came back inside.

"It's time."

Fran felt an icy pang in her heart as they traipsed down the winding path to Sophia's caravan. She had been deteriorating these last few months. Fran willed herself to find the courage to face yet another death.

Several people were gathered around Sophia when Jasper and Fran arrived. Some were singing, some were moaning, one child was crying. Gustav ushered the others out of the caravan so that Jasper and Fran could have a seat.

"Where is Helena?" Sophia asked Gustav.

"She is coming soon," he assured her.

Fran put her hand softly on the old woman's forehead. It was hot with fever. Jasper handed Fran a cold facecloth and she dabbed the cool fabric around Sophia's weathered skin. The old woman murmured her appreciation.

Fran could smell jasmine incense burning, and turned to see a small altar set up at the foot of the bed.

Sophia opened her eyes and looked up at Fran. She whispered "Jasper say you are great poetess. I want that you read me one of your poems."

"Oh, not really."

"Yes, really," objected Jasper. "I've heard at least seven by now. I love them all."

"He's biased," she whispered.

"So am I. Do it as favour for a dying lady."

Fran sensed a mixture of devotion and need pouring out from her grandmother's dark-skinned face. The need to serve Sophia superseded Fran's own discomfort at performing her poetry.

"Okay," she agreed.

Fran searched her memory for a poem that she could recite and that felt fitting for this moment, close to the end of a great person's life. A poem she'd written and sang recently sprang to the forefront of her mind.

"Okay. This one is called *Ancient Lore*. It's actually a song, not just a poem," she clarified. She glanced over at Jasper.

"I didn't know you wrote songs," he said, wide-eyed.

"Yes, I've written a few," Fran replied, feeling herself flush.

"You get band to record her song, okay, Jasper? Promise?" said Sophia.

Jasper nodded and stroked the old woman's forehead.

"Don't promise anything until you hear it," Fran warned.

"Shut up and sing," Jasper chided, flashing a playful grin.

Fran drew in a long, slow breath to find the first note of the haunting Celtic melody. She began to sing in her pure, soft tones.

*Life feeds itself through my weary bones*
*And takes and gives in one night alone*
*I am the one who has been before*
*Through roots of legend, and ancient lore*

*This quake now upon us*
*Brings epilogues of promise*
*Pray for the lullaby*
*Before we all say goodbye*

*I see in this land*
*A friend is at hand*

*That carves me a staff*
*Then shows me the path*

*I am captured by light*
*Then cast into the night*
*The somersault begins*
*On great waves of chagrin*

*I now choose to be here*

*Standing alone with that fear*
*Finding ways into my mind*
*Are the great loves of all time*

*Life feeds itself through my weary bones*
*And takes and gives in one night alone*
*I am the one who has been before*
*Through roots of legend, and ancient lore*

When she finished the song, Fran looked up. She wrote the song at a time when she had felt alone in the world and was looking for solace. The song had come to her fully born; words and music, no editing. It was a gift from an unknown muse.

Fran sneaked a glance at Sophia and there was pride in that sunken smile and a shimmering lagoon of love in her steady gaze. Jasper wrapped his arm around her waist.

"It's beautiful," he said. "And your voice is incredible, so pure, huh Baba?"

Sophia touched her knee and whispered, "No more undercutting your art. You insult the muse when you do that, hmmm?"

Fran felt the fire of truth in those words. It was that incessant gremlin of self-doubt; a parasite of her life force and creative fire. She nodded in silent pledge to Sophia.

"Do you know where your name comes from?" whispered Sophia, willing herself to keep speaking.

"Where?"

Sophia gazed over at Gustav, "Tell her."

Gustav sat forward on his chair, "We think Jiri name you after his best friend at school … Francesca. She was Jewish, no?"

Sophia nodded.

He continued, "He was many times bullied at that school. She understood him. She saw his smarts," Gustav explained pointing to his temple.

"I saw a portrait he did of her …"

"He kept all his portraits! That is good, he kept that part of him. He was so good at his art. We knew he would be great artist or inventor."

Sophia's cataract-eyes glistened in their opaque way.

"He make many pictures of Francesca, huh? She was godsend to Jiri, always there for him, when so many others shun him."

"Like you, hmm?" Sophia whispered. "… always there for him."

Fran felt a throbbing in the back of her throat as she re-lived the ragged misery that his life had become. It was true. She had been there with him through the crushing blow of abandonment and the smouldering remains of his last years. For years she was the only lifeline between that dangerous world outside the house and his fragile mausoleum of a life. No one had ever appreciated her in the way that Sophia just did.

The door to the caravan cracked open and Helena stepped inside. They made room for her near the bed. They greeted each other in loving silence and then sat holding hands. Fran could again sense the presence of her father close by.

"Meeting both my beautiful granddaughters has meant everything to me. I am glad I live this long. You are my blood, my family, and I live on now because you have known me."

The comment rendered them both speechless. Indeed their grandmother's presence would leave an indelible mark for the rest of their lives.

They stayed there into the cold half-light of dusk, huddled in prayer and gratitude until she finally, and almost unnoticeably, took her last breath.

CHAPTER 51

As Gustav's melancholic notes echoed through the weeping willows, Fran and Helena scattered their father's ashes over the sunken, empty Olino gravesite. Over a hundred people had gathered for a double memorial service for both Sophia and her long-lost son, Jiri.

While most people in the community never knew Jiri, they all sat in rapt attention as Fran recounted the story of his life. As a community, they gave into their compassion as she unfolded his journey from Olino to Austria, to Hitler Youth, to his "death" in the Sahara Desert and then onto Canada.

While the wound of the Holocaust still festered in the souls of those in attendance, the fact that one of their own had saved a few Olino lives allowed them to forgive Jiri's betrayal and the renunciation of his roots.

After the tribute to Jiri, the community turned their attention to his mother, the woman who had survived the camps and thrived across the seas from her own son all these years. There was story after story about Baba Sophia, grandmother to everyone at Olino. She had clearly been a container and guide to those going through dark times; both compassionate and unrelenting in her quest to help them find the truth.

After the double service, family and guests wended their way back to the meeting hall. At the entrance someone had set up an altar. Fran studied the faded photo of Sophia and her baby. Her fifteen-year-old face was blurry, but Sophia's stance belied an eternal vibrancy that would be her lifelong trademark.

In another photo to the left, she was about twenty-three-years old, wearing a bejewelled headdress, a puffy-sleeved blouse and an ornately patterned, ruffled skirt. She was holding her prize plaque for winning the Czardas Dance contest.

To the right was a photo of Jiri at fifteen years of age. He was standing next to an easel, a paint brush held in mid-air, while he contemplated his unseen subject.

Someone had scattered orange marigold flower tops around the edges of the altar table and was burning Nag Champa incense from a green, clay holder that was inscribed with the Sanskrit word for Peace. A sketch of Jiri's parents, Karl and Sophia, was taped to the back wall.

The well-worn Alastair Crowley Tarot Deck and Sophia's crystal ball sat next to her exquisitely carved figurine of Santa Sara. Under Santa Sara was a postcard someone sent Sophia from Rome, back in the 1980s. It was of the famous Pietà sculpture in St. Peter's Basilica in the Vatican. The Michelangelo sculpture featured the Virgin Mary seated in her long robes with the bloodied corpse of Jesus draped across her lap.

Something about the sculpture transfixed Fran for several minutes. Then her spell was broken by the sound of a toddler shrieking with delight across the room. She noticed a stack of the magazines that featured Sophia's regular columns about arts and culture. One article was entitled: "The Link Between Creative Freedom and Economic Well-Being." On one side of the magazines were her silver ankle bracelets and the antique book of quotations. It was open to a quotation by Mark Twain that read: *Forgiveness is the fragrance that the violet sheds on the heel that has crushed it.* The words sent a shiver down her spine.

Now that the memorial service was over and guests stood chatting and eating sweet breads, Fran felt a wave of exhaustion run through her.

As she studied the altar, the impermanence of things seemed to burn a black hole in her heart. Sophia was gone from her life forever. Fran would never talk to her again; never hear her laugh, never feel the love emanating like the sun from her ancient eyes.

Fran would also never see her father again. She would never see Laszlo again. He was gone. They were all gone, like passing clouds soon to be forgotten.

She glanced over at Helena and Jasper talking together by the window. One day they would both be gone, too. She looked down at her own hand, so animated and full of life now, but one day would also turn to ash.

Fran stared at the Tarot deck and decided to flip over the top card. It was The Tower card. Although she didn't understand the symbolism of the Tarot, there was something about the image of the lightning bolt striking a dark, brooding tower with people falling to the ground that held her attention. Memories of September 11th filled her heart and mind.

She rocked back on her heels as if impacted by a force beyond her understanding. It cracked the dam. One droplet at a time started to seep from the fracture. The droplets then became a stream of water, and soon a torrent of waves. She slipped into a small alcove and stood in the dark. Her shoulders heaved silent sobs. A few minutes later she felt a hand on her shoulder. It was Cecelia, the dancer.

"Francesca, its okay to cry here. We at Olino are born to wail, and you are now one of us," Cecelia smiled.

Fran half-smiled, not quite knowing how to respond but touched that this woman who had been her nemesis was somehow including her in the Olino creed.

Cecelia took her hand and whispered in broken English, "We all miss Sophia. I love her so much. I am dancer because of her. She teach me everything."

Fran's eyes widened wondering what it would have been like growing up with a woman like Sophia to guide her.

They stayed there together holding each other listening to the sound of Gustav's violin until Fran's sobbing finally subsided.

It was three weeks later when Fran, Jasper, Helena and Effie arrived at the Vienna airport for their trip to Canada. The Olino community had allowed Fran and her sister to choose from some of Sophia's treasured few possessions. She had chosen the figurine of the goddess Santa Sara and knew she would gift it to Marguerite. She had also gratefully accepted a shawl, the Tarot deck, a silver ankle bracelet and the tiger's eye necklace.

In addition, Fran had an entirely new set of clothes in her suitcase, handmade with the help of Cecelia and two of Jasper's cousins. Fran had given away all her Canadian clothes to the women of Olino. It not only lightened her load but it was a way of appreciating them. She did it partly because they were intrigued by the muted tones, the fine fabrics and the trendy design and partly because none of her clothes fit her anymore. Fran's body had transformed into womanly curves and the tomboy had somehow wandered off to other explore other worlds. She now relished wrapping those newfound curves in the crimson, blue and gold fabrics of her clanswomen.

While the four of them waited to board the flight, Fran noticed people noticing her and she liked the feeling; not because she felt proud of how she looked but rather because she felt she was honouring the essential human need in all people to witness beauty in one's surroundings.

Fran remembered how rough the last flight felt and searched through her bags to find the nausea pills. She couldn't find them and there was no time to shop for more.

When the airplane took off Fran breathed in that whispering way that Marguerite had shown her. Jasper was peering out the window. She hadn't bothered to mention her fear of flying. In these last few months their merging had coaxed a quality in her that she was just beginning to understand. In his body flying was a pleasure, an intrigue of landscape, free movies, and three-course meals. In his world this pressurized metal tube blasting through the skies could actually land safely like hundreds do every single day of the year. In his world she found a way, just as in hers he had found a way back to a place he needed to be. Flying, for the first time since she was six, was as she experienced it now ... a safe passage back home.

## CHAPTER 52

"And here I am now," Fran said stretching her jet-lagged body. "Does that give you enough to work from?"

J.P. hit the stop button on his digital recorder. "Wow. That could be a mini-series."

"I suppose I got carried away."

"No, it was all great. Totally fascinating."

"Good."

"So, you're back to slay the dragon then?" J.P. queried.

"We'll see," Fran shrugged.

"I have a feeling it will be a piece of cake for you."

She had to grin and as she did she caught her reflection in a mirror. Her habitual furrow seemed gone. Instead she saw a rootedness in her body, in the earth.

"Take from it what's useful for your article, and as a reminder, we could really use your help to win the case."

J.P. nodded, "I'll do my utmost and I'll get you the proof before we go to print."

Fran nodded and shook his hand.

"I am grateful to have spent this time with you, Fran."

"Call me Francesca," she insisted.

"Francesca," he said, bowing his head. "It suits you."

She shook his hand and turned to leave. She noticed that her clan had just entered the lobby and waved. As she walked towards them Francesca turned and said, "Send me the proof by a week Monday, yes?"

"Yes! Absolutely," J.P. reassured her.

"Good."

## CHAPTER 53

About a month later in Vancouver, spring was bursting through. The myriad of pink-blossomed cherry trees offered their colors to the God of the royal blue sky. Yellow, red and purple tulips stood tall guarding the greens of the Marine Drive golf course.

Nelson Gaulin was entertaining a potential new partner, Reg Cooper, for a round of golf. He hoped Reg would join him in the new accounting firm he was launching. He planned to entice all the top clients from Freeman & Wilson to bring their business to the newly established Gaulin & Cooper.

After the game the two men sat in the lounge for a post-game whiskey; two silver haired men with Palm Spring tans courting each other, looking for ways to improve their lives of privilege.

Just as they got settled, two attractive women entered the lounge, both wearing their shades and golf visors. Nelson and Reg looked over at the same time.

"Hey, I've never seen either of them here. I'll take the brunette, you can have the blonde," Reg Cooper chuckled to his buddy.

"You're on," replied Nelson as he surveyed the tall blonde who stood with the authority of a commanding general.

The women both looked around the lounge, spotted the two men and started walking directly toward them.

"Hey, the cards are playing right into our hands. They're coming our way," Reg observed.

"Excuse me, are you Mr. Nelson Gaulin?" asked Sheila Wilson as she approached their table with her air hostess smile.

Nelson's grin grew wide as he wondered if his reputation as a great lover amongst the wives of the golf club members was somehow preceding him.

"As a matter of fact, I am," he replied.

Sheila was in her mid-thirties and had shoulder length, blonde streaked hair and wide-set blue eyes that exuded confidence, intelligence and sensuality all at the same time. Her grey pencil skirt and cream colored blouse swayed gently around her curvy physique.

Nelson looked over at the other woman who was just taking off her sunglasses and visor.

Reg waved toward the nearby chairs and said, "Ladies, please join us."

His smug grin fell like an avalanche when Nelson saw her face. His lips tightened and he squared his shoulders to the two women.

"Actually, we're in an important meeting right now," he asserted.

Reg looked over at his friend, shocked that he would turn down an opportunity to meet two such hot women. Maybe he was playing hard to get.

"This will only take a moment," Fran said as she reached down into her bag and produced a manila envelope, "Hi Nelson, nice to see you again. And you are?" she said reaching out her hand.

"Reg Cooper."

"Nice to meet you. My name is Fran Freeman and this is my lawyer Sheila Wilson."

"Oh, you're Fran Freeman!" Reg replied, eyeing her up and down.

Fran smiled at Reg and looked over at Nelson as she handed him the manila envelope.

"It seems we now have evidence; letters of testimony from concentration camp victims that George Freeman saved. Also the Wiesenthal Foundation has zero evidence that George was ever a war criminal. We also have testimony from our family doctor that my father signed off on Wrightway audits after he had been clearly diagnosed with onset dementia."

Nelson squirmed in his chair.

Sheila added, "You may also be interested to see this witness statement. It's from Gordon Weise, one of the former Freeman & Wilson partners. He has provided us with evidence that suggests you tricked Fran Freeman into signing off on another Wrightway audit, plus ..."

"Hold on there, honey!" Nelson said, red faced, "I did no such thing and one person's witness statement isn't going to prove that."

"Actually, since Gordon made a statement he convinced three of the other partners to come forward."

Nelson's chest sank and his eyes took on the look of a caged animal. "You have no right to come in here and make these accusations."

Reg jumped in, "Actually, Nelson, this is all rather interesting to me. What else do you have in that little manila envelope of yours?"

Fran added, "We also have proof of your ongoing sexual liaison with the CFO of Wrightway, Mary Ann Redwood, emails and voice mail recordings. There appears to be a paper trail of the bribe you received from her to falsify their accounting records. We have filed copies with your lawyer and the judge."

The two women flashed delicious smiles down at Nelson.

Fran gingerly placed the manila folder on the lounge table in front of Nelson.

The two men exchanged an uncomfortable glance, then Reg knocked back his whiskey and said, "This looks like a matter between the three of you. I'll catch you later, Nelson."

"Listen, Reg. This is all a counter-attack, there is no way they have that kind of evidence. Let's get together tomorrow. I'll buy you dinner at the Flying Horseman."

"I'm booked up the whole of next week, but I'll have my secretary give you a ring when my schedule clears up. Ta ta, ladies."

With that he grabbed his camel hair coat and hustled his way out the side entrance.

Nelson's eyes narrowed as it dawned on him that Fran Freeman chose this time and place to deliver the evidence. His big deal was being destroyed in one spectacularly well-planned swoop. As images of the impending humiliation, public outrage, loss of financial wherewithal, and even a possible prison sentence loomed before his eyes, Nelson held his forehead and was seized by a pounding, dizzying headache.

"How dare you invade my privacy like this!" he growled like a wounded beast.

"How dare you bankrupt a forty-four year old company and put 107 people out of a job!" said Fran, her stare intense, as they turned to leave. There was something supremely knowing in her gaze that was altogether different than the woman he'd known before. It was a gaze that could, like a tsunami, drown self-aggrandizing manipulations in a single wave. Nelson felt trapped like a rat in that look.

"See you in court," added Sheila.

And with that, the two women exited out the grand mahogany doors of the most exclusive golf course in town.

## CHAPTER 54

A few weeks later the doorbell of the Gaulin residence chimed like a medieval toll bell. Nelson was expecting the courier from the pharmacy. He had recently ordered another, more potent, anxiety pill prescription.

When he peered through the spyglass, however, four people from Freeman & Wilson stood on the landing side by side: Peter Wilson, Meili Cheng, Gordon Weise and Nisha Gujral.

"Tell them I'm not well and get rid of them!" he growled at his wife, Janine.

Nelson stood just out of view wearing his coat and hat as Janine opened the door.

"Hi, Janine," Gordon said. "Is Nelson here?"

"Yes, but I'm afraid he's not well," she said, her eyes darting to the side.

"I imagine the stress of this situation is challenging, but maybe a mini 'Truth & Reconciliation Commission' will help him feel better.'"

"Perhaps it would. I'm so glad you could come over."

In that moment, Janine did something unprecedented in the history of her marriage; she stepped back and allowed them to enter the house.

Gordon stepped past Janine into the front hall, "There you are Nelson. You look like you're just about to go out."

Peter, Nisha and Meili all surrounded him.

Nisha added, "We just heard about the new evidence from Fran's lawyer and it's pretty compelling."

Nelson took a step back and almost toppled over the hat tree, "Listen, guys, it's great to see you, but I'm incredibly late for a meeting right now."

"This meeting is more important, Nelson," Gordon warned him.

Nisha added, "Yes, we've come to let you know that Fran shared this new evidence with all the ex-Freeman & Wilson employees. And, at our last meeting, about forty-six out of the 107 of them are willing to be part of a class action suit against you."

Nelson looked like he'd just been hit by a baseball bat. He pushed through them toward the door, dizzy from the new information.

"None of that evidence has been proven in a court of law yet, what makes you think you could even begin some kind of class action suit?"

Meili took a step sideways to block him, "Because several employees came forward to Fran's lawyer upon hearing the evidence to corroborate it."

Meili had always been such a mouse-like woman, especially in the presence of the omnipotent Nelson Gaulin.

Peter was buoyed by her defiant behaviour and added, "Yes, and we heard details from Jackie, Susan, Robert, Simon and even Steve. Plus, George's caregiver came forward and she told us about where you got the photos."

Gordon added, "After they all gave evidence, there was very little doubt in the minds of most of the employees that you had masterminded this whole fraud."

Janine arrived with a tray of mint tea and almond biscuits for everyone and ushered them into the sitting room.

"Oh thanks, Janine. That's so sweet of you," Gordon said as he started peeling off his trench coat and looking for a spot to hang it on the hat tree.

Nelson glared at her.

A few weeks ago Fran had requested a confidential meeting with Janine. Before Fran even opened her mouth, Janine knew exactly what she was going to say. It was no surprise that her husband had seduced Fran along with several other women at the firm. She both admired and feared the young woman's courage to face her with the information. Part of her had wanted to bolt from the meeting. But something about Fran's demeanour made her stay. She made an irresistible plea, coming forth in full disclosure, seeking atonement and offering recompense in whatever way she could to Janine.

Perhaps she stayed because at the root of it Janine felt a glimmer of possibility: a guilt-free way out of her unhappy marriage. With both morbid fascination and bullish resistance battling it out inside her, Janine faced the train wreck that was her husband's life.

She left the meeting saying she needed a few days to digest the information. With the support of a few trusted friends and the advice of her lawyer, Janine had agreed to their plan. On a quiet Sunday she had given Sheila Wilson access to Nelson's office and his computer.

While Janine was only too aware of Nelson's rogue nature, she just couldn't bear the public humiliation of a divorce and a full-blown law suit. Yet, it was now clear that the media would be soon descending on them if Nelson kept insisting on his innocence. Janine, even more than all the other parties concerned, wanted a low key resolution as quickly as possible.

As the four guests settled themselves in the sitting room, chatting away with Janine about the importance of mint as a digestive aid, Nelson stood in the corner of the hall, unable to move. His demeanor was like that of a chameleon lizard, frozen on the spot in hopes of disappearing into the scenery.

Finally, Nisha stood up and helped Nelson out of his raincoat, and guided him to sit in the Indian rattan fan chair. The once almighty Nelson slumped back in the regal chair looking like an errant twelve-year-old; the irony apparent to everyone.

Several boxes of cookies later it was clear that Nelson had stranded himself on an island of delusion. They forced his hand and he agreed to drop his suit against Fran Freeman. In return, the employees agreed to see if they could settle out of court, regarding the class-action suit. Since Nelson and Janine were wealthy, there was a possibility for some much needed financial restitution.

Surprisingly, there was a group consensus in that sitting room on that day. Making amends was, for that moment in their lives, more important than winning.

CHAPTER 55

The sky was clear over Vancouver's inner harbour revealing a spectacular view of the downtown skyscrapers towering over a sunlit ocean, which swirled toward the distant Gulf islands to the west. The realtor, Wenda Simpson, felt a slight chill up her spine as she drove back up the winding roads that led to the top of the British properties. She remembered the last time she showed Freeman Manor.

A lovely young couple from the United Arab Emirates sat in the car with her, enjoying the unfolding view as they drove higher and higher. She pulled into the circular driveway of Freeman Manor and parked near the front entrance. This time the trees had been cut back, which gave the house a sense of openness again.

"As you probably heard, this is an estate sale," she informed her clients, "the heir to this estate has recently re-done the place. And I can tell you it's quite an amazing difference. I'm sure it will sell immediately."

The young man's Dubai family wanted to establish residency in Canada.

"It most certainly is," he replied as he surveyed the front of the house.

Wenda continued, buoyed by his comment, "As your other realtor may have mentioned, Freeman Manor has always been a landmark. When it was built back in 1972, its innovative architecture put it on the front cover of *Canadian Homes Magazine*. Photographers regularly came here to capture its unusual features, such as the curved roof, spiral columns, and the green tinted picture windows. The owner was …"

"We know who the owner was," interrupted Mohammed.

"Didn't he help save some people from a concentration camp during World War II?" asked his wife.

"Why, yes he did," replied Wenda. "I believe that was in *The Global Reader* recently."

She pressed the doorbell and heard a sing-song tone. No answer. Soon after Wenda wedged the key into the brand new front door lock. It opened smoothly.

Inside Wenda was stunned to see how exquisite the house looked, returned now to its original glory. Mohammed and his wife walked from one floor to the next and around the grounds, talking excitedly in Arabic to a family member on a cell phone. As they wandered around the basement area, Wenda sneaked a peak into 'the room' that had spooked her. The hole in the wall had been fixed and light was now shining in through the ground floor window. No sense of dread, just a sense of relief filled her body as she walked back up the stairs. Whatever presence had brooded this space had now disappeared.

Two weeks later Wenda pulled the SOLD sign out of the ground and handed over the keys to the new owners. Fran, now four months pregnant, watched as the couple entered their new home. She stood next to Wenda in the circular driveway and said goodbye to the place that had been her home till her father died. Like a war-torn mother, the house seemed to emanate a sense of gratitude back to Fran for being reinstated as a place of nurturing and wholeness again.

## CHAPTER 56

"Two goat cheese and pecan salads," announced Fran as she slid into the booth at Selby's. She was now five months pregnant and although the morning sickness had died down, she was now dealing with horrendous pressure pains in her pelvis. She shifted around in her seat trying to get comfortable.

Their favourite waiter raised one eyebrow and said. "Substitute the red onions for cilantro?"

"But, of course," grinned Marguerite as she pulled out a sheet from her briefcase. "Here is the band's schedule. You go all down the west coast, across to the Midwest, then you do a whole east coast tour. It's quite the coup."

Fran frowned as she sipped her water.

"You don't look as thrilled as I feel."

"Yes, I have mixed feelings about being on tour during my last trimester of pregnancy."

"Yes, it's a tight schedule."

"And lots of bus travel. I'm not sure how I'll be feeling."

"You can decide closer to the time."

"Plus maybe it's unseemly for a pregnant woman to be up on stage," Fran said rubbing her belly.

"On the contrary, when I saw you belting your songs and poetry last night … woohee! Full with the promise of new life. Mesmerizing. Truly it was. Pregnancy looks good on you. It doesn't always look good on everyone … but on you … it's a whole other dimension. You are like the sixth dimension, ha!"

Fran beamed and breathed in the compliment like a whiff of fresh sea air "The sixth dimension? Too funny. We sure brought the house down, though."

"That you did."

Fran flinched and rubbed her lower back.

"See how it goes on tour. At any rate, you'll be back well before your due date and before Helena arrives."

"Yes, did I tell you she found a location for her factory on the North Shore?"

"I heard. She emailed me."

"I'm helping her do the financial forecasting."

"Good. That reminds me, how is your seminar coming along on *Financial Management for Artists?* I think Lynette scheduled you for Wednesday the 3rd."

"Oh yes … that is coming along."

The two salads arrived and they ate in silence for a few moments.

Fran added, "I love it all, and it's all a bit much. Do you know what I mean? Being pregnant, starting a consulting business, growing a relationship, moving into our new condo. I keep letting go of the handlebar, but I feel like I'm on that triple loop Mindbender sometimes."

"That's the wildest rollercoaster in the world!"

"Ha! Of course it is. I just forgot how much I love it," Fran said rolling her eyes.

"Remember this time last year? You had a whole different set of hurdles to overcome than you do now."

"Yes, I felt like the world was out to get me."

"That's how you said your father viewed the world."

Fran felt a shock of recognition. "Yes. Like father like daughter."

"But now those problems have mostly vanished from your life."

"True," Fran mused as she sipped a tart-tasting lemonade.

"And this time next year, you could have a whole new set of problems."

"Does it ever stop?"

"Yes!" Marguerite replied holding her fork in the air for dramatic effect.

"When?"

"When you're pushing up the daisies!" she replied stuffing her mouth with lettuce.

Fran picked at her salad as she remembered the souls resting peacefully in the Olino cemetery. Yes, indeed, she thought. No problems in their worlds.

Marguerite added, "The good news is that you don't seem so overwhelmed by the new problems."

"I suppose I have more coping tools now."

"Absolutely. It's the upside of getting old and gray," Marguerite said as she proudly pointed out a new streak of gray hair at the crown of her head.

"I'm getting a few of those, too," Fran said looking at herself in the mirror behind Marguerite. She imagined herself being as old as Sophia, sitting by the fire sharing stories with her grandchildren. She added, "Since meeting Sophia I'm not as scared of getting older as I used to be. Strange isn't it?"

"Excellent!" Marguerite said almost shouting. "Here's to getting wonderfully, fascinatingly, ripeningly older!"

They clinked glasses and slumped back in their seats laughing. Several people at other tables glanced over at them. Fran held up her glass to an elderly couple at a nearby table and they responded with a toast of their tea cups.

Fran surveyed the clouds snuggling in against the green-fringed slopes of the North Shore mountains.

"I still don't understand something Sophia said right after September 11th. I keep thinking about it so it must have significance for me right now. You'd probably have an interesting take on it."

"What's that?"

"She said 'look for the gift'."

Marguerite nodded, "In reference to September 11th?"

Fran nodded.

"Hmmmm, well, crises often seed reinvention."

"How so?"

"You can see it when you look back on history. Crises and tragedies often fuel cultural development because people are more open to new ideas. For example, they estimated that the Plague in Medieval Europe killed a third of Europe's population. Many who survived took the inheritances of their dead relatives and pledged the money to scientists, researchers, artists, and philosophers in hopes of preventing another outbreak. That funding in essence seeded the Renaissance, a cultural movement that affected all aspects of society. Another example is the Holocaust."

"How could there be a gift in that?"

"Some people suggest that it helped fuel the Civil Rights movement. In fact, the way we view human rights now is unprecedented in the history books. Racism, classism and sexism were the norm for centuries. People often forget that."

"Yes, I never thought about that before. It's probably true. So, what about September 11th? I haven't figured that one out yet."

"Definitely it's fuelling a consciousness shift around power and energy structures in the world."

Fran sipped her lemonade trying to get her head around what all that meant. "Sometimes, though, people just let the negativity consume their lives, like my father did."

Marguerite countered, "Did he? Or did he pass on a creative legacy to you and Helena and all those who benefited from his entrepreneurial efforts?"

"And architectural efforts," Fran added thinking of the mansion on the hill that he had designed and built many years back.

"Your father was a genius of creativity, it sounds like to me. Sometimes I think those who dare to be the most creative are those who sometimes must face the darkest shadows."

The waiter came to clear their plates.

"That's interesting. You know that is one of the greatest insights I've had in the last year: seeing and appreciating my father in so many new ways. I used to judge him so much."

Marguerite smiled in that half-eyed way she often did, the way that navigated Fran so often through her ocean of mistaken assumptions.

"Honor thy father and mother … for they gave you life," Marguerite announced as she leaned back. "Think about it. The gift of life alone is worth a thousand appreciations."

Fran sighed as she digested the words, "Even though they made mistakes?"

"Do you know any people in the world who have not made mistakes?"

"Are you saying I'm going to make mistakes as a parent?" Fran said in mock innocence.

"Yes."

"Bummer."

She watched a family of four, a mother, father and two teen boys, eating at a nearby table. The parents seemed annoyed at the boys for fighting over a handheld video game. *Honor thy father and mother for they gave you life.* Those words smouldered just below her skin. The sacrifice it is to bring a child into this world, she mused, as she struggled to breathe through the growing discomfort in her belly. *What might my life look like if I let go of all the hurt and resentment I have felt for decades toward my parents?* As she imagined that possibility, a whoosh of energy rose up and Fran felt her baby kick for the very first time.

## CHAPTER 57

Her baby boy sleeps in the curve of her arm as Jasper drives the rental car across the border into Slovakia. She re-reads the note on her lap. It's from the parent finders office. It arrived as they were heading for the airport: *A Ms. Roberta DeLeon has now registered seeking re-connection with her daughter, Fran Freeman.* The phone number is in the United States.

She stares at the Washington State area code. It is close to Vancouver but they won't be back for weeks. Fran doesn't know if, or when, she should call.

Jasper pulls the car into Olino. Gustav and the community swarm them. He throws his new grandson up in the air, thrilled to be meeting him for the first time. He places a violin bow in the toddler's hands.

"Can he play yet?" Gustav asks hopefully.

"Papa, Adam is only twenty-two months old, give it some time," replied Jasper.

"I start playing in the womb!" exclaimed Gustav.

"He started in the womb, too." Fran assures him. "Jasper played guitar for him and I every night before going to bed."

"Okay, so he plays guitar. As long as he is musician!"

They walk toward the Olino cemetery. There are many changes like indoor plumbing and waste water treatment.

"Some still won't use the indoor plumbing." Gustav laughs.

"Why not?" Fran asks already knowing the answer.

"We like to wash in running water from nature. Is only way to truly purify. But we get used to it over time. We thank Jiri, too. Just like he once promised me, he finally brought back riches to Olino," he says winking at Fran.

Father and son talk about the new violin he is making in the wood-working studio. Fran and Adam wander down to the pond. Sophia's new tombstone stands right next to the sixty-year-old one with Jiri's name on it. The only new part of Jiri's tombstone is the date of death. Instead of 1943, it has been re-engraved as 2001. She lays down two small bouquets of freesias on each gravesite and stands in silence.

Fran cradles Adam as they sit on the bench admiring the weeping willow tree that caresses the silky smoothness of the pond's surface. She hears the hum of crickets in the nearby pond, and Adam reaches out to touch a silky winged creature fluttering by. She hears a distant voice whisper "butterfly."

She turns around to see who said it, and all she sees is the breeze blowing away some of the flowers that she had placed on the tombstones. She feels a chill run down her spine and a strangeness in her chest.

As Adam wraps his arms around her neck, the two of them look back again at the two tombstones, mother and son together again with their descendants whole and healthy. She feels compelled to whisper a quote she has memorized for an upcoming speech. It is the last quotation that is underlined in Sophia's book. It is by the eighteenth century poet, Rainier Maria Rilke:

*You must give birth to your images*
*for they are the future waiting to be born.*
*Fear not the strangeness that you feel.*
*The future enters long before it ever happens.*

## Acknowledgments

During the many years that it took me to research and write this book so many people supported me on the journey. I had the privilege of crossing paths with literally hundreds of people who have made my life richer and who influenced the course of this book.

I would like to thank: Peter Nagy, Evert Moes, Aaron Breitbart of the Wiesenthal Foundaton and Marek Hojsik and Laco Oravec of the Milan Simecka Foundation for their research; Gerda Wever-Rabehl, Patrick Bermel, Dan Millman and Donaleen Saul for their writing guidance.

I would also like to thank Moira Broom, Dan Poynter, Elaine Allison, Stephen Hammond, 1106 Design, Ulrich Frietag, Doug McKegney, Ron Coleman, Lorraine Rieger, Carol Ann Fried, Gillian Maxwell, Catherine Berris, Jovanka Buchanan, Betti Clipsham, Jane Skea, Kannara Daniel, Adelle Bernadette, Jana Stanfield, Tobi Lange, Daniella Sorrentino, Phyllis Harbour-Murphy, Maureen Jack-LaCroix, Mahara Brenna, Julie Blue, Sharon Abbondanza, Luke Barber, Matt Weinstein and Playfair, Abheeru Ricard, Remi Thivierge, Paul & Kathie Scott, Prasad Rangnekar, Garry Gallagher, and The Osho International Resort.

Finally, I am grateful to David Scheffel for his feedback and for *The Gypsies of Svinia;* Patricia A. Williams for *Once Upon a Lifetime…* (The Time Broker, Inc.); Jean Shinoda Bolen for her work on men's and women's archetypes, Joseph Campbell and Christopher Vogler for their story wisdom, Sidra Stone for *The Shadow King* (Nataraj Publishing); Byron Katie *End the War with Yourself* (Byron Katie International, Inc.); Eva Kor for her courage to forgive; Rudolf Vrba for his memoirs and testimonies; Dr. Ian Hancock for his feedback and for *We Are the Romani People* (University of Hertfordshire Press); David Whyte for his poetic inspiration; and Marion Woodman for her groundbreaking insights regarding the Divine Feminine.

## Author's note

This book has been inspired by a number of true stories. The initial story was suggested to me after my father's death when I found a hidden box of photos, documents and some journals. Yet, this book is a work of fiction. It is not a biography or an autobiography. The names, characters, places and incidents are the products of my imagination. Yet, truth is stranger than fiction and I would never have imagined this book unless the essence of these stories actually happened.

While there may be some Roma blood in my family tree, from what I can gather they have not lived in a traditional Roma way for generations. My father grew up amongst carneys, musicians, artists and entertainers of mixed heritages. I chose to highlight the plight of Roma, artists and others during the Holocaust because I felt their stories were less well-known and needed to be told. I also wanted to tell the story of the backlash against Germans after the war, and the number of people who did try to stand up for what was right, since their stories are also less known and needed to be told. If there are errors or inaccuracies about the Roma people or any other group identified in this book, I welcome your feedback for the next edition.

Some Roma still use the word Gypsy and others won't tolerate it. I use the word at times to offer an entry point to those unfamiliar with the newer term of Roma. The persistence of the use of Gypsy may be because there is no single Roma equivalent that is universally agreed upon. This is slowly changing over time through discussions and academic study. Any spellings and usages relating to the Rom, Roma, Romani or Gypsies were based on geography, history, conventions and political affiliations current at the time when the story takes place.

## About the Author

Carla Rieger is a creativity catalyst. She has been the director of **The Artistry of Change** (www.artistryofchange.com) since 1991, a Vancouver-based consulting firm working with organizations, companies and individuals to use creativity to access higher performance states. Her academic background includes adult education, theatre, mediation and conflict resolution, creative writing, and organizational development.

Additionally, Carla has been an actor, playwright and artistic director of several theatre troupes. She has previously self-published three nonfiction books: *The Power of Laughter, Speaking on the Funny Side of the Brain,* and *The Heart of Presenting,* as well as three audio programs on *The Artistry of Change, Managing Change with a Sense of Humor,* and *Captivate Your Audience.* Her work as both a speaker and performer has been featured on radio and TV, and she is a regular columnist in several trade journals.

During her forty to fifty speaking engagements per year, she addresses groups from 10 to 4000 people internationally on a variety of topics related to her books and to enhanced creativity.

Carla has written dozens of short stories, plays and sketch comedy pieces. In addition she has written and performed in her own one-woman show entitled *Dancing Between Worlds. The Change Artist* is her first full-length novel.

## Discussion Questions

These questions are designed as a way to stimulate discussions about the book, and can be useful for your book club, university class, or reading group.

1. What parts of the story affected you the most?

2. What was unique about the various settings of the book (both in the present and in the past)? And, how did these settings enhance or detract from the story?

3. What specific themes did the author emphasize throughout the novel? What do you think she is trying to get across to the reader?

4. Do the characters seem real and believable? Can you relate to their predicaments?

5. Which character do you most relate to?

6. Which character had the most impact on you, and to what extent do they remind you of yourself or someone you know?

7. How does Fran change or evolve throughout the course of the story? What events triggered her greatest changes?

8. How does the father character change or evolve throughout the course of the story (as an old man, as a young man during the war, as a boy running away from his past)?

9. How does the grandmother character change or evolve throughout the course of the story? What events triggered her greatest changes?

10. In what ways do the events in the books reveal evidence of the author's world view?

11. Did certain parts of the book make you uncomfortable? If so, why did you feel that way?

12. Did this discomfort lead to a new understanding or awareness of some aspect of your life you might not have thought about before?

13. How do you interpret the title, The Change Artist? How much of a Change Artist are you in your life?

14. The author makes the case that artistry, both practiced and appreciated, can transform your life. How has that been true or not true in your life?

## Invitation to the Reader

If you'd like to learn more, please check out
*www.thechangeartistbook.com*

There you can:

- Read Frequently Asked Questions
- View Upcoming Events
- Post a comment on the Blog
- and more...

Are you on Facebook? Feel free to "become a fan" on
*The Change Artist* page. Simply type "The Change Artist"
into the Facebook search engine.

Breinigsville, PA USA
22 September 2009
224537BV00002B/1/P